The
KEYSTONE

A. M. Dean is a leading authority on ancient cultures and the history of religious belief, whose expertise in late antiquity has earned him posts at some of the world's most prestigious universities. An abiding interest in the human tendency towards conspiracies, together with a commanding grasp of the genuinely mysterious contexts of real history, inspire the breadth and focus of his creative works. His first novel, *The Lost Library*, launched to great acclaim in 2012 in sixteen territories worldwide.

Find out more information about A. M. Dean's books and other activities at:

www.amdean-books.com

And be sure to follow A. M. Dean on Twitter @AMDeanUK for regular updates, news, contests and literary chat.

Also by A. M. Dean

The Lost Library

The

KEYSTONE

A. M. DEAN

PAN BOOKS

First published 2013 by Macmillan

This edition published by Pan Books
an imprint of Pan Macmillan, a division of Macmillan Publishers Limited
Pan Macmillan, 20 New Wharf Road, London N1 9RR
Basingstoke and Oxford
Associated companies throughout the world
www.panmacmillan.com

ISBN 978-1-4472-0952-2

3 5 7 9 8 6 4 2

A CIP catalogue record for this book is available from the British Library.

Map artwork and cave drawing © Raymond Turvey

Typeset by Ellipsis Digital Limited, Glasgow
Printed and bound by CPI Group (UK) Ltd, Croydon, CR0 4YY

The
KEYSTONE

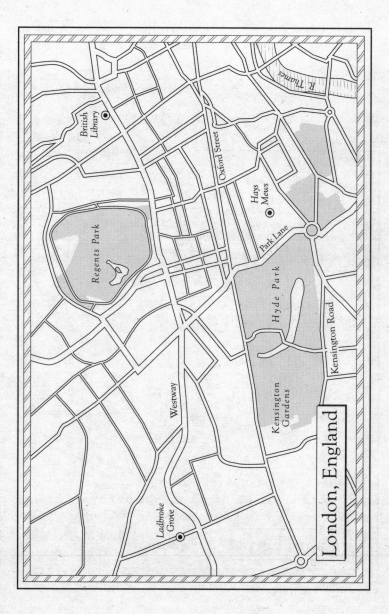

London, England

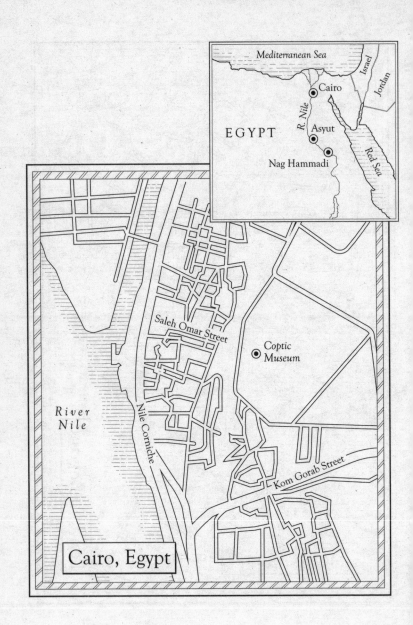

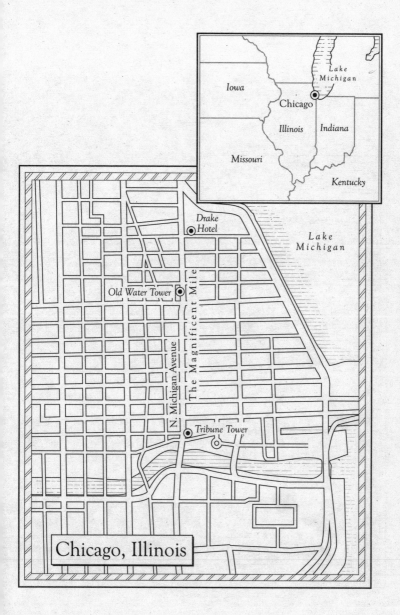

PROLOGUE

AD 374 – Egypt
The Egyptian Desert

Tarasios of Luxor stared into the face of the taller man's fierce, cold eyes. The sharpened edge of the engraved pugio pressed against his throat was already drawing blood, and the pressure of the blade on his larynx choked his breath. No matter what came next, he knew that this encounter ended with the blade being given a sharp jolt by the powerful man, cutting through his throat and sending him out of this life. That much was a certainty. His earthly journey was already over.

But there was still hope for good, even great good. He would be free, and his liberation would be the cause's surety.

The taller man, who held a military bearing and whose well-worn garments bore imperial insignia, grabbed at Tarasios's hair with his free hand.

'Your companions have left you, little man. Your pathetic followers have fled like desert rats into the sand.' He spat the words with a cruel venom.

'They know what persecution means,' Tarasios answered

back, forcing a defiance into his tone in the face of his certain death. 'They know what you and your men will do to them if they're caught.'

The officer smiled, satisfied. 'Good. At least their fear is justified. Perhaps there's some knowledge in these "Knowers" after all.' He peered deep into his victim's eyes. He expected to see terror there. Hopelessness. Panic. Instead he saw only resolve, and his fury rose in response.

'Tell me where they've gone,' he demanded, forcing back Tarasios's head and pressing the blade's sharp edge further into his protruding neck. Blood began to seep across the metal surface. 'Tell me where your friends have run to, and I will spare your worthless life.'

The knife still in his throat, a confident smile curled the edges of Tarasios's mouth. 'My life, as you call it, is already saved. I am free.' Defiant against the pain, he forced his forehead down and stared directly into the persecutor's eyes.

'I will tell you no more. Do what you must.'

The soldier waited only a moment longer. The man would give him nothing – nothing but delays, distraction and heretical talk. Nothing worth putting off the inevitable for, not any longer.

With a powerful, swift motion, he wrenched the knife sharply to the right, severing tendons, vocal cords and arteries in a single motion.

Tarasios's eyes bulged, but he did not remove them from his attacker's face. As the blood poured from his throat, he watched the world fade to black in peace. He was already free.

*

Twenty minutes later, a nineteen-year-old compatriot, nearing the point of exhaustion, continued his fevered run. The sun was already beginning to set over the distant dunes, but Eunomius knew the dusk gave him little advantage. The persecutions of his people were government sanctioned and the officers had at their disposal horses, weapons and highly trained soldiers. They would be close behind. He only prayed that Tarasios had been able to delay them long enough to give him the time he needed.

The key had to be hidden before they found him. That was all that mattered. The ignorant soldiers only wanted his brethren, all those who had followed Tarasios and his truths. In their pathetic desire to eradicate the Empire of unwanted beliefs, they had no idea what was really at stake. Today, Eunomius would use that ignorance to his advantage. As long as he could hide the key, he would accept whatever they chose to do with his body.

His lungs burning from exertion, at last he came upon the spot the group had chosen two kalends past, before the persecutions had fragmented them so desperately. Eunomius slowed to a jog. Before him was the ideal hiding place, one that would ensure the key's safety for years – even generations. For as long as was necessary.

Catching his breath, Eunomius navigated by memory rather than the illusion of his eyes, and clambered to the entrance, stepping into the darkness of the cave. Navigating his way through the blackness by feeling along the wall with his fingers, at last he arrived at the cleft in the rock that he knew was there. Kneeling, he reached beneath his cloak and removed the small jar containing the object. After pressing it to his forehead in devotion, he pushed as far into the cleft as his arm would allow and deposited his charge.

Drawing back, he brought all movement to a halt. Outside, he could hear the sounds of men approaching. They had found him. In a matter of moments, his body would be theirs.

Though the darkness was complete, Eunomius closed his eyes, raising his hands to shoulder level, and uttered a familiar prayer as a feeling of peace swept over him. His initiation had taken place only two years ago, when the world had seemed a calmer, more tolerant place. He had never suspected that the ultimate liberation would be delayed in this way, nor that he would be given such a critical role in preserving it for posterity. But these were the ways of the fleeting world and this fallen, wretched life. He was honoured to fight for a higher cause.

His prayer finished and his duty complete, Eunomius opened his eyes and stood. Filled with resolve, he backtracked to the entrance of the cave. After the darkness of its depths, even the hazy brightness of dusk was blinding. He took a moment to absorb the fleeting rays before climbing down, away from its entrance, and taking his final position at a dark opening in the nearby stone, before which the men would find him.

Their arrival came swiftly. The sounds Eunomius had heard were replaced by the vision of approaching soldiers as he stood his ground on the diminutive ledge. The group assembled below him, and from the edge of his vision Eunomius tracked the motion of two who climbed up the stone, striving for positions on either side of his post.

It was perfect. He was ready for his freedom.

Gazing into the clutch of men, he met the stare of a taller soldier whose garments marked him out as their leader. Concentrating intently on the man, Eunomius took a deep breath and shouted with full force the only word that mattered.

'*LIBERATION!*'

Even as the shout echoed off the stone hillside into the desert sands, a sword appeared at his right, glistened a moment in the evening sun, and with a swift flicker severed his head from his body and his life from the wantonness of the physical world.

The Modern Day – eight months ago

In the dark, solitary room, Albinus sat shaking, his whole body a mass of profound agitation. He could turn on the lights – in the windowless room they would not betray him – but the darkness felt safer. He held the cordless phone tight against his cheek, its rounded edge pressed firmly into his jawbone, the dialling tone droning in his ear. Sweat ran in rivulets down his face, dripping off the tip of his nose and making the phone slippery in his hands.

What have I done? What am I doing?

He was terrified, but there seemed no other choice. What was being planned was too terrible, its consequences unfathomable. His conscience would never let him live with the guilt if he did not make contact with someone who could stop this before it began.

Liberation was not meant to be purchased at such a cost.

In the darkness, he unfolded the scrap of paper on which he had scribbled the number for the FBI's public line, refreshing his memory with the green illumination of the phone's keypad. A moment later, his fingers nervously pressed into the digits.

The phone rang once. Twice. By the third and fourth rings his pulse began to increase. *Someone's got to answer.* A feeling in his gut told him he would not have another chance to make his call.

After the sixth ring, the line connected. Albinus's breath stopped.

'*You have reached the FBI automated reporting service . . .*'

His heart sank. An automated line. This was not what he had anticipated. Maybe it should have been, he suddenly realized; but second-guessing himself was too easy a trap for despair.

He could not abandon his only hope.

When the message was complete and a long tone signalled him to start, Albinus sputtered his anxious words into the phone. He had prepared himself for a conversation, not a one-way summary.

'I'm, I'm . . . my name isn't important. I have information . . . on an attack. Chicago. Something terrible . . . from the Church of Truth . . .' He gasped, his breath seeming to fail him, words insufficient for the magnitude of his message. 'A terrible set of events is coming. You have to stop it.'

The leadership assembled in an air of urgency. The Great Leader was seated, his closest aides gathered around him, to deal with the defection that threatened to put decades of preparation at risk. The date that loomed only months away had been fixed as their target, symbolic and infused with too much meaning to be abandoned, and movements all across the globe were now advancing.

'It's Albinus,' one of the brothers offered, hesitantly. He pushed the name out of tight lips, his Italian accent struggling with its strange, foreign shape.

'He's always been weak-willed,' added another, his Spanish inflection contrasting with the Italian's, 'but we never thought he would go this far.' His broad shoulders alternated between a frustrated droop and an angry, flexed tension.

'How far, precisely?' The Great Leader kept his tone firm. He did not need the others' anger overtaking their focus.

'He's gone to the FBI.' The man who answered stood directly opposite him, his arms firmly folded across his chest. If he felt any emotion at all, his features did not show it. 'We've had it confirmed from the inside. He left a tip this morning. Used our name. Mentioned an attack. They're going to be on watch.'

The words provoked a deeper tension, broken only by the Italian who spoke the obvious implication, his eyes more afraid than upset. 'Our shield of secrecy is broken. This "veil of anonymity" as you called it – it's gone. *Andato.*'

The Great Leader absorbed the words, the slight pulsing of flesh at his cheeks the only evidence of the grinding of his teeth beneath. The compelling vigour of his features – the intense eyes, inset beneath a brow whose gentle lines bespoke wisdom and experience, with cheekbones shaped enough to suggest power without being so angular as to seem vicious – now seemed hidden behind a sheen of concentration.

7

Finally, he peered up at his men.

'Albinus must be stopped. Tonight. Co-opt the Arab if you need him. We can't have this man telling the authorities any more than he already has.' He turned directly to the Italian, whose frustration visibly transformed into a resolve to match the Great Leader's own.

'Don't be gentle. Show him just what happens to defectors from a righteous cause.'

The slender man's face switched to pleasure. He knew the order gave him carte blanche over just how much pain and suffering could precede Albinus's execution. He rose, together with three of the others, each nodding reverently and turning for the exit.

The sterner man opposite the Leader stood firm.

'And our plan?' he asked. 'The cause itself?'

The Great Leader looked long into his eyes. The customary intensity of his own was now back in full force.

'Another approach will have to be devised,' he answered. His confidence was not shaken.

'Silence is no longer our ally. It's time to make other friends.'

Part One

THE PRESENT
SUNDAY, JULY 1ST

CHAPTER 1

Hays Mews, London

In the early morning silence, the creaking floorboard tore into Andrew Wess's consciousness like a siren. At first his groggy head took it as the last traces of whatever dream he had just escaped, the strange creak of boards and shuffling of papers the leftovers of scenes his mind had concocted in sleep. Glancing at the large clock opposite the armchair in which he'd passed the night, he registered the early hour. It was far too early to be up.

Then he heard the noises again: a repeat of a creaking floorboard, the sound of drawers being opened and papers shuffled. Andrew's back stiffened. The sounds that had roused him from sleep had not come from his dreams. These were distinct and real, and his taut skin immediately went cold.

'Wake up,' he whispered to the woman asleep on the sofa next to his chair. Their impromptu sleep on the sitting-room furniture had come after a late evening of conversation that had been more engaging than either had anticipated. After a

11

lifetime of tête-à-têtes, they could still keep each other totally enthralled for hours on end.

The woman's head rested against one of the settee's padded arms, her sleep deep.

'Emily, wake up,' Andrew repeated, stepping lightly towards her position, his voice still hushed. 'Someone's in the house.'

In the darkness, the two men found navigation of the semi-detached townhouse a challenge. Each carried a pen light, but they had surveilled the area thoroughly and were aware that residents in the elegant neighbourhood were prone to report unusual activities to the police, so they kept their use to a minimum.

'This way, it looks like her office,' one man whispered to the other. With a nod of his head he indicated a doorway to the right, behind which lay the makeshift office of Dr Emily Wess's London home. They had already located and searched a similar room which served as her husband's study, but had found nothing. This, however, was the room with real potential. It was her work they were interested in, or rather, her possessions. She had acquired only two days ago the object of which they now intended to relieve her, and she had taken possession of it without having the faintest idea what it really was. They, however, knew its real value, and their leader had charged them to reclaim the one object that would enable them to undertake the greatest work in their history.

Now it was somewhere here, in the dark of her home office, waiting to find its way into their hands. Ideally, they would have come when the house was empty, rather than at night when its occupants were asleep so close by; but the chances of her leaving the object unattended were slight, and they did not know how long she intended to keep it in her possession before transferring it to its new owners. No, a nighttime operation was what the situation demanded. She would wake in the morning to find the item gone, never knowing just what it was she had truly lost.

Emily's eyes sprang open and without further demurral she sat upright to face Andrew, crouched on the floor in front of her. Before she could speak, he reached up and held a finger over her mouth, ordering quiet. 'Shh,' he mouthed. Cupping his hand to his ear as an instruction, they both listened. The sounds coming from Emily's office down the corridor were soft, but clear – sound travelled through the old house's paper-thin walls as if they weren't there.

Someone was rifling through her desk.

Andrew rose slightly and sat himself on the sofa next to Emily, grabbing her shoulders and turning her squarely towards him.

'I'm going to see who it is,' he said boldly. He scanned the room, assessing his options, as Emily leaned in and whispered into his ear.

'Don't even think about it. We don't know who it is. They could be dangerous.'

She reached across the sofa and grabbed the cordless phone from the end table.

'There's a bolt on the sliding door at the end of the corridor, just there.' She motioned towards the entrance to the front room, keeping her voice as soft as she could. 'Go slide it closed, quiet as you can, and lock it. I'm going to head to the closet and phone the police.' The walk-in storage closet nestled between the front room and kitchen was enormous, almost an additional room secreted into the wall, and so over-full of linens, clothes and supplies that it would do a decent job of muffling her voice.

Andrew's heart was thumping painfully, unaccustomed to switching so rapidly from sleep to stress. He looked to Emily, caught her familiar eyes – he had known them for so long, seen them in so many settings.

He gave her a firm squeeze on the arm, relinquishing the sentiment to the needs of the moment, and pulled her towards the edge of the sofa. Emily nodded, rose on bare feet and tip-toed into the closet, slowly pulling the door closed behind her.

Though Andrew Wess was terrified, a nighttime break-in something he had never experienced, the protective instinct was stronger. He and Emily had matched wits since their childhood, had played and sparred and fought as equals. But whenever she had been in danger or in pain, Andrew had always been her protector. He was the one who bandaged the scraped knee, who fended off the neighbouring bullies and then taught her to do the same.

The sounds continued, and the childhood memories fled. Convinced that Emily was well hidden, his motivation changed. Locking them in and hoping for the best wasn't in his nature, and ridding the house of the intruders became Andrew's priority. He scanned the room, looking for anything he might wield as a weapon. The sconces on the fireplace were too small to intimidate, much less pose any real threat if intimidation didn't work. The corner lamp was too unwieldy and cumbersome.

Then, in the room's far corner, the perfect resource. *God bless you, Em.* Though he had never tried the game in his life, Emily's love for golf suddenly became one of her greatest virtues: her well-stocked bag of clubs was perched in a corner nook. He had teased her so many times about her love for the sport. When he'd got the intruders out of the house, he'd have to be sure to offer a good apology for that.

Andrew stepped lightly across the floor and extracted a suitably heavy driver from the bag, then made his way quietly into the central corridor. With each step, the sound of muffled voices and shuffling papers grew louder, and closer.

CHAPTER 2

Hays Mews, London

In the midst of Emily Wess's office, one of the men suddenly froze. His hands were still tucked midway through a large pile of folders and documents, and for an instant he questioned whether this was real. The doubt didn't last. He knew what he held in his hands: success.

Simon had always been a practical man, but in moments like this he could not help the fact that emotion demanded an equal share of his attention. All his labour and service in support of their cause were aimed at a spiritual end, after all, and Simon had always had a spiritual side. In this moment, nothing could diminish the significance of what they were here to claim. It was the greatest work he had ever undertaken, and it would mark out his life's finest achievement.

'I've found it.' The words came out as a whisper. Despite his sense of success, he was not a man who would allow his awe to overcome his attention to circumstances. The woman and her husband were almost certainly asleep in the house, and speech needed to be kept to a minimum.

As the second man turned towards him, Simon drew the padded folder out from the larger stack in a drawer of the artisan desk. A moment later, it lay open and they both peered down at its precious contents.

A single, ancient sheet of browned paper, wrinkled with age.

'You're sure?' The second man studied the page, puzzled by the antiquated lettering that covered its surface. He was naturally mistrustful, a characteristic that had served him well more than once in his difficult life; and at the moment his innate disbelief seemed justified. 'It doesn't look like a map.'

The first man scrutinized the document to its smallest detail. His partner was right: it didn't look like a map. But the script was familiar, matching the penmanship in the Book – the ancient journal that had been their unerring guide for as long as he could remember – perfectly.

'I'm positive.'

The other man still wasn't convinced. 'I don't understand how that's supposed to get Arthur to the keystone.' If they returned to their leader without the authentic map, the repercussions would be severe.

Simon looked up at him, his face suddenly bitter. He wanted to smack him for his inexcusable irreverence, but at the moment he was more concerned about the noise even a whispered rebuke would generate. They had spoken enough. He shot his partner an angry look.

The man stopped protesting. He was used to being rebuked so Simon's glare didn't upset him. Besides, there was something different about his partner. The fierce man, whom he had never seen quake, however dire the circumstances, was physically shaking with excitement. His eyes almost sparkled, even in the darkness.

Andrew Wess shifted a few steps further down the corridor, finally pausing beside the door to Emily's study. Inside, the sounds of drawers being shuffled through had been supplanted by whispers and the scuffling of feet, then more recently by stillness.

As he approached, Andrew's fear began to give way to anger. He'd heard of the rise in burglaries in London, and could picture a pair of teenage thugs just inside the small room, drunk or drugged and acting on the assumption that whatever they wanted in life they could simply steal. Never mind the damage, or the fear they might instil in others. The thought infuriated him. Back home in Ohio, they still took hooligans out behind the proverbial woodshed for a good Midwestern, small-town 'discussion' with the local community. He didn't know what they did with them in London, but he was absolutely not going to let them run free through their lives.

As he stood just outside the door, his fury drove him to impulse. Taking a breath and marshalling his courage, he spun to his left and thrust himself into the door frame. It was a mistake, but one he didn't have the experience or maturity to appreciate.

'What the hell are you doing in our house!' he thundered, raising the club high in his left hand, its titanium-plated, wooden head almost scraping the ceiling.

The fact that the intruders were not drunken teens registered in less than a second. Andrew's surprise at the sight of the two physically towering men standing over the desk was superseded by the shock of two rapid gunshots that broke the nighttime silence, even before the last word had thundered off his tongue. The man closest to him had drawn his pistol with remarkable speed and fired without hesitation.

Andrew Wess dropped to the floor, his heart perforated by the bullets and his life already gone.

'*Fuck!*' The gunman stepped forward and nudged his pistol against Andrew's lifeless body. The two wounds glistened like rosettes on his T-shirt, a black pool of blood already appearing beneath him.

'Dammit. He's going to be pissed.' The gunman didn't mind his partner's constant insults, but the Great Leader's were harder to bear.

A moment later his face registered another, more immediate cause for concern as the sound of the gunshots continued to reverberate in the air.

'Come on, time to go. We can't get caught here.' They hadn't intended to be discovered, and certainly not for this operation to generate casualties. But circumstances were what they were, and had to be accommodated.

The other man nodded, and enclosing the precious page back in the folder, tucked it securely under his arm. Stepping over the lifeless body of Andrew Wess, the two sprinted down the stairs to the rear door and disappeared into the labyrinthine streets of Shepherd Market and greater Westminster.

*

From the back of the walk-in storage closet, Dr Emily Wess let the tears stream down her cheeks as she waited for the men to depart. Their words had come through the thin walls softly but clearly, and burned their way into her mind with clarity and permanence. Even through her emotional agony, she knew she must cling to them.

She did not recognize the intruders' voices, she did not know what they wanted or what they had found. The words that they had uttered made no sense and she did not know what delusions had led them into her home.

She only knew that two gunshots had been followed by the noise of a body falling, and there had been no sound from Andrew since.

CHAPTER 3

Córdoba, Spain

'The Disciple said, "Why do we not rest at once?"
The Lord said, "When you lay down these burdens!"'

In the middle of the circle a ceremonial oil lamp flickered a wavering light. The outdated mode of lighting was intentional, the gentle flame it produced an important part of the ritual. The bodies surrounding it swayed in rhythmic motion, each clad in an identical velvet robe of a dark crimson, almost black. A low, bass tone was sustained by some of the participants, while the others joined in the words of the familiar incantation, drawn from their copy of the Book.

'The Disciple said, "How does the small join itself to the great?"
The Lord replied, "When you abandon the works which
cannot follow you, then you will rest."'

The ancient words, uttered in reverent monotone by the practised tongues of their devotees, resonated through the dimly lit space. Only through careful focus could the initiate see the symbols chalk-drawn onto the floor, surrounding the lamp. Two snakes, entwined in a loop – the oldest of their images, the *ouroboros*, employed since the beginning. It was also the most familiar, worn by each member in the form of a silver ring on their left ring finger, where others put wedding bands. On the floor it was surrounded by celestial spheres, arranged in careful hierarchy. A sun, cresting a tree. All ancient images, faithfully recreated, representing the journey towards illumination into which he was about to be joined.

This man sat, cross-legged like all the others, but stripped bare except for a pair of white shorts. Only when the Initiation Incantation was complete would he be clothed in the robe of the Knowers and drawn into a greater truth than any he had yet experienced. Only then would he discover the self beyond himself, the spirit beyond body.

'The Traitor cried, "How is the spirit apparent?"
The Lord replied, "How is the sword apparent?"'

As the sacred words continued, a messenger in lay clothes appeared at the fringe of the circle. Hesitantly, he made his way around its edge until he came to the hooded figure of its local Leader, seated in the incantation ring with the rest of the members. It was all but unheard of to interrupt an incantation, especially an initiation, but the circumstances at hand were not ordinary. The Spanish Leader would want to know. Even if it meant a momentary distraction.

Crouching down, the messenger leaned in close to the hooded figure's ear. *'Mi señor,'* he whispered during a momentary lull in the chanting. In the circumstances formal titles were required. The seated figure inclined his head towards him.

'Master,' the messenger reported, 'the manuscript has been obtained. Our brothers are on their way to the Great Leader as we speak.'

Beneath his heavy hood, the regional Leader allowed himself a contented lift of his eyebrows. This was the news he had been waiting to hear.

'Very well. The time has come to put our plan into action,' he said softly. He lifted his right hand, calmly placing his open palm on the courier's chest. The ancient, intimate gesture was reserved for significant moments of parting, and this moment qualified.

'Contact the brethren abroad, tell them it's time to begin the exodus.' Then, recognizing that the event commanded a more formal remark, he sat firmly upright and spoke with reverence.

'It is time for them to come into the light.'

Having received his charge, the messenger inclined his head and stepped away from the sacred scene.

Exhaling a long, satisfied breath, the Leader turned his attention back to the matter of the moment. The Initiation Incantation was at its climax, and he joined his words to those of his brethren as they united a new life to their midst.

'The Disciple asked, "How is the light apparent?"
And the Master replied, "Only when you are bathed in it forever."'

CHAPTER 4

Hays Mews, London

Emily Wess sat on the sofa in the living room of a house that had, until only hours ago, sheltered both her and Andrew. His body, which since the shooting had lain on the floor in the doorway to her study, was being loaded into a body bag and placed on a trolley by the Metropolitan Police Forensic Services.

'Dr Wess, I'm terribly sorry to have to continue with these questions at such a difficult moment.' Detective Inspector Joanna Alwell broke a silence that had seemed longer than it was. 'But I'm afraid I do have a few more matters I need to go through while these events are still fresh in your memory.' Alwell had been in her rank over three years, but these moments never became any easier.

Emily nodded, but made no other reply. She had removed herself from the scene as the men started their work. The hot tears that had flowed down her cheeks all morning were drying, but the sight of Andrew's lifeless body being manhandled by emotionless men in sterile suits was too much for her to bear.

She had known Andrew since her childhood, and could no longer remember a time when she had not considered him part of her life. Even now, with her career meaning they saw each other only rarely, she had never felt this decreased the closeness between them. His was a life that was always a part of hers. He had been the childhood strength that had helped a tomboyish little girl – still unsure of herself and far from the beauty and forceful self-composure she would later gain – find confidence and strength. Andrew was younger by almost ten years, but something in him had always been sure of every step he took and unafraid of those that were ahead. If Emily had come to love adventure, it was because she had been so strongly influenced by this man who had loved it since his youth.

And that was exactly who she had become: a woman driven by the unknown, who craved the mysterious and unexplained. Her father had taken Emily and Andrew to a science museum's exhibit on ancient Sumeria in her mid-teens, and her life had changed. Ancient history became her new passion, and she and Andrew had spent more weekends than she could remember recreating historic scenes from ancient Rome, or forging new expeditions of discovery in the park behind her family's Logan property.

Andrew had pushed her creativity, her enthusiasm, her strength. Suddenly, in the face of her loss, Emily found it hard to think of any dimension of the woman she had become that he had not influenced.

It was a crushing, defeating, tormenting realization.

DI Alwell leaned forward in her chair, professional yet

compassionate, drawing Emily's attention back to her questions. 'You're certain there were two men?' She glanced back over her jottings from an earlier moment in the conversation, the near-verbatim notation of interviews a standard practice with the Met's Homicide and Serious Crime Command. 'You said you didn't actually see the intruders. Could there have been more?'

'No, there were two.' The flat tones of Emily's soft, Midwestern American accent lent themselves to her simple insistence. Though she had wept for much of the time that Alwell had been on the scene, Emily had done so quietly, her emotions stirring so deeply within that they seemed beyond the hysterics the detective might have expected.

'One's accent was south London,' Emily added, 'the other sounded vaguely Irish.' She wiped a stale tear from her cheek, trying to focus on the details. On her lap, her interlaced grip was so tight that her well-manicured fingernails went a stark white.

Alwell nodded. 'Okay, good. That's very helpful. Do you remember what they were speaking about before the gunshots?'

'At first we only heard footsteps and the shuffling of papers. They were a couple of doors down.'

Emily Wess's normally upright posture was slouched, her auburn hair falling loosely around her shoulders. It was clear to the inspector that she was a woman for whom grief was as unfamiliar as it was uncomfortable, and the shell shock of the morning resonated in her appearance and voice.

'They were searching through your house?'

'Through my office. Either they didn't know we were here,

or . . . no, someone's always here at night. They must have thought they were being quiet enough we wouldn't be woken.'

Emily paused, her emotions threatening to swell. She wanted more than anything else to make a phone call, but the inspector had been insistent that she answer her questions first.

'Now, you say you hid yourself in the closet, just there,' DI Alwell continued, motioning towards the linen closet. 'Were you able to hear anything once you were inside?'

'Not perfectly, but enough. It was late, so the house was silent, and the walls here are paper-thin.' Suddenly, Emily could hear Andrew bemoaning the poor insulation of the old house when he'd first seen it, thumping a fist against a wall and mimicking an echo carrying the sound to every room. *Paper-thin.*

She rubbed her fingers against her temples, forcing a regained composure. 'Though they kept their voices low, I could catch a phrase here and there. They mentioned finding "the map", which they said could be used to find a "keystone", whatever that is. The Irish one quizzed the other to make sure they'd got what they came for, and the man from London was confident.'

DI Alwell took down Emily's words in an efficient shorthand on a pad in her lap. 'Map . . . stone . . . that's a wonderful amount of detail, Dr Wess.'

Emily nodded vaguely. 'Memory's not a problem.' She'd had a near-photographic memory her whole life, and her auditory recall was almost as clear, which on most days she considered an asset. But in the circumstances, she knew it meant she would never be able to remove the sounds of this morning from her mind. They would be with her, in all their horrible clarity, for life.

'I would give anything to forget these details.'

'I understand,' Alwell replied automatically, 'but every detail you tell us can help us find the men who did this to your husband.'

'Cousin,' Emily corrected her, her gaze remaining fixed. 'Andrew was my cousin.'

CHAPTER 5

The British Museum, London

'Michael, pay attention and switch on the box!' The venerable frame of William H. Gwyth appeared in the office doorway of the Distinguished Research Fellow in Coptic Antiquities at the British Museum. Gwyth personified the stereotypical old-fashioned scholar, as innocent of concern for trends in fashion as he was for trends in thought outside his realm of specialism. He remained at the helm of the Department of Ancient Egypt and Sudan, which he had piloted for seventeen years, despite now being four years older than the museum's official retirement age of seventy-six.

Michael Torrance looked up from his desk, ignoring the command. 'The box', he knew, referred to the television, and he had too much work to be distracted by it. Gwyth was an eccentric, always insisting that everyone drop everything at his whim.

'Switch it over to Channel Four,' the octogenarian commanded, stepping further into the room. Sensing Michael's disinterest, he gave a demonstrative wag of his arthritic hands. 'Don't make an old man ask again.'

For the briefest moment, Michael debated internally whether resisting the distraction was worth the scolding he would receive if he didn't comply. Realizing it wasn't, he withdrew a remote from his desk drawer and switched on the tiny television that sat perched in the middle of the bookshelf opposite. His office was traditional and dignified, and the television appeared incongruous with the immense desk protected by its muted, burgundy felt mat, surrounded by overly full bookshelves that lined every wall and once-organized stacks of paper that reached up from the shelftops to the ceiling. Michael Torrance had considered the office a second home for only the past six months, but with the clutter it could have been six years.

'What warrants such a worldly distraction this morning?' he asked as the old television gradually faded its images into view. William Gwyth was not known for his love of television, modern culture, or indeed much of anything that dated later than the ninth century AD. Everything else was generally marked as a 'modern innovation' and dismissed just as decisively.

'That,' Gwyth answered, pointing to the small screen. Michael turned his attention to the television, on which a news report was headlined with the unlikely phrase: 'Gnostic terrorist.' His face contorted in surprise.

'Gnostic terrorist?'

'I thought that might get your attention,' Gwyth replied, a satisfied smile on his dry lips. 'Seems a juvenile in the States has been arrested for some terrorist something or other, and claims to be one of your Gnostics.' He lifted a well-wrinkled brow towards his surprised colleague. 'Not something one sees every day, is it?'

Michael held back an obscenity. His field of study was hard enough to separate from the realm of cultic mystics and spiritualist nonsense in the public mind. Having Gnosticism attached to terrorism, even if only in the sphere of the media, was absolutely the last thing he needed.

The television switched from a shoulder shot of the newsreader to an arrest photograph of a man in America. Gwyth's condescending 'juvenile' was an observation well made: the man could not be more than twenty-five. His bruised face made him look pitiful, though Michael saw a smugness that the bruises didn't conceal. Bullet points on the screen indicated he'd been arrested in possession of a sniper rifle and claimed to be involved in a 'sacred mission' about which no further details were conveyed.

'Maybe you should ring up the station,' Michael's boss offered, already turning to walk away. 'You might be able to add "Anti-Terrorism Consultant" to your growing list of accolades.' Michael heard Gwyth's self-congratulatory laugh as he departed down the corridor.

He kept his eyes on the screen a few moments longer before switching off the television in annoyance. On days like this, he wondered whether his career shift had been a good move. He could have gone anywhere in life, done anything, and had already followed more career paths than some. He had formerly been an architect – or, more accurately, had become a qualified architect only weeks before a sudden shift put him on the historian's track.

That shift had come in the form of a woman. For a man of good English stock and above-average intelligence, with a career on the horizon and a life-long desire to 'make his mark' pressing at him since childhood, being swayed off course by love had surprised everyone in Michael's circle of friends, including Michael himself. He'd abandoned almost every romantic relationship he'd had since his teens on grounds that 'career comes first' and his plans for life trumped the momentary impulses of romantic emotion; but with this woman, things had been different. The man who was never swayed, was swayed. The architect with an internship nearing completion and qualifications already in hand, had fallen for a historian and then fallen back into history himself.

Michael had trod the path of history earlier, during his undergraduate days, before the lure of higher salaries and a natural curiosity with structure and form drew him away. But only seven weeks after his wedding, Michael had opted to leave the architectural world as swiftly as he had joined it, returning to university to take a PhD in the subject that had been his first interest. Now, sporting a doctorate in Coptic Studies and a zest for his new career, he focused on Gnostic social history and the fringe movements of early Egyptian Christianity as part of a prestigious year-long fellowship with the British Museum. The thirty-four-year-old's fascination for modern structures of steel and glass had not waned, but the lure of other interests had taken pride of place.

It was a lure that inspired deep and zealous commitment. A recent consignment of third-century BC Nile Delta pottery had pressured the whole department into a long working weekend, and Michael had even committed to sleeping in the corner of his office, reluctantly staying away from the comforts of home and bedding himself down with a thin pillow and a few blankets in order to make the most of early mornings and long working nights. His wife hadn't even protested. She was a woman of zeal herself, and knew it when she saw it.

But despite his own energy and that of the scholars around him, Michael was gradually learning an important fact: there was idiocy everywhere. The fool on the television wasn't miles away from the stupidity of the group that had sent him the letter that now lay unfolded on his desk. He'd been trying to shake their persistent requests almost as long as he had been in post, but still they continued to write. 'For reasons of academic research', a 'scholarly collective' of which Michael had never heard was requesting access to the museum's Coptic manuscripts collection. Though the terms were vague, it was not an unusual request. Groups constantly requested access to such materials, and the museum regularly granted it, but this group stood out for its persistence. Michael had already denied them access on no fewer than five occasions, on grounds that they had not provided him with any evidence of a genuine scholarly intention or adequate credentials to handle such ancient materials.

But some people couldn't take a hint, however formally it was stated.

All at once, Michael chuckled at the strange absurdity of his morning. A group of fools in Britain seeking access to priceless manuscripts, while a lone fool in America claimed to be a 'Gnostic Terrorist'. *The ancient Gnostics were as far from modern-day world terrorism as night from day*, Michael mused. A bit of nonsense that was a momentary object of predictable media misrepresentation.

Sighing, he tossed the letter into a bin at his feet and pushed the whole matter from his mind.

CHAPTER 6

Hays Mews, London

Detective Inspector Joanna Alwell's head sprang up. 'Andrew Wess wasn't your husband?'

Emily shook her head slowly, hardly noticing the other woman's surprise. The detective's reddening face foiled her effort to control a quickly mounting embarrassment. 'I'm sorry. I was told you were married, and I assumed from the identical surname . . .'

'I kept my maiden name when I married. Andrew is my younger cousin from back in the States. He's been visiting us these past three weeks. He'd never been to London.' Emily's words faltered, nostalgia creeping in, uncontrolled and unwelcome. When she continued, her voice wavered. 'We used to spend our summers together, out in the woods, all through our childhood. Climbing trees, building forts. Whatever the summer brought.' Her words began to choke in her throat.

DI Alwell gave her a moment, regaining her own composure, then steered her back towards the events of the morning.

'So these men broke in and attacked your *cousin*, in order to steal a map. A map of what?'

'It doesn't make any sense,' Emily answered. 'When your colleagues asked me to look through the desk and see what was missing, I noticed immediately what the men had taken. It was a file containing a manuscript I've been examining – a recent acquisition I'd made for CUA.'

'CUA?'

'Catholic University of America, in Washington DC. I'm a visiting professor there for the year, during my sabbatical from Carleton College in Minnesota. One of my chief roles is to acquire new materials for the university's special collection. This stay in London was for me to collect this manuscript and bring it back to Washington. My husband's family home here in the city is a convenient hub for us, especially since he's here for a twelve-month post.'

'Your husband is British?'

Emily nodded in the affirmative, and DI Alwell took down the detail.

'So these men broke in to steal a manuscript,' the detective added a moment later, looking up. At least there was a clear motive. 'Is it valuable?'

'To historians, of course. But in monetary terms it's hardly worth stealing. The university purchased it from a private collector here for just over £7,500.'

'That's not exactly pocket change.'

'Maybe not. It's a matter of perspective. The last acquisition my office made was of an eleventh-century parchment. Our bill there was $600,000. We only got this one so cheaply because there's some debate over its authenticity. It might be a later forgery.'

Alwell raised an eyebrow. 'I had no idea old documents went for so much.' She took the details down in her notebook. 'So the intruders took this ancient map and left?'

'It's not a map.'

'You said—'

'I said that's what they called it. The manuscript is a mid fifteenth-century French text recounting the history of a settlement in the Languedoc. I have no idea why they referred to it as a map. There's nothing on it but text, and none of that text relates to geography.'

Alwell took down these details, too. Whether they made any more sense to her than they did to Emily was impossible to determine from a face that had practised professional dispassion for years.

'What happened next, Dr Wess?'

'That's the moment Andrew yelled out and stormed into the room. A second later, the gunshots came. The men didn't linger after they'd killed him.' Emily fought for composure. 'They took the manuscript. Left by the rear entrance.'

Concluding her notes, DI Alwell looked up at her. 'Is there anything else? Anything at all?'

Emily shook her head in the negative – her first and only lie of the morning. For whatever reason, something pushed her to keep quiet about a fact that she knew changed the contours of the scene before her, perhaps dramatically. She knew it was important, but she could not bring herself to tell it to the officer.

Alwell sat up in her chair, tucking her pad into a pocket on her uniform. 'There's one last thing to attend to. The US Embassy needs to be informed of your cousin's death,' she said. 'You can do this yourself, Dr Wess, or I can do it for you, though you'll need to be in touch with them directly at some stage.'

Emily nodded at the latter option and the DI attempted to offer a consoling smile. 'All right. That's enough for now. You've been tremendously helpful. I know you've been anxious to get to the phone. Is there anyone we can call for you? Anyone you might want to talk to first at this difficult time?'

Only one name came to Emily's mind, and she announced it to the detective without hesitation.

'Michael Torrance. I'd like to speak with my husband.'

CHAPTER 7

The Outskirts of Terrasini, Italy

'This is the whole shipment? Are there other crates?' Mustafa Aqmal looked over the three boxes before him without gazing up at the courier.

'No, it's everything.'

He removed a full-sized Kabar from a sheath at his waist and used the military knife to cut the cord binding the first wooden crate. Lifting the lid, he carefully examined its contents, ensuring all was as he expected it to be, before lowering the cover gently back into place. He repeated the process twice, once for each of the remaining crates, before finally turning to the courier. The cigarette dangling from Aqmal's thin lips accentuated every action with a puff of thick, curling smoke that seemed to wrap around his heavily accented words.

'Where did you source the compounds?'

'The principal ingredients from my source in Gattières, in more than ample quantity. This you can see.' The courier's accent was stronger than Aqmal's, he spoke a muted African French in which his 'th's came out as soft 'z's.

'The final elements for the reaction are from his associate in Germany. Just as you instruct. Nothing from anywhere on the watch list.'

Aqmal had been specific: all countries designated on the Terrorist Watch List were to be strictly avoided.

'And the circuitry materials?'

'Also from Berlin,' the man confirmed. The courier spoke quickly, wanting to please his buyer. He also felt the rising desire to complete the delivery and get away as swiftly as possible. Something about the man's tone during their phone conversations had set him on edge, and meeting him in person only renewed that discomfort. The courier knew nothing about the individual before him, but something intangible suggested a darkness he did not wish to explore. And the man had horribly vacant eyes that seemed to stare right through him. He wanted to get away from those eyes as fast as he could.

Aqmal gazed long at the three boxes. They contained all the supplies his mysterious clients had requested, and from sources that wouldn't raise suspicion. His promise of an efficient and untraceable delivery had thus far been fulfilled. His aim and theirs was met.

Almost.

'Who knows of the shipment?' he asked. 'Who is aware these materials have been brought here?'

The African courier, used to being questioned, had his answers well prepared. In the hierarchy of black-market transactions his work was critical, but his position as low on the totem pole as it was possible to be. To stay alive and in business, he had learned years ago, meant always to be prepared to give a full accounting.

'I brought them myself. I take my uncle's boat from Toulon to Cannes, and last twenty-four hours in that death trap' – the courier motioned towards a small 1986 Ford Transit parked a few metres away – 'driving to Genova, then down to Arezzo and past Rome. This morning I take a ferry from Napoli. I know the captain, and for a little cash he takes me on board, no question, no inspection, and sets me down in Ficarazzi, away from port traffic.' The man finished his report, self-satisfied at his labours. 'That these crates are here,' he added, 'is only known to two men in the world: you, and me.'

Aqmal nodded, the motion of his head distracting the courier from the slight movement of his hands.

'Good. But I'm afraid that's where you're wrong. Their existence here is known only to one man. Me.'

The courier was momentarily confused. 'But I—'

It was then that he saw Aqmal's right hand, raising the Kabar up to chest height. This time the blade was not pointed towards the packing cords. What moments before had been a tool was now a weapon, wielded by a man whose haunting eyes bore directly into him, devoid of any emotion.

With a certainty that came from too many years working on the market, the courier saw what was coming, and even as he bolted to dodge the blade, a helpless 'Non!' escaping his lips, his mind knew where this moment led. His presentiment was fulfilled in the sudden lunge forward of Aqmal's lithe frame, forcibly halting his attempted escape. The Arab man grabbed his torso with his free hand and forced the knife between his ribs, piercing his heart without a sound.

As the courier dropped slowly to the ground, his final contribution to the shipment was accomplished.

CHAPTER 8

The British Museum, London

The ancient telephone on Michael's desk vibrated as it rang, sending the papers around it into a flutter.

'Hello?' he answered, lifting the receiver to his ear while his eyes remained glued on a photocopied article. Most of the office calls Michael received were quick matters of routine business and he'd learned to multitask without losing his focus.

'Is this Dr Torrance?'

'Yes.' He used his free hand to highlight a segment of the article that struck him as potentially significant.

'Dr Michael Torrance, of the British Museum?'

'The same.' Another highlight, a quickly circled key word. A turn to a new page.

'Dr Michael Torrance of 46 Hays Mews, Westminster?'

Michael finally paused from his reading. 'Yes, I'm Michael Torrance. Who is this?'

'My name is Detective Inspector Joanna Alwell, with the Specialized Crime Division. I'm phoning you on behalf of your wife, Dr Emily Wess.'

At the name of his wife Michael shot up in his chair. 'Is she all right?' A not unfamiliar sense of panic grabbed at him.

'Yes, Dr Torrance, your wife is safe and unharmed. But I'm afraid there's been an incident at your London home, involving her cousin.'

'What type of *incident*?' Michael's body was rigid with instantaneous worry. Emily's life over the past five years – ever since her discovery of the ancient Library of Alexandria – had been far from predictable and rarely sedentary. What had begun then as a historical exploration had culminated in the exposure of a global conspiracy that had gone as far as Washington DC and the Oval Office, beginning in a college common room and ending in an FBI debriefing room. It had been Emily's first great 'adventure', as she cherished calling it, but it had not been her last.

There was a lengthy pause following his question, and Michael heard words being exchanged quietly, away from the phone. Eventually, the detective's voice returned.

'Dr Torrance, I'm going to pass the phone to your wife.' A moment elapsed, and a different voice came across the line.

'Mike?'

'Emily! Are you okay? What's happened to Andrew?'

'He's dead,' she answered flatly, numb and too drained for any more tears. 'Two men broke in this morning and shot him.'

Michael faltered. The sense of panic returned.

The only words he could think to offer were, he knew, totally inadequate. 'Em, I'm so sorry.'

'There's more,' she continued. 'After they shot him, they stole the manuscript I'd just acquired.'

Michael's mind struggled with the report. 'They killed him for your manuscript? Why would anyone do that? What kind of manuscript?' He tried to anticipate the various possibilities.

'One which, until this morning, I hadn't thought was anything special. A fifteenth-century document, maybe forged, from the Cathar Gnostic community near Mont-Louis.'

As she spoke, something turned over in Michael's stomach. Taking into account the television report he'd seen only fifty minutes before, this was the second time within the hour that mention of violence and Gnosticism had been strangely paired together.

Coincidence.

'Are you still at home?' he asked, coming back to himself.

'Yes. The investigators are finishing up and starting to leave.'

'Don't move,' Michael instructed, already rising from his chair. 'I'll be there as fast as I can.'

CHAPTER 9

Chicago, Illinois

The man whom some knew as Walter retrieved a new cell phone from his pocket and dialled a long series of digits from memory. The line took only a few moments to connect. The phone on the other end did not complete a single ring before being answered.

'I'm listening.' No greetings were exchanged. No names would be used. The protocol had been discussed and rehearsed many times.

'It's time.'

From Walter's seat at the Palm Court restaurant of the Drake Hotel, Chicago's 'Magnificent Mile' was framed in picturesque view through large, tinted windows. Even as he made the call that would set the final phase of their plan in motion, he knew this place was the perfect stage. Lining the six-lane Mecca of consumerist self-indulgence were endless shops, ranging in their degree of glamour from Ralph Lauren, Tiffany & Co. and Luis Vuitton, to the Disney Store and the Purple Pig. Even in the early morning, the street bustled and tourist-shoppers jostled excitedly from one glass door to the next, caught up in the surroundings and willing to pay twice the actual value for items they only here realized they couldn't live another moment without.

Walter looked on the scene with unmitigated disgust. Everything about the sight repulsed him, from the fat, materialistic shoppers who scuttled about like insects below, feeding on the dung heap of decadent materialism, to the buildings themselves, which stood like dazzling, shiny monuments to gluttony and delusion. Even the so-called 'religious' buildings of the Mile had fallen prey to the convoluted idolatry of the age, with the Archdiocese of Chicago's complex blending seamlessly into Saks Fifth Avenue, leaving considerable doubt as to whether there was any real difference to the philosophies exemplified within them.

If anything was proof of the Great Leader's interpretation of the End, this was it. The world was lost, dead, over. Anything good was long since gone, leaving behind only . . . only, *this*. A sour taste formed in Walter's mouth.

The silence on the phone became conspicuous, and he turned his attention back to the exchange.

'Release the video.'

The slightest pause, then the brief, expected response. 'Consider it done.'

Walter said nothing further, and a moment later the line went dead. The diminutive script had been followed to the letter and the men on the other end would know precisely what to do. The video they had prepared a week earlier would be released and the public face of the plan set in motion. Truth would begin to be spoken in darkness, and the elect would at last be set free.

Just as had been intended for nearly two thousand years.

Walter took a sip from his water glass and a bite from the single slice of plain bread he'd ordered from a visibly unimpressed waiter a few moments before, turning the small phone over in his hand. He raised his gaze from the street to the buildings lining the avenue to the south, his eyes settling on the site that had been selected long ago. Its location was ideal: accessible, along the scheduled route, and the central structure of a gardened square where the Mile was at its widest and the greatest concentration of people would be assured. Its elevation was perfect. At just over 150 feet it was tall enough to ensure wide exposure, without being so high as to diminish the impact or effect.

Even the design was fitting. On a street that glistened with everything modern, this building looked old. Almost ancient, so much like their own cause.

With no need to linger further, Walter set the cell phone down on the table, wiping it clean of his prints. He would leave it as he departed, a tool that had served his purpose and was no longer required. Gazing back through the window, for a brief moment the scene before his eyes changed. He saw a vast, fiery cloud; glass fragmenting the sun as it fell like rain; bricks loosing their connected clutch and turning to vapour. He saw ash and dust and an impact blast stronger than any natural wind. He saw the future, and it filled him with an excited satisfaction.

When he blinked, the vision was gone. Before him was once again the glitz of the present, yet his satisfaction remained.

CHAPTER 10

Hays Mews, London

'Emily, my God.' Michael's comment came the moment he entered their London home, seeing her standing before the sofa. 'I'm so, so sorry.' He rushed to her side and embraced her with all his strength.

'I really don't know what to say.' Michael surrounded her with powerful, reassuring arms.

'Neither do I.' Emily pressed herself into his embrace, the physical consolation going further than words. When she came out of it, she sank into the sofa and Michael took a seat next to her, keeping her hand reassuringly contained in one of his own. He passed his other hand through her shoulder-length hair, still uncombed from the previous night's unrest.

Around them, the remaining personnel from Homicide Command, together with the last huddle of forensics officers, busily concluded their work in the plush house. Michael's family home at 46 Hays Mews had been a surprise gift to the couple after their marriage – as an incentive, Michael and Emily had both suspected, to ensure they regularly came back to England to visit. This morning it seemed cold and clinical, the forensics officers in their paper suits only adding to the awful ethos of a home that had become a crime scene.

Emily's distress was apparent, and the tender flesh around her eyes made it clear that she had wept through most of the morning – though there were no tears now. For his part, Michael's sudden sense of guilt was visible in his features. Of all nights to have chosen to stay over at the museum, stiffly catching a few hours' sleep on the cot in his office in the name of a late night's work and an early start.

'I've run dry of tears,' Emily announced, breaking the awkward silence. 'It's like my emotions have gone numb, Mike.'

'You've been through a shock. God knows you'll need some time, Em, to absorb it all.'

Her emotional state was hard to imagine. Emily and her cousin had been close, to a degree he had rarely witnessed in what amounted to semi-distant relatives, and though Michael had only known him since his own wedding, he had long since learned why Emily's love for Andrew was so strong. He was affable, boyishly enthusiastic about everything and yet surprisingly deep, overwhelmingly caring. Michael had come to consider him his own family in more than just a legal sense, finding in Andrew the welcome brother he'd never had.

He knew his current shock would give way to a terrible grief. Emily's must be . . .

He clutched her hand more firmly, the action the only replacement for words he couldn't find.

'Michael,' Emily finally said, raising her head and angling

to face him directly, 'there's something about this morning I can't understand.'

He didn't know how to answer. Loss, trauma . . . these were things that went beyond understanding.

'The men who broke in and killed Andrew,' Emily continued, 'they were after the manuscript I had here in the house.'

'You said so on the phone.'

'They killed him . . . for a *manuscript*.' The colour returned to Emily's cheeks as she repeated her point, and it was a red that matched the anger in her words. 'For a manuscript it makes no sense to kill for.'

Michael could see the emotions shifting in her expression: grief, anger, rage, sorrow, all cycling over her features with increasing intensity.

Suddenly, her gaze was sharper.

'They called it a map,' she said, speaking almost to herself. 'A map. That was important to them.'

'Maps attract interest, Em. Maybe they thought it would lead them to something.' Michael tried to keep his voice supportive. 'The thieves could have been anyone. Black-market dealers. Treasure hunters.'

The words triggered a memory, and Emily's mind was suddenly filled with the memory of the childhood treasure hunts that Andrew had staged for her, tucking small toys and sweets into crooks in a woodshed or perching them on the branches of a tree, providing riddles in the style of Dr Seuss poems to lead her to her prize.

Her eyes filled with moisture, but she turned to Michael with resolve.

'It makes no sense, Mike. The manuscript wasn't a map.'

'Wasn't a map?'

'It was text, nothing more.' A tear broke over Emily's right eyelid and rolled down her cheek, but she did not alter her gaze.

'Em, I'm so sorry. That they would kill Andrew for a, a . . . mistake.' It seemed to make the brutal act even worse.

Emily squeezed her eyes closed, the rage and grief almost too much; but beneath them was a distinct memory. The memory of one intruder questioning the manuscript, recognizing it was only text; and of the second man, dead certain it was more.

When she opened her eyes they were red, but determined.

'No, it wasn't a mistake.'

Michael tried to comprehend her defiance. 'But if it wasn't a map?' He let the question linger.

Emily sat forward.

'Sometimes there's more to a document than meets the eye.'

CHAPTER 11

Hays Mews, London

'More than meets the eye?' Michael asked. 'Emily, I'm not sure I know what that means.' It was starting to seem likely that her grief was getting the better of her reasoning.

Emily, however, clung to the detail and its possibilities. Perhaps, in the midst of the burning question, she would find a temporary respite for the emotions of the morning.

'There were two men here, Mike,' she announced, wiping her cheeks dry. 'I heard most of what they were saying in the office, and one of them asked the other if the manuscript was a map. He pointed out that it didn't look like one.'

'A mistake,' Michael repeated.

'That's just it: the other one was convinced. He knew he was staring at text, but he saw something else.'

Michael let out his breath, recognizing where she was leading. 'More than meets the eye . . .'

'Exactly.'

Emily paused, collecting her thoughts, then sat up straight, blinking the moisture from her eyes.

'Mike, I don't know exactly what this means, if anything at all, but one thing I don't believe is that Andrew was killed for some random break-in, or thieves stealing the wrong document.'

'Emily, I know it's awful. I loved him too, but—'

'No!' Emily stood as the word came out, almost a yell. Michael went silent, stunned by her sudden ferocity.

'I won't accept it,' Emily said, her voice quieter but the tears returning. 'I do not accept it. There is more going on here. Andrew did not die for nothing.'

Her husband sat quietly. He couldn't fault his wife's grief, but he felt it was leading her to irrational conclusions. 'Em, even if you were right that there was more to this manuscript than just text, what difference would it make? These men wanted their "map", and they got it.'

Emily seemed to stare down at him far longer than the few seconds her silence actually occupied, before responding with two quiet, firm words.

'Not quite.'

Michael's brow wrinkled. Rather than explain, Emily turned and walked away from him. It was time to share with her husband the piece of information she'd kept from the investigators. Walking to a bureau at the side of the room, she slid open a small drawer and extracted an archival file. Returning to the sofa, she stood before Michael.

'What those men apparently didn't realize, was that the document they were after is not a single page long. It's two. And the second page is right here.'

CHAPTER 12

Al Bukamal, Iraq

At the north-eastern corner of the small freight yard at Al Bukamal, near the American Al Asad airbase, a small van turned into the grounds and began to weave through the narrow lanes between cargo containers and packing crates. The vehicle moved slowly but deliberately, the driver knowing his route precisely.

Two minutes after it had entered the lot the van pulled to a stop near the opposite corner, in front of a coffee-skinned man who had surveilled its approach carefully.

Ebion watched the driver exit the cab. His companion was on time.

'You made it,' he said, matter-of-factly. The driver was casually dressed, his blond hair cut crew-style and his features sharp. He shook Ebion's hand with a firm grasp, powerful and significant enough to symbolize something more than mere formality. Then he nodded towards the metal shipping container positioned at Ebion's feet.

'Everything's in order?'

'Just like you wanted it. The device is packaged in the small inner box, and the items around it are standard possessions, liked you asked for.'

Surrounding the box that contained the device, itself measuring only one foot by two feet by fifteen inches, were canteens, cookware, clothes, tools and various other items that would routinely accompany a soldier returning from a long posting abroad.

'And the inner container?'

'Lined like you requested. It won't stand up to heavy-duty scanning, but there's enough lead grafted to the interior to throw off a light X-ray.'

'No need for it to stand up to anything stronger,' the soldier said. 'My effects will be going with me on the personnel transport later today. There won't be anyone on the plane but us, all military. I'll be surprised if it even gets X-rayed.'

'If the outer crate is opened, the device's housing looks almost exactly like a standard metal supply box. It shouldn't attract attention. But if someone opens that . . .' Ebion let his voice trail off.

'The plan will work either way, whether I make it to Chicago or not. You and I both know that.'

'Of course.' Ebion admired the soldier's dedication. He was another true devotee.

The details confirmed, the two men loaded the crate into the van and the soldier moved towards the driver's door, ready to depart. He turned back to Ebion, scanning over the man's traditional dress and recently added beard, short and sandy and trimmed in the customary manner.

'I'll be damned if you don't look as fucking Iraqi as the best of 'em,' he muttered, smiling.

Ebion was pleased at the remark. As one of the few brothers who felt at home in the other-worldly culture of the Middle East, or 'Ancient Asia Minor' as the brethren called it, he had been uniquely qualified for this mission. Neither he nor his American passport considered him to be Iraqi, but as the son of a mixed marriage he had always felt a connection with his mother's homeland. That this connection could now be used to further their cause was confirmation of the higher purpose to his life.

Crafting the device according to the exacting specifications required had taken substantial effort on Ebion's part. Thanks to front work put in by locals who knew more of the anti-American scene in Iraq than he, contacts with the right people had been made in advance. The timer and firing mechanism were integrated into a metal casing that contained two empty cylinders, each of a slightly different size, crafted to hold the proper amount of the powerful compounds already waiting across the sea. They had been constructed with the same materials, sourced from the same regional providers, as two devices that had recently been employed in the volatile Diyala province. He had even managed to locate one of the men who had constructed those devices, employing him to help ensure that the mechanism for his own was recognizably similar. That was a critical detail, and Ebion was satisfied it had been met.

The assembly markings scribbled on various elements in the device were also, critically, written in regional Arabic, ensuring that the proper cultural connections would be evident.

'Leave ends in two hours,' the soldier said, stepping up into the cab. 'Transport goes wheels-up ninety minutes later.'

'Then safe travels, and good luck.' Ebion took his hand again through the cabin window and shook it with genuine admiration. The soldier glanced back, suddenly reflective, as the van's engine rolled over into life.

'Did you see the video?'

'Sure did,' Ebion answered. 'I watched it online this morning. Almost indistinguishable from the genuine article.'

'Gonna scare the shit out of 'em back home. I've heard the government's taking it seriously.'

Ebion merely nodded.

'It's perfect.'

CHAPTER 13

Hays Mews, London

'There's a second page?' Emily's revelation came as an unexpected bolt to Michael.

'Andrew and I were looking over it last night,' she answered. 'Since you were staying over at your office for the working weekend on your new delivery, he had my sole attention for a good grilling. You know how curious he's always been about our work.'

Despite her trauma, Emily took comfort in being able to say 'our', and stepped closer to Michael. His shift of career into academia – and, in particular, ancient history – following her adventures five years ago, had been a welcome joining of the minds. He'd proved just as good at it as she'd known he would be, and she often found herself wondering if his talents wouldn't catch him up to her academic stature a little faster than pride might prefer. But today, in this moment, that affinity was a welcome support.

'I was pointing out a few of the document's peculiar phrases and vocabulary,' Emily said. 'When we were finished, I put it in the drawer nearby. It was late.'

Michael looked at the folder in Emily's hands. The purpose-constructed manuscript file was nearly an inch thick, foam padding protecting the ancient document within.

'Can I see it?' he finally asked, motioning towards the file.

Emily took the folder to the dining table where she could lay it open carefully, motioning Michael to follow.

Contained within the lining was a single page of yellowed parchment, covered in carefully penned, medieval French script. Whoever had written the text had done so in a thick, black ink that had only slightly faded with age. The scribe had been diligent: there were still faint signs of the shallow indentations he had scored across the page to ensure straight and even rows of text.

As Michael examined it, his curiosity grew. To his right, Emily's eyes reddened at the sight of something that was now more than an object of historical interest. This page bore some connection to the men who had killed Andrew. It was the only connection she had.

'You can see,' she said, stepping closer and forcing out her words, hoping that emotional overload might be avoided through a concentrated focus on the facts, 'the script is of a style that would have been common in the fifteenth century. We've tested the parchment to confirm roughly that age, but we still suspect a later forgery. A forger could have had access to older materials. Molecular ageing can't be faked.'

'It's in good condition, Em.'

'I know, and that's surprising, since it obviously wasn't a

terribly important document when it was written.' Emily motioned towards a crossed-out correction, midway through the page, her mind supplementing the narrative with words she didn't speak.

An unimportant document, typos and all. Of all the things to die for.

'A rewrite?' Michael questioned, examining the marking.

'Just the one, in a passage on a series of shops in a town market. The original phrase translates as "thirty-two hands south-west," but it's been crossed out with a correction of "thirty-five". That wouldn't have been allowed in a formal document. This might have been a draft, or something for local use.'

Bastards.

Michael's head bobbed in understanding. 'The text itself, what's it about?'

'A pretty typical historical reflection on a Cathar community in the Languedoc countryside.'

'Cathar,' Michael repeated, looking up from the ancient document. That reference again. Emily had mentioned it on the phone.

His thoughts not yet fully formed, Michael found himself muttering, half under his breath. 'Hard to not see a pattern.'

Emily studied him. 'What do you mean?' Something in Michael's expression beckoned – a glint of a puzzle he wasn't quite sure connected.

'I'm not sure I should speculate,' he caught himself, 'given your emotional state.'

Emily's expression instantly went hard.

'Don't you dare coddle to my "emotional state"!' she snapped. 'Emotions are about all I've got right now, but if you've got something more, you're damned well going to tell me!'

Michael took the scolding calmly, recognizing his poor choice of words. Emily was not one to be condescended to. For all her strengths, it was one thing she was never willing to accept, especially from him.

'I'm sorry. You're right. But bear in mind, it's probably all just coincidence.'

'I will once you tell me.'

'For months, right up to this morning,' Michael started, his discomfort at the speculative line of thought showing through in his posture, 'I've been pursued by a group seeking access to Coptic texts at the museum. Coptic *Gnostic* texts, dealing with various sects of the fourth and fifth centuries. Nothing unusual on its own, but then this morning my boss tells me to switch on the telly, and there's a news report of a lad in the US who's been arrested, calling himself a "Gnostic terrorist".'

An unexpected comment. Emily felt a slight increase to her pulse.

'But, that's back in the States.'

'I know. Coincidence, like I said. But then, this same morning, men break into our house and steal a document recounting the history of the Cathars, a French *Gnostic* sect.'

Three curiosities, all in a row, all with a common theme. Emily could see the intrigue, but it was too much coincidence to be consoling, even amidst the grab-for-anything hopefulness of her raw emotions.

'They can't be connected,' she said. 'My manuscript is about the Cathars, who had no real connection to the old Egyptian Gnostics. They were in a different part of the world, and they lived a millennium later.'

'But they felt themselves to be a continuation of those earlier groups,' Michael pointed out, for the moment strangely compelled by the curious ties between the three events that had consumed his morning. 'And they held the same basic Gnostic beliefs: a radical division between body and spirit, a belief in the saving power of true, secret knowledge. In the request I rejected this morning, a letter by an Arthur Bell sought the museum's manuscripts that dealt with precisely those themes.'

Emily froze, her skin suddenly clammy.

'What did you say?'

Her eyes drilled into his, shaped by a new emotion Michael could read as if it were transcribed on her forehead.

Shock.

'Which part?' he asked.

'The name, of the man who wrote to you.'

'Arthur Bell,' Michael repeated.

'The map . . .' Emily muttered, her memory surging. 'They said the map was what he would need.'

'Who would need?' Michael was now completely lost.

'They never said his last name.' Emily grabbed her husband's shoulders and turned him squarely into her face.

'But they mentioned his first. I can't forget it. The name was Arthur.'

CHAPTER 14

Hays Mews, London

Whether Emily was driven more by grief or by reason Michael could not say. What he could not deny, however, was that the connections he had suspected were gaining hints of being something more. The sensationalist labelling of an American news report to one side, the fact that a man called Arthur was behind the attack on their home and the theft of a Gnostic manuscript, while at the same time a man called Arthur was harassing him for Gnostic manuscripts at the museum, was a little too much for coincidence.

'Are you sure of the name?' Michael asked. If it was a misremembered detail, there might not be any connection at all.

'I'm positive. I can still hear their words, muffled by the linens in the closet.'

Michael's doubts faded. Emily's memory could rarely be faulted. It was an attribute that had helped her excel in academics from her youth. It had also been extremely annoying in their marriage, though most of the time Emily politely pretended that she didn't remember every single faux pas committed by her husband since the first day they had met.

Michael's voice took on an edgier tone.

'Listen,' he said, sliding the paper evenly between them, 'you told me before that Catholic University suspects this manuscript might be a forgery, right? That's why you were able to buy it so cheaply.'

A nod in affirmation.

'Well, if that's the case and these men were as certain as you say that they were looking at a map, then maybe their certainty might be a clue. Maybe it's a forgery after all. Maybe the text is fake, designed to conceal what's really here.' Michael pointed down at the second page.

'A map,' Emily whispered.

'There are plenty of ways that could be done.'

Emily's mind started to speed through the possibilities.

'If it's a later manuscript, all sorts of avenues open up. The seventeenth and eighteenth centuries were filled with coded documents, layered inscriptions and the like.'

Suddenly, Emily's shoulders sagged. She let her head loll forward, her appearance deflated. Michael could see the self-defeat start to spread over her features, and suddenly more than anything in the world he wanted to keep it from taking possession of her. Emily was a Midwestern girl-done-good, a woman who had risen to the top of her field thanks to a strength and resilience that seemed, to others, unending; but above all else Emily was his wife, and he knew there were weaknesses, too. Fragility. The appearance of her frailty brought out every protective impulse Michael had ever possessed. He reached out a hand, took her by a wrist, and placed the ancient manuscript in her grasp.

'I don't think so, Em. I think there might be more to this, and I know you'd want to chase up any possibility.' He signalled to the page.

'The men who killed Andrew thought there was more to this manuscript. The fact that they didn't take this second page means we have a way to find out whether they were right, and maybe find a link to whoever they are in the process.'

Emily stared at the antique lettering covering the browned page. Michael softly touched her chin, turned her face towards his.

'We've got to figure out what this text is hiding.'

CHAPTER 15

FBI Field Office, Chicago

The woman at the head of the long table called the meeting to order with an efficient, 'Let's begin, boys.' Angela Dawson's words, spoken with a familiar authority, were barely out of her mouth before the rapid-fire comments of the briefing began. The commanding woman, her first silver hairs beginning to make their appearance among a host of brown but with the posture and strength of a woman half her age, was accustomed to speaking to everyone in the department as her 'boys', and they were all – male as well as female – used to hearing it.

'The threats on the ground are, so far as we can tell, the routine for any run-up.'

'All the relevant sources are being monitored.'

'The wires are lively. Same shit as before most events, most of it. That's good. Familiar means fewer surprises.'

The city's famous Fourth of July parade was less than seventy-two hours away, and given the calibre and number of dignitaries participating, oversight of security rested in their hands.

Special Agent Ted Gallows, sectional head of foreign intelligence assessment, leaned back in his chair. His words were marked by a strong Boston accent, a constant reminder to everyone around him – if his general brusqueness and ability to make everyone in his presence immediately uncomfortable did not do the trick on their own – that the imposing man's roots were not in the Midwest, but in big city, east coast intelligence operations.

'Most of our attention's been on the Big Three, as it's been for the past week. The Swords of Righteousness, the Church of Truth in Liberation and the Soldiers for Justice have all issued threats on the parade, and each has yielded background data that suggests their threats could amount to more than just words.' Gallows spoke the dramatic words nonchalantly, leaning back in the large chair.

As usual, threats had been flowing in for weeks – a routine happening in the run-up to any major public spectacle. The current bomb-threat count was seven, while declared assassination intentions stood at three and included the mayor, the police commissioner and the head of one of the city's most conservative churches, all of whom would be participating in the procession. There had even been one threat to situate a sniper atop the Willis Tower, still better known as the Sears Tower, picking off as many people as ammunition would allow. That there would be a special contingent of religious leaders in this year's parade – a 'Unity Procession' as the Governor was billing it – meant that the pro- and anti-religious threats had been coming in thick for months. Most of the threats were hoaxes. Separating the dross from the rest was the group's chief aim.

'The Swords of Righteousness have issued ultimatums here before,' Deputy Director Dawson noted, glancing down at her notes. 'Two years ago.'

'Almost to the day. They threatened to "devastate and destroy" the Fourth of July parade the year before last.' Gallows leaned forward, the front legs of his chair coming down with a sudden thump. 'A day after their video arrived, our agents located an improvised explosive device in Fourth Presbyterian on East Chestnut.'

'Currently there's a general threat posted anonymously on two tourist websites for this year's parade, claiming an "explosion of wrath" will come from the Two Prudential Plaza tower twenty minutes in.' The detail came from Special Agent Laura Marsh, one of the principal members of the anti-terrorism squad. Her sandy-blonde hair was cut relatively short and her hazel eyes seemed to flare with intensity.

'But our suspicion is that these are mock copies, playing to the group's former MO.' A *modus operandi*, once known, was easy to imitate.

'All the same,' Dawson interrupted, 'I trust we've scoped out the building and heightened the security detail on site.'

'We've coordinated with the Chicago PD's Bureau of Patrol to ensure the whole block has heightened force presence for the next three days,' interjected Alan Mayfair, another of the Division's sectional heads, a man known for his obscure demeanour and penchant for speaking briefly and rarely. 'The force's Intelligence Service is working with us on expanded safety checks.'

'It's pretty much the same with the Soldiers for Justice,' Marsh cut back in. 'The threats have come in the form of online postings to local discussion groups, but the IP addresses on the posts trace to a series of cyber cafes where we're aware hoaxers congregate. Chances are good these are idle threats, but we've sure as hell got the resources to see where they lead.'

The stature of the FBI's Chicago Division was a matter of pride to the agents who staffed it. Still technically a 'Field Office', a cachet that would otherwise suggest something small, mobile and situational, the massive complex the Division now populated at 2111 West Roosevelt Road was anything but temporary. The Chicago Division Field Office had a reputation that was second-to-none within the Bureau. Not only was it the heart of the most effective counter to criminal activities in the nation – a reputation that harkened back to its work to bring down the Chicago Outfit and post-Prohibition mob activities in the 1930s – it was also one of the country's most active hubs of activity in defence of the national security.

'What about the other group, this "Church of Truth in Liberation"?' Dawson asked.

'Our knowledge there is scant at best,' Ted Gallows answered. 'We wouldn't know about them at all, had it not been for an anonymous message left on the anti-terrorism tip line almost eight months ago. No follow-up was possible: the callback number was a dead line, and the information too general to bump it up the priority chain for detailed scrutiny.'

'But the name has been in our files since,' Marsh added, 'and especially as the few details in the message mentioned Chicago and some kind of attack, we've been keeping our eyes open here.'

'It's not a faction that's ever shown up on our radar before,' followed Gallows. 'Our background research has them as some kind of New Age religious group originally based in Los Angeles. Their rhetoric's mostly about enlightenment and spirituality, but they have no track record of violence.'

The Deputy Director, however, had seen the video.

'Boys, that's no longer a safe assumption.' She clicked a small remote on the tabletop and the grainy internet video began to play on a wall-mounted display.

'If this so-called Church of Truth in Liberation doesn't have a past in terrorism, it sure as hell looks like they're trying to forge a future.'

CHAPTER 16

FBI Field Office, Chicago

The video started to play the moment its first frames appeared on the monitor.

'As you all know,' Dawson said, narrating as they watched, 'this was posted online within the past twenty-four hours. The source of the posting was well concealed, and half a billion dollars of equipment notwithstanding, we still don't know its origin – but it's what first caught our attention as a genuine threat.'

She let the others watch as what was in most ways a traditional Middle Eastern activist cell video advanced on the screen. Dawson knew they had seen it already, had scrutinized every detail; but examining it together brought a common focus around the table.

'Every word's in Arabic, but the phrases are awkward even in translation.' She looked at her notes and read aloud. '*We proclaim to the Western mind that the fallen age is over. Corruption will cease and the body will be forgotten when the light of liberation will shine; and we will bring this liberating fire upon you.*'

'Shit. I flunked philosophy in college,' an agent muttered, the dense phrases meaning nothing to him.

It was Brian Smith, sectional head within the Directorate of Intelligence, who summed up the situation more constructively.

'Not exactly your ordinary Middle Eastern rhetoric.' *To say the least*, his expression seemed to add.

Everyone knew the language went on to threaten the United States, and 'a major event in the Midwest' in particular, in equally strange terminology.

'No, it isn't,' Dawson affirmed. 'And it's damned difficult to see how a foreign threat like this relates to a New Age religious sect here in the States, whether or not a dead end, anonymous tip spikes our curiosity.'

Laura Marsh turned from the screen back to the others. She'd watched the video at least twenty times that morning, and had played a key role in connecting it to the Church. 'It's the curious phrasing that marks this threat as real, and gave us grounds to make the connection with the Church of Truth in Liberation. The video itself doesn't self-identify any group affiliation, but in amongst the taunts of "death to the American lie" and other friendly rants were a few key phrases. Phrases that wouldn't have caught our attention had it not been for the arrest in New York last night of Harry Pike.'

'The one the media billed the "Gnostic terrorist"?'

'One and the same.'

'He's barely more than a kid,' Ted Gallows picked up, 'and no signs yet he's got enough brain cells in his head to count even as that. He also hasn't claimed to be part of any group, but a scan of the emails on his home computer revealed an association with the Church. And then, during police interrogation he started to use a few, well, let's just say significant phrases.'

'Phrases that also occur in this video.' Special Agent Marsh took the remote from Dawson and clicked a quick series of buttons. Three bullet points appeared on a massive LCD screen at the side of the room.

'It's here that the connection became concrete. These three phrases appear in Arabic in the video, and were uttered in English, word-for-word, by Pike.' The whole room looked over at the three phrases.

> *The light of liberation will shine.*
> *The body will be forgotten.*
> *The fallen age is over.*

'The phrases are innocuous in themselves,' Marsh continued, 'hardly more than inflated rhetoric. But now we've got a man in New York, aligned with a New Age sect here in the States, using exactly the same language as a terrorist group overseas that's threatened our local region. It's a hell of a red flag.'

No sooner had Special Agent Marsh's words been spoken than the door to the situation room slid open and a uniformed agent entered, moving quickly to the Deputy Director's side.

'This has just come from downstairs,' he whispered. He handed her a folded page and left the room as surreptitiously as he had entered. A moment later, Angela Dawson looked up at the agents around the table, their curiosity piqued. Her maternal features seemed entirely to have disappeared, and she looked every inch the Bureau's warrior-at-the-helm.

'Your red flag has just got itself a partner,' she announced, looking in Marsh's and Gallows's direction. 'Investigative forces outside of Baghdad have just reported losing the trail on a burst of cell activity near Ramadi. They've detained two cell members, who were quick to fold under questioning. They've revealed that for the past two months they'd been co-opted into the preparations for an attack to take place on American soil. Chicago was specifically mentioned as the target.' Dawson spoke her next words with significant emphasis.

'When asked for their motivation, both men answered, "The fallen age is over."'

CHAPTER 17

Ladbroke Grove, London

Number 214 Huxley Street appeared like any other house in the neighbourhood, and in most ways was. It was two storeys, only two rooms wide, and constructed of a faded red-brown brick that was common down the whole lane.

The room in which Marcianus had gathered with four of the brethren was on the first floor, and the curtains over its sole window were tightly closed. The space was lit by a row of specially installed fluorescent fixtures, hung low so as to maximize the light they shed on the large, metal worktable that filled most of the room. On the table lay a set of flat plastic trays, each an inch and a half in depth, together with a large collection of small bottles, vials and meticulously labelled containers.

'Open it up,' the Great Leader ordered. 'We've been waiting long enough.'

At the far end of the table, two Knowers opened the red folder they had obtained early that morning, and with gloved hands extracted the single page contained in its foam lining.

The strong blue-white glow of the fluorescent lights washed some of the colour out of the ancient manuscript, but even in the antiseptic environment of their workshop it had a majesty about it. Everyone in the room felt an appropriate awe.

'Still doesn't look like a bloody map,' one of the men whispered, almost inaudibly. But Marcianus heard the comment, and smiled.

'By now you should know not to let appearances distract you,' he answered in full voice. 'You know how the old writings put it: "There is nothing hidden that shall not be revealed."'

The man looked as if he was about to ask a question, but a gesture from the Great Leader cut him off. He wished to supervise the remaining preparations himself. His life was going to be a blur of activity over the coming days; he should cherish this moment, revel in its sanctity.

Marcianus was, at heart, a simple man. He had always believed that simplicity was the greatest virtue to attaining spiritual enlightenment, even if that simplicity often had to be wrapped in complex arrangements of organization. At the centre of it all, a man's soul had to know the truth, plainly and simply, as Marcianus always had. It was why their founder had seen in him a suitable successor; it was why men and women all over the world submitted themselves to the truth he could deliver. And it was why, when he had finally seen the true simplicity of the world's end, the way forward had become so clear to him. The time of preparation was over. His life's ultimate mission had become tangible: to show the brethren that the End was already here, and transform the great Liberation from a thing of expectation and hope into a concrete, present, ultimate reality.

'Get the mixtures to the right consistency,' he ordered.

Close to his own end of the table, two brethren mixed together liquid ingredients in each of the three plastic trays. An old, leather-bound journal was held open on a display mount between them, and the men concocted their solutions from the recipes written in an ancient hand on the brittle pages.

The Book. The document that had so long been their guide – and this was the original, no less. This sacred volume was as close as the Brotherhood came to having a sacred scripture.

The brethren who worked on the chemical mixtures took their time, ensuring that the amounts and proportions of each ingredient were measured exactly. The process had taken just over twenty minutes, but at last one of the chemists looked up at Marcianus.

'Master, the solutions are ready.'

The Great Leader nodded and motioned to the men at the far end of the table. Reverently, the man on the left picked up the manuscript and passed it to the Knower nearest the first tray.

Marcianus paused. All his life he had had to tone down his love for speaking in lofty rhetoric, so suitable to their heritage, in order to make sure his message reached those who needed to hear it, speaking instead in comforting tones and un-intimidating phrasing. It was his politically necessary condescension to the requirements of his office. But tonight, he was surrounded by true devotees, fully aware of the grandeur of their actions. He could speak with all the loftiness the moment deserved.

'Let us reveal tonight that which has been hidden for so many generations,' he instructed, standing proudly before his men.

The chemist's hands trembled. The moment was almost too much. He knew there would be only one opportunity. If it didn't work, if he hadn't mixed the solutions precisely right, the manuscript would be destroyed and their opportunity lost forever. There would be no second chance. Nervousness turned his courage cold, and he froze, motionless.

'Begin the exposure!' Marcianus commanded again, pointing to the tray.

Jarred out of his immobility, the chemist performed the Great Leader's bidding. With all the self-assurance he could muster, he plunged the ancient parchment downward, submerging it in the solution that crept around its edges and drowned it before their eyes.

CHAPTER 18

Montelaguardia, Italy, AD 1755

'What do you mean, you've written it down?' Talano asked, incredulous. 'How can you write down what you know must never be written?'

'Don't worry, brother,' Mario answered. 'It is not written the way you think.'

His compatriot was not satisfied.

'For close to forty generations this knowledge has been passed down by word of mouth alone. Held sacred in our memory. Unwritten memory. Who are you to change this?'

'Who am I?' Mario Terageste questioned reflectively. 'I'm no one, only a soul seeking freedom just like you. But our liberty is less and less secure with every day that passes.'

'We'll survive.'

'You've always been an optimist, Talano.' Mario smiled at him. 'Me, I've always preferred alchemy, and a good dose of reality.'

His fellow Knower looked down at the strange concoction Mario had fashioned in a large copper bowl. Sparkling flecks of the minerals he had crushed and prepared still glimmered in the nearby mortar.

'Do you really think that what you've written won't be discovered?' Talano was edgy and wanted reassurance. 'If it is, anyone might find the way . . . before the appointed time. Before the End.'

Mario held up a page of old parchment. 'Tell me what you see, brother.'

Talano scrutinized the sheet. 'Why do you tease me?' he asked. The page that Mario held was blank. 'I see nothing.'

'Then neither will anyone else,' Mario replied, smiling.

Setting down the parchment, he moved over to his desk and extracted a small leather-bound journal in which he kept his notes.

'The means of revealing my work, I'll record here. This will be our heritage, my brother. Once again our Brotherhood is persecuted fiercely, but once again the future shall be secured.'

Talano continued to examine the page, still worried.

'Now it's your turn,' Mario added. 'The map needs a cover.'

He walked across the room and handed Talano a quill and ink pot.

'How much do you know about the Cathars?'

CHAPTER 19

Central London

'The group that's been requesting my department's manuscripts at the museum has been hard to track down.' Michael Torrance and Emily Wess were little tested by the slow pace of their Hackney cab. The lunchtime traffic in central London barely moved, with streets that had first been designed to convey horses and the occasional carriage straining under the pressure of modern transport. But the back of the cab was quiet, and gave them the chance to reflect without distraction on what little they knew about the situation emerging out of Emily's cousin's murder, as they made their way towards a site that would help them study the manuscript still in their possession.

'The man who sent in the requests,' Michael continued, 'this Arthur Bell, described their interest as scholarly, but didn't put much effort into concealing that it was his community's religious interests that were really motivating him.'

'What sort of religious community considers ancient Gnostic manuscripts important? It's scholarly turf. We're not talking about copies of anybody's sacred scriptures.'

Michael didn't need to reply. Gnosticism as a distinct religious movement had died out centuries ago, as they both knew perfectly well.

'Apart from one or two cultures with historical connections,' he pondered aloud, 'such as the modern-day Mandaeans, the only groups claiming Gnostic heritage today tend to be New Agers caught up in the easy mysticism of long-lost secrets and ancient rituals. And of course, they don't have the Lord's faintest idea what they're actually talking about.'

'Is that what you think Bell's group are – New Agers? You looked into them?'

'As much as I could. Google didn't give me anything useful off his name, and as he never mentioned a title for this "ancient religious community" I didn't have much to go on. But the nature of the request, together with the lack of credentials and the allusions to religious life . . . everything in me says they're a clique of nouveaux spiritualists, trying to validate their views by gaining access to fragments of real history.'

In other settings he would have shown more reserve, but alone with Emily, Michael made no attempt to keep the distaste from his voice, and the slightly upper-class English accent that could so easily sound consoling now did a fine job conveying his distaste. He saw the whole New Age movement as a joke – groups of vague, socially popular beliefs that had no history of their own, trying to claim the background of antiquity for whatever system of thought pleased their adherents in the present. He viewed the ideology as self-indulgent and the misuse of history as academically distasteful. If it turned out such a group was behind Andrew's murder, he'd have a whole new reason to loathe them.

Emily's feelings on the topic were not as sharp. She considered his words as the taxi turned a sharp corner onto Curzon Street.

'If your suspicions are correct, then we might have a starting point for figuring out why they were after my manuscript.'

'How's that?'

'New Agers love claims of hidden wisdom and secret knowledge, and this manuscript appears to be one thing, while scholars think it might be another.'

Michael saw where she was leading.

'The kind of thing that fascinates most New Age groups. Arcane, hidden mysteries. Mystical revelations. Concealed truths a forged text might contain.'

'And if this group really *believes* that there are secrets hidden in this text,' Emily tapped the folder on her lap, 'then it just might be something they're willing to . . . go to extremes for.'

There was an uncomfortable moment of silence that followed her allusion to Andrew's death. Michael could almost see the thoughts swirling through her mind: visions of spiritualists seeking enlightenment intertwining with memories of summertime hikes and late nights sharing secrets, nestled into sleeping bags gathered around a campfire.

He reached across the bench seat and took her hand.

'One way or another, Em, there's one place where we have the best chance of finding out.' He motioned out of the window with a lift of his head. As Emily raised her own, the unmistakable facade of the British Museum came into view.

'If there's something on that page worth killing for, I promise you we'll find it.'

CHAPTER 20

Ladbroke Grove, London

All eyes were drilled on the chemist's hands as he pressed the page into the liquid solution, forcing it down with his latex-gloved fingers so that it was fully submerged in the clear bath.

'We expose it to this first solution for twenty seconds,' he noted, his partner keeping his eyes on the second-hand of the room's wall-mounted clock. His voice was timid, but with the conviction that came from having plunged past the point of no return, it gradually gained strength. 'The Book insists the exposure time is critical.'

The brethren continued to eye the manuscript as he held it beneath the surface of the solution, though it underwent no visible change during the tense wait. When his partner announced 'Now', the man lifted the manuscript from the first tray and swiftly plunged it into the second, again ensuring its complete submersion.

Marcianus was enrapt. Though the scholars from whom he had stolen it believed the manuscript to date either from the fifteenth or the sixteenth century, he knew that it had been crafted on the afternoon of July 14th, 1755, at the hands of the great alchemist and Knower, Mario Terageste – the same man who had written the Book – in a small workshop in northern Italy. He knew that it had then been hidden by a cluster of adherents outside of Montelaguardia, near Perugia, and its location safeguarded for nearly two centuries, until it was discovered in 1942. It had since passed through the hands of three caretakers before being acquired by Lady Catherine of Endsleigh, remaining in her well-secured collection ever since, until a carefully spun negotiation with the Catholic University of America had produced a sale. That sale had yielded the first point of vulnerability in the manuscript's safe-keeping in over two decades, and Marcianus had seen his opportunity to act.

'It stays in this second bath for forty seconds.' Marcianus, together with his brethren, counted each passing second with anxious anticipation. At first, the document seemed to undergo no change, but from the fifteen-second mark he noticed that the ink seemed to be getting lighter.

Lighter.

'It's fading,' he remarked, an outstretched finger pointing to the lightening text. Whatever chemical reaction was causing the change, it escalated quickly. By the time the forty seconds were up, the writing of the eighteenth-century scribe had completely vanished.

The ancient page was entirely bare.

Marcianus felt a heady wonder, potent almost to the degree of nausea. He had always known, always believed, that what had been promised by the Elect of past generations was true;

he had never doubted that their instructions were authentic and would lead to the new and final revelations. But to see the ancient document change, to know the map was coming, was no less thrilling for its being so long expected. Every decision, thought, act and expectation of his life was being validated, here and now.

'Now the final solution.' The chemist lifted the page from the second tray and deposited it in the third. 'The Book says it must stay in this solution for at least two minutes.'

Marcianus found the wait all but impossible. Pushing aside the chemist, he moved to the table edge in front of the third tray, looking down directly on the document. The blank page seemed to tease him in its emptiness, daring him to doubt or disbelieve.

The Great Leader had no intention of doing either.

'There,' he gasped a moment later, losing all but a touch of his usual composure. 'Look!' The other four men pressed in around him and every eye locked in on the waterlogged page.

On its surface, dimly at first but with increasing clarity at each passing second, a new series of inked lines began to appear. First a long, almost straight line alongside a far less geometric counterpart. Then a third and a fourth, and soon the page was covered in the kinds of irregular lines and shapes that conveyed the imperfections of natural geography. Labels began to appear, written in a script similar to that which had formerly covered the whole page, though in a different, far more ancient language.

'We have it,' Marcianus pronounced as the page continued to take on its new form. 'The ancient map is ours at last.'

CHAPTER 21

FBI Field Office, Chicago

'What have we learned?' Deputy Director Dawson asked, calling the group to order. The special task force was reassembled in the situation room of the FBI's Chicago Division complex. In the two-and-a-half hours that had passed since their larger heads of squad meeting, their teams had worked without pause on scoping out the Church of Truth in Liberation.

Ted Gallows was the first to reply. He was, as always, propped back in his chair with the front legs up in the air.

'Despite the link, through Pike, to the video broadcast from somewhere in the Middle East, everything we've found on this Church points to a low-impact religious group. Our background checks confirm the initial reports from the morning. The group's got no background in terrorism or violence of any kind. Not so much as an aggressive protest or threatening letter in their entire history.' He scratched at his chin, kept under a deliberate five-o'clock shadow that was as much a part of his uniform as his blazer.

'The only taint on an otherwise flawless reputation,' Gallows continued, 'is the message left all those months ago, and with no ability to follow up, we have no idea whether it has any credibility.'

'That doesn't mean they're clean.'

''Course it doesn't. The old adage is true: absence of evidence is not evidence of absence. Or, at least not solid proof of it.' Gallows tried to sound accommodating, which he accomplished only with difficulty. 'It's possible they've simply been successful at staying off our radar.'

'For how long?'

'The group was founded in 1961.' Special Agent Laura Marsh leaned forward as she spoke. She felt a strange competitiveness around Gallows that she didn't feel around anyone else, almost certainly occasioned by the fact that he gave no appearance of being the slightest bit impressed by anything she did, positive or negative.

'Their founder was a man named M. Laurence Mahler III. He was something of a freelance archaeologist, by all accounts, spending his family's money travelling to dig sites all over the world. Tracing his group's history has been a challenge: they don't appear to have any public front. No website, no publications, no listed buildings.'

'So you've gone to the computers?'

'It was the logical next step. Based on the few names and key terms we knew from the video and the records of Pike's arrest in New York, we've been able to construct a useful email sweep. Each time a message comes up as a match, the database incorporates its language and key terms, and the net widens.'

The procedure was a standard operation, made so much easier with the relaxed restrictions on government surveillance of its own citizens since 9/11, and Laura's efficiency in staging the electronic sweep was hardly going to impress her colleagues. Still, she took pride in her work, and her evident sense of confidence came from knowing she did it well. She had taken a Master's Degree in political science and sociology before enrolling in specialist training for the FBI, and though she'd never taken a degree, or even a course, in computing, she'd grown up with technology and had always been adept with it.

'You've had success?' asked the Deputy Director.

'Enough to give us a little more to chew on. Direct correspondence between members appears to be the principal way of informing new recruits of their history, so by linking their messages together we've been able to learn the rudimentary facts.' She looked down at her notes. 'Mahler started his group as a religious fraternity, believing he was providing new access to an ancient Gnostic, mystical tradition.'

'Gnostic,' Ted Gallows interjected, 'was the same word used by the Pike boy in New York, to describe himself.'

'So the man the press dubbed "the Gnostic terrorist" is definitely connected to this group?'

'Absolutely.'

'This emphasis on Gnosticism,' Agent Marsh continued, bringing the discussion back to the group's history, 'is the key principle of the Church of Truth in Liberation. Mahler claimed to have found some ancient document, some book, that gave him the means of access to a much more ancient tradition, and he ditched the familiar New Age crowd of the 1960s to delve into his new – or by his accounts, old – alternative.'

'This Mahler is still at the helm?'

'He died in 1979. His successor was an even more secretive man named Arthur Bell, who's apparently still their leader.'

Angela Dawson's intensity grew. 'So, we have a concrete individual behind the threat?'

'Only a name behind the group, and no info on him yet. And remember that the Church of Truth in Liberation hasn't claimed responsibility for the video,' Gallows answered.

'Well, shit,' the Deputy Director answered curtly. She tapped her fingers on the tabletop before deciding to explore another avenue. 'So our background detail is scant. What do we know about their beliefs?'

Special Agent Marsh answered. 'Even less than we do of their history. They seem intentionally guarded about discussing their beliefs in anything other than person-to-person settings. The only touches we get are brief mentions referring to their beliefs as *disciplina arcani*, which apparently means "hidden teachings" – things never to be written down, only passed on by word of mouth. And their emails suggest they take this seriously.'

'So we know *nothing* about what these people believe?'

'At this stage, only that they foster at least basic Gnostic teachings.'

'Which are?' Dawson gave a shrug that suggested she had only ever heard the term in passing.

'Yeah, I had to ask too.' Gallows swivelled his chair to the fourth person in the room, who until that moment had remained silent. He was a well-groomed man in nicely pressed slacks and a green sweater – an old-fashioned look that clashed with the stark, modern surroundings of the FBI briefing room. 'You remember Bruce Atherton, of the University of Chicago's anthropology department? He's liaised with us before on sect identification.'

Marsh and Dawson nodded in recognition. The Director waved for him to speak.

'The basic tenet of Gnosticism,' Atherton began with a practised directness, 'is a radical soul–body dualism: a belief that the spiritual world and the physical world are distinct and diametrically opposed. The material world is base and evil, and the spiritual holy and good.'

'Isn't that what most religions preach?' Marsh asked. 'Doesn't Christianity teach that the spirit is different from the body?'

'There's a difference between seeing body and soul as distinct and seeing them as fundamentally contradictory. Christianity teaches that the material world is fallen, but can be redeemed. Genuine dualism of the sort we see in the Gnostic groups of history insists they are naturally, eternally in conflict. The physical is not meant to be saved: it is meant to be eliminated, cast away, so that only the spirit remains.'

Angela Dawson tightened her grip around a pen. 'Destroying the physical? What you're saying isn't out of line with the mentality of a group that might threaten to wreak havoc on a city.'

'Maybe not,' Atherton answered. 'But violence is uncharacteristic of most Gnostic history. The term "Gnostic" itself means "knower", and Gnosticism is really a generic term for spiritual knowledge.'

'How does knowledge relate to the dualism you were just describing?'

'The knowledge about which the ancient Gnostics spoke was a secret, saving awareness. Different groups described it in their own ways, but it generally had something to do with a mystical awareness of the true nature of the universe, which enabled the Gnostic initiates themselves to renounce the material world and move towards the spiritual – to be liberated from fallen existence and become free in the spirit.' He stopped for a moment, then added, 'Gnosticism wasn't a violent movement. It was, in fact, heavily persecuted by a much more violent empire that viewed it with suspicion. Most Gnostics were peaceful and contemplative.'

Dawson leaned over the table. 'That may have been true of your Gnostics in the past, Dr Atherton. But these Gnostics today are threatening destruction on this city, one of them has just been arrested in New York with a sniper rifle, and there are apparently connected operatives from a Middle Eastern terrorist encampment on their way here – men who have sure as hell exercised violence in the past.'

She turned towards Special Agent Marsh. 'We need to know more about their agenda. If they won't write about it, then there's only one way to get the intelligence we need. You've got to get me a member of the Church of Truth in Liberation.'

CHAPTER 22

The British Museum, London

Feeling the same rush of excitement he always felt when he walked through the vast classical entrance to the British Museum, Michael swiftly led Emily through the ornate foyer and into the Great Court, its 1,656 panes of glass swelling over what amounted to the largest covered square in Europe. Directing her around the cylindrical Reading Room at its centre, he wound her through a seemingly endless series of galleries, until they at last came to an unassuming doorway.

'Most of the office will still be working on cataloguing the new Nile find,' Michael noted, passing a keycard through a scanner on the door. There was no formal placard; only a small label near the card reader indicated it as the entry to the working facilities of the Department of Ancient Egypt and Sudan. Michael waited for the lock to spring open, then he and Emily passed beyond the gaze of a public who had barely noticed their passage, their eyes enthralled with Pharaonic statues and millennia-old wall carvings.

'The department's preoccupation means the whole group

will be out of the laboratory. That should give us a little privacy with the equipment.' He placed a hand tenderly on her shoulder and pulled her into his world.

The departmental corridor was narrow and unremarkable: with no need to impress visitors with either style or upkeep, it provided solely functional access to a series of offices and workrooms. Michael's own office, the third door on the right, was flanked by those of his departmental head, William Gwyth, and a second fellowship recipient. Beyond these, another row of doors housed staff ranging from scholars and cataloguists to web designers.

Emily had been in the department only once, shortly after Michael's appointment, and then only to see what his office was like. She didn't know the surroundings.

'It's straight on, Em, just at the end of the corridor,' Michael said, motioning her forward.

A few moments later they had reached a set of shaded glass doors, clearly newer than the others in the corridor. 'Research Laboratory' was etched on the left, and to the side was another card reader. Michael slid his card through as before, this time adding a six-digit code on a keypad.

'Security's a little tighter here than for our offices, given the kit inside.'

An electronic beep signalled the successful entry and the door latch released, the lights in the room beyond automatically switching on.

The moment she entered, Emily could see why the extra security was in place. The laboratory was a storehouse of technology.

'Out in the galleries we may have one of the finest collections of antiquities in the world,' Michael said as they entered, 'but in here we've got some of the most modern technology to study it.'

Even given their present circumstances, Michael felt an energy in this setting and a surge of pride in his surroundings. His mind had had a hard time taking in the dimensions of the museum's collection when he'd first arrived – more than seven million artefacts from every continent on the globe, his own department housing over 140 mummies, sarcophagi and thousands of items that helped fill the two miles of public galleries – but the technical research provision was almost as impressive.

'That wall's the radiography equipment,' he said, pointing across the white linoleum floor to the room's far side. 'The bulky set-up there is the X-ray tube and exposure structure. Over there's the spectrographic equipment –' he motioned towards the museum's proprietary multispectral imaging platform '– and on that side of the central worktable is one of our newest toys: the CRS.'

'CRS?'

'Computed Radiography Scanner. We just got the CRx Flex scanner upgrade this summer. The big brother of older film-based X-ray developing.'

Emily took it all in, her own research rarely exposing her to such equipment.

'Everything works?'

'Everything but whatever that is in the corner,' Michael said, pointing towards a cumbersome piece of unidentifiable equipment, covered in a clear plastic sheet, 'and that's only because I don't know how to operate it.'

'Don't worry', Emily tried to force an encouraging look onto her face, still unsure how to feel about their errand here. 'If we have to go beyond the tools you do know how to use, then finding whatever may be hidden in the manuscript is going to take a lot more time than we have at our disposal.' She extracted the document folder from her bag and opened it on one of the central worktables.

Michael stepped to her side and began to pore over the manuscript's surface.

'If there's something hidden there, it'll be something physical.'

'Obviously,' Emily answered back, a little too testily. 'If the text were all that mattered, they could have just gone with a copy. Scanned images of the manuscript have been available online for more than a year.'

'On the physical side, it looks fairly clean. There are no signs of overwriting.'

'A palimpsest? No, that would be too obvious.' The words were barely spoken before Emily's face registered her regret. Michael was not to blame for what had happened. He didn't deserve her anger or her attitude.

'I'm sorry, Mike. It's just the whole—'

'Don't worry,' Michael interjected. 'I understand.' He raised a hand to her cheek, softly reinforced his care.

Emily took a deep breath, forcing down her gall. Sheathing her hands with a pair of white cotton gloves from a box on the table, she picked up the page.

'To make a palimpsest manuscript, scribes would use a sharpened blade to scrape the original ink or paint off the document's surface, so they could reuse the parchment for a new text.'

She held up the manuscript, repositioning a bright examination lamp so that it shone through the page.

'What makes palimpsest manuscripts interesting is that the erasing process never quite got rid of the underwritten material, even if they followed the scraping by washing. If you look closely enough, signs of the original text are usually evident. Some fairly amazing materials have been found that way. The Vatican has a copy of St Augustine's commentary on the Psalms, written over the top of Cicero's *De Republica*. Then there's the famous Archimedes Palimpsest at the Walters Art Museum – a whole prayer book copied over the top of two ancient and otherwise unknown scientific tracts.'

She pointed towards the edge of the page, and then to various blank sections between paragraphs and at the end of shorter lines. 'It's in these empty spaces that palimpsest manuscripts like those usually give evidence of their past. With the Archimedes Palimpsest, for example, you can't clearly read the underwriting without the help of some modern technology, but in the margins and empty spaces of the prayer book a close eye can still make out the shadows of old handwriting and scientific diagrams.'

'But there's no underwritten text here,' Michael noted, watching the lamplight flow through the page without revealing the slightest trace of phantom characters behind the inked scrawl.

'No. And in any case, it wouldn't be a good way to conceal a secret map, or anything else. The visible evidence of something else in the document would inspire curiosity – not what you usually want, if you're aiming to keep secrets. Palimpsests were created for reasons of economy, not secrecy.'

Suddenly, Emily's resolve seemed to disappear, her deflated, distraught look returning.

'Maybe Andrew's killers knew what they were doing after all. Maybe their map was only on the first page.'

There was something close to agony swelling in her voice, and Michael sensed her slipping.

'Don't give up just yet. You mentioned at the house that this manuscript might actually be from the seventeenth or eighteenth century, right?'

'Estimating, of course.'

'Well, that may give us something more specific to look for. Throughout Europe in those centuries, alchemy was rife and secret texts something of a feature of the age.'

'Alchemy?' Emily raised a suspicious brow.

'At least in the practical, chemical sense. Its practitioners often believed they were toying with mystical elements, but most practical alchemy was nothing more than basic chemistry.'

Emily pieced his observations together. 'So, a better way to conceal text on a page would be some sort of – invisible ink?'

'Why not? A chemical concoction that's invisible to the naked eye, but which another chemical agent, known to the scribe and the intended recipient, would reveal.'

'In that case,' Emily said, her enthusiasm for his idea

mounting, 'we'd need to look for some way to expose that hidden ink.'

'The easiest way to do that is to submit the page to a barrage of multispectral imaging,' Michael answered. 'Most basic chemical compounds from antiquity were mixed in doses far more concentrated than today. They should have a strong enough signature that a good dose of one or another band on the light spectrum ought to set them glowing.'

He picked up the manuscript again and gave Emily a resolute look.

'It's time to play with the lights.'

CHAPTER 23

The British Museum, London

A moment later, Emily and Michael were positioned before the museum's home-built multispectral imaging platform. A black support board held the manuscript beneath a guillotine-like frame on which a digital video camera could be positioned at just the right height. Two panels containing banks of specialized lights loomed like great arms at the sides, which Michael manoeuvred to a position nine inches above the document's surface, aimed obliquely from either side. Emily dimmed the room's main lights, while Michael powered on the system and pressed his finger to the first of a bank of small buttons.

'The first band is basic ultraviolet,' he said, 'masked in standard black light.' As he spoke, a bluish light shone out of the panels, casting an unearthly pallor over the old manuscript. The edges of the ancient lettering seemed to dance under the strange colouring, giving an illusion of depth that made it hard to focus on the text. But it was, despite the new ambiance, the same writing as before.

'See anything?' Emily asked.

Michael shook his head, and placed his hand gently on her shoulder, turning her away from the document. 'Don't look at the page itself, Em, look at the monitor.' He signalled to a computer terminal displaying the feed from the digital camera above the manuscript. 'If there are chemicals – an invisible ink, for instance – reflecting UV light, those reflections still aren't going to be visible to the naked eye. We need to use the camera to translate reflected UV light into a colour we can see.' He tapped a few sequences on the keyboard. The display changed, its colouring vaguely transformed. 'I've had the computer replace reflected UV light with visible shades of red. The brighter the hue, the more UV light being reflected off the page.'

They both studied the screen before them. While parts of the page cast back a redder glow than others, there was nothing in the image that portended a hidden text.

'There's nothing there,' Emily observed quietly.

'Let's try pure green,' Michael offered. 'While UV is the most common wavelength for showing up chemical signatures invisible to the naked eye, the museum has had a fair bit of success recently with isolated wavelengths within the RGB spectrum. Pure green, pure red. Narrow-band light reflects off different agents in different ways.'

He flipped a few switches on the scanner, and the light emitted from the two panels switched to a concentrated, alien green. But again, the new lights and their colouring revealed nothing on the computer's display. He switched to a third setting, then a fourth, but in each case, only the shade of the manuscript's surface changed under the alternating beams.

The text remained alone, unchanged.

'Damn it!' Emily's remark was not that of the dispassionate scholar encountering negative results. What little hope she had for some way out of the meaninglessness of the morning's tragedy was fading, the bright beams of the spectral imaging lights casting her disappointment in glaring colour.

'Don't give up just yet. There may still be something here. One more colour to go.' Michael switched the controls so the panel emitted a pure blue beam – so dark as to appear almost violet to Emily's eyes.

A slight gasp emerged from Michael's mouth.

'Would you look at that . . .' On the display, something new had appeared. Criss-crossing the page, not as straight lines but waving strokes, were a series of extremely faint, barely visible lines that had not been there a moment before.

'I can't make it out. It's too light.' Emily's expression was completely changed. She stared at the display with an intensity fuelled by sudden hope.

'Can you adjust the beams, make it any clearer?'

Michael tapped at the controls, but he knew the effort was futile. 'This is the final wavelength we're capable of with this equipment.' He adjusted the enhancement settings on the computer, but the phantom lines on the page did not become any clearer. They remained an agonizing tease: not enough to read whatever was hidden on the page, but enough to be absolutely certain there was something more there.

'Hold on, Mike, there may be another way,' Emily suddenly announced. Her eyes were still fixed on the display, her thoughts moving almost too fast for her to keep up with them.

She let the unformed ideas come out as she had them.

'Chemical compounds aren't the only way a clever alchemist could try to conceal a message. Assuming he had a decent knowledge of metallic properties, he could have diluted a powdered metal alloy into a clear base. Some sort of solvent could be used by the recipient, either to oxidize it or somehow discolour the metal, revealing the text.'

Michael's face betrayed his surprise.

'Metallic oxidation? Em, that's a little—'

'If that were the case,' she cut him off, keeping her thoughts in motion, 'there would be a metallic signature, but it wouldn't necessarily be chemical in nature.'

She hesitated, then stopped, letting out the remainder of her breath. Her technical expertise had met its limit. An idea, but no answers. When she turned to look at Michael, she expected to see the contours of pityingly supportive patience she knew the far-fetched notion deserved.

What she saw instead was the studious expression of a man with a new idea.

'Or,' Michael said, his words slowing, his own mind still piecing together the details, 'it could be a metal that simply doesn't reflect the light wavelengths we have at our disposal. Some alloys absorb light, rather than reflect it. But if it's metallic, then it might well appear on an—'

'X-ray,' Emily said, her face suddenly bright. She turned around and faced the bank of radiographic equipment on the opposite wall. 'And you've certainly got the tools for that.'

CHAPTER 24

Ladbroke Grove, London

Marcianus, tightly surrounded by the four Knowers, continued to direct his stare unwaveringly into the tray containing the carefully prepared third solution. The chemical reactions caused by the three liquids, the recipes for which had been passed down within the Brotherhood for nearly 200 years, had achieved their aim, and the details of the ancient map continued to crystallize before their eyes.

If apocalypse meant 'an unveiling', then this was a genuinely apocalyptic event. The unveiling of the map meant that the location of the keystone was itself coming out of hiding, and soon he would be able to hold it in his own hands.

The centuries were crying out to Marcianus. Men had lived in every age, awaiting this aim, and as the ink on the old page dissolved, its hidden text taking form, the long wait came closer to its end. The timing was tight – the symbolic significance of the Fourth of July had given them their target, and everything had been timed accordingly. It was a manageable push. Other preparations had been completed ahead of schedule; this, however, had been the first opportunity to claim the manuscript. And wherever in the world it might point, Marcianus would have time to follow its directions and reclaim the key before the appointed moment arrived.

His sight blurred slightly with his noble thoughts, as his mind moved from the page before him to the implications of its discovery. It was when he brought his thoughts back to attention and refocused his eyes on the document that he saw it.

Or rather, he didn't see it.

The newly revealed page contained a series of meticulously made, hand-drawn sketches, each contained in a box or panel, outlining a step in a carefully planned route. Each step was annotated with descriptions of its major geographic landmarks, measurements of distance and basic travelling instructions. But, as he leaned down over the tray and looked more closely, the most important step – the conclusion, the climax: the actual resting place of the key – was not indicated. The annotations in the final panel referred to 'the steps to follow', but nothing followed. There was no next, no more. The directions simply stopped.

The Great Leader felt an adrenaline spike of helplessness as he grabbed the ancient document out of the tray, lifting it up to eye level and scanning every detail with a panicked urgency.

'Master, we're not supposed to remove it from the solution for another thirty seconds,' the chemist protested, watching the page drip the pinkish liquid across the tabletop. 'The instructions are very precise.'

Marcianus ignored the protestation. His eyes were wide with disbelief and anger as they scanned the page again, and then again.

Finally, lowering the manuscript and turning to the two brethren who had obtained it, he spoke with barely restrained outrage.

'It's not here!'

He was met with blank, uncomprehending stares.

'The location of the keystone is not indicated on this page,' he continued, lifting up the document and wagging it at the two men. 'It only shows the beginnings of the journey. You imbeciles have brought me half a map!'

The brethren cast their glances between the manuscript and each other before daring to look into the face of the Great Leader.

'Get the hell back to the house!' Marcianus shouted, before they could speak. 'Get back to the house, and get me the rest of my map!'

CHAPTER 25

Archbishop's Residence, Washington DC

Cardinal O'Dowd, still in his formal attire from the Mass he had celebrated earlier in the morning, ran his finger along the crimson piping that formed the border of his simar. Before him lay the formal invitation received from the Illinois Governor two months ago. He had delayed long in responding, his disdain for such gatherings palpable. How he loathed the useless pomp and ceremony, the frivolous conversations uttered as if there were real meaning to the words. The pretensions of unity where none really existed, where little was actually desired. Such events flaunted all the trappings of religion, but were in reality nothing more than political showpieces meant to kowtow to fickle public sentiment.

Still, there would be ramifications for absence, and a certain denial of personal proclivities came with the office.

'Mary,' he bellowed through the wood-panelled office door towards the small desk staffed by his diminutive assistant. 'Phone up the Illinois Governor. Tell him I've had a last-minute opening in my calendar. I'll be able to participate in his procession, after all.'

CHAPTER 26

The British Museum, London

It took Michael little more than five minutes to power up the General Electric CRx Flex scanner that sat on the opposite side of the room, together with the computer terminal attached to it. He had gained a decent amount of experience with the device over the past six months, using it to see through pottery jars and to read etchings on the interior of clay panels too fragile from age to be opened.

Today, with a little bit of luck, he would use it to find a map hidden away on a page of ancient text.

Keying the machine to cycle up and setting it for basic image capture, Michael attached the manuscript to a phosphorus plate and fitted it onto the X-ray exposure unit.

'Time to put this on,' he said, grabbing a lead-lined apron from a hook next to the machine and passing it to Emily, taking another for himself. When they were both protected, he entered a few keystrokes on the control panel of the Seifert Eresco 200 X-ray tube. A moment later, a small red indicator light began to blink. Millions of X-ray photons silently and invisibly beamed through the manuscript.

Fourteen seconds later, the red light switched off.

'That's all there is to it.' Michael removed his protective apron.

'How long will it take to develop?' Emily asked, hanging her own back on the hook.

'That's the magic of the CRS: we don't develop, we compute.' Michael gently removed the manuscript from the plate, setting it back in its foam-lined folder. His excitement was obvious.

'The scanner can read the plate in a couple of seconds.'

He walked over to the scanner, now fully powered up and awaiting its input. A horizontal slot on the front of the white device allowed him to insert the plate, and the settings he had already configured caused the system to whir to life and immediately begin its scan.

'It's time to see what's here.'

The machine whirred with the sounds of electronic life, but Michael's calculation was soon proven wrong. Five seconds passed, then ten.

'Okay, okay,' he said, sensing Emily's anticipation, 'maybe I was overstating the machine's speed. It takes more than just a few seconds.' She rolled her eyes at him, anxious.

In the end, it took seventy-three seconds. On the seventy-fourth, the CR scanner beeped a soft confirmation tone and the monitor on the terminal changed from a maintenance screen to a blank display window. In under a second it filled that window with the X-ray image of the manuscript.

'Holy hell,' Michael gasped. 'You were right.'

Emily caught her breath as she stared into the screen. On

the display, beneath the manuscript's original text, now faded by the X-ray image, were the vivid lines of an entirely new document. Lines and curves created geometrically irregular shapes, filling three boxes on the page and annotated with small notes in Latin script.

'A map,' she said aloud. 'The men were right.' Andrew's killers had known something she didn't. Her cousin had paid the price.

Michael leaned towards the screen, his eyes growing wider as he looked over the map several times.

'Em,' he said, 'I know this map.' He pointed at the display, his finger shaking with the shock of the mystifying realization.

'And what's more, so do you.'

CHAPTER 27

The British Museum, London

Emily scrutinized the computer display with her full attention. The X-rayed image glowed an eerie bluish-white on the monitor, the hidden map standing out in bold, black strokes.

Try as she might, she didn't yet see what appeared familiar to Michael, though his sudden intensity had her expectation readied.

'How can I know the map?' she asked. 'This document is, at the very least, 250 years old.'

'Look closely,' Michael answered. 'Look at the flow of the lines in the second-to-last panel.' The map was divided into three square panels, each appearing to contain a segment of a longer journey.

Emily centred her attention on the hand-drawn geography of the panel he indicated.

Focus, she commanded herself. *He's seen something. What is it?*

'Concentrate on the location of the river and the contours of the land masses,' Michael prompted, pointing at the marks on the display. 'This location may not have been famous in the ancient world, but it is today.'

Emily's eyes danced over the monitor. Three small tributaries of a larger river snaked their way over the page, and contour lines indicated a mesa outcropping with cliff-like edges.

Suddenly, the details clicked into place. Recognition. A tingle seemed to start in Emily's spine, working its way through her arms.

'My God,' she exclaimed, her voice a tense, spellbound whisper, 'that's Nag Hammadi!'

Michael nodded. 'Without question.'

A rough drawing of the location of one of the twentieth century's most important manuscript finds glared up at them from the radiographic display. The Nag Hammadi Library had transformed the archaeological and historical worlds, its collection of ancient codices among the most significant ever discovered. Michael's amazement and his confusion were no less pronounced than Emily's, and he pointed to the edge of one of the oblong shapes indicating a mesa.

'Unless I'm mistaken, that's the cliff where the document stash was discovered in 1945.'

'This is unbelievable,' Emily said. The cold shiver that had begun in her back now consumed her whole body. She had hoped, desperately hoped, that they might find something that could make Andrew's murder more than a hapless accident, something that could imbue her cousin's death with the slightest meaning. Maybe even show up some way of tracking down those responsible.

She had never expected . . . this.

'But it's more than just a map to Nag Hammadi,' Michael said, continuing to scrutinize the monitor. 'This map points past the library, to something else.' He moved his finger to the final panel. 'Nag Hammadi is the final waypoint, but the destination itself is here.'

'Can you zoom in?' Emily asked. After a few drags of the mouse Michael enhanced the display on the map's final segment.

'It's another bluff, further into the desert.' Emily studied the details. 'I don't know anything about it.'

Michael squinted his eyes at a scrawl near the 'X' indicating the map's point of destination. The strange luminosity of the X-ray made it hard to read, but the two words near the marker stood out on the page. While all the other inscriptions were penned in Latin, these two, and these two alone, were in another language altogether. Coptic. The language of the Graeco-Egyptian inhabitants of North Africa in the ancient world.

The chief language of ancient Gnosticism.

'Can you make them out?' he asked, pointing to the two slightly blurred words. 'The second word looks like *ohne*. Coptic for rock. The first is – I can't quite make it out. *Shoshl*?'

Emily shook her head, her amazement growing. 'No, it's *shosht*.' She pointed towards the small difference of letters. 'Which means "key".'

Michael nodded, and all at once the meaning hit him. '*Ohne* means rock, but it could just as easily be translated as "stone".'

114

It was Emily who put the two together.

'Keystone.'

Her voice was a mystified whisper. 'The men who killed Andrew said this was a map to a keystone.' She looked directly at her husband. 'They were right.'

CHAPTER 28

Hays Mews, London

The man who called himself Simon swilled a long drink from the bottle he held angrily in his hands. At 160 proof, the alcoholic content of the imported Stroh Original Rum was 80%, as close to pure alcohol as drinkable liquor comes, and he felt invigorated by the burning sensation on his lips, tongue and throat.

The man's real name was Edward Stills, and the fact that the manuscript's second page was not here was not the worst news of his day. He had been taken to task by Marcianus with absolute ferocity. He had been humiliated, called inept, threatened with expulsion. But worse, he had failed in his divine charge. Reclaiming the map was his unique role in their sacred purpose. His spirit lived for this holy task, and when he had stood in this house early in the morning, he had been so close to fulfilling it. Yet he had failed. That knowledge was far worse than any threat the Great Leader could make.

Simon's day would get worse. From the kitchen counter he surveyed the wreckage around him. The home of Emily Wess and Michael Torrance was in shambles – he had ripped it apart, looking for the missing page. The brethren had already liaised with a contact in the Metropolitan Police and confirmed that no manuscript had been collected as part of their investigation, which meant that Wess had to have kept it back.

And that meant Wess had to know something.

Taking another long, fiery draw from the bottle, Simon carried it from the kitchen to the living room, surveying the ransacked contents a final time. There was nothing here.

Dammit.

Yet he had to press forward. In light of his failure, there would be new work to be done. He was not about to give up.

As he turned to leave, he took a final swig from the bottle, then smashed it against the door frame and tossed the shattered remains back into the room.

If he couldn't give the Great Leader the map, at least he could give him the woman who had it.

CHAPTER 29

The British Museum, London

'Do you know what this means?' Emily's deep-blue eyes were filled with a new mix of emotions as she spoke. The grief and the pain were still there, still vivid, yet among them were the traces of a resolve that was taking new life inside her.

'What it means?' Michael finally took his eyes from the scanner's display. He was certain of their discovery's remarkable dimensions, but substance and meaning were two very different things.

'Apart from the discovery of a manuscript pointing to the Nag Hammadi find, and beyond it, centuries before it was known to scholars?'

'Apart from that.' Emily waved aside what might amount to one of the major finds of an academic's career. 'This means we have a lead. A lead in Andrew's murder.' She grabbed Michael's forearm with a firm hand. 'The *only* lead.'

He stared long into her face, suddenly realizing the true shape of her excitement. This was not an academic astonishment over a significant find. Emily was struggling after any-thing that would ease her grief.

'Em, all this does is prove the thieves who killed him weren't as inept as we thought. They knew they were looking for something that was more than it appeared to be.' He reached out for her, knowing his words would bring her more distress. 'This discovery doesn't bring us any closer to the men who did it.'

'But it does.' Emily found herself growing angry that he didn't see this new material for what it was. 'They said the map was the last thing that was needed for them to find the key-stone. We now know that the map points to that keystone, whatever it is. We know what they're looking for, and where it's located.'

'Emily, that still doesn't amount to anything.'

'It damn well does!' she shot back. 'It means we know where they're going!'

Her face was red, and Michael saw the anger and the frus-tration there. He'd thought that helping Emily uncover the map might shed some light on their situation, but his concern over where this was leading was growing. If Emily's greatest scholarly strength was her unending drive, it could also be her biggest emotional hindrance. She was not a woman who knew how to give up, how to accept defeat, especially the meaning-less, horrifying defeat of a crime she could do nothing to change.

Michael knew that responding with his own frustration would only worsen the situation. He forced himself to speak with a calm, controlled logic.

'The very fact that we have the part of this document that reveals its end-point, rules out tracking them, Em, if that's where these thoughts are leading you. Whatever this "keystone" may be, these men don't seem to know where it is. Look how far they were willing to go to get this map. Breaking and entering. Murder!'

Emily almost snapped back in frustration, but caught herself. Michael was right, though the thought had already occurred to her. His words, however, led her in another direction. Not a chase. A preemptive manoeuvre.

'They don't have the map. We do,' she reiterated, 'which means only we know the location to the object they've already killed to obtain. Without this map –' she motioned towards the manuscript '– they aren't going to Egypt.' Then, the inevitable. 'We are.'

'Emily, what you're suggesting is ridiculous,' Michael finally answered, giving the shock of his wife's suggestion a moment to fade. 'I know you're upset, but what the hell is there to be gained by going off to Egypt in pursuit of . . . of whatever this map is pointing to?'

'Don't talk to me about pointless,' she snapped. 'A man, barely more than a kid, murdered in our house, *that's* pointless! But the men who killed him did it for a very specific reason: to find this keystone.' She pointed towards the Coptic inscription on the last panel of the map, still shimmering on the display. 'Now you and I have what we can assume is the only map in the world that points to what those men want. It's as close as anyone can get to having a way to find them.'

'But how, Em? For God's sake, we don't even know if this is all real!'

'It's real enough that this Arthur Bell, whoever he is, was willing to go to some pretty awful extremes to get it, Michael!' Emily no longer tried to constrain her irritation, her raised voice echoing off the metallic laboratory equipment.

'But I've told you already, without this page, the man doesn't know where he's going.'

'Something tells me he's not going to stop looking!' Emily yelled. 'Think about it. He's been obsessed over this thing, writing to your office for any clues your collection might have – how many times did he write?'

Michael hesitated slightly. 'Five, maybe six.'

'Six times! Then he somehow finds out about this manuscript, and pieces together both that CUA has bought it and that I'm on the acquisition. Finds out where we live. Has men break in and steal it, whatever the cost.'

'Emily, don't let anger cloud your—'

'He's going to keep looking, Michael!' Emily pounded her fist down on the aluminium worktable, the sound shaking the room. 'He's going to keep looking until he finds a way to get to this keystone.'

'And?' Michael's own voice was now raised to match his wife's. 'And then what? Where does this get us?'

Emily drove her gaze into him. 'To Egypt. To the "X" on this map. To the keystone that Arthur Bell wants.' She took a few deep breaths, allowing a moment for her meaning to sink in, then spoke with an absolute resolve.

'We take what he wants. Then we let him come to us.'

CHAPTER 30

The British Museum, London

'Let me be quite sure I understand you', Michael finally answered. 'You want to follow this map, so that the man who orchestrated Andrew's murder to find it, will want to come after you *again*?'

'It's that, or we just let him disappear,' she answered. 'And that's out of the question.'

Emily checked her intensity, softening her tone to a genuine emotion. 'Apart from you and my brother, Andrew was the only man in my life. We may have been family, but we were each other's closest friends since grade school. You know that. My sense of humour, my love of adventure, my confidence in sparring with others – it all comes from Andrew.' As she spoke, her eyes began to glisten with tears that almost fell. 'I'm not letting him die in vain, Mike. Not if I can help it.'

Seeing her grief return, Michael's anger fled. He grabbed Emily's arms, offering her his strength.

'The police, Em. They're not going to sit on a murder of a US citizen in the middle of London.'

'But they're also not going to hop on a flight to Egypt,' she protested, wrenching free a hand and using it to wipe the moisture from her eyes. 'You know as well as I do that they're not going to follow a lead as abstract as an ancient map on half a manuscript.'

'That's really what you expect us to do, then? Fly to Egypt, see where this thing points?'

Emily tightened her features. 'It's not the first time I've had to travel abroad to try to make sense of a death with little to go on. And last time turned out well enough in the end.' Her defiance was back, and the allusion to her pursuit of the vague clues leading to the Library of Alexandria after the murder of a colleague five years ago was not lost on Michael. She'd left Minnesota with only two scraps of paper and an elderly man's cryptic instructions, and had found herself tracing a path from America to Britain, to Egypt and Istanbul and even further afield. And she had found what she was looking for.

'I made that trip alone,' Emily added, pointedly. 'If I need to, I'll make this one alone, too.'

'You made that trip alone because neither of us knew what you were getting yourself into,' Michael answered, remembering the worry that had captivated him for almost a week. It was a memory he had no intention of reliving.

'This time, there's no way I'm letting you out of my sight.'

Despite the bitterness of the moment, at Michael's words Emily's expression was suddenly warm. Relieved.

'You'll go?'

'On a fool's errand to Egypt?' Michael caught himself. The chances of such a trip providing anything other than a distraction from the potency of Emily's grief were, at best, remote. But maybe a distraction was enough.

'Well, if one fool is going, I might as well go too.'

'Damn right,' Emily answered back, rushing to him with an outpouring of gratitude. Their lips met, and they embraced in a long, tender kiss.

The emotion of the moment came to an end with the piercing ring of Emily's mobile phone. Reaching into the pocket of her Salvatore Ferragamo jacket, she clicked on the Black-Berry without glancing at the caller ID, and held it up to her ear as she pried her lips from Michael's.

'Yes?' Her eyes were still locked on her husband's.

'Em, oh shit, are you okay?' A panicked woman's voice erupted from the phone's small speaker.

'Yes, yes, I'm okay,' Emily answered, coming into the moment. *It's Grace.* She mouthed the name of their nosey and entirely too exuberant next-door neighbour, Grace Willis-Chapman. 'You've heard about Andrew.'

'Andrew? No. You can tell me later.' The woman's tone was frantic. 'Tell me you're all right!'

'I'm fine', Emily answered. 'But I don't understand, if you don't know about Andrew, then why are you—'

'Your house!' Grace shouted into the phone. 'Something's going on at your house. Half the Met is parked outside your front door!'

CHAPTER 31

First Class Lounge, Paddington Station, London

Marcianus sat comfortably in the British Rail lounge, a drink positioned at his side and the departures display directly in front of him. A few well-dressed City businessmen sat spaced throughout the room, generally self-absorbed but not out of earshot. The time constraints of his travels, however, hadn't allowed for a more private meeting.

In a plush seat at his right, and visibly more anxious, was Simon. His face bore the red-eyed, glassy hue of a man who'd had too much drink, and for the briefest moment Marcianus wondered whether the man's failure had been self-induced.

'You're absolutely certain it wasn't there?' he asked, as he had done twice before.

'Yes. I passed my eyes and hands over every inch of that house. I can absolutely guarantee that the second page wasn't there.'

The Leader ruminated on the meaning. 'Then she has to know, or at least be suspicious.'

'My thoughts also, Master.' Simon said the final word softly.

He did not wish to attract undue attention through their reverential language.

'We know she collected the manuscript yesterday and was keeping it at her home until she could transport it to Washington.' He tried not to let his irritation come through in his voice. 'Since the second page isn't there now, she must have taken it with her when she left this morning, after the police.'

'Which she wouldn't do if she didn't sense it was important.' Marcianus rattled his fingers across his knees, a pair of grey cotton trousers absorbing the sound.

Simon hesitated. 'The existence of the map is a closely guarded secret, known only to us. There are no signs on the document.'

'She might know what it is, she might not,' said his Leader, 'but it's not worth the risk of hoping she doesn't. If she's got even the slightest suspicion of what the document contains, she'll follow it up. You've sure as hell given her some motivation, killing her cousin.' Marcianus stopped the rattling of his fingers and checked his anger, knowing that any further scolding of his assistant would be counterproductive. Instead, he leaned towards Simon. 'I don't need to tell you, it would be disastrous beyond all description if she were to locate the keystone before us.'

Marcianus gave him a moment to absorb his meaning, then glanced across at the departures listing. The express line north was marked for boarding in five minutes. Anticipating the short walk to the platform, he downed the remainder of his drink and began to rise.

'I'm co-opting the Arab for this job,' he said curtly. 'I

didn't want to bring him back in, but he's nothing if not effective.'

Simon started to protest. This was his mistake, he should be the one to resolve it.

'But to use him again . . . is that wise?'

Marcianus's irritation rose again. 'You said you wanted to deliver the girl to me, right?'

'Of course.'

'Then setting up my meeting with the Arab is how you do it.'

Simon sighed, then nodded a grudging assent. His face, however, continued to betray his discomfort.

'Don't worry,' Marcianus added, beginning to move towards the door. 'I won't tell him anything more than he needs to know. Just enough to help him find Dr Emily Wess and rid us of this nuisance before she becomes a more serious problem.'

CHAPTER 32

Hays Mews, London

The tasteful interior of the house Michael's family owned in Westminster had become something else entirely. It was now a mess of broken furniture, overturned shelves, torn carpeting and dismantled cabinets.

'It's everything,' Michael exclaimed, his shock increasing as he surveyed the wreckage. 'They've destroyed everything.'

'I'm afraid so, sir,' a police officer answered, stepping over a broken lamp. 'Every room, including the garage. There doesn't appear to be anything the perpetrators didn't touch.' He attempted to offer a consoling look, failed in his effort, then walked away and resumed his duties.

Michael's attention turned to the sofa, now bereft of its cushions with its backing slashed open. His mother had nursed him on that sofa; he remembered building forts from its pillows as a pre-teen. And earlier that morning, he had sat on it to console his wife at the loss of her cousin.

Emily stood in the corner of the room, unmoving. Her eyes

took in the destruction through an expression that seemed to be looking past it.

A second official approached Michael's side, this man a uniformed detective.

'Truly sorry about all this, Mr Torrance,' he said, rather pitifully. 'I know it must be a shock. You've up-to-date insurance cover?'

'Sure, of course.' Michael barely registered the man's questions.

'At least that's something. We can make a call into the assessors to help with the clean-up and claims filing, but it'll have to wait. We've some complications to deal with.'

Michael's attention coalesced on the word. 'Complications?'

'This is still a murder scene. The forensics team did most of its work this morning, but we're going to have to treat this as an extension of the earlier crime.'

The detective stopped himself from going into too many details. 'Any idea what an intruder or intruders might have been looking for, especially coming back a second time?'

Emily was suddenly at Michael's side.

'It could be anything,' she said, a subtle glance commanding Michael's silence. 'There are plenty of valuables in here. Maybe something caught their eye during the night, and they came back to grab it.'

The detective reflected a moment, then politely nodded his head. 'Again, my sympathies for all this, for both of you.' He waited the obligatory moment, respectful, then stepped back into the disarray.

Emily grabbed Michael's hand and drew him to the corner

of the room. She spoke in a whisper, trying to keep their conversation unnoticed.

'Do you believe me, now?' She waved her hand over the scene before them. 'Andrew's dead, our home is in tatters. Like I told you before, Mike, they're not going to stop looking for the second half of their map, or for the object it points to in Egypt.'

Michael's attention was back on the wreckage of his family home. So many memories destroyed. So much security, stability, stolen away.

His wife was right. These men, whoever they were, were not going to stop searching for their keystone. But the fact that loomed in his mind at the moment was one that now felt far more threatening.

They weren't going to stop looking for Emily, either.

It was suddenly possible that Emily's plan to keep a step ahead of them wasn't as crazy as it had sounded in the museum.

'Yes,' he finally said, turning to her. 'I'm convinced. And one thing I'm sure about: I'd rather stay in front of these guys than meet up with them face-to-face on terms like these.'

Emily clenched his hand tightly.

'But,' Michael continued, 'I'm not willing to go this route without some help.'

'Who could possibly help us with something like this?'

Michael's gaze showed a growing confidence, his hand already sliding into his jacket for his mobile phone. 'There's only one person I can think of.'

CHAPTER 33

American Embassy, Grosvenor Square, London

At precisely 4.18 p.m., a small cell phone tucked into the pocket of an uninhabited blue blazer buzzed to life. The MP3 configured as its ringtone began to broadcast the *Navy Blue and Gold* through the phone's tiny speaker, but the man who should have answered was not in the room.

Twenty seconds later, the mobile phone continued to vibrate. Then, as the digital ringtone looped back to its beginning, a door six feet away swung open. Chris Taylor charged through to his desk and the jacket slung over the chair behind it. A moment later, he had his phone in hand.

Glancing at the caller's name on the display, he answered with a wide smile. 'Mike! It's been a while.'

'Too long,' Michael Torrance answered back, and like that the two friends were connected. Michael had met the Chicago-born FBI agent during his time as an architectural intern there, when Chris was still serving in the Chicago Field Office, before he had climbed up the ranks and received his transfer to the embassy. Back in their mutual Chicago days, Chris had found his way to one of the Irish pubs that Michael frequented in lieu of any proper English equivalent, and the two had got to know each other over flat Guinness and traditional bar conversations on the extensive plight of modern society. Their friendship had lasted through Michael's departure for Minnesota, and Chris had served as a groomsman at his wedding. When Michael arrived in London for his fellowship at the British Museum, his first social port-of-call had been to visit Chris at his new surroundings in the Embassy.

'I thought we weren't on till next week?' Chris spoke through the phone. He and Michael met at least once a month for drinks and a chance to spend an evening on their own. 'Men's night out' was a cherished tradition.

'You're right, we're not,' Michael answered. 'But I need to see you sooner. Is your schedule at Fort Raptor flexible?'

'Fort Raptor' had been their nickname for the Embassy since Michael had first visited. The vast grey-brick cube had once seemed a venerable monument of power in the midst of a city of pomp and circumstance, but with all the added security features and patrols since 9/11, it now seemed considerably more like a prison block dropped into the centre of a populous business community. Barriers diverted traffic and pedestrian flow around the complex, cameras poked out of every crack and crevice. The massive gilded aluminium eagle with its thirty-five-foot wingspan mounted high over the entrance had caught Michael's attention as he approached. *Whether or not that's meant to remind me of majesty and freedom*, he'd joked, *with these grey skies, hung over these grey bricks, it looks a little more like a raptor ready to attack*. 'Fort Raptor' had been christened the same day.

Chris took only a moment to deliberate Michael's vague request. 'Sure, bud,' he answered into the phone. 'What's up?'

He knew that on the far end of the line, Michael would cringe at the nickname. Chris Taylor prided himself on being as American as a man could be without actually turning into Uncle Sam, and his propensity for referring to everyone as 'buddy' was a favourite pet peeve of his English friends. A few months ago, Chris had shortened it to 'bud' in Michael's case, in taunting acquiescence. The short form, Michael had noted soon afterwards, was far worse.

The teasing tone went out of Chris's voice as soon as Michael began to allude to the morning's events: Andrew's murder, the stolen page of the manuscript and the secret map hidden within the portion that remained, the ransacking of their house on Hays Mews. Michael's words were guarded, but even the broad strokes were dramatic.

'Damn, Mike,' Chris offered once the brief description was complete, with real concern in his voice. 'You've phoned up our guys, right?'

'Yes, the investigators took care of that for Emily. That's not why I'm ringing you.'

'If not that, what?'

'We're going to Egypt,' Michael answered. When Chris didn't respond, he continued. 'Emily is convinced that the map represents a lead we can follow – a lead the police won't – that might get us closer to Andrew's killers. And Chris, it's clear to us that something bigger is at play here. Both of us want to know what that is.'

The tone of Michael's voice left little question: he was

asking for Chris's help. His role in the bustling infrastructure of the American Embassy on Grosvenor Square was as a specialist consultant on international intelligence, and the position reflected his special set of talents. He'd once been Navy, joining up with the Reserve Officer Training Corps in college, but after his tour he'd moved eagerly on to the Hoover Building in DC. His Naval experience had revealed a strength in intelligence analysis, and since joining up with the FBI, Chris had developed a specialism in anti-terrorist intelligence in the Middle East, largely through an adept ability to read between the lines of intel reports and develop an insight into the intended actions of opponents.

'Chris,' Michael finally said, 'we need you to help us make sense of what's going on.'

Chris listened closely. So too, he knew, did many others. Words didn't echo off the walls of the Embassy: they were gathered, recorded, analysed. His cell phone was clean, but the office walls were not. And though Chris didn't suspect that Michael was suggesting anything illegal, he knew that he, as an FBI agent, couldn't openly discuss the circumvention of a domestic police investigation on UK soil.

'Let's talk about this properly,' he offered. 'I want you to fill me in on the rest of the story.'

'Name the spot.'

Chris knew a public location would suit best, and he could think of none better than the place he and Michael had shared their first drink on British soil. A formal monument to all the pomp and splendour of London.

'Meet me at the Savoy, one hour.'

CHAPTER 34

FBI Field Office, Chicago

Harry Pike was tired and deflated. His arrest the day before in New York City had been more physical than he had anticipated. His wrists were bruised from the cuffs pressed against them and the left side of his face scabbed from an extensive flow of blood. Though he had cast down his rifle ahead of the first command from the arresting officers and given himself up without the slightest protest, he had been thrown onto the pavement with force and held there under the firm pressure of an officer's boot. When finally it lifted off his back, relieving the pressure on his spine and ribs, he was raised to his feet by a fierce pull on his cuffed wrists and dishevelled hair, and thrust towards a waiting police cruiser with all the gentleness of a wrestling spar.

Once processed and in formal custody, the situation had been different. The detention and correction branches of the New York police force were well-oiled machines, and they operated with clinical efficiency. He had been taken from interrogation room to cell and back again with politeness and protocol. He had been cleaned, and fed, and his wounds dressed. He had been addressed as 'Mr Pike' and asked if he was comfortable each time his handcuffs were removed or replaced. Outside the frequent interrogations, he had been left largely alone.

All of which had changed dramatically three hours ago. Without warning, his small cell in the Brookline Detention Complex was stormed by three non-uniformed men, a hood thrust over his head and his hands newly bound, this time far too tightly and without the pretence of concern for his comfort. He was marched out of the building, into a car, and a short time later prodded up the steps of what turned out to be a small jet. Not once was he informed where he was being taken.

Two-and-a-half hours later the process was repeated in reverse, and when his hood had been removed a few moments ago, Harry was in another anonymous interrogation room, location unknown. The walls were brick, coated in a thick layer of turquoise paint, and a vague aroma of pine floor cleaner lingered in the air. A long mirror covered most of one wall, and a dented metal table stood in the middle of the room, to which his hands – still cuffed – were now chained. His handlers were already gone, leaving only two women and a man in the room with him. On the opposite side of the table, the man sat. A thick file was closed on the table in front of him. The lights in the room were too bright. He had a strange, inexplicable urge for a Pepsi.

'Where am I?' Pike asked.

'That's not important.' The man spoke firmly. 'I will also

point out that that will be your last question. This is to be a one-way conversation. I will ask, you will answer.' A pause, then, 'Let's practise: tell me your name.'

'My name is Harry Pike. From New York.' Pike wasn't sure where the man's accent was from. It sounded like Boston. *Am I in Boston?*

The man let an uncomfortably long silence pass after the answer, keeping his eyes fixed on Pike's. The young man squirmed in his cuffs.

'That wasn't difficult, was it, Mr Pike? Keep cooperating and this will go smoothly.' Boston let another pause fill the room, then, abruptly, 'At what point did you join the Church of Truth in Liberation?'

Pike returned a look of surprise. 'What Church? I'm not—' His mind raced back to the moment of his capture. There had been so many agents, so many guns. He'd been scared, but not that scared. *I wasn't that scared, was I?*

'Don't pretend with me, Mr Pike.' The man tapped a finger on a thick folder that sat before him, keeping his gaze immobile. 'We know you are a member of the Church of Truth in Liberation. We know you are in routine correspondence with various Church members, and we know you've received personal guidance from the Church's leader, Arthur Bell.'

Pike, a devoted but still immature young man at twenty-seven years of age, began to show the first signs of being flustered. 'I don't know why you're—'

'Please,' Boston cut him off again, holding up an open-palmed hand. 'Do us both a service, and don't try to deny what we both know to be true.'

Man talks fancy, Pike's mind noted, put off despite his growing fear. *A man shouldn't talk fancy unless he's somebody.*

He went quiet. The questions from the arrogant agent made him feel a little off balance, yet he knew his role was already accomplished. He didn't have to do anything, or say anything more. He'd played his part, and the Great Leader would make sure that his labours – and whatever might happen to him now – were not in vain. Harry had a profound trust in his Leader.

'You are aware that Arthur Bell is dead?' the interrogator suddenly asked, leaning forward.

The words instantly eroded the supports of the young Pike's self confidence. 'No way!' he protested, visibly upset. 'It ain't true. You're a lying sonovabitch!'

'So you know him, then.' Boston eyed the young man, eyebrows raised. Pike went motionless, and his world began to crumble.

Special Agent Ted Gallows had been given the lead in Harry Pike's interrogation, and it had started well. He was in control. The suspect was wavering.

'You're *lying*,' Pike repeated. His throat seemed to have gone dry, leaving his voice cracking out its words.

Gallows leafed through his open file until he came upon a page that seemed to attract his attention. He thumped an extended index finger on it. 'This is the operational report from the op that took Arthur Bell down only forty-five minutes ago,' he said, appearing to scan through the document. 'Shot fourteen times.' He lowered the page and gazed into

Pike's eyes. 'That's what happens when you find yourself on the wrong side of an FBI SWAT team.'

Pike didn't answer. His face couldn't conceal a hopelessly racing mind.

'We pieced together his identity and location from your words and emails, together with your video.'

Harry Pike's colour went from pale to pure white.

Good, Gallows thought. *That's the edge. He relies on the man. Get rid of his support.*

'Arthur. Bell. Is. Dead,' he repeated, emphasizing each word distinctly. He replaced the page into the folder. Pike need never know that it was merely a printout of one of Gallows's emails. There had been no operation, no team, no execution. The FBI still had no idea who Arthur Bell was, or where.

Gallows allowed his demeanour to betray nothing of that reality. He fostered a well-practised little smile, as if amused at the opportunity to rip Harry of his hope.

Harry Pike was now entirely white, his skin clammy. 'Liar,' he whispered, but the statement was void of power. Everyone in the room, likely including Pike himself, knew that he didn't believe his objection.

Ted Gallows slammed a fist down on the table, the blow echoing loudly in the concrete enclosure. 'Listen to me, you inept little fuck: your leader's gone. There's no point in trying to protect him any more. All you can do now is make things better for yourself. Cooperate. Help us out, and we might be able to take a trip to Guantanamo Bay off the cards.'

'Guantanamo?' Pike's eyes stretched fully open.

'You're billed as a terrorist, and a known associate of a

terrorist leader,' Gallows announced. 'Gitmo's a given for a member of a terrorist group. You've already got your ticket in.' He leaned forward and spoke with a practised menace. 'And very few people get a ticket out.'

'But we're not terrorists!' Pike protested.

Gallows sat back down into his seat, the faintest trace of a satisfied smile visible at the edges of his expression. 'That's good to hear. Why don't you tell me just who you are.'

CHAPTER 35

The Savoy, The Strand, London

The glamour of the Thames Foyer Dining Room in the Savoy might have distracted Michael and Emily with its opulence on any other occasion, but today they were both drawn to only one sight in its interior. Chris sat at a table across the room, looking much like he had the day Michael first met him in Chicago: fit and jovial, with tight features that seemed always to be on the cusp of a smile – or, as was more often than not the case, a joke. His hair was still cut Navy-style, though he had given up his uniform for an equally unchanging ensemble of beige khakis with a blue blazer over a grey turtleneck.

As Michael and Emily approached, Chris set aside his imported American beer, which he insisted on drinking from the bottle rather than the provided glass, and stood to greet them.

'Mike!' The word came with a genuine smile. 'And I'm so happy to see you as well, Emily.' Chris walked around the table to greet her, and after the formal handshake wrapped her in an unrelenting bear hug. 'I'm so sorry to hear about your cousin.

We'll get to the bottom of this, don't you worry yourself about that.'

Emily accepted his hug, then nodded. Chris was a kind and sincere man. She appreciated his words.

'That's why we're here,' Michael said as the group sat. 'To get to the bottom of this.'

'On the phone, you sounded convinced you have a way forward.' Chris took another swill from his beer.

'We do,' Emily answered. 'You remember what Michael told you about the manuscript Andrew's killers broke in to steal?'

'The one you say contains a map? Yes. Impressive stuff, too, from the bits and pieces Mike shared.'

Emily opened her bag and extracted a folded sheet of printer paper. A high-resolution printout of the X-ray displayed the ancient map. 'This is what was hidden on the second page of the document, the page they didn't manage to steal.'

Chris took the paper and examined it with a professional efficiency. 'You know where this is?' Though always outwardly casual and convivial, Chris was a talented tactical officer and was used to piecing together bigger pictures from small scraps of intelligence.

'That's only the second page,' Michael answered, 'and presumably most people would need the first to get them orientated. But in the centuries since this was drawn, the location in that panel –' he pointed towards the second-to-last hand-drawn box on the page '– has become rather well known to scholars of ancient history.'

'It's the region of a small village called Nag Hammadi,' Emily said. 'Have you ever heard of it?'

'Sorry. I'm no scholar of ancient history.'

Emily pushed herself back into her seat. The opportunity to orientate Chris would draw her focus back to history, which was about the only thing that kept the alternating rage and grief from flaring up and taking possession of her.

'In the winter of 1945,' she began, 'two peasants were about ten kilometres from the village of Nag Hammadi, digging for fertilizer. One of those peasants, a man called Mohammed Ali, made the discovery that would turn out to be one of the most important finds of the twentieth century.'

'Wait,' Chris interrupted. '*Mohammed Ali?*'

'Not the boxer, Chris,' Michael sighed, shaking his head.

'Damn you both!' Emily snapped. 'This isn't the time for jokes. You can piss about later, if you're up for that.'

Chris caught himself, for the first time realizing just how raw Emily's emotions were. She carried herself with such composure that they stayed well hidden, but he should have anticipated that heavy grief.

'I'm sorry, Emily,' he said, 'really.'

She took a deep breath, calming herself, a nod acknowledging that it was as much her nerves as anything Chris had said that had set her off. When composure had been reclaimed, she continued.

'Mohammed found a large earthenware jar buried at the base of a boulder near a cliff. Specifically, he found it at this cliff.' She pointed to a line drawn on the map. 'When he saw that it was old, and sealed with pitch, he was afraid.'

'Afraid?'

'The al-Samman clan are superstitious, like most traditional peoples. Mohammed was worried that the jar might contain a *jinn*, an evil spirit.'

'But the thought of treasure outstripped his fear,' Michael added. 'Drawing up his courage, Mohammed shattered the jar, and inside he and his friend found a stash of very old codices.'

'These papyrus books had leather covers, and they were very, very old,' Emily said. 'Some were deteriorated into flakes, others in fairly good condition. But Mohammed and his partner had no idea what they were. They went back to their village, and the codices were distributed to various people in the community. Mohammed threw his portion into some straw near the stove in his hut, and his mother, not realizing these were priceless fourth-century treasures, never seen in the sixteen hundred years since they had been hidden in the sand, used some of them to fuel the fire for their food.'

'Bet she regrets it now!' Chris interjected, amazed. 'They must be worth a damned fortune.'

Michael gave him a warning glance, trying to suppress Chris's intractably upbeat air. Emily's face reddened.

'They're literally priceless,' she said firmly. 'Thank God that eventually bartering and attempts to make pocket change by Mohammed's friends led to collectors realizing what had really been discovered. Though it took a few years, all the surviving codices were collected and assembled, and today they reside in the Coptic Museum in Cairo. They're widely agreed to be one of the two most important manuscript finds of the last hundred years – the other being the library of documents found at the Qumran settlement near the Dead Sea.'

'The Dead Sea Scrolls? Those I've heard of.'

'They were found only a few years later. It's a coin toss as to which find has been more influential in the scholarship since.'

'The entire field of Gnostic studies has been fuelled by these ancient manuscripts,' Michael added. 'Nearly everything we knew about Gnostics and Gnosticism prior to Nag Hammadi was from second-hand reports and the pens of ancient writers who had worked to discredit them. With the Nag Hammadi find, we had for the first time a library of Gnostic texts written by the Gnostics themselves. A whole new world opened up.'

'This is amazing,' Chris said. He looked to the printout of the map. 'Your manuscript contained an invisible map to this find?'

'Not precisely,' Michael corrected. 'This map uses Nag Hammadi as a waypoint, but as you can see, its "X" marks a different spot.' He tapped his finger on the final panel. 'That location is marked "Keystone".'

'And what's a keystone?'

Emily hesitated. 'We . . . we don't know.'

Chris's eyebrows rose and he looked at her quizzically.

'But,' Emily added, 'we know it's what these men are looking for. They talked about using the map to find this keystone – and obviously, they're desperate to get to it. Andrew, ransacking the house . . .'

Chris took a long drink of his beer, draining the last of its contents. When the bottle was set aside he leaned forward and put both his elbows on the table, gazing straight at Emily.

'So, I get that the map is ancient, and important. I get that it points to something that your cousin's killers want. I get that you want to do whatever you can to make them pay. But what I don't get is why you want to follow this map. What's your bigger plan?'

'My plan is to draw these men to me, in a way I can control.' Emily leaned forward to match Chris's gaze, her eyes intense and determined. 'They've proven they're not going to leave us alone, not if they're willing to come back to the scene of their own crime, on the same day, looking for this. So we don't wait for more attempts: we move a step ahead. Once we've got what they want, they're damned well going to come after it. We can make sure we're ready, and use it as a trap.'

'And how are you going to do that?'

'I have no godforsaken idea.' Emily said the words with such angry force they sounded like a rallying cry, despite their content. After a few seconds she added, only slightly less emphatically, 'But I have every intention of figuring it out.'

Chris stared at her a long moment before leaning back.

'So, I've heard what you've had to say. It's interesting, the X-ray-secret-invisible-ink thing is pretty cool; but your plan is dangerous, unresolved, and potentially suicidal.'

'And?' Michael asked.

'And I'm totally in, obviously.'

Emily let out a held breath with a rush of relief.

'Thank you, Chris!'

He smiled at her. 'When do we go?'

Michael reached across the table and dangled his cell phone before Chris's face. 'I'm already dodging the obligations of my own work, and we managed to get our passports out of what's left of our house . . . If you call the Embassy now, is there any chance you can take some leave starting this evening?'

CHAPTER 36

Witley Tea Rooms, Slough

Mustafa Aqmal was a tall, lanky man with dark, oily skin matched by dark, oily hair. His nose, by proportion to the rest of his face, was enormous and beak-like, and both its size and awkward shape were emphasized by sunken cheeks and seemingly non-existent ears. He kept his black hair smartly combed, and the natural oils of his scalp gave it an almost polished sheen. He wore an olive-green suit without a tie, and the boniness of his frame was visible through the fabric.

In his general demeanour he appeared to most people in the Western world as a fairly standard example of what an Arab in Western attire was expected to look like: generally like a westerner in the same garb, but not quite fitting into either the clothes or the surroundings. It was a look he cultivated carefully, for fulfilling a stereotype helped to make one invisible, which was almost always Aqmal's goal. Only when one stopped to look closely did one begin to sense something more to his image. His slender fingers danced with a certain, deliberate grace; his lanky limbs moved with precision. He never seemed to look directly at anyone or anything, yet the surety of his gestures bespoke a man who was familiar with every detail of his surroundings at all times. In the rare moments when one did make eye contact with him, Mustafa Aqmal's brown eyes seemed hollow – but it was not the hollow of emptiness. The hollow of his eyes was like a vacuum, forcibly depriving everything around them of light.

Marcianus had always hated those eyes. Since he and Aqmal had first met three years before, they had always filled him with a distinct unease – a feeling to which Marcianus, from his own position of power, was not accustomed. What was worse, Aqmal seemed to know that he had this effect upon Marcianus.

Marcianus walked towards him now. The corner table of the Witley Tea Rooms off Bath Road in Slough was secluded, and the establishment itself largely quiet – though not empty enough to make their meeting memorable to the staff or other patrons. Marcianus watched as the spindly figure of Aqmal sat strangely in the booth seat, sipping from a water glass. He approached and sat opposite him.

'*Assalamu alaykum,*' he said as he sat. His Arabic was raw, but his greeting passable. The other man could take it or leave it.

'*Wa alaykum assalam,*' Aqmal answered calmly. He moved his gaze from the window to Marcianus, and the two men's eyes met. Marcianus squirmed despite himself. Aqmal's features seemed to flash the tiniest of satisfied self-adulations.

'I was not expecting we would meet again,' he said, keeping his gaze on Marcianus. 'Your call came as a . . . surprise.' A sip from his water glass. A long pause.

'Neither was I,' Marcianus answered. 'Everything I mentioned on the phone is new, since we last spoke properly. It's my luck you happened to be in the country.'

Marcianus struggled to keep this rhetoric friendly. He despised the language of 'luck', every ounce of his will desiring to say what he really meant: *Your being in the country is a fortuitous confirmation of my divine plan.* But he knew that it was with more comfortable, approachable words that he would gradually exert his familiar grip of control.

Mustafa Aqmal nodded a slow, acquiescent nod, his face betraying no emotion.

'I hope it does not mean that my previous work for you has been for nothing.' As Aqmal spoke, he wove his long, thin fingers in front of him. He kept his eyes slightly downcast as the words came, speaking into the tabletop, carrying on his conversation with Marcianus as if with a phantom – as if the man were not sat mere feet from him. It was an unnerving tactic, and Marcianus recognized the subtle manoeuvrings of a man whose position, in his circles, was as influential and revered as his own.

'We allied ourselves with your project,' Aqmal continued, 'because you promised us a strike on the beast. An attack on the Western infidel. It would be most unfortunate if that promise were not to be fulfilled.'

Marcianus answered dismissively. 'That's not an issue. Your strike will still come, and it will be fierce. But we need to eliminate this little . . . hiccup . . . before we can proceed.'

He worded his comments carefully. It was essential that Aqmal remain on board. The Arab man's aims, which the

American government openly and rightly called terrorism, did not interest Marcianus in the slightest. The man was simply out to enact his rage: to strike out at the oppressors and the impious. Make them bleed and suffer for their wrongs. 'A weakened foe falls more easily,' he had said when they first met.

Marcianus had brought him on board because that image was required, with all its associations. Apart from that, Aqmal had proved himself helpful more than once. He could be so again.

That is, assuming the whole arrangement wasn't derailed.

'The woman has intercepted part of our plans,' Marcianus said. 'She's a risk. We need to eliminate that risk so we can proceed.'

Aqmal nodded. 'If that is all that is involved, it will not be difficult.'

'She has made travel plans. She intends to fly to Egypt in two hours, and we've got to stop her.'

Aqmal took a long breath, considering. 'It will be far easier to do in Egypt than here in Britain. If their flight is in only two hours, by now they'll be in the airport. Too much security to act there, unless you want to draw attention to yourself.'

'No. We must remain as invisible as we can.'

'Who is she travelling with?'

'Wess is with two others. Her husband, Michael Torrance, is booked on the seat next to her.' Marcianus paused. Torrance had already represented an obstacle, a wall against their interests, though one whose importance had been superseded by recent events. Or so Marcianus had thought, until he had discovered that Torrance was married to Emily Wess.

'The next seat over has been booked on the same reservation, under the name Chris Taylor,' Marcianus concluded.

'Who is that?'

'He is an FBI agent stationed at the American Embassy in London. A former Navy officer.'

Aqmal's lips curled back, and he looked up squarely at Marcianus. 'The FBI? I thought you'd kept the American government out of this.'

'He's a friend of the husband,' Marcianus answered. 'His involvement only reinforces the need to put an end to this, and to them.' He leaned across the table, bringing his head as close as possible to Aqmal, and spoke in an urgent whisper. 'Will you offer your assistance once more? I'll give you one of my men, more if you need them.'

'Yes, and no.' Aqmal all but gnarled his answer. 'I will help, if it will further my cause through yours. Though the matter must be dealt with quickly – I have other obligations. Twenty-four hours, no more.'

'Fine.'

'But,' Aqmal added, 'I will not travel with one of your men.'

'You want to seize them yourself?'

'No. I do not wish to go alone, but neither do I wish to be accompanied by one of your . . . lackeys. You have requested the last-minute aid of the leader of my organization. Me. I expect the assistance of the leader of yours.' He let his gaze linger, unblinking, on Marcianus's face.

Marcianus said nothing. He had hoped not to be further sidetracked from his essential work, but if personally accompanying the Arab was the only way to get him to assist them again, he had little choice but to comply. He nodded his assent silently.

'Then our next stop is Egypt,' Aqmal said, smiling sinisterly back at him. 'We'll wait for them when they land. Then, at the first opportune moment, we'll take care of your little hiccup, once and for all.'

CHAPTER 37

Above Southern England

By 11.45 p.m. two flights were approaching cruising altitude above the southern-English countryside, one twenty minutes ahead of the other and on a faster flight path. The early Egyptian morning would greet them both, though it would rise on groups with starkly different ambitions.

From their triplet of seats on British Airways flight 155, Emily, Michael and Chris settled into their journey with a sense of optimism. Though the day had begun with tragedy, it was ending with action. Emily was convinced that locating the object to which the ancient map pointed would provide them with the tool required to entrap Andrew's killers. As they had before in her life, the relics of the past were finding their way into her present, and not simply as objects of antiquated curiosity. She did not yet know precisely what was located at the destination on the manuscript, she did not know what the term 'keystone' meant. But whatever it was, she would use this piece of history to change history – to ensure that the sad saga of her cousin's murder was not the last chapter of his story. There would be justice. There would be resolution.

Ninety miles to the south and slowly gaining a wider lead, Aqmal and Marcianus sat stoically aboard an EgyptAir jet. For Aqmal, the mission ahead would be quick and decisive: tracking the trio just long enough to get out of range of the countless observant eyes of the city centre, three bullets – if his aim was true – would finish them off in time for him to catch a lunchtime flight back to England.

For Marcianus, however, the path ahead was more than merely practical. It was divine. Those who threatened to overturn his great aim would be thwarted. The remainder of the map would be reclaimed. The keystone would be retrieved. And then he would fulfil a divine purpose two millennia in the waiting. His people had wound their way through history, hidden in the dark corners of the flow of ages – and all for this: to stand at the end of the world, the End of All, and be set free.

CHAPTER 38

Montelaguardia, Italy, AD 1756

Working as quickly as his nervous limbs would allow, Mario Tera-geste wrapped his journal in an old cloth and placed the bundle in a small wooden box. He took two iron nails in hand and secured the lid with a few blows of his workman's hammer.

How quickly things came to a head.

Talano had already been taken, the officers sweeping into his home two nights before. They had been predictably merciless, beating his wife before him without so much as a second's hesitation. She had fled to Mario's small shopfront as soon as the officers had left with her husband in tow. Collapsed on the wooden floor of his apothecary's shop, she had relayed the brutality and horror of Talano's capture.

By now he would be in prison. If a trial ever came, it would be purely for show. The man's fate had been sealed the moment he was arrested, and Mario knew the two brethren would never see each other again in this life.

'And I shall fare little better,' he reminded himself. He was not so deluded as to pretend that his future was not as certain as Talano's.

Taking the wooden box in hand, Mario exited his shop by the rear door and did an about-face. To the side of the door frame was a wooden panel which he removed gingerly, knowing its contours and supports. The board granted access to the foundations of the small building, and over the course of the previous hours Mario had dug out a deep pit directly beneath its centre.

Crawling towards it on his belly, he dropped the box into its new resting place and began to shovel the displaced dirt over the top of it.

'My little book is secure,' he muttered once the hole had been refilled, scooting himself backwards and out of the crawl space. The work Talano and he had done would outlive them both.

Part Two

MONDAY, JULY 2ND

CHAPTER 39

The Temple, Chicago

Fourteen candles were arranged in the traditional circular formation at the centre of the temple floor. Though what the brethren called a 'temple' was in reality only an empty industrial warehouse, the lack of outward form did not trouble the believers. The true Temple, they unbendingly believed, was the great Spirit. The prophecies had announced for centuries that when the End was come the physical world would be over, and they would be freed to live wholly in the spirit: their greatest and purest aim.

That had been the most awe-inspiring, and unexpected, dimension of the Leader's revelation. They had been waiting for the End for generations, for the event that would mark the complete breakdown and destruction of the world and the time of their emancipation; but it was the Great Leader who had seen that the End did not have to be considered in physical terms. There was no need to wait for the environment to collapse or world war to obliterate man's potential for life. The End was moral, spiritual. Everything good and sacred that the divine spark of life had preserved in the world was already gone, obliterated by humanity's greed, vice and perversion.

In a few moments the Liberator would speak. He who would make real what the Church had preached for decades, what the wider Brotherhood had known for generations, and what the illumined had awaited for millennia.

After the End, release.

Before he would ascend the makeshift podium, however, the Truth Incantation would be chanted. Words without truth meant nothing. Knowledge without truth was only deception.

A robed Knower chimed a small bell, and at once a hush came over the large crowd. Then, with well-honed skill, a deep droning tone began to emerge from the kneeling masses. As the melodious chanting filled the warehouse temple, the lips of the readers chanted the sacred words above it.

> 'We are come to proclaim what is, and what was, and
> what will be;
> We are come that man might understand the invisible
> world beyond that which is seen;
> We are come to proclaim the immovable race of perfect
> humanity.'

Those who had not already done so donned their dark robes as the incantation began. As the first group of readers finished, a second picked up the next refrain of the ancient mantra.

> 'He who is ignorant is deficient
> And his deficiency is his terrible ruin,

For he lacks that which would make him perfect –
But this we shall give.'

Walter Janus, whose name in the Church was Cerinthus, but who had come to be known by every gathering in the world as the Liberator since the ultimate plan had begun to be enacted, stood as the words continued to reverberate hauntingly off the metal walls and ceiling high above. He was exhilarated by the common chant, and knew his words to the gathered brethren would be important for their encouragement. But before he encouraged them, he would take his own strength from the truths they sang.

He inhaled a confident breath as he approached the podium. All around him, enlightened lips cried out prophetic words.

'Ours is the book which none find it possible to take,
For the Light is reserved
For those who will take it and be slain.'

CHAPTER 40

In Flight, between London and Cairo

'So,' Chris said, turning towards Michael after their in-flight meal had been served, consumed and cleared, 'it's time for Harvard to enlighten Navy on a few of the more esoteric details.'

Michael had one arm wrapped gently, protectively, around Emily's shoulder, while the fingers of his other hand rattled along the opposite armrest. Now that they had finally got a meal into them, he felt his exhaustion. He was desperate to fall into even the flitting sleep that Emily had finally managed in the seat to his right, but his mind was too consumed with the questions of the day and unknowns of the way ahead. Emily's emotions had finally drained her into sleep; perhaps Chris's interest would at least provide Michael's mind with something to occupy itself.

'You do realize, I didn't go to Harvard?' he responded, for at least the thirtieth time in their friendship.

'I won't hold it against you,' Chris answered, smiling. 'Point is, you need to be filling me in on a bit more of the background to this little trip. Give me the details, as scholarly as you want to make them.'

'Where would you like me to begin?'

'Start from the beginni—' Chris cut himself off. 'No, on second thought, you're an academic and this flight's only five-and-a-half hours long. Why don't you just give me the highlights. I know nothing about Gnosticism.' He lifted the edges of his mouth and openly spread his hands. 'Consider me an empty canvas. Paint a clear picture.'

Michael adjusted his position in the small seat, gently taking his arm from Emily's shoulder.

'We're talking about a movement that spanned centuries, covered multiple continents, incorporated dozens of philosophical and religious paradigms and cultures. To set the stage we'd need to go back to the ancient Greek philosophers, to Plato and Aristotle—'

Chris stopped him abruptly with an open palm, raised like a traffic officer halting a rush-hour onslaught.

'You've had thirty seconds, and you've already lost me.'

'Chris, this isn't a simple question. History is complex.'

'Imagine for a moment that you had to describe everything in a single phrase.' Chris was used to receiving bullet-point intelligence briefings. What couldn't be said in a sentence usually couldn't be said at all.

'Boil it down to its real core. Just what are we talking about here?'

Michael hesitated. He'd always hated reductionist simplifications, but he also recognized that Chris wasn't the type to warm to a scholarly lecture.

'The ultimate aim of Gnosticism,' he finally said, 'was the liberation of the soul from matter.' He opened his mouth, took in half a breath as if preparing to continue, but caught himself before another word came. With a look of surprise on his own face, he gave an unexpected gesture to Chris. *That's it. There you go. Your one sentence.*

'Liberation from matter?'

'The groups we call Gnostics were diverse and eclectic, but to one degree or another they were all after the same thing: a true knowledge, or *gnosis*, of the universe. They believed that knowledge allowed a person to become aware that the material world is a deception and only the spirit is true. It was a knowledge that was believed to lead to an eventual liberation from the material world and entrance into the pure realm of Spirit.'

What he was describing felt familiar to Chris. 'You've just described half the population of the state of California, and every New Ager I've ever met.'

'Right,' Michael answered, understanding the joke but too distracted to laugh. 'This philosophy has been rather influential in the New Age spirituality of the past decades. It's been so popular, in the ancient world and now in the modern, because a belief that true life lies outside the material realm allows you to have a pretty free and easy approach to the world. If all this physical stuff is just a shell, a cage, a prison, then your behaviour towards it will reflect that. The material world doesn't matter. It's a lower entity, to be discarded.'

His eyes were becoming heavy as he spoke, the pace of the day finally starting to catch up with him.

'Doesn't sound so bad,' Chris replied. 'Plenty to dislike about the physical world, isn't there?' His tone stayed light, but Michael sensed his question was sincere. 'Disease, suffering, death. Why *not* look down on it all?'

'Gnosticism was shunned by the early Christians, as well as by the Roman Empire, because of just that,' Michael answered. 'What you're saying sounds logical enough, even reasonable. But it's an understanding of the world that Christians could never accept. They were teaching that the world was broken but could be healed and redeemed, but the Gnostics were teaching that it was flawed to its core and needed to be escaped. There's a big difference between liberation from sin and liberation from matter.'

Chris pushed his large frame into his seat, trying unsuccessfully to stretch a few extra millimetres into its recline. Michael's words lingered.

'And the group we're after,' he at last asked, 'that's their aim, then? This "liberation from matter"?'

'They certainly seem to strive for some connection with Gnosticism,' Michael answered. 'Though what that is, we don't really know.' He yawned. It was a good sign: perhaps he would be able to sleep for a few hours before they landed.

'You don't know?' Chris asked.

'Not yet. I guess I'm rather hoping this "keystone", whatever it turns out to be, might provide some kind of explanation.'

Now it was Chris's fingers that tapped on the plastic armrest between them.

'Whatever the connection is, it can't be good.'

Michael was startled back to attention. 'Why do you say that?'

'Because what you call "liberation from matter" sounds to me an awful lot like death.' He leaned in to Michael, softening his speech. Emily was still asleep, and he didn't want to wake her with these thoughts. 'And they've already "liberated" your relative, haven't they? If their aim is more liberation, then this, this . . .'

As his voice trailed off, Michael completed the thought.

'This can't be good.'

CHAPTER 41

Maadi, Outside Cairo

Forty minutes after their flight had landed, Michael, Emily and Chris were in a rental Mitsubishi Pajero and headed south through central Cairo. Michael and Chris had finally agreed to end their conversation in favour of rest, and just under four hours of sleep had provided them with a new energy. Economy-class rest and airline food weren't the best antidote to adrenaline-induced exhaustion, but they weren't entirely bad, either.

Emily's sleep on the flight had been surprisingly peaceful. She had drifted towards it with a fear that it would arrive as a series of nightmares she couldn't bear to face: pictures of Andrew's smile; the gunshots echoing in her memory; blood on the floor; the body bag, wrinkled and bulging with the contours of her cousin's body. How he had been so proud, so boyishly vain, about his care for that body . . .

But her sleep had been calm. Perhaps her mind, like her body, had simply been too tired to continue. It had shut off, and sleep had been a welcome respite from thoughts and memories. She had awoken as the small breakfast was being served from the aisle, pleased to see that Michael and Chris had not gone the whole flight without rest.

Twenty minutes after securing the rental and taking to the Egyptian roadways, the trio had made it onto the Circular Road that circumnavigated the great city, and by 6.15 a.m. they had cleared the southern city limit. Where the Circular Road became the Mehwar Al Moneeb, Michael, who occupied the driver's seat, took an exit for what Chris insisted was an essential first step in their journey: a supply stop. He had researched availability before they left and back-seat-drove until they approached a service station that sat opposite the vast Carrefour serving the Cairo suburb of Maadi. Michael pulled the car into the station and was charged by Chris to fill up the tank, as well as a reserve canister, while he and Emily crossed the street to stock up on a supplies list containing the items Chris had deemed essential.

'We need food and water. Terrain maps for the region. Some basic tools – at least a shovel and a knife. We need flashlights for after nightfall.' He had rattled off his list for what seemed the entire drive through the city. 'Packs, flares, maybe a tent . . .'

'Chris,' Michael had protested, 'we're not going on a month-long Saharan expedition here. The site on the map is only twenty or thirty kilometres into the desert, and there may well be roads running close by.'

Chris had summarily dismissed the comments. 'God willing you're right and we'll be in and out and home for supper. But plans don't always go the way you intend. The desert can be

. . . inhospitable.' He had concluded his remark by flopping back into his rear passenger-side seat and continuing his list. 'A good compass, something for the sun . . .'

Michael now topped up the fuel tank and canister and screwed the caps tightly on both. Once he had secured the canister into its niche in the SUV's rear interior, he entered the service-station shop and purchased three carrier bags filled with snacks: sandwiches, protein bars, power drinks, fruit that looked days past its sell-by date. Petrol-station rations, he remarked to himself, were remarkably consistent the world over.

He paid the teller, exited the shop and walked across the tarmac towards their car. As he did, Chris and Emily returned from their shopping, carrying two rucksacks and two shopping bags filled with their stash. Under one of Chris's arms was an enormous container of water, with smaller bottles dangling from it.

'Find everything on your great master list?' Michael asked.

'Everything's a check, save one item.'

'What's that?'

'We're going to need a gun.'

Michael had always held a particular loathing for guns. Weaponry in general seemed out of place in human society, too harsh and terrible; and though he knew his position was naive and his hesitation more emotional than logical – history, after all, tended to be the storyline of those with the best weapons – he couldn't help the awful feeling that came to his stomach whenever they came up in conversation. Guns were the worst of all. All physical contact was removed with a gun. Man had devised a way to end another's life remotely, impersonally. It was the absolute victory of the inhumane.

'A gun?' he forced himself to ask.

Emily's look was unreadable. Michael couldn't tell if her thoughts echoed his own.

Chris's position, however, was unmissable. 'You didn't think this little cat-and-mouse game you two have dreamt up was going to keep you ahead of the danger, did you?'

They both remained silent.

Chris shook his head. 'We need a weapon. We're lucky, we won't need to use it. But that's not a chance we're leaving to fate.'

His point made, Chris drew his attention back towards the matter at hand. Looking away, he glanced towards the petrol-station building with a nod to Michael. 'You've been inside?'

'It's a little private shop.'

'What's the station worker like?'

'He's a local. The shop might double as his house.'

'Perfect', Chris said. 'Give me five minutes.' With that, he walked towards the station entrance and disappeared inside.

Michael turned to Emily. 'So, here we are.' He walked to her side near the front of the SUV and put a hand on her shoulder. Chris's most recent comments had done something to chill both of them.

'Still sure you want to go further with this? There's no shame in backing out now.'

Michael was right. They could stop, turn the rental around and be back at the airport in an hour, flying home to safety.

They could avoid the danger, the uncertainty. Maybe the men who had killed Andrew and ransacked their home would move on. Maybe they would be safe, in the end.

But none of that was certain – any more certain than what lay ahead here. And here there was still hope. Hope of finding . . . *something*.

Emily did not answer. Instead, she set down her shopping and thrust her fingers into her handbag. A moment later, their printout of the hidden map was unfolded and laid flat against a side window of the car.

'It will take us about another six hours to get to Nag Hammadi,' she said firmly, though Michael could not miss the slight tremor to her voice, 'assuming you drive well and we don't have traffic. Then, to get here –' she used her thumb to point to a spot near the mesa where the famous codices had been discovered '– should take us about another thirty minutes.'

Emily passed the map to Michael, then unfolded a geographic survey chart she and Chris had purchased from the store across the street. After a few seconds of examination, she found the section that interested her.

'According to this, there are a few single-track roads that wind through the area, but we might have some off-roading and something of a hike ahead of us. Still, if we push on we should be in Nag Hammadi by two o'clock, and hopefully to our destination by three. We'll have plenty of time before nightfall.' She held the map closer to Michael's gaze and indicated the area.

With Emily's practical direction behind him, he pushed thoughts of retreat from his attention and focused on what

lay ahead. 'Sounds good. We can set off as soon as Chris
retur—'

He was cut short by a firm slap on his back.

'As soon as I what?' Chris asked, his face screwed up in
mock innocence.

In an instant, Michael's hesitations all returned. 'Did you
get your gun?'

'Gun's a no,' Chris answered. 'But the shop wasn't a total
waste.'

He reached beneath his blazer and slammed a heavy-duty
Becker utility knife down on the hood of the SUV. Its seven-
inch blade's matte-black coating matched the Mitsubishi's
paint job. 'Amazing what a little sweet-talking and a wad of
good old American cash can get you round here.'

CHAPTER 42

Maadi, Outside Cairo

Throughout the dialogue between Emily Wess, Michael Torrance and Chris Taylor under the service station's large canopy, two men in a small Daewoo Nubira a few hundred metres down the road had observed them diligently. The cab of their car was filled with the thick, acrid smoke of the Turkish cigarettes Mustafa Aqmal smoked almost without cessation. Marcianus's eyes were red from the saturation, and he had sat himself in the rear of the car, rather than beside his counterpart, to distance himself from the smoke's source. It proved only a slight help; yet Marcianus wasn't about to let the distraction steal his focus. His attention remained wholly on the three people they had followed from Cairo International Airport. Their every move, their every gesture, attracted his complete attention.

On the seat next to him in the rear, a long Hakeem 8mm Mauser rifle lay like a portent, fully loaded. Aqmal had arranged for the car to be waiting for them in Cairo, and its boot contained a collection of firearms for the two men: two Helwan

9mm handhelds, together with the older Egyptian rifle. 'It may be old,' Aqmal had noted when Marcianus first caught sight of the antiquated gun, which had once been a staple of the Swedish and Egyptian militaries but had ceased production in the 1960s, 'but it's as accurate as anything made today.'

Aqmal now tapped out a cigarette in the car's already over-full ashtray, and in a single, uninterrupted motion extracted another from a pack in his chest pocket. 'From this point on, they're clear targets,' he muttered, striking a match to flame and lighting the cigarette with a long, inward draw of breath. 'The city is behind us and after a few more miles they'll be on the open road.'

'Fine,' Marcianus acknowledged, his tone dismissive. He did not take his eyes off the group.

'Once they're out on the motorway, we let them drive a short time, get to the proper outskirts of the city. It shouldn't take more than five, maybe ten minutes. Then we drive them off the road and take care of business when they're stopped.' Aqmal drew in another deep breath of the grey smoke, and exhaled it into the cloud filling the car. 'Or, we can just shoot them as we drive by. Up to you. In either case, we make the matter quick. My connecting flight to Niger is in four hours.'

Marcianus ignored the Arab. What he was seeing take place at the service station was far more important.

'Look at that,' he whispered, pointing through the side window to the conversation taking place between Wess and Torrance. She was holding a paper against the side of their rented SUV. *Is that the second page of our map?* Marcianus watched as she passed the page to the man, then extracted a survey chart from her bag and pointed to various locations. She did so with a certainty and clarity.

She knows where she's going. The details of the route were concrete in what was obviously an agile memory.

'There's more to this woman than I'd anticipated,' he muttered to himself.

Aqmal cut himself out of his smoker's reverie and glanced at him through the rearview mirror.

'What do you mean?'

'I mean, she's not just optimistically following a string of clues.' This time it was Marcianus who spoke without deigning to return the gaze of the other man. 'Look at her. She clearly knows exactly where to go. They've assembled provisions. They have a definite plan of action.' Marcianus's intention had been to have Aqmal execute Emily Wess and the two men, then retrieve the map and collaborate with the brethren to determine where it pointed and organize a trip to reclaim the keystone. But as he watched the confidence of Emily's gestures, their preparations and the certainty of expression on all three of their faces, Marcianus realized he could save time and effort by taking a different approach.

His heart raced, the ultimate aim of his whole life suddenly closer than ever to being in his grasp. *Of my whole life.* Nostalgia swept in to match the moment's potential. From a childhood in India, the son of an American Peace Corps devotee that dedicated his family's life to bringing good to others, the young Arthur Bell had felt himself a missionary for as long as he could remember. But he'd felt early on that his father, and all those like him, had got their mission wrong. What good did their charitable works ultimately accomplish? Perhaps the natives lived a few years longer, died a little less malnourished, but nothing could stop that death, and no one was offering anything to liberate them from the wretchedness of life.

That sense of the meaninglessness of worldly compassion had stayed with him as he moved to the States for college, and had been what drew him to Laurence Mahler. Here was a man who cared not for the body, but the spirit. The counsel he gave did not provide comfort for the horrors of this world: it provided a freedom from it. Arthur had clung to him like a divine father, and given his whole life to Mahler's new Church. Mahler, in turn, had taken him in like a son and a close second in the Church's growth. He had called him Marcianus, after one of the earliest members of the Gnostic family whose legacy they continued, and had helped him become a man who would lead others to spiritual freedom.

How proud the old man would be, were he still alive today, to see how far Marcianus had come.

'Our plans have changed,' he suddenly announced to Aqmal. 'We will follow them. They know where the map leads. There is no point in my wasting time figuring it out after taking it from her. This Emily Wess woman will walk me right to the keystone.'

CHAPTER 43

The Temple, Chicago

Taking the final step up the wooden platform, the Liberator looked out over the gathered brethren from his elevated position at the centre of the temple. In the faint light their dark velvet robes and hoods merged into a sea of barely discernible form.

That his life had come to this point was a miracle of the divine. Every time he donned the velvet robe, thick and heavy, luxurious in every way, he thought of his childhood, spent in third-generation, hand-me-down clothes borrowed or stolen from whichever family his sorry excuse for a mother had befriended for the moment. If he tried hard, he could remember a few images from his earliest years, when he was told they had had a home of their own and a father to look after him and his sister, but all that Walter could truly remember were the constant shifts between the trailers or apartments of whomever his mother had decided was her 'man friend' for the time being. He'd had no father; he'd generally wished he had no mother.

That was how the Great Leader had found him. Nineteen years old, addicted to whichever drugs he could afford, preferring the streets to another night in the sorry abyss of 'home'. Marcianus had met him at a restaurant. Walter hadn't been in it, of course – it was far too up-market for his lack of pedigree – but he'd paused in a walk down the street to gaze through the window at the well-dressed patrons inside, and had caught sight of him. Walter remembered the man's inconspicuous appearance, as well as the look on his face as he registered Walter's presence through the glass. Marcianus had stood up from his meal, exited the restaurant and introduced himself. A moment later he had drawn Walter inside, to his booth, seemingly unfazed by the disgusted looks of the waiters who recoiled at Walter's grungy appearance. The kindly man had reached out to him, offered him food, invited him to sit and speak; and Walter had sat there in unwashed clothes, still half-stoned, with two men who gave him their food and spoke to him as a friend. And in that moment, Walter encountered the first man who seemed actually to care for him.

My name is Marcianus, the man had said kindly, *and this is Simon. And we believe there is more to your life than . . . this.* He had pointed to Walter's dirty appearance and unwashed hair, but, strangely, Walter had not felt offended or judged. He had felt only hope. The man's voice soothed him, his words encouraged. He had told him of a better meaning to his life, of a spirit that was pure, despite his circumstances. Walter had been completely drawn in and his life had changed. The greatest moment of his nineteen years had come when, not long later, he had been absorbed into the Church completely, initiated and blessed. The Great Leader had even given him a new name, Cerinthus, and with it he had begun a new life.

In the years that had passed, he had ascended higher and higher. Then, when the Great Leader had revealed his vision, had discerned that the End for which they were waiting had already come, the culmination of his life had arrived. Marcianus had chosen him to be the Liberator. He had given him the greatest task a member of the Church could receive. His actions would bring freedom to all the Elect.

Those Elect were now before him, filled with anticipation.

'Knowers, brethren,' he began from the platform. 'We draw ever nearer to the great moment, to our great triumph. In less than a day and a half, the Elect will at last be free!'

His booming voice reverberated off the rafters and walls. The brethren followed the Church's established etiquette and did not respond to his rallying words with cheers or cries, but the feeling of excitement in the expectant, hushed room was tangible and electric.

'Hidden so long in the earth, the promise made by our ancestors is about to be fulfilled. They left us a way to accomplish in our day what circumstances did not permit them to do in their own. Their gift to us is the key, the key to unlock the words of life.'

The electricity in the room flared and a few of the brethren could not restrain their cheers of delight. Walter allowed them their spontaneous burst of enthusiasm. Looking down on the crowd, he could see elderly women, young men, even children. The Church did not discriminate. Any who were willing could find the true light, and liberation would be offered to all.

'And so we rally here, my brethren, awaiting full revelation of the long-concealed, long-awaited words.'

Cerinthus reached into a deep pocket and extracted his own copy of the small journal known as the Book, painstakingly copied by hand onto thick paper pages, bound and tied with a leather cord. He raised it high over his head.

'The Book shows us our past! But far more than this, it gives us instructions for the final day. When we follow its guidance, when we act, then we will wait no more. It is time for us to be set free from this mortal coil!'

He shouted his words with genuine emotion and urgency. His activities over the past days had been done with one aim: to ensure that the raw materials for this work were ready when the time came. He was satisfied they would be. If the truth required a little lie to ensure it was not hindered, so be it. That had been the cunning foresight of the Great Leader's new plan. Come out of the darkness and feed the world deception in order to keep it from consuming what is noble and good.

He had heard from their contact in the FBI earlier in the day. The deception was working. The bait was being taken.

His chest swelled and he brought his full energy to the heart of his rallying speech.

'I assure you, my illumined brothers and sisters, of one thing above all: the light of liberation is ready, and it will offer the release that lifts our souls to heaven.'

Another cry went up in the darkness. Hands came together and applause won out over decorum.

'The world will hold us captive no more!' Walter bellowed

at full force, raising his arms in a gesture of unmitigated triumph.

And as he did, the people's cries of victory could not be contained.

CHAPTER 44

Nag Hammadi, Qena, Egypt

At 2.42 p.m., Michael pulled the Mitsubishi Pajero off the Al Nagda in downtown Nag Hammadi, turning sharply onto El-sadat. Emily navigated from the passenger seat, a large map unfolded on her lap. Chris, who had slept for most of the long drive south from Cairo, had awoken thirty minutes before and seemed intent on regaling his partners with a running commentary on everything he saw out of his back-seat window. Though his skill set meant he would take the lead once they were in the desert itself, the drive down the Egyptian motorway he was content to leave to the others.

'You want the left onto Al Hekma road,' Emily said, 'then two and a half blocks and right onto Masr Aswan Al Sree.' Michael peered closely at the road signs as he drove. Street names in the small town were not well marked, and his familiarity with Arabic script was rough at best.

'Just prompt me when to turn,' he noted to Emily. 'That might work better than relying on me to read the signage. These Egyptian street names are too much for me.'

She offered a small smile, her own familiarity with Arabic only slightly stronger than his. 'The names might sound impressive to foreign ears, but sometimes their meaning is more basic than you'd expect. As near as I can tell, the name of the main road we'll take translates as "Roads and Bridges Administration Road".'

'Rolls off the tongue in both languages,' Chris shot at them from the back seat. His sense of sarcasm had not drained, even during the long drive.

'We'll take that until a crossover to the Giza-Luxor highway, which runs along the edge of the fertile, irrigated region by the Nile, and the beginning of the arid desert itself. It should take us about twenty minutes to get there.'

'It's about time,' Chris muttered. 'Real desert. We've been in Egypt all day, and I still haven't seen a single sand dune. A real let-down, if I'm being totally honest.'

Emily tried to ignore his comment. Chris's persistent humour was beginning to grate. She didn't suspect him of insensitivity and she knew he took the matters to hand seriously, but the constant joviality was hard for her emotions to bear. If it was his way of bolstering her under the circumstances, it was not having the desired effect.

Emily set aside the survey chart and again unfolded her printout of the ancient map. The destination, the location of the 'keystone', was clear. The other texts on the panels, written in a more familiar Latin, were instructions for arriving at that goal. The modern chart that Emily held on her knees made the ancient guidance, intended for those travelling by foot and without the overview of the area that satellite mapping could provide, unnecessary. Yet she still marvelled at the handiwork and ancient detail.

'North, then four hundred steps to a great stone,' she translated aloud as they drove. 'Past the bluff with three even peaks.'

'Someone clearly took a lot of care to provide precise directions,' Michael noted.

Emily's attention was rapt in the phrases scribbled here and there along the route. In the final panel, at the bottom of the page, ran a solitary line.

REGULAE QUONDAM SPECTATAE

This Latin inscription, unlike all the others on the document, was not obviously connected to any segment of the map's indicated journey.

Emily looked up at her husband, repeating the line out loud. '*Regulae quondam spectatae.*'

Michael squinted as he drove, his mind quickly providing a rough translation. '"The directions formerly seen"?'

'That's how I make it out as well.' Emily's eyes continued to scrutinize the text. 'What do you think that might have meant?'

'I've no idea,' he admitted. 'It's a little more cryptic than "turn right at the big rock". Though thankfully, we shouldn't need to worry too much about it.' He reached across and rattled the modern survey map, still sat on Emily's lap beneath the printed page. 'I'm more interested in our current drive. You got as far as our crossing the Giza-Luxor road. What then?'

Emily brought her attention back to the present. 'From

there we switch on the four-wheel-drive and turn into the desert itself. Chris gets his dunes and we start navigating by the scrawls on a centuries-old set of directions.

'And from that point on, the roads no longer have names.'

The drive through the stretches of the habitable green belt west of Nag Hammadi took almost precisely the twenty minutes Emily had predicted, and at the crossing with the Gaza-Luxor highway they were confronted with all the sand dunes Chris could have hoped for, though even he checked his humour as Michael switched the SUV into off-road mode and crossed the highway onto a sandy track Emily identified from her map. As they left green landscapes and paved roads behind them, the severity of the Egyptian desert suddenly became tangible and real, and the contrast stark. The highway drew a perfect border between landscapes a sane man unfamiliar with Egypt might think could only exist on separate continents: on one side lush pastures, green trees, and all the signs of industry, culture, society and life. Then, thirty feet to the left, a landscape of deadening brown, other-worldly curves and intersecting lines of sand, devoid of any indications of life or human presence.

For the first time in their journey, Chris was speechless. As the terrain of inner Egypt, unchanged through the millennia, filled his vision, he simply gawped at the overwhelming sight.

For forty minutes they drove, at an increasingly slow pace, as the sandy track turned to barely more than a path leading towards a series of golden bluffs twenty miles into the sand. Eventually, even the path disappeared and the trio found themselves driving over untrodden dunes and flats.

'Up there,' Emily finally said, looking up from her map and pointing towards the base of a bluff 200 metres ahead of them. 'Stop us as close as you can to the base of that cliff.' Michael nodded in affirmation and eased the Mitsubishi to the point where sand met the uneven rocks rising towards the base. Switching the tired SUV into park, he left the engine idling in order to keep the air conditioning fresh.

'This is it, gentlemen,' Emily announced, folding up her map. 'As close as we're going to get to our destination by car. From here on, we go by foot.'

CHAPTER 45

Nag Hammadi, Qena, Egypt

If Marcianus had been expecting keen agreement from Aqmal on the change in their plans, he was quickly stripped of his delusion. No sooner had the Arab man shifted the car into gear and begun to follow Emily, Michael and Chris out of Cairo, than he began to voice his discontent. That discontent was now at its peak, as they watched the vehicle they had been tracking move off into the orange-brown dunes.

'Absolutely not,' Aqmal finally said. Marcianus tore his gaze from the trio's car and glared angrily at Aqmal in the rearview mirror.

'Excuse me?'

'This is not what I agreed to,' Aqmal emphasized, waving towards the vehicle ahead of them as it veered around a dune and out of sight. 'The plan was to kill them on arrival in Egypt. We've already delayed, but I'm not continuing this trek any further.'

He slowed the small car to a halt, then disengaged the

clutch and reached for the rifle, checking that it was loaded and ready.

'Your ignorance is blinding you,' Marcianus answered back, enraged at the other man's insolence. 'Ingenuity is not to be ignored, even in one's foes. It's to be taken advantage of. I will let them lead me to the keystone.'

'Keystone?' Aqmal's eyebrow was raised. That was the second time Marcianus had used the word. He had never heard mention of it before this conversation.

'It's an . . . artefact.' Marcianus spoke simply for the man whose renewed involvement in their plans he was fast coming to regret. 'A significant artefact. All you need to know is that it's extremely important to me and to my people, and Emily Wess knows where it is.'

Aqmal took another drag from his cigarette before extinguishing it, his motions emphatic and deliberate. The rifle was loaded and ready. He could take out Michael, Emily and Chris from fifty metres, he was fairly certain.

'The desert, a keystone. I should have fucking known better.' At last he turned to face Marcianus with his full gaze, his hollow eyes stern, glaring back at him from his awkward angle in the front seat.

'The answer is no. I agreed to a quick trip into Cairo. In and out, as a favour to you. Nothing about going into the desert after some pointless piece of history. It's ridiculous I've let you drag me this far. We end this, now.'

Marcianus drew in a long breath through flared nostrils. Their current deadlock was a classic example of why a cause could have only one leader. Strong wills did not intermix. He realized now that Aqmal was intractable. He would not change his mind, nor alter his precious plans in order to accommodate the new advantage they had at their disposal. Their discussion had come to its productive end.

'I want to thank you, Mustafa,' he said calmly, exhaling his long breath. Aqmal, attempting to light another cigarette before driving further after their prey, did not remove his gaze from the windscreen. 'For the help you have been to our cause. Your role in procuring supplies was essential, and your Arab background will prove more helpful than you know. And you have helped bring me here. For these things, you will always have my thanks.'

Aqmal grunted disinterestedly. He did not notice Marcianus slightly alter his position in the seat behind him, nor the subtle motion at his waist.

'But I'm sorry your mind is so fiercely made up on our present course. That is . . . most unfortunate.' As he spoke, Marcianus finished removing his belt. It was not the ideal weapon, but a gunshot in the car would be loud and messy.

'What is at stake matters more than your plans. And it matters more than you.'

Before Aqmal could answer, Marcianus lurched forward, raising the belt over the seat-back before him. Its two ends wrapped around his clenched fists, he caught Aqmal's neck in the resulting loop and snapped the makeshift garrotte backwards, pulling the Arab's head flush against the seat's headrest. Immediately, Marcianus realized that the belt's width prevented it from functioning as a proper garrotte, and he hadn't had enough distance to snap the man's neck.

Aqmal's life would have to be choked out of him.

Marcianus raised his knee and pressed it into the seat-back, using the extra force to pull more firmly on the two ends of the leather noose.

The Arab man fidgeted frantically, struggling with both hands to gain purchase beneath the belt strap, but Marcianus's grip was too tight. Feeling his larynx collapse and sensing his vision start to lose clarity, Aqmal stared up at the rearview mirror in helpless terror.

Marcianus stared back, gazing a final time into the hollow, brown eyes that had so long set him on edge.

'May your spirit be free,' he said, his voice almost a chant. He pulled back further on the belt.

A moment later, Aqmal's eyes rolled back in his head, his breath and his motion fully gone.

Marcianus released his grasp, and the Arab man's head slumped against the dash.

CHAPTER 46

The Open Desert, North-West of Nag Hammadi

It took Emily, Michael and Chris fifteen minutes to array themselves for the hike that lay before them. As much as they could prepare within the SUV, they did: the landscape outside shimmered with the undulating distortions of heat rising off the sand, and even if it were not over 110 degrees of desert heat outside, the cliff in front of them would still have represented a daunting prospect.

Chris insisted that they begin by each drinking a bottle of water, then filled up the two rucksacks with the essential supplies for the hike ahead: water bottles, the flimsy plastic torches that had been the best he could find in the Cairo hypermarket, a compass, whistles, a folding spade, flares and a field first-aid kit. He strapped the utility knife to his belt, slung one of the full packs onto his back, then handed the other to Michael. Finally, he handed each of them a broad-rimmed sun hat. The hats were not exactly outdoor-grade specimens. Chris had found them in the 'Garden and Patio' section of the Carrefour.

'I feel like you ought to offer me a pina colada with this,' Michael teased as he put the fake-straw creation on his head. In the bright sunlight, with a climb and excavation ahead – things that stirred Michael's historical and archaeological interests to their fullest – he couldn't help but allow a bit of Chris's tireless positive spirit to affect him.

'Sorry, Mike. Wasn't on my list. You should've said something.'

Emily offered a dismissive shake of her head, but even she couldn't protest the light-hearted banter at this moment. The map had brought them here. She felt discovery close enough to claim in advance. There was reason for hope.

'Come on, you two,' she said, matching their tone. 'I'll buy you both a drink once this is over. For now, we hike.'

Michael smiled at her. The accession to humour was a good sign.

The two men had assembled at her side a moment later, and Emily cast another glance over the ancient map.

'It shouldn't be far,' she said, squinting in order to read the page in the bright sunlight. 'The map puts its "X" at the edge, just over there.' She pointed to the left of their position, where a slight fissure in the cliff-face created a texture of light and shadow.

The trio stared up at the scene before them. Then, without further ado, they stepped away from the car and towards a cleft in the forbidding cliff that few human eyes had seen in the past two millennia.

All around them the desert burned hot, the sun scorching

the earth, the sands parched and barren. The only sounds of life were their own, and in the vastness of the Saharan wilderness around them, those sounds amounted to almost nothing at all.

CHAPTER 47

Boston

The Reverend J. Barry Packard desperately wanted to be freed from the pointless obligation. He did not see the purpose of his participation in the futile event. He wanted to stand amongst those who knew his true heart and beliefs. To celebrate the real triumph, not gatherings of those whose purpose was of no consequence, who had no true hope or real vision.

'Please,' he pleaded into the phone, 'let me decline. I would rather be on the ground incognito, amongst our own.'

'It's out of the question,' the stern voice came back through his handset. 'Your participation is essential. This event, this date, they were chosen for a reason. The Governor's Unity Procession on the day of independence, with the spiritual leaders of so many people gathered together . . . the symbolism is dramatic. You represent a sizeable community. They will be all the more inclined to participate if you are there, and active. You know this. We've discussed it before.'

'It just doesn't seem necessary.'

'You don't believe a sign should accompany our end? Something to send a message to those left behind?'

Packard breathed long. He supposed he understood. 'I just, I just want to be at the heart of things with the others.'

The Knower on the other end of the line offered soothing words. 'Do not worry, Brother Packard. You will not be alone in the procession: other brethren will be there, at your side, as well as out among the masses. When the time comes, you will be clothed with us, you will stand with us, and you will be freed with us.'

CHAPTER 48

The Open Desert, Egypt

The hike up to the rough terrain at the foot of the cliff was gruelling. The distance from the SUV to the base of the sheer, stone face didn't appear to be great, but the climb up the rocky protrusions of earth was steep and the footing uneven. Twice they had had to stop to catch their breath and hydrate from the water bottles in their packs. When, after fifteen minutes in the glaring sun, they had finally entered into the shade provided by the fissure in the enormous cliff-face, Emily, Michael and Chris breathed a collective sigh of relief.

It was a relief, however, that dissipated as fast as it had come.

'More water,' Chris instructed, forcing a bottle into Emily's hands and gesturing to Michael that he was expected to drink up as well. Both complied, the exertion from the hike taking far more of a toll than they would have expected. The heat burned away their energy mercilessly.

Chris was not as exhausted, but his extra physical strength left his mind able to focus on more than securing a stable footing and finding strength for the climb. That focus had, over the past half-hour, produced a growing concern.

'Not sure either of you are going to want to hear this,' he finally said, 'but I don't see anything up there.'

He motioned up into the relative blackness caused by the tall fold in the rock. The fissure ran vertically up the face of the sandstone cliff, rising perhaps fifteen or twenty metres towards the skyline. It created an inverted 'V' in the stone, in the shade of which they now stood.

Michael examined the terrain closely. He didn't want to admit it, but he couldn't see anything either. The folds of stone hidden from the sunlight were pocketed with smaller grooves and peaks, but looked markedly like the surface of the cliff-face as a whole. The fissure before them looked as barren as the rest of their surroundings.

Suddenly he was hit with a thought more debilitating than his exhaustion. There might not be anything here at all. The map could be a hoax. Or it could simply be wrong. Maybe there was no keystone at all. And in the midst of these thoughts, Michael recognized a more disturbing fact: that none of them bothered him as much as the thought of what that realization would do to Emily.

'Maybe we haven't got the location quite right, need to fine tune our position,' he finally said. 'Bear in mind, the map is hand-drawn. We can't be absolutely sure of the scale.' He tried to keep his tone positive.

A moment of silence passed. Emily said nothing.

Chris finally gave an annoyed, exasperated sigh. 'Fact is, the map's damned old and may be totally inaccurate. Maybe it was too much to hope for.' If the map's 'X' didn't actually mark the spot, then the keystone could be anywhere: the possibilities were so supremely vast they might never be able to find what they were looking for.

'This is bullshit,' he announced a moment later, his frustration plain. 'Are we sure this is even the right cliff?'

Michael turned to face him, trying to project a strong and immediate desire for him to silence his concern.

'Come on, Chris. Where's that joking optimism gone? You've been so positive till now.'

'It's hot. I get cranky when it's hot.' Then, mid-whinge, Chris finally captured Michael's meaning, saw the imploring look in his eyes. And he noticed that Emily had not yet said a word.

'Desert looks a lot better from inside the car window,' Chris added, trying to withdraw his discouraged tone. 'But you're probably right. I'm sure we'll figure it out.' He felt no conviction behind his words.

'The two of you can stop cushioning your words for my sake,' Emily finally said, breaking her silence. She did not remove her gaze from the cleft in the rock as she spoke. 'You think I'm not aware that this looks bleak? You think I'd rather not be comfortable, at home, instead of sweating through my bra and having my eyes burned by the sun?'

The two men were silent for a long, tense draw.

'I'm sorry, Em,' Michael finally said. 'It's just that our prospects here are looking dismal, you've got to admit.'

'Give it a few minutes before you give up,' Emily answered. At last she broke her gaze from the scene and turned to the two men.

'Michael, do you remember how Andrew soaked in scenery whenever we'd travel together?'

Surprised at the question, Michael nodded hesitantly. 'Like a boy who saw everything for the first time. Always amazed.'

'Always amazed,' Emily confirmed. 'And this, this is pretty amazing.' She gestured to their surroundings, her eyes glistening: the vast desert behind them, the ancient cliff in front. Light and darkness playing off the folds of orange stone. 'So if nothing else, let's take a moment to just look. To be amazed. We, after all, are seeing this for the first time.'

Emily's sudden emotionalism was unforeseen, but both men assented. As Chris surveyed the cliff, the heat and the frustration seemed to lose their grip over him. It was, he had to admit, the most breathtaking geography he had witnessed in a long time.

It was Michael whose eyes finally caught something more than beauty before them.

'What is that?' he asked, extending an arm and pointing finger.

Emily and Chris followed the line from his finger to the face of the cliff.

'Look just there,' he instructed. 'There, where that fold in the stone gets darker in the shadows.'

'I don't see anything,' Emily replied. Chris's frustrated look mirrored the sentiment.

'Look closely. Just left of the mid-line. Focus. What do you see?'

'It's dark, like the rest.' Emily squinted her eyes, straining for vision.

'No,' Michael corrected. 'It's dark, but not quite like the rest.'

'Okay, it's darker there. Almost black.'

It was Chris who finally recognized what he was seeing. 'A cave!' he announced. 'It's the mouth of a cave.'

Michael nodded, smiling. 'Exactly. And if I'm not mistaken, it's positioned *precisely* at the spot indicated on the manuscript.'

CHAPTER 49

'What have we learned?' Angela Dawson asked the question in predictable fashion. The interrogation had gone on all night and through the early morning hours, and they all felt it had reached a satisfactory conclusion. With the arrival of the new day, it was time to debrief. She and her two agents assembled in a small office near the suite of interrogation chambers. At her request, Special Agent Brian Smith joined them for the discussion, having observed Pike's interrogation from a traditional vantage point behind the room's one-way glass mirror.

'The parade is definitely the target.'

Ted Gallows had extracted the key information from Harry Pike only minutes after he had folded at the threat of a life in Guantanamo Bay. The long hours since had been spent probing him for every detail he was willing to give up – and those he wasn't.

Gallows's interrogation of Pike had been the kind of instinctive operation that defined the Special Agent's career and style. His research was always meticulous, his planning careful;

but when he walked into a room with a suspect, he went on instinct. Notes and profiles had their place, but nothing matched the feeling one got from the look in another man's eyes, or the changing sheen of perspiration on his skin, or the patterns of his breath.

Gallows had conducted his first suspect interrogation only three months into his work with the FBI, now over eleven years in the past. He'd been a novice to the art, though he had studied it thoroughly. When he had walked into the small concrete room containing a man suspected of being a minor financial operative in a corporate embezzlement scam, Gallows had read every document outlining his background, suspected connections, and all the dots the FBI couldn't act upon until they'd been connected with corroborating support. He'd been able to get the suspect to provide those connections after only forty minutes, his work apparently done. But something had stopped Gallows from leaving the room. The man sat awkwardly at the interrogation table – not quite at the right angle or with the right demeanour. He seemed confident of his gestures yet hollow in his speech, as if he had trained himself to speak with human emotion, but lacked the emotion itself. Gallows had sensed something more to the man. That intuition had led to a probe, which had led to an investigation, which had ultimately discovered the suspect to be the chief hit man for a group whose corporate aspirations were far loftier than simple embezzlement.

Since that day, Gallows had learned to trust his instincts and let them guide his interrogations. Pike's had been the same. And, as before, following his instincts had produced results. The man might appear a dimwit, might actually be one; but he was connected to something more than a group of ideologues or gun nuts. There was a real force to the Church of Truth in Liberation, and real substance to their threats.

'We're no longer dealing with a hypothetical threat,' he said. 'Even if we don't know the full details, this is real.'

All four heads around the table nodded in unison.

'And it appears to have been meticulously planned,' Laura Marsh added. 'The fact that Pike doesn't know all the details makes that fact even clearer. Whatever else the Church of Truth in Liberation might be, it's carefully organized. Information is compartmentalized and individual members only know what pertains to them.'

Dawson turned to Brian Smith. 'Do you believe Pike when he says he doesn't know the precise nature of the attack?'

'I do,' the section leader answered. He, like Ted Gallows, was formerly stationed at the Bureau's main headquarters in Washington DC, and he comported himself with the dignified-if-stoic air that came with having risen high, fast. 'Special Agent Gallows's interrogation was thorough, and Pike was broken. I don't believe he was holding back.'

'Pike slipped several times,' Gallows continued. 'His references to the Middle East made it clear that he doesn't know much about just what links the Church has there, but left me with no doubt that it does.'

'His comment on "having learned plenty from our Arab friends" didn't leave much to the imagination,' Dawson recollected.

Smith leaned forward. 'And it puts Pike's knowledge entirely in line with what we saw on the video released yesterday.'

'So we've singled out the parade, and the Middle Eastern connection,' Dawson summarized. 'What can we hypothesize about the method?'

'If we go with traditional terrorist approaches, the most likely candidates are either a suicide bomb on the ground or some kind of attack from the air.' Marsh pondered the various possibilities. 'The latter is significantly harder to orchestrate, but we all know it's been done before. And we all saw how devastating it can be.' Though there were no buildings on the Chicago skyline to match the former World Trade Center towers in New York, it was still home to some of the world's tallest.

'Alert the FAA,' Dawson ordered. 'Tell them we have a credible threat on the parade, type unknown. There need to be extra precautions taken with regional airspace, just in case.'

'Meanwhile, we need to step up sweeps for a ground-level attack,' Gallows added. 'Establish extra waypoints along all the roads within a six-block radius around the parade route, check every car for explosives. Set more men on the ground, seeking a portable device.'

'We have no idea what we're looking for. It might not even be a bomb.' Smith's comment seemed to interrupt the growing energy with a dose of more pessimistic reality. 'We shouldn't rule out a well-positioned gunner, or a political assassination. There will be hoards of dignitaries in the parade.'

Deputy Director Dawson ruminated on the statements for

a few moments before standing. When she did, Gallows, Smith and Marsh followed suit.

'At least this gives us something to work with, however vague. Get our men on the ground mobilized, and start running scenarios for how such an attack might play out – the most likely methods, locations, times, specific targets.' Dawson turned from Gallows to Marsh. 'You get your team fully onto the Middle Eastern connection. I want to know just who they, and we, are really dealing with. Divert whatever resources you need.'

CHAPTER 50

FBI Field Office, Chicago

It was when the FBI agent, the arrogant one who identified himself as Gallows, had mentioned the Great Leader's anti-American sentiment, that Harry Pike had known he was lying.

'We know his rage against America was strong,' the agent had declared in the hours that followed his having convinced Harry that the FBI had killed Mr Bell. 'It was only a matter of time until he tried to act on them.'

With that, that irrefutable lie, Harry had realized he was being deceived. He did not know the Great Leader any better than most other brethren, but he knew that Bell was as apolitical as any man he could imagine. There was no more a drop of anti-American blood in his veins than in the hearts of the founding fathers.

The FBI man was lying. They did not know the plan. Did they even know who Mr Bell really was? Was he still alive?

That question, that possibility, had cemented Harry's resolve. Though he had buckled for a moment, it had not been too late. He had realized that his role was still critical

– perhaps now, at this late hour and in these unexpected circumstances, more critical than ever. Every cause required martyrs, and this was his martyrdom: being here, captured by the FBI, saying what needed to be said. He would miss the glory, but it would be possible because of him.

And he had played his role well, in the end. He had told them what needed to be told, pointed them where they needed to be pointed. And they had believed him. The poor country boy who had bent under pressure had given up all the details he had at his disposal, and they had sopped them up like a sponge.

As Harry Pike was now escorted to his cell, he smiled with genuine satisfaction. He imagined the agents were gathered in another room even now, sweating their little heads over the meaning of his every word.

CHAPTER 51

The Cliff-Face, North-West of Nag Hammadi

The point of blackness that Michael had located was situated in the deepest fold of the rock, twenty-five metres above the disjunction of desert sand and the stony face of the cliff. Given the heat and the steep, uneven footing of the terrain, it proved to be a longer climb than twenty-five metres would have suggested.

As Emily, Michael and Chris advanced past the ninth metre, the slope of the stony ground changed from what could be considered steep to what was properly a cliff, and their advance switched from a careful hike to a precarious climb.

'I don't suppose you packed anything for this?' Michael asked Chris as they stared at the rock face above them.

'I've got a few ropes,' Chris answered, 'but a cliff ascent wasn't exactly in your pre-departure sales pitch.' The rocks loomed high, blocking out the sun.

Emily had already set herself to the work of the climb. The near-zero humidity kept her palms dry, allowing a firm grip on the sandstone surface, and the pocketed face of the cliff provided hand- and foot-holds that were not entirely unlike the artificial versions on the climbing walls at her gym.

'Em, be careful,' Michael said, watching her rise above his eye level. 'There are no mats on the floor here.'

She glanced down at him. 'Take your own advice, and start climbing.'

The climb proceeded slowly, but their group made progress. After taking enough time to survey the scene and determine that the ropes would do them little good – without carabiners or belay equipment, they couldn't do much in the way of rigging – they advanced in a slow free climb up the face.

Michael was the least prepared of the three for a freestyle climb. Though he occasionally approached the wall at his fitness centre near the British Museum, it wasn't his favourite activity and he had nothing close to the experience of his wife. Chris, likewise, couldn't claim extensive background in climbing, but his military past had rendered him well enough equipped for the terrain they were facing. They chose to put Michael between them, keeping their positions close as they ascended, so that Emily and Chris would be able to offer assistance from above and below if he needed it.

Michael concentrated on the basics: keeping three points of contact on the rock at all times, using his hands as locks and thrusting himself upward with his legs. The actual push wasn't the challenge – it was the need to find the right set of natural grips that would give him enough purchase to keep his balance as he slid his legs along the cliff-face, searching for the right holds for his feet.

The climb had proceeded well for a good fifteen minutes, and Michael was gaining confidence. Swinging his right leg outwards, he anchored his foot on a small ledge. His hands holding firm, he released his left foot and brought it below his central body mass, edging the toe onto a small, triangular protrusion of stone. His position stable, he transferred his weight onto the left foot and pushed upward.

It was then that things fell apart.

The sound of stone snapping was sharp against the silence of the surroundings. Before Michael could fully register its source, the rock beneath his foot broke away and his body plummeted downwards.

An instant later Michael was hanging from the cliff by only his hands.

'Michael!' Emily screamed, looking down from her perch a few feet above. Michael clung to the cliff-face, unable to respond, his face pressed sideways against the stone. His hands rapidly losing their strength, he tried to cling to the rock with his torso and counteract the shift in balance that came from his legs dangling free in the air above Chris's head.

It took all his strength to keep himself attached to the cliff, but he knew he couldn't keep it up for long.

'Hold on!' Chris shouted, 'I'm coming.' He pushed himself upwards with two muscular thrusts of his legs, and a second later had his face even with Michael's knees. Securing his own lock on the sandstone, he reached over and grabbed Michael's legs, pushing upwards to give him support. The angle, however, gave him little leverage.

'I'm coming down,' Emily yelled. Locking her hands onto

grips at her waist, she lowered herself three feet and slid to her left. Her torso was now level with Michael's face, which was turning a darker red as the effort required to keep his grip restrained his breathing.

'Get his arm!' Chris called up from below. 'Take up some of his weight.'

Emily secured her footholds and reached an arm to Michael's position, attempting to grab him at the armpit and hoist upward.

Michael's fingers were numb, and he could no longer tell how tightly his grip was clutching the stone. He felt a slipping at his chest, and realized he was losing his position.

'Slipping!' was the only word he could get out. The motion began to combine with vertigo and lack of oxygen, and the world began to spin.

Emily leaned as far to her left as she could reach. Driving her hand between Michael's right arm and the cliff, she gripped around his shoulder and pulled.

'That's as much as I can shore up!' she shouted at Chris. Her voice was frantic. Michael's body was in motion. If his grip fully gave, there was no way she would be able to support his weight with one hand.

Chris repositioned his feet, moving to a spot directly beneath Michael. Keeping one hand locked on a grip for balance, he reached up and wrapped the other around Michael's shins, pushing upwards.

Michael released a breath as the pressure of supporting his whole weight with his hands was relieved.

Chris continued to push upwards and inwards, guiding

Michael's left leg towards a free ledge near his knee. He set Michael's shoe on the stone, then released his grip. Emily followed the motion, and when Michael had finally got a foothold, she placed his hand on a suitable grip, keeping it covered in her own.

'Got it?'

Michael nodded, too shaken to speak. The adrenaline flooding his muscles caused the surface of his legs to twitch.

'Gonna hold?' Chris shouted up. He looked past Michael to Emily, who only nodded. Chris's own breath racing from the exertion, he could see her face was still caught in a look of terror.

Damned near dead, the whole lot of us, he thought to himself. *Not a good omen.*

'We should head back down,' Emily said between heavy breaths, gradually regaining her own composure. 'This is too much without some better equipment.'

'No!' Michael retorted, gaining back his breath. 'We're almost there. The cave can't be more than another five metres up the rock.' He took a series of deep breaths, calming himself. Then he looked straight into his wife's eyes.

'We keep going.'

CHAPTER 52

The Cliff-Face

The climb continued for another fifteen minutes before the small ledge positioned below the black hole in the rock appeared close enough to touch. The steepest part of the face had been at the bottom, though after Michael's slip they had slowed their pace, the precariousness of the climb registering fully.

Chris climbed steadily, but he had begun to feel a new tension, and its source wasn't entirely in Michael's near fall. He looked back, out and over the desert behind them. They were so alone, their position so remote.

Despite the blazing heat, Chris suddenly shivered. Whether it was due to his well-honed suspicion or simple trepidation, an unmistakable thought filled his mind.

We're not alone here.

The suspicion had him looking over his shoulder every thirty seconds since, but there was no sign of anyone else in the area. No other cars were visible below, no other bodies or movements on the stone, no other sounds but their own.

Yet the feeling didn't abate.

A car could be behind any number of dunes. A man could hike a different route. Not everyone talks while they climb.

There were possibilities for being tracked that wouldn't allow the lack of evidence to bar the thought from Chris's mind.

When, a few minutes later, they crested the ledge that protruded out beneath the mouth of the small cave, Chris was anything but comfortable. He surveyed the surroundings intently.

'We're here, after all these centuries,' Emily said, wiping a sweaty brow. She took a step forward, admiring the sheer fact of the cave's existence. 'From a computerized X-ray in London, to a cave in the desert.'

Michael placed a dusty hand on her shoulder, gripping tightly. His near-death experience on the climb still had his heart racing, but he could see the change in his wife's demeanour. Whatever came next, at least the map had led *somewhere*. That it wasn't a hoax or a fraud at the very least confirmed that Andrew's death was no accident. There was a bigger story at play, they were standing in front of the proof of that; and that fact alone seemed to bring Emily some consolation.

Michael turned his attention to Chris. 'Any instructions, boss?'

Chris forced himself to break off his continual scanning of the terrain behind them and turn towards the cave's small entrance. Scoping out the situation, he took off his pack and extracted the three flashlights. Distributing two to Michael, he gave instructions with military authority.

'When we first get inside, leave the lights switched off. The contrast between the brightness out here and the darkness in there is going to be more dramatic than night and day. Give your eyes a few minutes to adjust.'

Michael nodded, passing one of the torches to Emily. His wife, however, didn't seem to notice it. Her look of consolation and comfort had given way to an intense concentration, on precisely what, Michael didn't know.

'You okay, Em?' he asked, for a moment worried that the loss of Andrew might be taking hold of her emotions again.

'I'm fine, I'm fine,' she answered. Her tone, however, said otherwise.

Eventually, she broke her vacant gaze into the distance and turned to face her husband. 'You two go in first. I just need a minute.'

Michael let his eyes linger on her, then clutched her hand. 'Take whatever time you need. Chris and I will take a first glance at what's waiting inside.' He leaned forward and gave her a hurried, though tender, kiss, then turned back to the entrance of the cave.

'Well, my friend,' he said to Chris, his pulse driving with excitement, 'there's no time like the present.'

Without further delay, he and Chris took their first steps into the darkness.

Emily could hear their mutterings as they kept still for the few minutes needed for their eyes to adjust. As she waited, her mind raced – but not with thoughts of loss, nor with the emotion that Michael suspected. She was preoccupied with something else entirely.

This is too obvious, too easy, her mind raced, harking back to earlier adventures in her life that had been led astray by following too simple a path. *For God-knows-how-long this key-stone, whatever it is, has remained hidden. Yet here we are, right at the point of discovery. A single map. A simple hike. A fold of shadow concealing a cave . . . but that's hardly enough.*

A moment later, Michael and Chris switched on their lights in the interior of the cave.

This can't be all, Emily's mind continued to race. *This doesn't feel like the final step in a puzzle. It feels like . . . like the first.*

Michael and Chris whispered from within the cave, but Emily did not hear their subtle comments. She only took note of Michael's voice when at last he called out to her at full volume.

'Emily,' he shouted, his voice tense. 'You're not going to believe what we've found here.'

But Emily's mind had already made the leap. She knew what they had discovered. The single, whispered word fell from her lips.

'Nothing.'

CHAPTER 53

Chicago

The lamplight by which Walter Cerinthus worked was dim, but it was enough. The basement workroom was a full storey underground, with no ray of natural light. Only a single mechanic's garage lamp hung suspended from an extension lead overhead, shining its light directly onto his cluttered table.

The local gathering was ready. Those who had filled the Temple earlier this morning had been unable to contain their excitement. Cerinthus could still hear their cries of anticipation ringing through his ears all these long hours later.

By now the Great Leader would be wrapping his hands around the precious key, and in a swift transfer would take it to the texts it would unlock. Already a beacon had gone out to the brethren of each locality, the calling sign that would draw the world's enlightened, the whole Brotherhood, together at last. Were some already here? Had the gathering already begun?

He looked down to the work of his hands. He must not

allow himself to be distracted by the grandiosity of events as the device that was his principal charge was nearing completion. Its components had been gathered from all corners of the world, surreptitiously brought to Chicago to enable his assembly. With all the vials and elements collected before him, he felt himself something of the mad scientist in his laboratory, though there was nothing mad about him. Cerinthus was as sane as any man who had ever lived. Perhaps even more than most, for he, unlike so many, knew his mission and his role in the world. And he knew what was coming, and that it would be a surprise to his brethren, defying every pious expectation.

He took up one of the jars from a box to his left. While many contained powders, this one contained a liquid. Donning his gloves and tightening the cords on his mask, he uncorked the bottle, and held it above a funnel suspended over a small, ten-inch-high glass tube just over half an inch in diameter. There would be twenty-five such vials in all. Three, their scientists had determined, should contain this liquid.

He poured slowly, carefully, watching the level rise.

CHAPTER 54

Outside the Cave Entrance

'There is nothing here,' came Michael's confirmation a second later. 'The cave is barely four feet deep, not even that in width. The walls and the floors are sheer, smooth rock.'

Within moments both Michael and Chris had exited the cave, into which they had previously entered with such eagerness. Their expressions were frustrated and disappointed. At the same time, the sudden let-down had peaked their adrenaline levels, and the exhaustion they were feeling from the climb, offset till then by their excitement, was catching up with them rapidly.

'It's absolutely empty,' Chris affirmed. 'There's not a bend or fold in the walls, behind which anything could be hidden. Whatever might have been there . . . it's gone.'

As Chris spoke, Michael looked into the eyes of his wife, expecting to see her emotional tenderness transform into grief.

What he saw, instead, was determination.

'This isn't the cave,' she said simply, surveying the scene before her.

'Excuse me?' Chris answered in disbelief. 'It obviously is. It's well concealed, hard to access, and it's at the "X" on your ancient map.' He transferred his gaze to Michael. Whether Emily was prepared to hear it or not, reality was reality. 'Disappointment is sometimes hard to accept.'

'I'm not disappointed,' Emily interjected before Michael could absorb his friend's meaning and the two strive to offer their mutual consolation. 'I'm telling you, this isn't the cave. This isn't where the keystone is hidden.'

Chris threw up his arms in frustration and stepped aside to the outcrop's edge. He was still uneasy from the climb and the unnerving sense of pursuit that he couldn't shake. Finding the cave empty added a new layer of frustration, but the last thing he needed was his friend's wife denying the reality right in front of her eyes.

'What makes you say that?' Michael asked, trying to keep his tone tender but feeling the same frustration as Chris.

'This has been too easy,' she answered, finally looking towards both men. 'Yes, it required the map, yes the shadows hid it well, and yes it was a steep climb. But if you were trying to hide something for generations, for the truly long haul, this just doesn't cut it.'

'Have you forgotten that your husband almost died down there, on this "too easy" climb?' Chris protested, turning back towards them.

Emily motioned to the small opening in the stone. 'I'm not saying the cave isn't difficult to get to, or hard to find. But hard to find is not the same thing as impossible to find. We're looking for something impossible.'

'Oh, well if it's only impossible, then no problem!' Chris didn't try to hide his sarcasm. 'Come on, it's here, it's at the spot, it's empty. Somebody obviously got here before we did.'

Emily extracted the folded printout of their map from her pocket. She set the paper down on the ledge, and defiantly motioned the two men towards it.

'No, there's something we're missing.' She set her finger on the last panel, near the 'X' that marked, or didn't mark, the spot. Michael drew close and gazed at the page with her, and Chris, despite himself, followed suit.

'We've followed the instructions and made it here,' he noted as he joined their huddle and saw Emily's finger pressed to the page. 'You can't be telling me there's any doubt we're at the spot where that "X" is drawn.'

'No, I agree,' Emily affirmed. 'But there's got to be something more.'

'Wait a moment,' Michael interrupted. His eyes hadn't left the map, and as Emily's finger lingered on the 'X' in the midst of the drawings and text, Chris's comment suddenly caught his attention.

'Say that again,' he said, turning to his friend, 'your last comment. Repeat it.' Chris, suddenly unsure of himself, repeated what seemed an innocuous remark.

'We've followed the instructions and made it here,' he began. Michael cut him off before he could go any further.

'That's just it,' he said, his intensity growing. He leaned in closer to the copy of the document as he spoke. 'We haven't actually followed the instructions, have we?'

*

221

'There's more on this page than just an "X".' Michael reached down and lifted up Emily's hand. With a gentle nudge he repositioned her finger, setting it back down not on the 'X', nor on the hand-drawn landscapes, but on the text that annotated the journey the map disclosed.

'We didn't need these step-by-step instructions to find our way to this spot,' he added, looking up into Emily and Chris's faces, 'but we didn't consider that perhaps that's not all the instructions are for.'

Emily's features glimmered. Her fingers continued to rest on the hand-written text, and then, as she looked more closely, she realized Michael had positioned them on one text in particular: the final phrase of the map, offset from the rest, written by itself. The phrase they had not been able to make sense of before.

All at once, Emily understood his meaning.

'Mike, you're brilliant!' His face beamed back at her.

'You think there's something in those directions that will lead us somewhere else?' Chris asked, still confused.

'Not in the directions, generally speaking,' Emily answered, her own mind now running with Michael's observation. 'It's this phrase, the one that puzzled us earlier.'

She moved her thumb to reveal the strange line written in Latin script at the bottom of the final panel. The line that didn't appear to be connected to any specific point in the journey.

REGULAE QUONDAM SPECTATAE

'The directions formerly seen.' Michael repeated his earlier translation of the cryptic phrase. 'We still don't know what it means.' Even as he spoke the words, Michael felt his stomach tighten. 'Oh God, what if it's referring to the first page of the map?'

'The first page?' Chris asked.

'The page the thieves stole from the house. We thought we had the upper hand by having the map's final section, but what if it requires the first page to interpret?'

Chris didn't answer. If Michael was right, there was nothing they could do. They would be stuck in the desert with no guidance at all.

A silence followed, the air static with three minds pondering the situation. When it was finally broken, Emily's voice came as barely more than a whisper.

'Formerly seen. Formerly . . .' Her eyes rose to meet them. 'I don't think it refers to the other page. If a person had them together, he'd still see them both. The phrase "formerly seen" wouldn't fit the situation. The wording is too awkward.'

'It's old. Maybe it didn't sound as odd to Latin ears.'

'Latin may be dead, but it's not dysfunctional. It means what it says.' Emily let her mind wander through the possibilities until at last a new idea started to take shape.

'Maybe it refers to the original text, to the manuscript before the map beneath it was exposed? It's what would have been "formerly seen" on this page, or at least on its original.'

'The text about the Cathar community?' Michael queried, his face doubtful. 'Do I need to point out that we're nowhere near Mont Louis?'

'Forget the location, and forget the nature of the text's contents. The point is that they were one document, written by the same hand. Maybe the text the map was written beneath wasn't just a cover.' As she spoke, details began to return to her. 'And you remember that page: there was one phrase that drew your attention. One that was—'

'Struck through.' Michael remembered the single oddity on the otherwise flawlessly crafted manuscript.

'That's right. The mistake and its correction, which led us to believe the document was a draft or unofficial text. But maybe that error wasn't an error. It might have been a signal. Maybe those words are precisely "the directions formerly seen" that are referred to here.'

'Well, what were they?' Chris asked, confused but anxious for the point.

Emily closed her eyes, thought, and spoke confidently. '"Thirty-two hands south-west." The number was crossed out and replaced by thirty-five, but the original phrase had thirty-two.'

Another bout of silence descended, and this time it was Chris who broke it.

'A hand is a basic unit of measurement, isn't it?'

CHAPTER 55

Outside the Cave Entrance

Emily's features brightened as Michael ran with Chris's observation. 'A measure. Especially in ancient cultures, the hand was a commonplace rule. It's not exact, but it's reasonably effective for general lengths. The width of an open hand, usually a man's, measured from the tip of the pinky to the tip of the thumb.'

'So we have a measure directing us towards our real objective,' Chris affirmed, taking up the concept and pushing it forward. 'But what do we measure from?'

'From the "X",' Emily replied, standing upright. 'From right here. We're standing on the ledge outside the mouth to this cave. We need to measure off thirty-two hand widths from this spot, bearing a line south-west.'

Michael asked the obvious question. 'Which way is south-west?'

'Always be prepared,' Chris muttered, repeating his mantra as he fished a small plastic compass out of his bag. He made a point of elbowing Michael sternly in the ribs as he held it up to the light, his face aglow with a new optimism. 'That way,' he indicated, taking his bearing. His hand motioned upwards along the cliff-face, askance and twenty degrees to the right of their position.

Michael shook his head. 'No, I mean which way is south-west, according to that map.' He pointed again to the printed document.

Chris's expression was unreadable, and he simply held out the compass a second time. 'I've already told you, south-west is—'

'Today,' Michael interrupted. 'South-west is that direction today. But this map was drawn several centuries ago.'

Emily nodded. 'Two hundred, maybe two hundred and fifty.'

'And?' Chris probed.

'I'm sure you're experienced in magnetic field variations, as they affect map reading today?' Michael brought his gaze back to Chris's as the FBI operative nodded, perplexed.

'The variation between magnetic north and true north has to be figured into any computation made from a compass.' Chris looked down at the small, plastic device in his hand, catching a faint glimmer of where Michael was going, but not yet fully able to follow.

'And that variation depends on geographic location,' Michael added. 'As well as . . . anyone?'

Emily and Chris both gazed at him, neither daring an answer.

'Time,' Michael finally said, answering his own question. 'Magnetic declination varies over history. It won't be the same today as it was two hundred and fifty years ago. It's a factor we have to allow for all the time in historical digs.'

'This is your region, Mike,' Emily noted. 'Does that mean you know the figures?'

'I can only make a rough approximation, since we don't know the exact date the map was produced. But if your guess of two hundred and fifty years is correct, I would put the negative declination here at about ten or eleven degrees, more or less.'

'Which means?'

'Which means south-west on that map is south-south-west on our compass.'

Chris, now absorbed in the computations, glanced down at his compass and then held out his arm at a new angle. 'That puts it down that line.'

'Okay, that's the direction. It's time to measure. Use your right hand, Mike,' Emily ordered. She marked an 'X' in the sand of the ledge with the toe of her shoe. Michael bent down to comply, flipping his hand, pinky to thumb, again and again, working his way to the right of the cave entrance and further up the steep, stony landscape.

No wonder the instruction was written, not marked, Emily thought to herself as he worked. *It was not only meant to keep it hidden, but it's a scale too small for the map itself.*

After thirty-two measures, Michael stopped. Emily clambered up the rocks after him, balancing at his side.

'Em', Michael began, 'there's nothing he—'

'Shh!' she commanded, cutting him off. Everything in her told her they were on the right track.

Standing upright, clinging to Michael's arm for support, she surveyed the scene before her. Below, to their left, was the small cave, Chris still standing outside it. To her right, nothing but more rock. Above, the cliff continued, the stone folding, arching and bending into the darkness of shadow and light.

And then, as her gaze swept over the scene, her eyes caught the illusion.

From her new position, the gap between two large stone protrusions slightly above them came into view. And there, in the tiny space between, a spot of blackness. Her heart began to race. She took a step to her left and the angle changed, the hidden space disappearing. Two to her right, to the same effect. Only when she returned to Michael's side, at the spot exactly thirty-two hands south-west of the ledge marked 'X' on their map, did the tiny pin-prick of darkness above them become visible.

It was the entrance to another cave.

The speed with which the trio climbed to the new cave's entrance matched the enthusiasm that filled them after Emily's discovery. There was no ledge here, only the support of the two angular folds in the stone that kept the cave hidden from view below. Reaching them, out of breath and clinging perilously to the rock face, there was no opportunity for casual discussion. Michael, who arrived first, pulled his body into the darkness. Emily followed, and Chris brought up the rear.

In a matter of seconds, they had disappeared from the desert landscape, as hidden from view as the cave itself.

CHAPTER 56

Below the Cliff-Face

Marcianus reentered his compact car and wrapped his hand around a small satellite phone that sat near the steering column. He had parked roughly 100 metres behind the group's SUV, behind a particularly steep sand embankment, keeping his vehicle hidden from view. An excursion to the top of the dune, lying flat on his belly and peering over with a set of high-powered-zoom binoculars he had taken from the back of the car, had allowed him to watch the three bodies disappear into the dark cleft of the rock. He was amazed at how they seemed simply to vanish from view. From his vantage point, far below, there was no sign of a cave, no sign of anything at all. The cave below he could see, though it was far from obvious. But here – here they seemed simply to vanish into the stone. And once they were gone, nothing. Not a shimmer or a shadow revealed so much as a slight interruption to the face of the cliff.

It was a natural optical illusion of the most wonderful sort. *No wonder the keystone has successfully remained undiscovered for so many centuries*. His ancient forebears had selected its hiding place wisely.

Despite the overwhelming desert heat, his body shivered with anticipation. He was close, so very close.

He clutched the phone, dialled and held it to his ear. It had sat on the dash during his drive into the desert and the absorbed rays of the sun made it burn hot against his skin. He accepted the slight discomfort as if it were a challenge from some unseen power. So many things might now tempt him away from his course, but he would succumb to none.

'Things have gone even better than planned.' Marcianus began to speak the moment the line connected. 'They've led me right to the spot. It's in the region we had suspected. Their progress for the first stages matched the segments of the map we possess. Their movements since, I have no doubt, match the remaining.'

'Then you are set to obtain the stone?'

'Everything is on target. I'll give them a few minutes alone inside, provide them with a chance to do the grunt labour of locating and extracting it. And then I'll take what's ours.' He paused. 'How are preparations at the site?'

'Everything's in order,' the voice replied. 'The deception is working. I've just spoken with our link inside the FBI. Their attention remains where we want it. Their interrogation of young Brother Pike, though nearly derailed, has produced the results we intended. He fed them every detail he was supposed to.'

Marcianus took a satisfied breath. 'Excellent. Once I have the stone, we'll move to take the texts. You know what comes next.'

He clicked the line closed and pocketed the phone, his attention returning fully to the task at hand. Tailing Wess and her companions had not been difficult. They did not seem to have the slightest suspicion they were being followed, with the exception of the FBI agent, who constantly gazed out behind them as if looking for pursuers. But the man didn't seem to be motivated by anything more than a general fear. He scanned the surroundings, but never focused on Marcianus's carefully concealed position.

Marcianus had paused in his pursuit only long enough to dump the body of the former Arab terrorist out of the passenger-side door. Without life coursing through Mustafa Aqmal's veins, the heat of the cab would have caused a stench to arise quickly, and Marcianus had no desire to fill his nostrils with the evidence of decay. It was bad enough he'd had to kill the man. Marcianus despised dirtying his hands with the actual actions of death. It brought him all too close to the material weakness of this life, and he had made a personal vow never to dirty his hands with the actual act of killing, which could so easily be delegated to others. He had had to break his vow today, but there had been no other choice; and it would not be the last life he took before the day was over. At least the desert would provide a way to off Wess and her companions without having to do the deed with his own two hands.

Marcianus opened his door and exited into the sun. As he took his first steps towards the cliff-face and the climb that would lead him to the cave's entrance, he checked that a round was chambered in his Helwan, just in case choices eliminated themselves once again. In his left pocket he already had the device that would ensure it was only he who left the cave alive.

CHAPTER 57

Hotel des Rives, Paris

It had been arranged twelve months previously: the beacon would come in the form of two lamps, burning in the north tower of Notre Dame. The west face of the tower's midsection had paired doublets of narrow archer's windows, towering high above the ornate Portal of the Virgin. A single lamp burning in the left-most window would be the sign that the process had begun – a readying mark, to instruct the preparation of the local brethren. A second lamp, burning in the adjacent window, would command action: the beginning of the exodus itself. The courier from Spain would relay the instructions.

The first lamp had begun to burn two days ago. Then, this morning, a second light had shone out over the ancient plaza.

It was time.

Guy de Longerac sat in a wicker chair next to a small table outside the Hotel des Rives, sipping a strong espresso sweetened by a single, brown lump of sugar. The towers of the cathedral were perfectly framed in his vision as he gazed east across the Quai Saint-Michel and the slowly flowing Seine.

He was embarrassed to admit how much he loved this view – a classic 'scène parisienne'. He knew he should not love something so base, so worldly. Yet it filled him with a soothing comfort all the same.

'You see the second beacon as clearly as I,' he said in native French to the brother sat beside him on the cafe foyer, 'and you know as well as I what it means.'

'Yes, Master.'

'All is ready?'

'The Knowers have taken the responsibility of their higher station and informed the brethren of Paris, together with the few who live outside the city. All have made their necessary arrangements.'

'They can move immediately?'

'On command,' the French Leader's assistant answered. 'Funds have been made available to each. The moment I say the word, they will purchase tickets themselves.'

Guy accepted the report with a slight incline of his head. 'Very well. Tell them Praxean commands their immediate action.' The local Leader's ritual name carried absolute authority amongst the enlightened of France. He turned to face the other man. 'As for you and me, we will gather together our closest and perform the Initiation Incantation this afternoon for our two postulants. They must be illumined at once, and then depart with us.'

'As you wish.'

The man known only as Praxean to the twenty-six brethren of France – soon to be twenty-eight – sighed a long, calming breath. He took the final drops of coffee from the small cup, letting them roll slowly over his tongue and down his throat, his eyes falling again over the scene he had admired his whole life. There had been so many Leaders in France before him, all guarding the same secrets, all enlightening their followers with the same wisdom. Had they been consoled with the same scenes as he? Had they taken comfort in the grand antiquity of the stones, spires and ancient streets?

The thought hit Praxean suddenly. There had been so many before, but there would be none after. He was the last, and so was this moment. The last coffee. The last of Paris.

It was time to depart these worldly things, to make the exodus with all his brethren, and assemble at the gateway to eternity.

CHAPTER 58

The Cave

The Cave

Inner chamber

Outer chamber

After two minutes of standing motionless in the darkness of their new environment, Chris instructed Emily and Michael to switch on their torches. Their eyes had adjusted to the black surroundings as much as they were going to, and their anticipation was too great to sustain a longer wait. It was time to see just what they had stepped into.

The light of the three small bulbs filled the stone chamber with a soft, orange glow, the sudden change from darkness to light making the sight all the more startling. The trio stood in a minuscule, oblong cave barely wide enough to accommodate two men standing side by side, and apparently no deeper than five or six short strides.

'It doesn't look like it's going to take us long to search,' Michael noted, a tinge of foreboding disappointment in his voice, though he noticed that the walls here were more ragged than the smooth chamber they had examined below. At least there were possibilities.

Emily shone her lamp in every direction, allowing the movement of shadow and light to help her get a sense of the shape of the space. *Notice everything*, she commanded herself. *Every surface is significant. Nothing is ever as it seems at first sight.* The deciphering of the map's clue had brought her conviction, as well as a suspicion that it was not the last deception to be encountered.

She continued to pass her torch over the uneven surface of the stone walls, sweeping back and forth across their pitted facades. Her light was joined by the two others, but collectively they revealed the same thing: emptiness.

The second cave was looking just as empty as the first.

It can't be. It just can't be. Her thoughts were growing more desperate now, hope a stronger motivator than reality.

Keep looking. Her light passed from floor to ceiling, and she tried to work through an impromptu grid in her mind, covering every surface of the cave walls with her beam, examining everything intently.

Rock. Only rock, together with the round disc of her torch's light, and the fluctuating shadows it cast over the bumps and ridges in the stone.

It can't all end in light and shado—

Before the thought was complete, something caught Emily's eye. It wasn't an object, or a feature of the stone. It was the shadows themselves.

Across the chamber, the shadow cast by her torch did not match the visible lines of the surface.

A slight disjunction left a break between stone, shadow and light. It was almost imperceptible, but it did not escape Emily's analytical gaze.

She took a step forward. The shift in the shadows increased. *It's something. At least, it could be something.*

She took another step, her eyes wide. It was as if a vertical line drawn from floor to ceiling was distorting her vision, the stone on the left seeming to come into focus at a different rate than the stone on the right.

Emily switched the torch from one hand to the other and watched the shadows dance. It was then that her expression broadened.

'Over here,' she motioned. Michael and Chris promptly

238

turned to face her. 'Look closely. There, at the back wall.' She motioned to the innermost recess of the small chamber. 'When you look at it, it appears to be a single surface, but the shadows aren't right. It's almost as if . . .'

Emily took another step, and when she finally reached the cave's far wall she turned ninety degrees to her left.

Her sudden, broad smile was illumined by the beam of light her husband shone on her face. 'What is it?' Michael asked. 'Don't keep us in the dark.'

'Remember our little hunch about the manuscript, back in London?'

Michael nodded. 'More than meets the eye.'

'Not just on paper, Mike.' She beckoned the two men to join her, and they stepped to her side in the cramped space. Michael, the tallest of the three, had to crouch to keep his head from colliding with the ancient stone above him.

At the rear of the tiny cave, a fold of rock blocked from view a fissure that ran vertically through the stone. From every other angle in the small space, the cave looked to be a tiny hole-in-the-wall, little more than a room-sized shelter from the desert sun. But from the rear wall, facing sharply left, the fissure came into view and the true reality of the scene opened up.

'Is that . . . *another* cave?' Michael asked, taking in the sight.

'Or an extension of this one,' Emily answered, 'depending on how you choose to look at it.' She examined the slender entry carefully. 'It doesn't look man-made. Whoever originally found this cave happened across one that lends itself particularly well to concealment.'

Before them, the fissure opened up a tunnel further into the cliff. This second chamber beyond it was at least three times as long as the first, and twice as wide.

Chris beamed with excitement. 'The perfect hiding place just got better.'

'Let's start in there,' Emily instructed. 'Given the drive for secrecy, it's more likely that something would be hidden in there than out here.' One by one the trio entered the cave's second chamber. 'Since we don't know exactly what we're looking for, look for anything that isn't a natural part of the environment. Anything man-made, whatever the shape, size or material. It might be hidden in the walls, or in the floor – so step lightly.'

Michael rolled back on his heels, suddenly conscious of the sand floor and the possibility that he might walk right over the top of whatever it was they were seeking.

'Don't forget to use your hands,' Emily added as she and the two men began to survey the cave's interior. 'Caves are places of natural optical deception: crooks and folds in the stone, small clefts. Your eyes might miss what your hands won't.'

Unconsciously spacing themselves at rough thirds throughout the extent of the interior, Emily, Michael and Chris began to feel their way along the cave walls, from floor to ceiling, hoping for their lights or fingertips to make contact with anything apart from stone.

The search continued in near silence. The interior of the cave was surprisingly cool, especially given the heat of the desert outside, and their fingers began to feel the chill of the stone as they passed them over every surface they encountered.

Long minutes passed, before any sign of discovery broke their concentration.

'What's this?' Michael asked suddenly. His fingers had found a fold in the stone that concealed a small space behind it. 'I might have found something.'

In a breath, Emily was at his side.

'It's a nook behind this lip in the stone,' Michael said. Emily reached behind it, her fingers sweeping the walls of a six-inch-by-six-inch well, dusting the sand of its base. After a moment's search, she knew the space was empty.

'Nothing here, Mike.' She placed a hand on Michael's shoulder, a tender acknowledgement and brief moment of connection. 'Keep looking. That's just the sort of spot where something could be hidden.'

Or could have been, she thought to herself. *This cave is remarkably well concealed, but we don't know when this object was hidden here. How many centuries in the past?* The fact that others might long ago have claimed the mysterious 'keystone' suddenly leapt into her mind.

Back at her search a moment later, Emily soon realized that the small cave was filled with similar holes in the wall, crannies and clefts. It was a veritable treasure trove of obscure hiding places. Every one she encountered charged her with anticipation; but on each occasion she discovered only an empty well or a vacant fold in the stone. Countless hiding places, but nothing hidden.

'I'm not getting anything,' Michael muttered after a few minutes, his own experiences mirroring Emily's and his frustration starting to show. 'You know, it's quite possible there's nothing in this cave, either. We'd do well to be ready for that.'

Emily avoided answering the topic. 'Keep looking. If we don't find anything here, we'll head back to the front chamber and try there.'

All three continued to feel their way along the stone, but the situation seemed more hopeless by the minute.

'Hold on.' Chris's exclamation came suddenly. 'What's this?' The others turned and watched as he pushed a hand further and further into a small cleft in the stone wall. His arm disappeared up to his elbow, and then nearly to his shoulder.

Emily stopped her search and walked over to him. Michael quickly followed.

'Have you found something?'

'This little spot goes back further than I can reach. No, no wait. There's the end. My fingers have just hit stone.'

Emily and Michael sighed, almost in unison. A deep chamber, deeper than the others, but still empty.

'Wait a second,' Chris continued, his face puzzled. 'It's a much smoother stone than the others. Almost . . . soft.'

Emily's face brightened. 'Feel it carefully, Chris. What, exactly, does it feel like?'

'Smooth, a little porous, and—' Chris hesitated.

'And?'

'And round. There, yes. I can wrap my fingers halfway around it. It's a cylinder, or something close.'

Emily's heart suddenly beat faster than she had known it

to pulse in years, yet when she spoke her next words, she spoke them calmly, professionally. 'Chris, this object – is it movable? Can you lift it?'

Chris didn't answer, but she could see from his concentrated expression and the twitching of muscles around his shoulder that he was trying.

'*Gently!*' she instructed. Chris nodded, keeping his eyes closed and his concentration intense.

A moment later, he began to pull his muscular upper body back, and his left arm gradually, carefully, made its way out of the dark break in the wall of the cave. He moved at a snail's pace, realizing that whatever he held might be ancient and would almost certainly be fragile. With every inch, the antici-pation and tension in the small cave grew exponentially.

At last, his hand came into the soft torchlight of the inner chamber. Wrapped in his fingers was a small ceramic jar, rusty-orange in colour. It bore no markings, and was sealed with a small bowl, fastened upside down over its rim and sealed with bitumen.

The three explorers gaped in wonder, and a long silence followed as they stared at the find in amazement. The map had actually pointed them to its target, and after all these years.

It was Chris himself who finally broke the silence.

'I think we've found your artefact, my friends. And damn, it looks old.'

CHAPTER 59

The Cave

'What is it?' came Chris's next question. He set the jar down on the cave's sand floor with care and stared at it with a strange wonder. His arm ached from the extended reach that had allowed him to extract it.

Emily and Michael could only provide a technical answer. 'Normally, jars like this were used to store documents or collections of smaller objects,' Emily said. 'They were the packing crates of the ancient world. The keystone could be just about anything.'

'The answer, though, is in this jar, right?' Chris pointed to his find as he spoke. He felt a certain pride as he did.

'So it would seem.'

'At first glance, it looks remarkably similar to the jars found at Nag Hammadi.' Michael's historically orientated mind was working at full speed. 'It's far smaller, but it's the same general composition and sealed in the same manner.'

'I remember you told me about them being afraid to open

those jars, because they were sealed. Should we be getting the shakes about genies and evil spirits?'

'What we ought to be more worried about is how to transport this jar safely, without damaging it or its contents. Remember, it's been stationary for a long time. The document containing the map was at least two, maybe three centuries old. But this looks far, far older. On first glance I'd say somewhere around the fourth or fifth century AD.'

'We can't just open it and find out?' Chris was deflated by the sudden let-down.

'Here? Of course not! We're not tomb raiders. We need to open it in a controlled environment, where we can be sure it won't be destroyed by the act. The bitumen needs to be cut through carefully, the lid removed and special care taken with the contents, whatever they turn out to be.'

'That would be ideal, yes,' Emily interjected. 'But I'm afraid we have other priorities today.' Without another word, she picked up the jar in her two hands and with a swift motion smashed it against the stone wall of the cave.

'Em!' Michael shouted in shock.

'All right!' Chris proclaimed with extreme satisfaction, his voice overpowering Michael's protest. '*That's* what I'm talking about!'

Emily ignored her husband's horror and his friend's over-excited reaction. In her hands, the ancient jar shattered into a hundred fragments, the shards falling through her fingers to rest on the cave floor. The sound of shattering pottery echoed through the chamber.

What remained in her hands was a flat, polished stone. Or

not a stone, precisely. It was a ceramic object made by human hands, out of a different material than the jar that had contained it. The oblong, flattened surface sparkled in their torchlight, and Emily brushed away the dust that covered it from her dramatic act a moment before.

As her hand swept the debris from the stone's surface, she looked down at a set of intricate carvings that marked it. Four concentric rings formed a layered circle subdivided by thirty-three radial lines, spreading out from its centre like spokes on a wheel. Each of the ninety-nine small sections these lines created was filled with a different letter, each etched into the man-made stone in ancient Coptic script. At the centre of the carving was a small grouping of five letters, written over the top of three numerals.

ⲅⲁⲅⲉⲡ
3 2 5

Emily stared at the carving, her eyes unmoving, capturing every detail.

'What the hell is that?' Chris finally asked.

'It's Coptic lettering,' Michael noted breathlessly. His shock at Emily's act was overcome by his amazement.

Emily continued to stare intently at the stone's strange inscription.

'I'm not sure just what it is or what it means,' Michael added, 'but I don't think there's much doubt that it's what Andrew's attackers, and our map, call the keystone.'

From behind the huddled group, the distinct click of a pistol being cocked echoed through the cave.

'The keystone is exactly what that is,' came a new voice.

Emily, Chris and Michael spun around, the light from their torches falling upon a man none of them had ever seen, whose pistol was aimed directly at them.

'And now,' the man said, 'you will give it to me.'

CHAPTER 60

FBI Field Office, Chicago

Special Agent Laura Marsh rubbed her temples as she gazed at the glowing monitor on her desk, sifting through the materials a sixth time. Or perhaps it was a seventh. She had lost count as the continual scanning back and forth between dozens of open windows on her monitor, and twice as many paper folders on her desk, blended the acts of background research into a hazy blur.

The space in her head immediately behind her temples – the space no finger-rubbing or massaging could reach – ached, and not simply from the general challenge of piecing together background information on the Church of Truth in Liberation's Middle Eastern connection. It ached because something was not right. Something didn't fit, and when material didn't fit, Marsh's head throbbed.

There was something they were overlooking. The Church showed no signs of an international dimension, yet the information on their threat against Chicago – the video, the reports from Iraq, the intelligence from Pike – all spoke to a strong Arab connection.

The Arab connection in turn spoke to an anti-American drive, yet there was nothing whatsoever in the materials on the Church that indicated any kind of political, much less anti-American position.

But if there was an anti-American facet to the Church, that would indicate an ideological, power-driven motivation and support a supposed terrorist tendency; yet the FBI's own consulting anthropologist had said that the group's Gnostic leanings would orientate them against such things, driving them towards peace and enlightenment and the freedom of the spirit, not political power-plays and terrorist ideologies.

No, there was something here that didn't make sense. She was missing something. They were all missing something.

Marsh's eyes fell on a yellow page an agent had delivered to her only a few minutes before. A general sweep of cellular communications by the National Security Administration had flagged a number after a conversation pinged the terms 'video' and enough additional characteristics to register an alert. The NSA had, most uncharacteristically, shared the information with the FBI, and they had triangulated the phone's position. It had been found abandoned at a restaurant table in the Drake Hotel earlier in the morning.

A hotel immediately along the Fourth of July parade route.

The phone call was an important lead. It suggested local support and activity. But it was not the call that troubled Special Agent Laura Marsh. It was a small detail noted on the report: the phone was an Italian make, registered on Deutsche Telekom's T-Mobile network.

Chicago. Iraq. New York. Britain. And now Italy. Germany. The spread of the Church of Truth in Liberation seemed to expand dramatically with every lead they found.

Marsh rubbed her temples more fiercely still.

We're missing something . . .

CHAPTER 61

The Cave

'The keystone is exactly what that is. And now, you will give it to me.'

The stranger who had suddenly appeared in the cave spoke with a quiet firmness. His words were those of a man who felt his point made itself, without the need for gratuitous emphasis. He kept his gun levelled at the group. Since Emily Wess was the one with the keystone in her hands, he trained the barrel on her.

Chris's military training immediately kicked in and he swivelled to take up a body position directly facing the unexpected visitor.

'Who the fuck are you?'

'A question with an answer that doesn't matter,' the man said dismissively. 'All you need to know is that the keystone belongs to me, and I don't intend on leaving without it.'

'Belongs to you!' Emily couldn't restrain her exclamation. 'This is a piece of history. It belongs to no one.'

The stranger's features radiated his annoyance. 'You scholars are all the same. Everything is so abstract, so general.' The disgust he felt threatened to overwhelm him. 'Let's not belabour this. Hand it over. The keystone was not fashioned to sit forever in this cave, much less in some university library or museum – any more than were our most sacred texts. It has a purpose.'

The man's words, sparse though they were, struck Michael.

'Wait a minute, I know you.' He leaned forward on one knee, still crouched with the others. 'The rhetoric, the intensity. I recognize it from your letters to the museum. You're Arthur Bell, the man who's been asking for access to our manuscripts.'

The man twitched ever so slightly at the secular name. 'I told you before, my identity is unimportant. Just give me the stone.'

But Michael was now certain. 'You claimed you wanted those manuscripts for a "sacred purpose" too.'

All the muscles in Emily's body tightened. The individual who stood before her was Arthur Bell, the man responsible for sending those who had killed Andrew. They may have pulled the trigger, but this was the man who had set them on their course. The connection between the events in Emily's home and those in Michael's office were now concrete, and the man she most wanted to stop was standing only feet away from her.

'Arthur Bell . . .' she whispered.

'Old names are for old men,' Bell finally assented, 'not for men of spirit.' He looked upset to be called by the name, as if it were a remnant of an identity he had long ago given up.

'Give me the stone, woman.' He glared at Emily. 'You know all too well how far I'm willing to go for the liberation our holiest documents will bring.' He drew in a long breath, his eyes absorbing the rays of light that danced over the stone's surface. When they returned to Emily's face, they were cold.

Emily stared at him, frightened but unmoving. She couldn't hand over the stone, she had to delay him—

'Dammit, the stone!' Bell shouted. He held out a hand, expectantly. Emily tightened her clutch. They were cornered and there was little she could do, yet everything in her cried out to refuse. Cried out that this man could not win. Not again.

During the whole exchange between Emily, Michael and the stranger, Chris had kept silent. But silence, for the FBI agent, was anything but stillness. It was a tactical tool, to be played for advantage.

He could not get to his knife without being noticed – the sheath was on the hip closest to Bell and he would surely see any motion towards it. But there was another option. Chris had purchased a compact flare gun during their supply stop in Cairo, and the plastic pistol was tucked into his pack in case of emergency. The pack lay on Chris's opposite side, shielded from the other man's direct view. As Arthur Bell spoke with Emily and Michael, rarely removing his gaze from the keystone in Emily's hand, Chris took advantage of his position at the periphery of the man's vision and slowly, silently, moved his left hand towards the open pack beside him. Without a sound, he snaked his fingers through the loosely packed contents, until at last they came to grip the flare. It wasn't enough to kill the stranger, but it would be more than adequate to shock the pompousness out of him and throw him off his feet, temporarily blinding him in the cave's dark interior. Chris would do the rest himself.

Slowly, imperceptibly, he began to draw his hand out of the pack, fingers already in position around the flare gun's handle and trigger. He only needed not to be seen – not until the last moment, when he would aim the flare at Arthur Bell's face and fire.

'Give me the keystone,' Bell repeated. 'Or do I need to make the precariousness of your position more obvious to you?' His eyes were locked with Emily's, and he seemed to realize the strength of her defiance. There was one way to deal with that. Bell swung his right hand a few degrees away from her, bringing the barrel of his Helwan to a point squarely between Michael's eyes.

'The stone, or your husband meets the same fate as your cousin.' His face was determined. 'I am not by nature a violent man, but do not think that I won't resort to putting a bullet between your husband's eyes if it is the only option with which you leave me.'

Michael tensed, and at last Emily's resolve faltered.

'No – don't! I'll give you the keystone.'

Bell smiled at the woman's predictable weakness.

At Emily's words, Chris drew his hand the final few inches towards the top of his rucksack. Positioned above his knuckles was one of the small water bottles he'd packed from the hike, and as he tried to manoeuvre the flare gun out from beneath it, the bottle suddenly toppled and fell to the ground.

The sound of plastic thumping onto stone and sand filled the cave.

Suddenly aware of Chris's movement, and remembering the man was an ex-Navy FBI agent, Bell spun at him. Instinctively, he clamped down on his pistol's trigger and fired a shot towards the noise.

The 9mm bullet struck Chris at 1,100 feet per second, slamming the muscular man back against the stone wall of the cave. His head met the rock with powerful force, and as the blood began to pour from the bullet wound, Chris's clutch around the flare gun went slack. He dropped his torch with the impact of the shot, and before his head had fully bounced off the stone, he had gone limp. With a thud to match his large body mass, Chris Taylor collapsed to the floor.

Arthur Bell spun back to Emily, his patience now worn through. 'You were saying?' He reached out his hand again. This time, Emily did not hesitate. She leaned forward and placed the keystone into his waiting grasp.

Bell looked down at the object in his clutch, his eyes wide with wonder. He allowed himself only a moment's gaze, however, before pocketing his prized possession and returning his stare to Emily and Michael.

'Thank you for being so . . . cooperative. I wish I could leave you in peace, but at least I can assure you your suffering won't be long. I wish your souls a good liberation.'

With that, Arthur Bell simply turned and disappeared into the darkness.

The shock of the encounter, and its sudden ending, left Michael and Emily momentarily stunned into a motionless silence. As he retreated through the cave's front chamber, Arthur Bell's footsteps seemed to echo through the space.

It was only the sound of a sudden, sputtering cough, followed by a long, slow wheeze that broke through their stasis. 'Chris,' Michael whispered. Lunging to Chris's body near the cave's far wall, he and Emily rushed to the aid of their fallen friend.

Chris's form remained where it had fallen, motionless save for the faintest rise and fall of his chest, just discernible in the dim light. It was almost so slight as to deceive the senses, and they both strained to listen for the sound of breathing – each desiring confirmation that he was still with them.

Instead, their attention was repaid with a different sound.

The distinctive clank of metal against stone pierced the silence forcefully, its tone foreign to the cavernous quiet. Michael's head shot up, Emily's a split second later, just in time for the sound to be repeated, this time a little more vividly, more closely. Then again, and again, each 'clank' coming faster and faster upon the one before it, like an object bouncing against the stone floor and rattling to a halt.

'Did something fall?' Emily asked, straining to listen. The sounds began to overlap on themselves; then, almost as quickly as they had come, they stopped.

A cold terror suddenly gripped the pit of Michael's stomach.

'Oh hell, I don't think so.'

'Then what was that?' Emily persisted, her face betraying her own fear.

Suddenly, a hand shot up from beneath them. Whether it was the sound or merely the fate of timing, Chris's consciousness had returned to him and he grabbed at Michael's chest, clutching his shirt. His eyes were glazed, but he concentrated them on Michael.

'Get . . . down!' he wheezed.

His friend's command was all the confirmation Michael needed. Without a second thought he reached across to Emily, grabbing her forcefully by both shoulders. Without time to explain himself, he slammed her backwards onto the ground and threw his body on top of hers, wrapping his arms around her head and pressing his cheek over her face.

A moment later, the thunder came. With a percussive strength far stronger than the soft sandstone's ability to resist it, the small hand grenade that Arthur Bell had retrieved from his pocket and tossed into the cave burst to life, bringing the walls of the chamber collapsing down into a heap of rubble.

CHAPTER 62

The Cave

The blast of the grenade shook the cave's inner chamber with a seemingly impossible force. Cracks formed in the walls, rock broke away from the ceiling, and the bodies of Emily, Michael and Chris jolted violently. The room appeared to be falling apart around them.

Despite using his own body as a shield to protect his wife, Michael had expected the stone to shelve, break and crush them in a dark and deadly tomb; but the explosion was concentrated in the front chamber and the damage that reached them was mercifully less severe. As the sounds of crumbling rock steadied back into silence, he pushed himself upwards, releasing Emily's head from the vice grip in which he had been shielding it.

'Are you okay?' He grabbed for his torch and gazed into her eyes. She stared up at him, coughing from the dust in the air. They were both a mess, sand, dust and fragments of rock filling their hair and covering their clothes. The air in the cave was like a grey fog, and they both blinked profusely, trying to keep the grit from their eyes.

'I'm okay.' But the reality of the situation suddenly hit her. 'He bombed the cave.' Her eyes went wide. 'Oh God. Mike, check the front chamber.'

Michael reached for his flashlight, which had fallen a few feet to his right, then stood himself up and walked to the front end of the inner cave. The narrow fissure that connected it to the entrance was entirely filled in with stone.

'It's sealed,' he coughed. He set the light down on a rock and explored the rubble with his hands. 'Completely blocked.'

They were trapped. *And where is Chris?* Emily's mind raced from one terrifying reality to the next.

It was then that Chris coughed again. They both moved to Chris's location on the cave floor. He appeared unconscious, as he had before the explosion, though the blast had flipped him into a face-down position.

'Shine your light on his left side, I'll take the right. Look for the bullet wound.' Michael grabbed Chris's torso gently but firmly and rolled him onto his back.

Emily steeled herself for the worst as Michael rolled the body over. This was not the first time she had rushed to a man's aid after he had suffered for being at the wrong end of a gun. Her thoughts flashed back momentarily to her encounter, five years before, in a basement in Alexandria. There a man called Athanasius had met an undeserved end, had met it in her arms, and the experience would remain burned in her mind forever. She expected to see Chris's chest covered in blood, his grey turtleneck turning a rusty brown, caked with sand that stuck to the congealing flow. Would Michael be able to take the death? He had known Chris far longer than she had known Athanasius.

The moment the body came aright on the ground, her anticipated shock was replaced by confusion. Chris's chest showed no signs of his gunshot wound – no blood, no sand, no marks at all. Instead, only the upper region of his left arm was stained a dark colour and bore the unmistakable sheen of moisture, a moisture that pulsed from within.

Thank God, the bullet missed his chest. A flesh wound in the arm they could deal with, as long as the bullet hadn't hit his brachial artery.

Emily reached for the sleeve of Chris's shirt, grabbing the blood-soaked fabric just below his shoulder. It was already torn where the bullet had shredded the material, and she prised her fingers into the tear and forcefully ripped it apart.

The sound and the jolt together were enough to rouse Chris back to consciousness.

'What's going . . . where am . . .?' His head swirled uncontrollably, the words hard to form.

'Shh, keep quiet,' Michael commanded. 'You're still in the cave in Egypt. You were shot.'

Chris stammered slightly, trying to bring the cloud of his mind back into some semblance of order. Michael and Emily. Egypt. The cave. The small stone. He began to piece together flashes of the moments before he had fallen. The intruder. A gunshot.

'That bastard . . . actually shot me!' he finally exclaimed. He tried to sit up, but Emily pushed him firmly back down.

'Fortunately, only in the arm,' she said, 'and I'm no expert, but it looks like the bullet only grazed you. You must have lunged out of the way just in time.'

'But I went down.' Chris blinked his eyes. 'Unconscious. A grazed shoulder doesn't knock you out.'

'No, that was the wall,' Michael answered. 'You slammed back against it fairly hard after the gun fired. In your little battle between stone and skull, stone won.' He gently touched Chris's head, hoping to provide a small dose of his friend's own light-hearted comfort, but even the slight gesture sent a spasm of pain through the FBI agent's body.

'Hands to yourself!' Chris moaned, wincing from the torment. He took a moment to catch his breath, reclaiming his focus. His drive came not far behind.

'Have you looked at my head? Any serious damage?'

Michael shone his torch at all angles around Chris's head. 'No blood, no obvious damage. Looks like you're still in possession of whatever brains you had before.'

Chris tried to smile at his friend's humour, but contracting his facial muscles only renewed his agony. And he could see a worry in Michael's features that was for more than his current plight.

'What is it?' he asked, looking from Michael to Emily. 'What's wrong?'

'You . . . you don't remember?' Emily answered. 'The explosion? You warned us.'

Chris passed a confused glance to Michael.

'Apart from Arthur Bell getting away with the keystone,' Michael answered, recognizing the signs of shell shock in his friend, 'he also destroyed the entrance on his way out. Some kind of bomb, probably a grenade. For the time being, we're trapped in here.'

Suddenly, Emily's demeanour changed. She leaned forward. 'Don't get too discouraged, Chris. We're not finished yet.' She placed a hand over his lower arm, squeezing with a gentle encouragement. She then switched her gaze to Michael. 'There's a first-aid kit in his pack. Clean his wound as best as you can, then you and he can start looking for a way out.'

'The lady doesn't feel like offering a little help herself?' Chris asked, a half-taunting tone returning to his voice. But Emily was already turning away, retreating to the far corner of the cave's inner chamber.

'There's something else I need to do.'

Chris gave Michael another confused look, surprised at Emily's urge to move off.

Without knowing details, Michael sensed there was a good reason for her action. He smiled at Chris as he opened the first-aid kit and began the process of cleaning the gash in his arm. 'She gets like this when her mind is running. Maybe a little abrupt, but I'd suggest you follow my instincts and leave her to it.'

As they spoke, Emily moved fully aside. Though she was silent, her heart raced and her mind concentrated on a singular goal. *Do it now, before it's too late. While it's still fresh.*

Rummaging through her own pack, she extracted a small pad of paper with a pencil attached by an elastic band. Opening the pad to its first blank page, she sat down on the cave floor and set it flat on the sand before her. Holding her flashlight in her left hand, she put the pencil lead to the page with her other, and began to draw.

First one circle, then another around it. Then a third. A series of intersecting radial lines. A grouping of letters and numbers at the centre.

Emily's eyes opened and closed in irregular patterns as her hand worked. At times she looked at her handiwork on the page, at other times she wrote without the need for sight, the unfolding image on the page emerging from the vivid picture in her mind. That picture was clear, almost a photograph. And in this moment, it was perhaps their only way forward.

A ring of Coptic letters. Then another . . .

In the gentle torchlight, the surface of the keystone began to reappear.

CHAPTER 63

The Cave

Emily worked with undistracted devotion for nearly ten full minutes. The basic shape of the engraving on the keystone was a simple radial disc with its concentric rings divided by spokes, each resulting space containing a single Coptic letter. It was the ordering of those letters that she knew she must get right.

A nearly photographic memory is not the same as a photographic memory. Truly photographic recall is like having access to a genuine photograph: memories are recalled as images that can be looked over in the mind with the same clarity and detail as a physical photograph. Emily's form of near-eidetic memory functioned slightly differently. Memories were recalled as images, but the clarity of detail was not always readily available when their minutiae were studied. 'It's like looking at a photograph that's slightly out of focus,' she had once explained the phenomenon to Michael. Usually, if she concentrated her mind carefully and worked to remember, the haze would clear and the detail would come to her. But sometimes was not always.

It was for this reason that Emily worked with such singular determination on the cave floor. The three rings of ninety-nine seemingly random Coptic letters on the inscription were just the sort of detail that was prone to go fuzzy in her memory, and she was determined not to let that happen before she'd produced a hard copy of the stone's surface.

The time it took her to complete the task was slightly longer than the time it took Michael to dress Chris's wound, and by the time she had pencilled the final letter into its cell on her page, he had moved from his role as triage nurse to the task of seeking a way out of the cave. Chris, not yet quite ready to set his hands to that physical task, hobbled over to Emily's side.

'So, just what is it that was more important than seeing to my wounds?' he asked, his eyes still readjusting to vision.

The intensity of her work over, Emily allowed herself a relieved smile in response to his expected taunt. 'Just this. And I think you might agree, it was worth it.'

She held up the pad of paper and shone her light directly upon it.

'Is that . . . ?' Chris stared in disbelief.

'Yes. The keystone.'

'I told you to trust her,' Michael said, shooting an affectionate look at Emily from the far side of the chamber.

'That's amazing.'

'I only hope I got it right,' Emily said. 'Such a long sequence of letters without any obvious pattern. It puts even my memory in a spin.'

'What are they for?'

'I'm not sure, Chris.' Emily handed him the paper. 'I do, however, have a theory.'

'I kind of thought you might.' Chris's comment was sincere.

'I'm not sure if it would have come to me so quickly on its own, but our conversation with Arthur Bell was, let's say, revelatory.'

'I can't say I remember every word of our . . . *conversation,*' Chris motioned towards his injured head. 'Give me a quick refresher.'

'He wasn't overly talkative,' Emily continued, 'but twice he mentioned something that doesn't have any immediate connection to a small man-made stone found in the middle of the desert. I'm talking about texts. He mentioned documents first when he was trying to assert his right of ownership over the keystone, saying that it wasn't created to sit in a cave or museum, "any more than our most sacred texts". Later, his language was even stranger. He spoke of "the liberation our holiest documents will bring". I don't think it's coincidence that twice he slipped from mentioning the keystone to uttering comments about sacred documents.'

'The stone might be another map,' Chris speculated, 'some set of directions to another document. Or maybe some ancient key to a vault where a batch of texts is stored?'

'It could be, but I don't think so. Having spent the time it took to copy it down, I think the keystone is meant to be a tool. It doesn't point towards texts, it helps its user to read them. It unveils their meaning.'

As Emily mentioned unveiling, something in Chris's mind clicked. 'It could be a cipher.' He looked up from the page.

'In fact, given its design that would make a lot of sense.' His attention was captured in a new, direct way. Chris had worked with plenty of cipher technology with the FBI.

'It's got three rings of letters,' he noted aloud, looking over the image, 'which means it could be a basic two-tier transposition cipher, using the first ring as the coded text, the second as an interim layer of translation and the third as the final step to reveal the source text. Or a two-tier columnar transposition cipher.'

Emily's eyes glistened as he spoke. 'Exactly what I was thinking. Though perhaps not in such technical terms.'

'It'd be pretty basic stuff,' Chris pointed out. 'But hell, it's carved on the side of a stone in an ancient Egyptian cave and Mike's guess is that it's over 1,500 years old. I guess I shouldn't be expecting public key cryptography. But you'd still have to know what text it's meant to decode.'

'I have a theory on that as well.' Emily rocked back on her heels, her legs sore from crouching. 'Bell mentioned the keystone unveiling the meaning of his group's "most sacred texts", their "holiest documents". Now tell me, what do we know about this man?'

'He's a crap shot with a handgun,' Chris said sarcastically, though it was a fact for which he would be thankful for the rest of his life.

'He's a Gnostic,' Michael offered from the other side of the cave, still running his hands along its surface. 'Or, at the very least, profoundly interested in Gnostic documents. He's been trying to get hold of ours at the British Museum for months.'

'Right. Someone who takes ancient Gnosticism seriously,

as something alive today. And,' Emily pointed out, 'a man clearly interested in getting his hands not on copies, but on the original texts of ancient Gnosticism.' She leaned towards Chris. 'Now put yourself in the shoes of a man trying to live out some recreation of those ancient cultures. Which texts today would you call your "most sacred"?'

Chris's mind raced back through the potted history of Gnosticism he'd received from Michael on the plane, to the conversations about its legacy and recent discoveries he'd had with both of them during their journey. And it came eventually to the location where the most celebrated collection of Gnostic documents had been discovered – a location they had driven through only a few hours ago.

'Nag Hammadi? You're saying this Arthur Bell wants to get his hands on your Nag Hammadi Codices?'

'Like Michael said earlier,' Emily answered, 'the find at Nag Hammadi completely changed the way we view ancient Gnosticism. It was our first, and it remains our only, large-scale cache of authentic, first-hand Gnostic documents. Apparently this man believes those codices still have more to tell us.'

Michael's excited voice suddenly broke through the tangible awe of their speculations.

'Emily, Chris, get over here!' he shouted. 'And switch off your flashlights. Both of them.'

'Off?' Chris quizzed.

'Off. And look there.' Michael pointed to an almost unnoticeable seam running up the wall. As the torches went dark, his suspicion was confirmed.

'Light,' he said. 'It's weak, but that's definitely sunlight seeping through that crack in the wall. I think we might have found a way out.'

CHAPTER 64

FBI Field Office, Chicago

Laura Marsh gave a perfunctory knock on Special Agent Ted Gallows's office door as she stepped into its frame. Gallows looked up from his laptop monitor.

'Special Agent Marsh, what can I do for you?' He motioned for her to enter. As she did, she noticed that the two chairs to her left were filled with Alan Mayfair and Brian Smith, both of whom wore the serious expressions by which she knew them.

'Have I interrupted a heads of section meeting?'

'No, just an informal knocking of heads together,' Gallows answered. His tone was customarily abrasive, but he remained polite. 'Join us.'

He motioned towards a small settee next to the wall opposite his two counterparts and Laura promptly took a seat. She sat silently, waiting, but when none of the others spoke she decided to step directly into the topic that wouldn't leave her mind.

'We're missing something.'

'A lot of our work at this stage is stabbing in the dark,' Gallows replied. 'But we're making progress. Step by step.'

'It's not that. It's the incongruities in what we know so far that are troubling me.'

'Incongruities?' Smith looked directly at her, an eyebrow raised. His gaze was forceful, and though Laura felt uncomfortable beneath it, she did not cease pushing forward.

'Doesn't it strike you as odd that a group apparently based in America, made up of spirituality-loving Americans, is sending us threats via anti-American terrorists in the Middle East? Or that the contact being made between members is being carried out on European cell phones?'

'Sure, it's odd,' Smith answered, 'but it reinforces, pretty damningly, the fact that this Church of Truth in Liberation is connected to a Middle Eastern terrorist cell.'

Marsh fidgeted in her seat. Her temples throbbed. 'Then there's the whole nature of the attack. We're assuming something similar to the general operations of most Middle Eastern cells. But let's think here for a minute: what do we know about those? Whether they're lone bombers, suicidal pilots or extravagant assassination plots, they're all acts specifically designed to cause suffering. Not just death, but pain and agony.'

'That's always been a special favourite of extremist assaults. The tactic of terror, defined.'

'But Special Agent Mayfair, why the hell is a group dedicated to "the freedom of the spirit" and the liberation from suffering aiming to cause suffering of the very worst kind?'

Ted Gallows mulled over Marsh's words. 'Laura, you're overthinking the theological side of a terrorist situation.'

'Excuse me?'

'Trying to understand the full contours of their motivation has a place, but right now the reality is we've got a very short timeline on which to act. We need to be tracking down their operatives and determining the most likely scenarios for the attack. The parade is only a day away.'

'You,' Special Agent Smith cut in, his eyes now boring directly into Marsh's, 'need to stay on task, and at this moment that priority is ground logistics on patrol, surveillance, and the obtaining of their device, whatever it is.'

Marsh went silent. The three section heads were set in their focus. As Mayfair and Smith rose to depart, she cast each a slight nod, half in acknowledgement, half in acquiescence.

Once they had departed she returned her gaze to Gallows, who still sat behind his desk.

'We need some additional expertise,' she finally said. 'Someone who knows how to think a few steps ahead of these kinds of groups. We've got good minds and manpower here, but we need an expert in predicting terrorist movements, especially in a scattered intelligence situation.'

'I don't disagree,' Gallows muttered. 'In fact, I've been thinking the same thing.'

'In that case, I think we both know the right man for the job.' Marsh looked at him suggestively. A moment later, Gallows's brow raised in recognition.

'You want Chris Taylor? But the man's in London.'

'Don't tell me that in the circumstances the Bureau wouldn't be willing to expedite a return trip home.'

Gallows met her gaze. 'You're sure this is a purely professional request, Special Agent Marsh?'

Laura fought off a squirm. Special Agent Chris Taylor had left the Chicago Field Office for his Embassy posting shortly after Laura had arrived. There had been the slightest hint of romance in the air whenever they had been in the same room together, but any possibility of exploring it had been cut short by his departure. She was surprised Gallows knew of the past chemistry.

'You know as well as I do that Taylor is the right man for the job,' was all she said in response. Memories of romance could be entertained later, and she certainly had no intention of discussing her private life with Ted Gallows. 'Chris was sent to London because he precisely matched the profile requested there: an unparalleled ability in predicting terrorist activities from piecemeal intelligence data. His skills are second to none, and he has the ability to work something concrete out of our general data. Can you think of a better candidate?'

Gallows remained in Marsh's eye-lock a long moment before finally giving a nod of agreement. 'No, you're right. We ought to get him involved.' He rose from his office chair. 'Dawson's sure to approve the emergency transfer, and we can rush his travel. I'll have one of my men track down his current location and send transport immediately.'

'Thanks, Ted,' Laura responded, rising to meet him. 'In the meantime, I'll take your advice and get my mind back on the first priority. But I'm going to task a junior agent with some deeper research into what these strange intelligence connections might mean. I can't shake the thought that there's more going on here, and some more in-depth background research can only help Chris when he arrives.'

She had a local agent in mind – one who had a gift for finding the kinds of connections she felt must be hidden just beyond their view.

CHAPTER 65

The Cave

The thin streak of light Michael had discovered entering the cave's inner chamber had not been there before the explosion. The force of the blast had not been enough to collapse the recess in the stone, but it had been enough to crack and splinter its furthermost wall. The light creeping in through the stone revealed just how far the angular recess of the second chamber folded back on itself: its far wall was in fact facing the cliff-face itself. The shock waves from Bell's grenade had fragmented the shell, allowing exterior light an entry into the inner chamber for the first time in the thousands of years the cave had been in existence.

Chris approached, running his hands along the seam of light. He grunted with pain as he moved, but wasn't about to cower motionless in the corner.

'It's narrow,' he observed. 'Couldn't fit a sheet of paper through that. And there are no signs of it being anything more than a rift.' The thin ray of light coming through the stone brought the reality of the desert outside tantalizingly close, but it still didn't mean they had any way of getting to it.

'If there's a splinter here,' Michael answered, 'it means there might be weaknesses elsewhere.'

Emily stared at the tiny fracture of light. She hadn't felt claustrophobic before: not when they were in the cave in the dark, not when the bomb went off and they found the entrance blocked in. But as she saw sunlight out of grasp, the crushing feeling of being trapped started to well up uncontrolled. She had the sudden, horrible fear that this might be the last daylight she ever saw.

Chris extracted his knife from its sheath and began using the blunt end to thump against the stone of the cave's exterior wall, sounding for differences in the noise that echoed back. As he thumped near the slender crack that had formed, the sound was solid and deep. As he moved further away, it became deeper, less resonant, until at three feet away it was barely more than a muffled thud.

He repeated the procedure over the whole wall, moving out from both sides of the crack, stepping painfully and avoiding movement in his injured shoulder. When he was finished, he turned to Michael.

'Nothing. The rock's solid. The only weakness is at the break, but even there I'd make the stone to be a good eight inches to a foot thick. And it's not brittle.'

Michael waited for Chris to elaborate further, offering a solution.

'I'm sorry,' Chris finally said, noticing his anticipation.

'Short of a grenade of our own to blast it the rest of the way through, I don't see this crack turning into an exit.'

The tightness in Emily's chest constricted further. She commanded herself to keep calm, but Chris's announcement sent her breath into short, faster cycles.

Michael simply stared at the slender strip of light coming through the wall. With his friend injured and his wife growing closer to panic, he felt the burden of responsibility for getting them out of the cave alive fell squarely to him.

'We're not dying in here,' he suddenly announced. Swivelling on his heels, he turned to Chris.

'The small spade you packed at the car. Do you still have it with you?'

CHAPTER 66

The Cave

As soon as Chris had provided him with the collapsible spade he'd purchased in Cairo, Michael put the only plan he could think of into action.

'You're not going to dig us out,' Chris protested as Michael snapped the spade into its open position. 'Not through solid limestone.'

'I don't intend to. Digging isn't the only thing this can be used for.'

Emily's breathing continued in short, rapid breaths nearby, the effects of claustrophobia not growing any weaker. She watched Michael, his apparent possession of an idea the only thing allowing her to keep her breathing under control.

'The handle isn't long,' Michael said to Chris, 'but it ought to be enough to give us a bit of a fulcrum.'

Taking up the shovel without further explanation, Michael gripped it firmly in both hands. Aiming the metal edge at the thin crack in the stone, he rammed it forward with his full strength. The spade's edge caught the fragmented divide and sunk a full two centimetres into the crack in the wall. Michael pulled back, but the stone gripped the spade and wouldn't release it.

Looking around him, Michael grabbed a fist-sized rock from the debris and used it to pound the spade further into the crack.

Once it had jammed as far into the rock as it was going to go, Michael set down the stone. Taking a deep breath to gather his strength, he pulled sideways on the handle, then pushed forward with his full force.

Emily's breathing began to steady as she watched. She still didn't fully understand Michael's plan, but he was in action and the simple conviction of his movements calmed her nerves.

Michael swung his weight back, pulling on the spade's handle, then thrust forward again. Using the shovel's entry in the stone as the fulcrum point, he repeated the motion, prising it from side to side.

The movements seemed to yield no results for at least the first fifteen or twenty swings on the handle. But suddenly, as Michael pushed his weight forward with a grunt, sweat dripping from his forehead, the crack in the wall began to yield more light.

'My god, it's starting to give,' Chris announced.

'Emily,' he said, motioning to her, 'give him some help. I'll be useless at that with this gash in my shoulder.'

Regaining her confidence rapidly as the daylight beamed more strongly into the dusty chamber, Emily moved to a position opposite Michael and placed her hands on the spade's handle along with his. Together they heaved at the stone with their combined strength.

With each sway, the thin crack in the wall began to grow. The soft sandstone had been weakened by the explosion, and the alternating tension and thrust of the spade caused its remaining strength to falter. After a few moments of hesitation it cleaved with a sharp snap, and portions of the stone began to fall away.

Emily and Michael pushed again, fiercely. Three large segments of rock broke free from the wall and fell inwards.

'We're almost through,' Michael announced, his breath heavy. 'Here, let me get in there.' Setting aside the spade, he sat down before the weakest point in the wall, leaning back on his elbows with his feet at the base of the stone surface. 'Watch out,' he said to Emily. Then, pulling back his knees to his chest, he shot forth his legs at the wall.

The impact caused the wall to buckle, but not fall.

'Once more, Mike,' Emily encouraged, shielding her face from the small debris that flaked away from the stone.

Michael gathered together his breath, pulled up his legs once more, and kicked for all he was worth.

This time, the stone buckled. Large pieces of ancient rock fell outwards, breaking free from the wall and rolling down the steep face of the bluff.

The light poured into the cave unabated.

CHAPTER 67

The Egyptian Desert

The descent from the cave to the sand at the base of the cliff was laborious. After another forty minutes of work, Emily and Michael had been able to break away enough of the stone to create a hole big enough to pass through, but what awaited them on the other side was not a convenient ledge allowing for an easy exit. The drop was sheer, and their only way down was going to involve making use of the rope Chris had in his pack.

Chris himself was another story. The makeshift bandage Michael had applied to his shoulder had stopped the bleeding, but his left arm was effectively useless for a vertical descent.

'You're no good to climb,' Michael said abruptly, silencing Chris's automatic protests before they began. Instead, he used the military knife to cut off a six-foot length of rope and handed it to Emily.

'You said your time on the climbing wall would pay off one day. See if you can't fashion that into a harness.'

A few minutes later, Emily had wrapped the rope in loops

around both of Chris's upper thighs, then around his waist. Tying it firmly, she took a step back.

'This is going to hold?' Chris asked, peering down at her work.

'It'll hold.' Michael approached and attached one end of the longer length of rope to the harness, just below his belly.

'We'll lower you down as best we can. Just remember we don't have any harnesses up here; it's going to have to be pure body strength. So don't linger.'

Chris smiled, grateful for his friends' industriousness and eagerness to help. He also felt a degree of shame, at being the only one of their group that was professionally trained, yet the only one who'd been injured. He was now putting their whole escape in peril.

Michael saw his expression, and put a hand on Chris's good shoulder. 'A gunshot's not your fault, Chris.' They locked eyes, and Chris nodded in thanks.

A moment later, he was outside the new hole in the cave wall and being lowered towards the first ledge he could manage, some eight metres below. The rope would reach no further, so Michael tied off the upper end to one of the stones in the cave and turned to his wife.

'You and I climb the rope without the benefit of harnesses.'

She nodded her understanding. 'I can do it.'

'I'll wait until you're down with Chris, and follow,' Michael said. Then, wrapping his arms around her, he kissed her firmly and with full energy.

When he pulled his face away, his eyes were warm and encouraging. 'You'll be fine. And don't forget this.' He shoved her pack onto her shoulders, ensuring her sketchbook was safely inside.

Emily took a breath, stepped to the hole in the wall, and lifted a foot out into the daylight.

It took almost an hour to complete their descent. After making it down to the first ledge, with no way to reclaim the whole rope from its fixture in the cave, Michael climbed up and cut it at the fifteen-foot mark, giving him enough of a lead to be able to lower Chris step by step below them. He and Emily would help Chris to a convenient ledge or outcropping, then climb down to join him, take a breath, and repeat.

The stop-and-go motion of the reverse climb was slow and exhausting, the sunlight again beating away at their energy; but the method was effective. Without more than a few words passing between them during the entire descent, they reached the sand of the desert floor nearly two hours after Michael had first broken through the sandstone wall.

A few minutes later, they were back in the Mitsubishi Pajero, air conditioning never having been more appreciated by any of them in their lives.

It was Emily who finally broke their silence, wiping the dust and sweat from her face.

'We made it.'

The two men said nothing. They had been held at gunpoint and sealed in a cave; but apart from Chris's injury and the odd scrapes and scratches of the climb down the cliff-face, they were safe and well.

Michael twisted the key in the ignition and brought the car fully to life. Turning a sharp 180 degrees from the cliff, he headed them back towards the city.

Once they were on the paved Giza-Luxor motorway, Michael edged the Pajero up to 90 kilometres per hour and headed north. He breathed a quiet sigh of relief at the long tarmac stretched out before him: a sign of civilization and life after hours spent too close to death. The deeper relief came from the lush vision of green to his right – of thriving fields, tall Date Palm trees, of irrigation canals and small agricultural encampments amidst the greenery.

'We'll be back in Nag Hammadi in a few minutes,' he noted to Emily and Chris. The wounded man was lying down across the back seats. 'We can head north from there. What are our plans?'

'We need a little down time,' Emily answered. 'Chris needs to wash out that wound and bandage it up properly. Your field dressing has staunched the blood flow, but he's got to get it cleaned out if he's going to avoid infection. If we can do it ourselves it will save hours at a hospital, not to mention the police getting involved over a gunshot wound.'

She looked across to Michael. 'And I need to do a little research online – see what I can do to connect the inscription from the keystone to the texts discovered at Nag Hammadi. Until we have some better idea of just what Bell and his group are hoping to do with those documents, it will be hard to plan our next move.'

Their previous pass through Nag Hammadi provided Michael with enough experience to know they wouldn't find a hotel to suit their needs there. The larger town of Asyut, however, was only two hours up the river.

He pressed his foot down on the accelerator, and the trio drove north in silence.

CHAPTER 68

Gaddis Suites, Asyut

At the conclusion of their drive, check-in at the Gaddis Suites Hotel in downtown Asyut took Michael only ten minutes. Five later he, Chris and Emily were ensconced in a double suite on the sandstone building's fifth floor, with views overlooking the ancient town and the bluffs beyond.

'I call the shower,' Chris offered before he had even passed fully through the door. 'I've got sand in more places than just the cut on my arm.'

His grin beamed as he walked past Michael and Emily, pulling the bathroom door behind him. His upbeat attitude had clearly returned.

'I'll sort out the supplies from the first-aid kit so we can do up a proper dressing once he's out,' Michael said. He loosed the tie atop Chris's rucksack and emptied its contents onto the bed's overly floral covering.

Emily made her way to the small desk in the suite's sitting room, situated directly beneath a large picture window. An ethernet connection was provided via a port on the desk, and in a few moments she had extracted her laptop from one of her cases and signed herself online.

It only took a few minutes of navigation before Emily was able to call up high-resolution images of the Nag Hammadi Codices on her laptop. She began to scroll through page after page of detailed scans, her transcribed copy of the keystone's surface lying before her on the desk. As she scanned the images she continually passed her glance back to her sketch, hoping for a connection to make itself apparent.

'Finding anything?' Michael entered the smaller room and moved to her side. His eyes caught a fragment of papyrus photographed on the screen.

'Have you tapped into the resources of the Library of Alexandria?' He knew that the interface to the library's unparalleled collection was available to Emily anywhere she had an internet connection, and their current project seemed the ideal opportunity to make use of the almost inconceivable collection of historical and scientific information she had at her disposal.

'There's no need,' she answered. 'This is all available publicly on the internet. The scans were made three years ago by Forrester and Jakobson. Anyone who wishes can view them at will, though the publisher has kept a few folios from each codex unavailable. I suppose to urge us to buy the printed volumes.'

Michael peered over her shoulder, knowing his expertise in Coptic studies could prove helpful.

'That looks like one of the fragments of Codex II – a passage from the *Apocryphon of John*, by the looks of it. See, there's a reference to Sophia, the renegade spiritual power, seeking to create other beings after her own likeness.' He motioned to a cluster of Coptic letters towards the lower portion of the small, broken fragment of ancient paper.

Emily clicked her notebook's trackpad and advanced to the next image. Like so many before it, this was of a small fragment, containing only a few disjointed letters.

'I hadn't realized the texts were so fragmentary.'

'They're not all like this,' Michael said. 'Some of the pages have deteriorated, but the bulk of the collection is in remarkably good condition. Here, let me.' He gently nudged Emily's wrist aside and navigated the display to Codex I.

'That's amazing,' Emily gasped as the display loaded a large graphic, containing a complete page of ancient Coptic writing. The thumbnails along the top of the monitor indicated that all the pages to follow were equally as complete.

'It doesn't take too much scholarly acumen to appreciate why this find was so important,' Michael affirmed. 'The best hypothesis is that this was either the library of a Gnostic sect in the fourth century, hidden once the persecutions became too fierce, or of a Christian monastic community with Gnostic leanings who decided that continuing to harbour forbidden documents was simply too dangerous.'

Emily allowed herself a long, silent ponder. From the other room, the sounds of Chris stepping out of the bathroom echoed through the half-closed door. His voice followed, apparently engaged in conversation. Emily raised a questioning brow to Michael.

'Probably his mobile phone,' he said. 'It was buzzing all throughout his shower.'

Emily nodded, then turned her gaze back to the computer display. Something had gelled in her mind.

'The keystone,' she said, motioning towards her sketch from the cave, 'has to be a cipher connected to these documents. The problem is that there are so many of them. Twelve complete codices and remnants of a thirteenth, containing fifty-two separate texts. If we're going to figure out precisely what Bell wants, we've got to know which text to decode.'

She looked back into her husband's eyes. 'And then, we've got to get to Cairo.'

'You think that's where he's headed?'

'You know how insistent Bell has been about getting his hands on originals, not copies. If he's set on these texts, then he's going to go after the Nag Hammadi Codices themselves.'

Michael didn't answer. Bell's plans seemed to become more grandiose by the minute.

Breaking through the silence that had descended between them, Chris burst into the room, his mobile phone still clutched in his grasp. He had overheard Emily and Michael's final remarks, but his mind was filled with something else.

'You're going to want to hear what I was just told,' he said, his face grave. 'There's a whole lot more at stake than just some old documents in an Egyptian museum.'

CHAPTER 69

FBI Field Office Basement, Chicago

Agent Scott Lewis kept his face only eight inches from his desktop monitor, a bad habit that had already earned him a thick pair of glasses and a perpetually sore neck. But it was one he had been unable to break; it was simply where his eyes wanted to be, where he could wholly surround his vision with the tasks to hand.

Special Agent Laura Marsh was going to be intrigued, to say the least, by what he had discovered. The telephone numbers and locations reinforced her suspicions, but went a hell of a lot further than she'd anticipated.

He made an additional annotation in his file.

Through the intensity of his labours, Lewis did not hear the door to his underground office creak open. Only a footstep in the room itself caught his attention, and he turned a moment too late. A second earlier, he might have avoided the blow that cracked against his brow with what seemed a superhuman force. As it happened, his whole body flew back against his desk, thrown out of his chair. He could hear his ribs crack as his upper torso collided with the edge of the desk's surface, and he fell to his knees with a thud.

Before his body could topple forward, an unhesitating grip pulled at his hair and angled his head upwards.

'Have you reported any findings?' a voice thundered at him. With the swirling of his vision, together with the blue-white light of the fluorescent bulbs above his attacker's head, he couldn't make out the face.

'What findings?' he gasped in terror.

'Anything. Have you reported anything at all up the chain of command?' The hand yanked back hard on Lewis's hair, sending spasms of pain through his neck.

'No! I haven't got far enough for a report!' He struggled for breath, the angle of his neck making it hard to take in air. 'I was just assembling data.'

His eyes widened as he saw his attacker reach beneath a jacket and draw out a handgun with a silencer already affixed.

'No, don't, I—'

'Are you sure,' the attacker demanded, holding the gun against Lewis's temple, 'absolutely *certain* that nothing has been passed along?'

'I'm sure!'

The attacker looked at him, nodded, then acted.

A pin-prick of light flashed from the end of the gun's suppressor, disappearing as quickly as it came.

Lewis's body seemed to hover a moment in suspended animation before collapsing to the floor. The temple where the bullet had entered was disfigured by only a tiny hole of red. The other side of the agent's head was completely gone.

As his body rocked to the ground, his attacker stepped around him and grabbed the CPU from his desktop, yanking it forcibly from its cables and tossing it into a large duffle bag.

Before the long exhalation of Lewis's final breath was fully complete, his killer was gone.

CHAPTER 70

Gaddis Suites, Asyut

Chris moved to one of the lounge chairs in the sitting room, opposite the desk at which Emily and Michael were working. He sat on the edge of the seat and waited a strained moment for the others to turn to face him. Michael could see that Chris's muscles were tensed. Something in his phone call had clearly put him on alert.

'That was a friend and former colleague back in the Chicago Field Office. They're dealing with a major threat against the Fourth of July parade – one of the biggest in the country.'

'A threat?' Emily leaned forward in the desk chair.

'Presumed terrorist attack, specific type unknown. There'll be tens of thousands of people lining the streets, from dignitaries, politicians and religious leaders to families and children out to celebrate the stars and stripes.'

'Someone is threatening to attack crowds of *children*?' Emily asked incredulously.

'I'm told that every squad in the division has been tasked

to the threat in one way or another. Apparently there are Middle Eastern connections as well.'

The shocking details notwithstanding, it was Emily who asked the necessary question.

'That's terrible, Chris. But what does it have to do with us? You made it sound like there was some connection between your phone call and our activities.'

'There is. Apparently, the group responsible for the threat are identifying themselves as . . . Gnostics.'

'*Gnostics?*' The word fell simultaneously from the lips of husband and wife.

'Again, I don't have many details, but the threat's come from a church claiming to be made up of Gnostic believers. And it's more than just a local instance. There was an arrest in New York two days ago, some guy with a sniper rifle and a vendetta claiming to be a Gnostic as well.'

'The "Gnostic terrorist",' Michael muttered, his mind flipping back to the news report Gwyth had forced him to watch on the small television in his office the day before. He had laughed incredulously at the ascription when it flashed across the news report's captions. *Could it actually be true?*

'That's the one,' Chris affirmed. 'Apparently he's connected to what's going on in Chicago.'

A silence lingered as all three pondered the new information.

'To my mind, there's a real chance the activities there are connected to what's going on here – I mean, how many Gnostic groups can be breaking out into fits of aggression at once?'

Chris probed. 'It seems too much for coincidence. But I won't know until I get there.'

'Get where?'

'Chicago. They've ordered me to fly in and help. It's my old office, and suddenly they're in need of someone whose expertise is in predicting terrorist activities from spotty intelligence. That's been my specialty since I joined up with the Bureau. I've been given direct orders to return.'

'When do you go?' Michael asked.

'In about an hour. A helicopter is already on its way from Alexandria to pick me up, and from there I'm on the first Bureau express to the States.' Chris paused. Part of him wanted simply to stay in the hotel, sip a few cocktails and sleep off some of the pain from his wounded arm. A more important part, however, knew the significance of the call he'd received.

'You go, see if there's a connection,' Emily interjected, 'but we have to chase up what we've got in our hands here.' Both men turned towards her inquisitively.

'This Arthur Bell is clearly at the helm of whatever's going on here in Egypt and London. If there's even a chance he's connected to what's going on in America, it's all the more important that we find out exactly what he's up to.'

CHAPTER 71

Saleh Omar Street, Cairo

A small corner flat on Saleh Omar Street had been requisitioned to serve as the waypoint for the Cairo operation. Following Marcianus's phone call from the mouth of the cave, the eight members of the specially selected team had each made their way to the unfurnished apartment the brethren had purchased in a cash-only transaction a little over three months ago. The floors were now heaped with the supplies that would become necessary once the Great Leader arrived in the city, the keystone at last in hand.

The chemist and his associate had flown in from London. The remaining six had been drawn from the Brotherhoods of France, Spain and Italy. The Italian, who, like the chemist, was one of the higher echelons of the illumined – the Knowers, the true Gnostics – was also an expert in the fine Italian criminal talent of breaking and entering, while both Frenchmen were security and systems specialists, adept at disarming even the most advanced security systems. Of the remaining three men, all Spanish, one was a cryptographer with suitable translating skills for the task to come, and the two others would serve as the group's brute force and protection.

The Spanish technician's phone had rung fifteen minutes earlier, and after a brief conversation the line had been disconnected and the room fell into a quiet, tense anticipation. A moment later, a chime marked the arrival of an MMS picture message. The technician clicked through the touch-screen interface of the phone's display until the message was called up on the screen.

The keystone. Its greyish, almost silver surface shimmered in the slanted light of the desert sun. The Great Leader had obtained it as promised. He was on his way to them now with the original, but in the meantime there was work to be done.

It took the technician only a few minutes to transfer the image from the phone to his laptop, and then to print a full resolution hard copy on a portable, colour laser printer set up in the flat. The engravings on the keystone's surface were visible in perfect clarity.

A few moments later, he had called up the digital collection of the Nag Hammadi Codices. He laid the printout of the stone before him on the table, and allowed it to guide him through the texts. Within a minute he had located the correct manuscript. He smiled as he saw which one it turned out to be.

The fact that the online images were missing two pages was hardly a serious concern. It would have posed more of an obstacle if the group didn't know they would have their hands on the complete original shortly. They would do the bulk of the work here, online. The remainder they would do from the source.

The technician looked to the three numerals contained in the keystone's central panel. *3, 2, 5.* They marked out the sequence of letters to be decoded, and he followed accordingly, undertaking his work with care and transcribing out the key letters at the indicated intervals. The seven remaining brothers looked on anxiously.

When the process was complete, the technician had covered the sides of two pages in a long sequence of Coptic letters.

'Now it's time for the keystone to work its magic,' he announced.

Placing the pages with his sequence of letters on his left, he set the printout of the keystone's surface directly before him, and a blank page to the right. He then began the process of decrypting the text. Taking the first letter, he located the same in the innermost of the stone's three rings, then located the adjacent letter in the second and wrote this down on the blank page. He repeated the process for the second letter, then the third, and continued throughout the long sequence he had extracted from the 1,600-year-old manuscript. In all, the process took him a little more than twenty-five minutes.

'It's still just gibberish,' the Italian Knower said, disheartened. The new pages were simply sheets of more apparently random letters.

'I'm not finished yet,' he answered testily. 'There's another ring to go.'

With that, he reconfigured the papers before him, moving the new sheets of decoded letters to his left, leaving the keystone copy in the middle, and placing a new stack of blank pages to the right. He began the process again, this time locating the new letters, one by one, in the keystone's first ring, and writing down their counterparts in the third and outermost ring of Coptic text.

This time, the letters that resulted began to form words.

CHAPTER 72

Gaddis Suites, Asyut

The windows and floors of the hotel shook as the Sikorsky UH-60 sank down past nine storeys of hotel windows, lights beaming in the dusky darkness, guests within the hotel gaping out from poorly washed panes of glass. After a long, slow descent it settled onto the tarmac of the car park.

Emily allowed the thundering noise and display to distract her attention, but only as a temporary respite. Returning from the window, she sat back down at the desk as Michael conversed with Chris and helped him gather his things. She and Chris had already said their farewells, and her mind was now wholly occupied with the puzzle before her.

Her hand-drawn recreation of the surface of the keystone still sat on the surface of the desk, next to her open laptop on which the graphical scans of the Nag Hammadi Codices remained on display.

Emily was certain that the engravings on the stone must somehow point towards the correct text within the larger collection it was meant to decode. She just had to find it.

The obvious candidate was the central circle of the engraving. The three concentric bands each contained thirty-three symbols, which Michael had already confirmed were the thirty-two letters and one symbol of the Coptic alphabet. At the centre of the diagram was a bundle of five letters, written over the top of three numerals. The three rings, Emily felt certain, formed the cipher itself. It must be the contents of this central panel that indicated the text to be decoded.

She gazed long at the five-letter sequence at the heart of the diagram:

ΓΑΥЄΠ

She scanned the letters against every Coptic lexicon she could locate online, and all returned the same result: nothing. The word, despite its script, was not Coptic.

What can it be? Emily tapped her fingers anxiously on the desktop. She was certain these letters marked the required text, but clearly they weren't a description. Or a name. But could they be . . . an *incipit?* The thought hit her suddenly. Ancient texts were almost never referred to by discrete titles. Instead, they were almost universally referred to by their incipit, or the first words of the text itself. So ancient believers referred to Psalm 51 as the 'Have mercy on me', and early Christians, as well as traditional moderns, to the prayer taught by Christ not as 'The Lord's Prayer' but by its incipit: the 'Our Father'.

Emily returned to her computer display with renewed energy. Starting at the beginning of the collection, she scanned

301

through the first lines of each tract, looking for the five-letter combination from the centre of the keystone. Her heart raced, but a solid five minutes later she reached the end, having found not one that began with the letters she required.

I'm still missing something. She tapped at her forehead, willing an insight to congeal in her mind. *We're dealing with secrets here, with simple, ancient encryption.* She pored her mind over how this might affect the guidance provided in the central panel. *It can't be encoded, or that would require another cipher altogether. But could it be simply . . .* She stopped mid-thought, the idea so simple it almost didn't seem worth trying. But without other possibilities leaping out at her, Emily went for a second round of trial and error.

Navigating back to the first page of Codex I she began her investigation again, but this time she reversed the order of the letters on the keystone. Rather than searching for an incipit beginning Γ Λ Υ ε Π, she looked for Π ε Υ Λ Γ. The letters in this sequence still meant nothing in Coptic, but they might well be a beginning to a longer word.

It was only a minute later, at the heart of Codex I itself, that she found it. There, written in an ancient hand, was the incipit of a tract that began with her five letters:

ΠΕΥΑΓΓΕΛΙΟΝ ΝΤΜΗΕ ΟΥΤΕΛΗΛ ΠΕΝΝΕ

As Emily stared in wonder at the screen, Michael reentered the room. He was full of energy, enthused by the flurry of helicopter noise and the bustle of activity surrounding Chris's dramatic FBI pickup.

'I've just seen him off,' he said, walking towards Emily's side of the desk. 'His ride is en route to Alexandria and from there he'll be on a flight to Chicago within minutes of landing. I told him we'd phone every couple of hours, to check in and confirm we're all right.'

As he stepped up to Emily, he placed a hand on each of her shoulders and began a deep massage of her tense neck. It was the first time they had been alone since their adventure had begun.

'We're not going to be able to rest here too long,' he said. 'If we want to get to Cairo in good time we should leave tonight. It's at least five hours of driving.'

Emily tenderly removed his hands from her shoulders and spun round in her chair to face him. 'Mike, I know exactly which text they're after.'

He raised a brow, startled. 'How?'

'It's indicated on the keystone itself.' Emily motioned towards her sketch and laid a figure over its central panel. 'These five letters are an abbreviated incipit, provided in reverse. A simple false start to distract casual onlookers. Inverted, they form the opening sequence of one key text in the Nag Hammadi collection.'

Michael felt his own pulse begin to beat faster. 'Which one?' He leaned towards her laptop's screen, then gasped as he read the answer for himself. 'The *Gospel of Truth*.'

Emily turned her body towards his and beamed directly into his eyes. 'Could there be a more apt document for a group of modern-day Gnostics seeking truth and enlightenment?'

'It's as much a mystical text as one could imagine,' Michael affirmed. 'Filled with allusions to secrets, revelations and the mystical reception of truth and life.'

'And unless we get to it first, Bell and his men will take it by whatever means necessary. And if Chris is right that there might be a connection between what's going on here and the state of alert in Chicago . . . God only knows what Bell intends to do once he has it in his hands.'

CHAPTER 73

Montelaguardia, Italy, AD 1756

'It's time,' the guard grunted. He was dirty and burly, his outline framed by the dim lighting of the corridor beyond. 'Get up.'

He stepped into the dark cell and unlocked Mario Terageste's shackles, grabbing him firmly by the wrists and thrusting him towards the door.

Mario had known since he was first imprisoned that his execution would follow quickly. There was a quiet peace that came with the acceptance of this fact. He had managed to hide his journal before the officers had taken him, and he had sent a message out to the unknown brethren in the rest of Europe. He could do no more, except trust that one day they would find their way to his book, and that with it in their hands the centuries-old knowledge of the keystone and the sacred incantations would not be lost.

All of Mario's suspicions had proven well founded. Following the Great Earthquake that had hit Lisbon on the first of November the year before, levelling the city on All Saints Day and seeming to centre around the masses of faithful gathered in the formerly great – and now entirely destroyed – Lisbon cathedrals, public sentiment had taken frantic turns.

The aftershocks of the earthquake had spread over thousands of miles. Even in Italy the ramifications were dramatic. The shaking of the earth in Montelaguardia had been pronounced, but it was not the most portentous event. That claim was reserved for the fires of Mount Vesuvius, so active and so much a part of the Italian landscape. On All Saints Day, as the world had shook, its fires had ominously ceased. The great mountain erupted no more.

The people, of course, took the earthquake and its after-effects as a sign from God. The choir of saints, who had sent this wrathful catastrophe on the day of their commemoration, were clearly upset – though the precise object of their heavenly anger differed depending on whom one asked. Perhaps they were angry with the politicians, perhaps with the royalty; but the most common public interpretation was that the heavens were upset with the sectarians – with those who dared believe what should not be believed and threatened to divide the faith of the land. What else could be implied by the portentous date, the seeming concentration on religious monuments and the cataclysmic effects of the quake?

With increasing fervour over each month since, the people had heightened their purges of the religious 'deviants' who had brought on the divine wrath, and nowhere was the persecution fiercer than in the Italian heartland.

Talano's arrest had been the beginning of the end in Montelaguardia proper. His public execution had been its confirmation.

Mario's would be its culmination.

Part Three

TUESDAY, JULY 3RD

CHAPTER 74

The Executive Mansion – Springfield, Illinois

In the early pre-dawn hours of a cool and dark morning, the phone in the private apartments of Governor Aaron Wilson began to ring, breaking through a secluded silence. The Governor jostled a moment at the sound, hesitating at the dividing line between sleeping and waking, but as the ringing continued he was roused from his rest and stepped onto the thick carpeting of his bedroom floor. Stepping lightly into his personal study, he slid closed the door and took a seat next to the end table where a faux antique white phone continued its ring.

'Hello,' he answered, silencing the metallic chime with a lift of the receiver. 'It's early.'

'I'm sorry for that, but I trust you'll be Christian and forgive me the intrusion.'

Barry Packard. The Baptist minister sounded edgy, and Wilson brushed the remainder of sleep away at the other man's tone.

He needed the minister to be calm.

'Don't worry about it, I was up already. To what do I owe this call?'

'I want to double-check that everything is in order. I've got my men and my staff ready for the Unity Procession, but they're only . . . part of the equation.' Packard chose his words carefully. Too carefully, the Governor thought. The pauses were too long and far too noticeable.

'I assure you everything is in order,' he finally said, after the Baptist's words had slowed to a halt.

'My visitors,' Packard repeated the coded term, 'are already in motion, on their way.' He hesitated. He wanted his assurances to be more direct. 'Tell me, Governor, is this a secure line?'

No answer came, only the sound of key presses on Wilson's end of the phone. Then, 'We're clean.'

'Let me speak freely, Brother.' There was now a stronger edge to Packard's voice. 'I'm concerned about their entry into the country. I'm told there is a terror alert on in Chicago. That security's been bumped up.'

'Our source in the FBI is keeping me abreast of the security modifications at the airport,' Wilson replied, 'and none of them will interfere with our arrangements. Everything remains in order. As long as our people do not deviate from the agreed procedures there won't be any problems.'

'Won't so many, so similar, attract attention?'

'That's also been taken care of,' the Governor answered. He shouldn't have to explain himself.

At last the Baptist breathed a sigh of relief. 'Forgive me. Just a little nervous. You understand.'

'Don't be afraid,' Wilson answered. 'Everything's in order, and in twenty-four hours I'll see you. Be strong until then.' He paused, then ended their conversation in the customary manner.

'May you find liberation.'

A few moments later the Governor picked up the phone a second time, and on this occasion he ensured the line was secure before dialling. Seconds later, Marcianus's satellite phone began to ring in Egypt.

'The exodus is in progress,' Wilson confirmed once the connection was made.

'Can I assume it's moving forward smoothly?' the Great Leader asked from the driver's seat of his small car, the landscape outside the windscreen beginning to change from desert countryside to the built-up cityscape of his destination.

'Nerves appear to be frail in some quarters,' the Governor replied.

'Who?'

'Packard just called for reassurance.'

'Is he faltering?'

'I don't believe so.' Wilson kept his voice low, barely more than a whisper into the phone. 'I assured him the border crossing and customs have been planned for. The brethren will be able to enter without obstacles.'

On the opposite side of the globe Marcianus switched the satellite phone to his other hand, turning his car onto an exit ramp into Cairo. 'Keep him calm if he calls up again. And do what you can to make sure plans for the procession are kept in the headlines for these last twenty-four hours.'

'They're the main feature of most reporting.'

'Good. Keep me up to speed,' the Great Leader added.

The line clicked out. Governor Wilson set down his phone, slid back open the door to his study and returned to the bedroom, reclaiming his place at his wife's side and the visibly normal routine of the morning.

CHAPTER 75

FBI Field Office, Chicago

The first sign that something was amiss had been Agent Lewis's failure to report in at 4 a.m. as they had arranged. Lewis was as meticulous an agent as Laura Marsh had ever known, a man who marked punctuality in fifteen-second increments. When her office phone hadn't rung by 4.02, Marsh knew something was wrong.

Her suspicions were heightened when an SMS sent to his mobile garnered no reply. The only thing more reliable than Agent Lewis's punctuality was his responsiveness to cellular hails; but this morning, nothing. Not after the first text, not after the second. Two further markers that something was wrong, and one would have been enough.

Marsh made her way to the lift at the end of her eighth-floor corridor, and when the doors parted she entered and typed in the access code for the third basement sub-level. With a reassuring ping of confirmation the doors slid closed and the lift began its gentle descent.

What on earth could be keeping him? she asked herself as she felt the slight lightening of her feet that came with the descent. *Unless he's found something. And it would have to be something significant, if it would keep him out of contact like this.* She felt a flash of encouragement. Maybe the agent's silence was a positive sign, not negative.

The lift descended slowly, and the possibility of an optimistic read allowed Laura's thoughts to wander a moment in an entirely different direction. She noticed the rounded metal bannister that was attached to three of its walls at waist level, and her mind drifted back to the encounter she'd had in the same elevator over a year ago. It had been her first moment alone with Special Agent Chris Taylor, before his departure for the London Embassy. As the doors had slid closed she'd found herself side-by-side with the man she'd been secretly ogling for weeks. Laura had gripped the bannister tightly to keep herself steady, surprisingly overtaken by the intensity of emotions she felt in his presence.

Today, in the midst of everything else going on, the memory brought a heat to Laura's chest. Chris was arriving later today. She hadn't seen him since . . . then.

She laughed, shaking her head. Perhaps the tinges of romance between them had been more than faint, after all.

As the lamps marking the elevator's descent continued to shift, she brought her thoughts back to Special Agent Lewis's unaccounted-for silence.

I've got to pluck him out of whatever trance he's got himself into and find out what he's learned.

It took less than a second for Laura Marsh to realize that goal would never be met. The moment the lift doors parted at floor B3, any hope that Lewis's silence might be positive evaporated. The normally quiet, semi-dark, sub-level corridor was brightly lit, abuzz with a frenetic commotion. The crush was so dense Marsh could barely make it two steps out of the lift before being shoved aside by a senior investigator and overtaken by a house photographer. The hallway was packed to its limits with agents, staff, even members of the city PD.

'What's all this?' Marsh asked a nearby agent, similarly caught in the melee. His badge indicated his offices were on this floor.

'There's been a death. One of our agents was killed here, in his office, sometime in the night.'

Marsh's stomach clenched. Her temples began to throb – that knowing premonition that always came so painfully. Though she felt she knew the answer, she still had to ask.

'Who?'

'Agent Scott Lewis,' the man answered, confirming her premonition. 'He was killed in his office, his computer apparently bagged and taken. A real mess.'

Whether or not the man continued his description Marsh wouldn't know. Her mind racing, her ears muffling out the discordant sounds of the scene, she stumbled backwards, back into the lift, and blankly pounded her fist against the button to her floor. She closed her eyes even before the doors shut out the stark reality with which she was now faced.

The murder of Agent Lewis could mean only one thing. There was an inside link. Wherever else this sect might be, it was right here, in her building, at the heart of the FBI.

CHAPTER 76

Egypt

'I haven't seen such an intense look on your face since you were confronted with your choice of wedding gowns.' Michael offered the light-hearted jab across the Pajero's cab as Emily sat hunched over her laptop, a look of determined attention on her face. At his voice, the faintest traces of a smile formed at the corners of her lips, but she kept her gaze on the screen.

'As long as you're equally as concentrated on the road, we'll be fine,' she answered. They had been on the motorway for the past three hours and at their present rate would arrive in Cairo after another two and a half, at sometime close to 5.30 a.m. Before leaving Asyut they'd forced themselves to take two hours' rest in their hotel suite, knowing that the energy keeping them moving was mostly powered by adrenaline; but the sense of urgency in getting to Cairo had made even that sleep far from restful. They had departed Asyut as soon as they had showered, changed into fresh clothes and eaten as much of a meal as their minibar provided.

'The road has my undivided attention,' Michael answered, overarticulating his devotion to the task.

Ever since their drive had begun, Emily had been devotedly at work from the passenger seat. Displayed on the laptop, which she held perched on her knees, were two open windows: one displaying the high-quality scan of Codex I of the Nag Hammadi library, highlighting the folios containing the *Gospel of Truth*, and the other, on the right, a blank window which she was gradually filling with text. Her hand-drawn sketch of the keystone's surface she had attached to the dash, just to her left, by the unglamorous means of a piece of used chewing gum.

Once Emily had made the discovery that the five letters at the centre of the keystone indicated the tract to be decoded, it hadn't taken the two of them long to determine that the three numbers below it – 3, 2 and 5 – must define the sequence of target letters within the tract. The fact that the keystone then contained three rings of lettering indicated it must function as a two-tier transposition cipher, with the innermost ring the original symbol, the second its decoded result, and the third providing a second layer of encryption.

'Chris would be disappointed,' Michael had muttered as they trialled the sequence and found it to work, disclosing definable Coptic terms. 'It's hardly Bletchley Park material.'

'Try not to be too harsh,' Emily had reprimanded him. 'This is over 1,700 years old, and we have no idea whether the people who produced it were in any way mathematically inclined. For all we know, this was a simple system thought up by a faithful adherent of some religious community. Just a means to keep something hidden the best way he knew how or could think up.'

Emily had worked with only occasional interruptions from Michael during the three hours of the drive that had passed. It was slow going, but steady, and gradually the blank window on the right of her laptop was filled with the text that the *Gospel of Truth* had hidden from the world for so many centuries. Each word that she decoded she translated with the help of a Coptic–English lexicon on the hard drive, as well as the occasional insights and clarifications of her husband, producing an English version of the results.

She looked up a moment from her work, her gaze passing vacantly over the dark road scene before them, broken up only by the bluish-white beams of the SUV's halogen headlamps and the occasional oncoming car.

'Mike,' she said, 'I don't understand what this text is supposed to mean.' She glanced over her translation again. 'I can't make sense of what I'm reading.'

Michael made a gesture that reminded her he couldn't read from the screen while driving.

'It isn't a text,' Emily clarified, 'or at least, nothing narrative. All these terms we've decoded, it looks more like a list, and a strange list, at that. They're all plant names, oils, spices. Ingredients.' She finally looked up and stared at her husband.

'It looks, for all the world, like a . . . recipe.'

CHAPTER 77

O'Hare International Airport, Chicago

The FBI Cessna Citation Ten marked with tail fin number N3678B touched down at Chicago O'Hare well before the sun broke the Midwestern horizon. Cleared on a direct flight path from Alexandria and given a bypass of the airport's usual landing queue, the small jet kept its cruising speed until only minutes before it met the tarmac, and once it had landed taxied at twice the customary speed. It arrived at the small side terminal maintained by the US military only three minutes behind schedule.

The agent who had accompanied Chris Taylor on his express flight unsealed the door and dropped the staircase as the aircraft was still slowing to its stop. The sound of the twin Rolls Royce engines tore through the silence of the cabin as Chris was motioned to the door.

'Your car's already here, Special Agent Taylor,' the other man yelled over the roar. He motioned towards a black sedan pulling up alongside the plane, coming to a stop 100 feet away as the aircraft's brakes finally brought it to a halt.

Chris nodded, then descended the stairs and crossed quickly to the car. A rear door was pushed open from the inside and Chris grabbed it, thrust himself in and pulled the door firmly closed behind him.

The sudden silence of the sedan's well-insulated interior was a welcome relief. 'Damn, those engines are loud. I'll never get used to—'

He stopped mid-remark as he turned to face the man waiting to greet him in the car. It was a face Chris recognized from his days in the Chicago field office. A face of a far higher rank than he had expected for an airport pickup.

'Special Agent Taylor,' the man said, extending a right hand in greeting.

Chris extended his own in return. He had never been greeted on the tarmac by a section head. 'Special Agent Gallows. It's been a few years.'

'It has, indeed.'

'I have to admit, I'm a little surprised to see you here. I'd assumed one of the staff would pick me up, take me back for a briefing.'

'We don't have the time,' Gallows answered. Reaching into a briefcase, he extracted a thick envelope and set it on his lap.

'I'm briefing you now.'

CHAPTER 78

Egypt

It had taken Emily another hour of work to decode and translate the remaining contents of the *Gospel of Truth* from her sketch of the keystone. She didn't have all the pages available, but she'd decoded everything she could.

'It's complete,' she said to Michael. 'I've translated it as best as I can.'

'Still the same content throughout – a list?'

'Only the last phrase, in fact, the last three words, have any clear meaning,' Emily said. 'They're the incipit of another Nag Hammadi text, perhaps the most famous of all.' She looked at her screen and read aloud. The Coptic came out in disjointed fragments.

Michael repeated the words as Emily uttered them, and translated as she went. His eyes went wide as he recognized the line. 'Are you joking? That's the opening line of the *Gospel of Thomas*, the most sensational find of the whole collection.'

'Not joking,' she answered. 'The copy of the *Gospel of Thomas* in the Nag Hammadi collection is the only edition ever discovered. And it's definitely what's referred to at the end of this encrypted text. Everything before it forms three lists.' She scrolled up through her translation. 'Each has a header: "Stage 1", "Stage 2", "Stage 3". They're followed by groupings of ingredients, each followed by a numeral. They're mostly medicinal, chemical and culinary.'

Michael didn't have to feign surprise. 'Culinary?'

'I'm not sure what better descriptor to use. The lists include things like cardamom, cinnamon and different salts, but then various tree-bark oils and plant extracts. The boiled distillate of certain flowers and leaves.'

'Maybe some of those are culinary ingredients, but it's not a recipe for anything edible.'

Emily set the laptop on the dash and turned to face him. 'I'm trying desperately to make sense of all of this, but I'm ready to confess the pieces aren't yet falling together. Murder, arson, international pursuit . . . it's a long way to go for a collection of ancient recipes and a literary reference.'

Michael kept his gaze on the road, but his expression changed. 'That depends entirely on what those recipes are for. Em, you left out something in your summary, just now. Something important.'

Emily traced back through her words but let Michael continue.

'Bell and his group killed your cousin to get the map to the keystone. But that map wasn't a map, at least not at first. If Bell's men hadn't referred to it in your hearing, we probably never would have known to look more deeply into the manuscript. As it was, it only showed itself to be a map once we'd submitted it to some fairly high-tech examination, revealing what had been hidden beneath the surface.'

The hairs on Emily's neck started to rise.

'We used a scanner and ultimately an X-ray,' he continued, 'to see what had been written there centuries before. But obviously, such modern technology can't be the only way to reveal that underwriting. There must be a way of doing so without it, something that would have been possible in the centuries when it was penned.'

'A solvent.' The word escaped Emily's mouth as she turned her head back towards the dash, her eyes falling on the lists of ingredients the decoded text had revealed.

'And while your manuscript containing the map might only be a few centuries old, there is no reason that such a means of secret writing couldn't be much older.' He lifted a hand from the steering column and pointed to the Nag Hammadi texts on her screen. '*Much* older.'

Michael's observations clicked the puzzle pieces in Emily's mind into connected formation. 'That's why they're so keen on getting hold of the original manuscripts. They don't just want to decode this list. They want to use its ingredients to reveal something hidden beneath another text.'

'And we know which text they believe to contain that hidden writing,' Michael said.

'The *Gospel of Thomas*.'

Michael nodded in affirmation. 'You read me the opening line in Coptic a moment ago. Allow me to recite it back to you in English. *"These are the secret sayings which the living Jesus spoke and which Didymus Judas Thomas wrote down, and whoever finds their meaning will not experience death."'*

323

CHAPTER 79

The Coptic Museum, Cairo

Marcianus and his followers stood outside the Coptic Museum in central Cairo, waiting anxiously to get in. One of the Frenchmen was on his knees at a control box sixty feet from the door they'd selected for their entry, the other at a similar box on the opposite side of the building. Marcianus, together with the other men in their small cohort, stood near the first and observed their progress. Despite the difficulty in getting inside, speed mattered immensely. If they were spotted outside, hovering near the doors, their intentions would be obvious. The police response would be swift and dramatic.

The museum's security infrastructure was controlled by a dual circuit computer system, meant to ensure that it did not lose power even if one of its circuitry pathways was routed or disabled. This meant that cutting off the alarms and cameras would involve disabling both pathways simultaneously. If either was cut before the other, the remaining circuit would immediately send the whole complex into lockdown, simultaneously transmitting a wireless signal to law enforcement and museum security.

The two French brethren, whose lives had largely been dedicated to the fine art of foiling such systems around the world, had been impressed with the set-up. They hadn't been expecting such modern equipment in a part of the world not known for technological advancement, but Egypt's Supreme Council of Antiquities clearly knew what needed protecting.

Fortunately, the two Frenchmen had yet to encounter a security system they couldn't bypass, and their research into the further protocols of the Coptic Museum revealed a weakness as significant as the system was advanced: the museum relied almost entirely on the computerized protection the system provided. The night shift of live guards was only two – far fewer than was called for in a complex of this size. Once they got past the alarm system, making their way through the interior would be far less of a challenge.

But they still had to get past the technology, and fast.

Through Bluetooth headsets paired with cellular phones, the two brethren coordinated their operation precisely. Rerouting the circuitry in each control box affected the live wiring only when a small chip was removed from its clasp and reinserted across two different terminal feeds. The Frenchmen gave themselves a five-second, tandem countdown to the procedure, then simultaneously flipped the circuits.

Silence.

Acknowledging that the security protocols hadn't been triggered, they increased their pace and undertook the short process of rewiring the leads within the control boxes. Two wires disabled the interior cameras, three took care of the motion-detection system. Finally, a disabled circuit ensured that the vibration sensors in the display cases wouldn't be triggered by what was coming.

The Frenchman at the front box rose to his feet and turned to Marcianus, putting his tools back into his bag.

'*C'est tout.*' He nodded towards the door.

After the second French brother had returned, dislodging the lock on the museum's door, oiling its hinges and forcing it open, it was time for the Spaniards to take over. Marcianus gave the signal and they entered the dark interior, their suppressed weapons drawn.

Only the slight breath of the silencer's exhaust indicated that the guard stationed twenty feet inside had been dispatched into the realm of spirit. The footsteps of the Spaniards retreating further into the interior signalled that they were moving towards the second night guard's station, and would have him dispatched just as quickly.

Marcianus and his men were now free to roam the building, their only concern being not to let their torches make their presence noticeable from the exterior.

When it came to preparing for their operation at the museum, Marcianus had left nothing to chance. His team had made use of their equipment at the staging flat to decode as much of the manuscript as they could via the printout of the photo he'd sent, then assembled the necessary materials for the incursion proper. They had concluded by torching the flat, setting alight all their equipment, their papers and notes and the tools of their preparation. Even the photograph of the keystone had been destroyed; the original would be on hand in the museum for the final decoding that remained. The group burned every sign of their having ever been on Saleh Omar Street. Time would now be tight and they could not risk any leads being spotted or followed.

Their new surroundings were other-worldly – ancient stone pillars, recreated Coptic church interiors, display cases containing everything from ceremonial knives to mummified human remains – all made the more atmospheric by a darkness broken solely by the sweeping beams of their torchlight.

A wood-carved staircase took them, in due course, to the first floor. 'It's here,' one of the brethren said, motioning to their right, just ahead. The group stepped forward in silence, Marcianus the last to enter the room.

And then, all at once, they were before him.

In beautifully tailored glass display cases that filled the centre of the gallery, the Nag Hammadi Codices lay enshrined. For the better part of two millennia they were hidden in the desert, unknown to the world. They had been rescued from that oblivion only to be trapped in these new confines of glass and informational display panels, to be examined and studied by men who, despite all their interest, had no idea what they were or what they were truly for.

Today, however, the ancient manuscripts were in the presence of men who appreciated them for their real worth.

The Great Leader turned to the burly Italian Knower. 'Go ahead.' He indicated the case they required with a smooth gesture of his hand.

An instant later, the Italian had extracted a diamond-tipped glass-cutter from his satchel. There was no way it could make a cut clean through the two-inch security glass that formed the display case around the codices, but he had other intentions for the device. Gripping it in two powerful hands, he scored the glass in a criss-cross pattern along its upper and side surfaces, creating a latticework of deep grooves that weakened the glass's structure. Then, slipping the device back into the bag, he extracted an immense, steel hammer.

The other men instinctively moved back as the hammer came down. The sound of shattering glass filled the room, echoing off old stone monuments.

When all the shards had fallen, the Italian reached into the case and with a delicacy and reverence to match his brute strength, removed a codex mounted at an angle for easy display. With tenderness, he presented it to the Great Leader.

Marcianus allowed his gaze to linger on the document, stroked a finger over one of its priceless papyrus pages, and felt his spirit surge. The interlaced pattern of the nearly two-millennia-old papyrus reeds rubbed against his fingertips. The inked writing seemed to have almost physical, tangible contours. The scent of antiquity filled the Great Leader's nostrils.

He turned to the chemist. 'We're ready. Get your things set up.' Moving to the translator, he handed him the bound book. 'The two pages you still need are here. Finish the decryption, and get me the other codex.'

CHAPTER 80

Chicago

Chris could not remember precisely the last occasion he had spoken face-to-face with Ted Gallows. As he listened to the briefing in the back seat of the car, memories of their past interactions resurfaced. Gallows held himself with a strange, almost unnatural confidence. A strange character, unlikable in a generic sort of way, he was not so different from most section heads Chris had experienced – and he couldn't claim to like most of them, either. Chris had an inbuilt aversion to bureaucrats.

'You're aware we're working on a strict timeline,' Gallows said, continuing with the condensed briefing.

'I'm at your disposal, and happy to do what I can,' Chris answered, 'but you've not given me a lot to start from. "Slight on details" would be an understatement.'

'Our intelligence on all this has been slim, and what concrete details we have, have come late – some only within the past few hours.'

'You're sure of the Middle Eastern connection behind all this?'

'Just watch,' Gallows answered. 'Brian, run the clip.' He barked the order at one of the two men behind the half-raised glass divider towards the front of the car, and a moment later a grainy video clip began to roll on the car's small multimedia displays.

'This is the threat issued by the Church, via its Middle Eastern counterparts.'

Chris watched. The connection was as clear as one could hope for. The translated transcript he was handed by Gallows left little room for doubt.

'My interrogation of one of their members, arrested in New York a few days ago, confirms the intel. The two men detained by our Marines in Iraq yesterday have us pretty sure we're dealing with some kind of bomb. We're working at the moment to determine the most likely target areas and sweep the city as thoroughly as we can. But these people, they're good. They've planned this well.'

Chris flipped through the pages of the file Gallows had given him. 'Tell me where I stand in the operational hierarchy.'

'The Deputy Director has given you top-level clearance to all our intelligence and operations, and you'll have the full resources of the Field Office at your disposal. We need to know precisely how they're planning to attack – the wheres, the hows, and as many other details as you can predict. That's your first priority.' He reached to his side, then handed Chris another stack of files. 'Here's the rest of the background intel, everything we've been able to put together so far. Read it and you'll know everything we do about this group and its leader, Arthur Bell.'

Chris's body tensed. He couldn't have heard the name he thought he'd just heard. He sputtered out his next words.

'What did you say?'

Gallows stared back, a brow raised.

'That name . . . what did you say the leader's name was?' Chris pressed as far towards Gallows as the space of the car would allow.

'Bell. Arthur Bell.'

'Holy shit.' Chris slammed the files down on his knee. 'You've got to be kidding me!'

'You've heard of Arthur Bell?'

'Not just heard: I got this from him –' Chris motioned toward his bandaged shoulder '– no more than eighteen hours ago!'

Gallows's eyes went wide. 'You've . . . *met* Arthur Bell?'

'We got to know each other rather too intimately in the short time we spent together,' Chris answered. 'And I've got two friends back in Egypt who know where he's located.'

Gallows's head inclined slowly as he took in Chris's revelation, his fingers digging ever more deeply into the armrest of the speeding car.

CHAPTER 81

Cairo

'Are you sure you're ready to break into the world's greatest museum of Egyptian antiquities?' After their drive, Michael had sat next to his wife in the front seat of the 4x4, parked in the far corner of the Coptic Museum's main lot, as he asked the question.

Her response had been emphatic. 'You can't possibly be having reservations. Mike, these people, we can't let them get away with what they've done. Much less what they're planning to do.'

Michael hadn't required further affirmation. A moment later, a few supplies tucked into their pockets and their phones switched off, they were out of the car.

The main doors of the museum opened directly onto the frontal courtyard: too visible a spot, if breaking in would take them more than a few seconds, and neither had extensive experience in this sort of activity. Emily's work with a bobby pin on a cheap set of handcuffs in Istanbul five years ago was a far cry from the main entrance to a secure museum.

The side door, unlike the main, was sheltered by two large trees and offered a small amount of cover. They made their way towards it, Michael tucking the flare gun he'd retrieved from Chris's pack into his rear pocket. It and the knife were the only weapons they had at their disposal, and though the flare wasn't a gun, appearance might count for something. Bullet or not, Michael didn't think he'd like to be hit in the chest with a live flare.

They approached the side door silently, anxious to reach the trees that would provide cover for forcing their entry. But as they drew close, a new fact became clear. Cover was not going to be needed. The door was already ajar, with fresh scuffs near the lock indicating that its recent entry had been forced.

'We're not the first ones here this morning,' Emily said, her voice suddenly lower. She pointed at the door. 'They're already inside.'

But there was no going back. Pushing gently on the door, Emily watched as it swung easily and silently open. She took a step forward, through the door and into the dark corridor beyond. Drawing in a deep breath, Michael followed. Two steps and a tug on the handle later, the door was closed behind them and Emily and Michael were confronted with the interior of the Coptic Museum of Cairo.

Subconsciously remembering Chris's advice from the cave, both stood still a moment, allowing their eyes to adjust to the darkness. Only when the distinct forms of sarcophagi, inscribed pillars and display cases began to come into focus did Michael make for his small torch.

'No,' Emily whispered, grabbing his wrist before he could

switch it on. With Bell's group already inside, even the smallest flicker of light could give them away. 'We navigate in the dark.'

Michael nodded without speaking, pocketing the torch. He closed his eyes, calling the layout of the museum to mind. He had been here twice in his studies, precisely to gaze upon the Nag Hammadi Codices. He had nothing to match Emily's eidetic memory, but the reminiscences were strong.

'The codices are kept in Room 10, upstairs. The stairway should be about two rooms down that way.' He motioned to the left of their present position.

Crouching low, Emily began to move, Michael a few paces behind. Though neither of them knew precisely what they would do once they got there, they knew exactly where they were going.

CHAPTER 82

FBI Field Office, Chicago

Chris allowed the door from the underground garage to slam shut behind them as he followed Gallows into the FBI division building.

'The man who held us at gunpoint in that cave is the very man you say heads the "Church" responsible for this plot. He gave a cryptic allusion to using another name among his followers, but it was definitely Bell.'

They rounded a corner and headed up three flights of steps. Chris continued, breathless at the pace. His shoulder still throbbed.

'He was almost maniacally intent on getting his hands on what he called a "keystone", which turned out to be a small item of pottery covered in engravings. I found it in a recess of that cave.'

'*You* found this keystone?' Gallows was incredulous.

'And he took it. A feat that ended with me shot and nearly concussed, and the three of us trapped.'

Gallows seemed not to notice the details of Chris's plight.

Stories of agents facing danger were, by his expression, commonplace.

'Did you learn where he was going? What he intends to do next?'

'Only that it has something to do with ancient documents kept in Cairo. I'm not an expert on these things, but the people I was with, Emily Wess and Michael Torrance, are.'

'And where are they now?'

'Still in Egypt, following Bell.' He paused a moment, catching his breath. 'Ted, this could be the most important lead in your case. We know where this man is. We might be able to stop him.'

There was a long stillness between the two men. Gallows pondered, considering Chris's information.

'It's good you told me this,' he finally said, turning and continuing his ascent of the steep staircase. 'You're right, it might represent our first major break. But I want to process the data before we throw this blindly onto the table – check out the details and confirm what we can pursue. Leave it in my hands for the moment. I'll make sure everything gets passed up the chain of command.'

'Passed up the chain? This isn't some trifling bit of interesting dross, Special Agent Gallows. It's something we've got to act on, now.'

Gallows reverted to his air of hierarchical authority and pushed his way through a door to his floor.

'I told you, Special Agent Taylor, I'll deal appropriately with the information you've provided. In the meantime, I expect you to follow protocol and not speak of this to anyone else. The last thing I need are agents abandoning their details to chase up new leads before we've had a chance to assess them appropriately.'

Chris stared at the other man, reminded in full measure of why he had never liked bureaucrats.

'Now get to work on figuring out the Church's next move,' Gallows added, stepping into his office. 'I'll want to cover this new material with you in more detail soon. Until then, not a word.' He swung his office door closed in time to match his final command.

Chris stood before it, dumbfounded. Then angered. Then belligerent.

'Not a word, my ass,' he muttered, flipping through his pocket and extracting his mobile phone. Locating Michael's number from his contacts, he hit 'Dial' without hesitation. 'This connection is not dying here.'

CHAPTER 83

Downtown Chicago

The group of four huddled close. This was to be their final planning session before they moved out. Their go order would come in under thirty minutes.

'You all remember the steps ahead,' Ammon said as the others nodded. 'I'll take the device. You two –' he motioned towards the Arab brothers '– will be on armed watch.' He turned to the woman. 'You'll take the stock of additional weapons and the moment we're on location, distribute them to all of us.'

The device, the core of which had arrived from Iraq, had since been fitted out with its remaining elements in their workshop in Chicago. Its small dimensions, wrapped in bubbled padding and carefully concealed in only a slightly larger than usual rucksack, betrayed nothing of the violent, raw power it represented.

Ammon paused, glancing over the gathered group. 'Our brother on the inside will have set up the way. Don't forget, we keep to the map once we're inside – only the pre-arranged corridors and rooms'll be dark. We set foot in any others and we're spotted. Understood?' Three nods came back in the affirmative.

The group of four had been chosen for their devotion, loyalty and reliability. Ammon, known to the US Army as Staff Sergeant Paul Johnson, had been the unquestioned choice for team leader. He had brought the heart of the device over from Iraq among his personal effects, and that risk, together with his efficiency in managing it, had made the current operation possible. The remaining three members were each devoted, long-illumined Knowers. The woman, called Priscilla in place of her given name of Anna-Belle, was from the American Brotherhood.

The two other men were both Arab and to their team leader were simply 'the Arabs'. He was not a racist man and in another context might have approached them on more personal terms, but for their current operation it was precisely their ethnicity that mattered. Their dark skin, black hair and unquestionably Arab features were today their greatest asset.

'Once we're in position and secure,' Ammon continued, 'I'll arm the device and set the timer. Then we stand watch until the moment comes. That's our calling. Not one of us leaves here alive.'

CHAPTER 84

The Coptic Museum, Cairo

Two-thirds of the way up the angular, carved staircase, sounds from a room ahead gave away the location of the others in the museum. Emily froze when the first voices echoed through the expanse of the dark space, and Michael followed suit.

'Ahead, there,' she whispered lightly, pointing. She was already on edge, her adrenaline spiked since she and Michael had passed the first inert body of a dead security guard at the foot of the staircase. Bell's men were not only here, they were again leaving bodies in the wake of their pursuits. Emily grew only more determined as she considered that Andrew had not been an exception; he had simply been one more body along their trail.

'That's the direction of Room 10,' Michael confirmed, holding his mouth close to her ear.

She nodded, any doubt over their course of action having long since faded. 'What else is in there?' she asked, hoping for something large, something that might conceal their own entrance from whatever group Bell had assembled around him.

'Only manuscripts,' Michael answered. 'The Nag Hammadi collection, together with the Coptic Psalter.' The world's greatest find of Gnostic texts alongside the world's oldest preserved codex. The contents of the room were of incalculable value.

'How are the displays laid out?' Emily persisted. 'Size-wise?'

'Size?'

'Are any of them big enough to hide behind?'

'Not even close.'

'Then we go that way.' She pointed towards the adjoining room. It opened onto the corridor through a separate entrance, though the two galleries were connected by an open arch. She could only hope that the configuration of display cases and artefacts in the second room would afford them a concealed position. Necessity was clearly going to require that they interact with Bell's men, but she wanted to scope out the scene first.

They walked on the balls of their feet over the parquet floor, past the open entrance to Room 10 and into the next doorway.

Room 11: Pottery, Textiles and Cultural Artefacts. The room turned out to be precisely what Emily needed: large display cabinets contained stonework, pottery, fabrics – a wide variety of cultural accretions from a bygone age, some taller than her. In the left wall was the archway connecting to Room 10, from which the dim lights and sounds of Bell's group emanated.

'Over here,' Michael whispered, stepping past Emily and taking the lead. He directed them towards a tall case containing a historical map of post-Pharaonic Upper Egypt, replete with small artefacts highlighting the key agricultural techniques of the regions it represented. It was large enough for both of them to crouch behind, and just opposite the archway into the other room.

The ideal location to see and not be seen.

CHAPTER 85

The Coptic Museum, Cairo

Marcianus surveyed the work of his brethren like a protective father. Their activities had been in the planning for so many years. To see them come together before his eyes was positively entrancing.

The surface of one of the room's long, glass display cases had been covered in a white cloth and the necessary materials gradually laid upon it. The texts expert had located Codex II, containing the *Gospel of Thomas*, and the second tract was now on the makeshift work surface, open to its first page.

To its right, three trays had been assembled, surrounded by numerous bottles and vials the group had brought with them from the staging flat. They had more than would be required; but until the instructions for the solutions had been fully decoded, there was no way to know which would be needed.

As the translator called out the ingredients one by one, the chemist selected the jars from the ensemble of supplies. The numbers that followed each ingredient indicated relative proportions, and the chemist had opted for 20ml units. As he located each ingredient in turn, he scooped a corresponding number of precisely levelled measures into its respective tray. The main binding agent was to be an equal mixture of water and palm oil, both of which were at the ready.

Soon, the three solutions were taking form, scoop by scoop and drop by drop. All save for the ingredients they hadn't been able to decode prior to their arrival. The chemist turned to the translator.

'I need the rest.'

Nodding, the translator left his side and walked to the far end of the table. There, one of the brothers had opened Codex I to the first of the two pages that hadn't been contained in the online scans. Next to it sat the keystone, and beside that a sheet of blank paper. Marcianus hovered nearby.

'Call out the remaining ingredients as you decode them,' he instructed. 'There shouldn't be more than ten or twelve to go.'

CHAPTER 86

Ancient Egypt, AD 373

The young man who sat at work in the cellar of his mentor's small home hadn't yet chosen his name. He had been born simply Markus, and though he had always liked the name, he knew that entrance into the Brotherhood of the enlightened would bring with it many changes. Tarasios had told him he could choose a name for himself and that he should put careful thought into the selection. The name of the Elect marked them for eternity.

But today Markus had other priorities. His training as a scribe had unexpectedly placed him at the heart of what the brethren were calling 'Liberation's Preservation', and even as a new recruit he knew that it was an act of monumental importance.

'The persecutions against us are growing stronger and stronger,' Tarasios had told him, together with a group of others, a few months ago. 'Our hopes of proclaiming true freedom in the midst of the Empire are falling. Our very existence is threatened.'

The imperial forces were closing in. Brethren were being rounded up, tortured and executed. Whole communities were banished to 'exile', but everyone suspected that such exile referred to something more permanent than merely relocation.

So the project of preservation had been conceived. The incantation would be concealed. It would be secured away, preserved for the future – for a time when it could be used to its full glory.

Markus gazed down at the small stacks of pages before him and his counterpart, a fellow scribe called Paul. The other man's papyrus folios had already been prepared, the sacred words written upon them in an ink whose mystical properties caused it to vanish only seconds after it touched the flattened, pressed reeds that made up the paper.

Paul had already removed a quill, and with studied care he began to transcribe onto the 'blank' pages the words of Thomas the Blind's gospel, the original of which sat next to him. As the darker ink, which was also a special formula developed by the Brotherhood, dried, it left no sign of the hidden words penned beneath them.

Markus turned to his own task. The pile of papers before him contained no concealed text, but the words he would write would contain a hidden message.

He withdrew the keystone from a pouch around his neck and laid it on the table by the papyrus pages. He then unrolled the scroll – so sacred, so ancient. The brethren cherished the original transcription of Valentinus's Gospel of Truth as among their most revered possessions, dating back to a century ago, to the very beginnings.

Markus had been given a clear charge: copy the text onto the pages, modifying its wording and structure as required in order to encode the list of ingredients that a future generation would one day require.

The list had been provided by the alchemist. Markus turned to the first ingredient, identified its first letter, and fed it in reverse through the keystone's formula. The resulting encoded letter stared up at him:

Picking up his pen, he dipped it into a pot of thick ink, then set it to the page.

CHAPTER 87

FBI Field Office, Chicago

Special Agent Laura Marsh tried with all her might not to slam her office door behind her, but her usually steady nerves were well and truly frayed. She was used to pursuing terrorists, men who did terrible and appalling things. But she was not used to discovering them on her own home turf. In her own building.

Agent Scott Lewis was dead – killed, working for her. There was no question of accident or coincidence. He had been killed to silence his investigation. *Her* investigation.

The Church has someone on the inside, someone who believes this route might expose something important. The revelation made Marsh's blood course faster.

Laura Marsh was no close friend of Agent Lewis, and she felt a twang of guilt that she had always regarded him mostly as a logistical resource. She now felt a sense of duty, of the need to honour him following his death, as if there was an intangible obligation to chase up this lead out of respect for the man who had died trying to do so.

Lewis's killer had taken his workstation, which told Marsh one important fact: whatever he'd been working on prior to his death was significant. And that, Laura knew, gave her an edge. Lewis's discoveries could still help her investigation, even after his death and even with his computer gone.

It took Laura a few moments to log into the Field Office's central server with her admin credentials and locate the partition where Lewis kept his backups. The system automatically performed a synchronous backup of all employee work, and beneath his ID Laura found thousands of files that filled a carefully organized hierarchy of directories. The date and time tags allowed her easily to locate the most recent.

The last. *July 2nd, 11.57 p.m.*

She extracted the file with a command at the hash prompt.

tar -zxvf july02_2357.tar.gz

The decompressing contents streamed past faster than she could read them, until a few more keystrokes brought up the new file listing. The one that interested her was immediately obvious in among the others. 'Marsh_details.txt' sat midway on the screen, almost calling out to Laura.

Lewis, like most computing types, had an irrational dislike of word processors and graphical interfaces, which meant opening the plain text file into which he'd been entering his notes was a simple matter. In seconds it was displayed on Marsh's screen.

Her breath tensed. The first paragraphs contained fleshed-out versions of the details she already knew. But then Lewis had chased the mobile lead further, and directed email scans on European locations, together with a pairing of names of individuals on the European mainland who had cellular accounts with the same German network provider that had been in use on the phone found in Chicago. At the time of his death, Lewis had been able to identify at least forty individuals who matched both criteria, though he hadn't yet been able to get as far as any actual line or SMS tracing via the provider.

Marsh copied the listing of names to a new window and emailed them to herself.

At the end of Lewis's notes, his final remarks caught her attention. He'd returned to the Middle Eastern connection. His interpretation of the facts, however, were of a tone that no one else had yet expressed.

She read and reread a line that quickly burned its way into her mind. At the end of the file, Agent Scott Lewis's final written words glowed up at her.

'*The Middle Eastern relationship is too clear. Its concealment is perfunctory at best. It is a connection that wants to be seen.*'

It was the last observation Lewis had ever made. Laura tried to absorb its meaning, but realized she was going to have to examine his data more closely. Calling up the print command, she sent the file to her office printer.

A sharp beep signalled an error. Staring at the screen, Laura read a message that made her back go rigid.

FILE DOES NOT EXIST

Her breathing went shallow, and Laura backtracked out of the display. Entering the command for a directory listing once again, she called up the mirrored contents of Lewis's drive.

The directory was empty. All the files had been erased.

CHAPTER 88

The Coptic Museum, Cairo

The moment to act, Emily sensed, was going to come quickly. Turning to Michael, she bore her gaze into his eyes and telegraphed all the authority she could command. 'Give me the gun.'

'Gun?' Michael hesitated. The plastic pistol he'd taken from the car wasn't a gun. 'It's just a flare, Em.'

'Appearance counts for something. In this darkness, it'll be hard for them to tell the difference.'

Her remarks were a mirror of Michael's thoughts at the car. Suddenly, recognizing where their current scenario was leading, he wrapped his hands around hers. They were positioned behind a map case, too close to allow unnecessary whispers, but he had to do something to convey the emotions flaring inside him. He locked his hands around her fingers. Looking into her eyes, he tried to convey the mixture of love and concern he felt.

Emily softened. She loved this man more than she would ever be able to express. Not only because he was the man whose emotions fuelled her own, or the man who so obviously sought to protect her, even as he supported her and pushed her forward. But in this moment she loved him because, beneath the fingers that gripped her with such conviction, he was the man whose hands were passing her the flare gun. He was as resolved in their purpose as she was.

A silent connection. And then, the moment came.

Emily tightened the flare gun in her grip and repositioned her weight behind the display case. Glancing around its edge, she took final stock of the scene. Allowing her memory to catalogue the position of every man in the room, every object and every route of motion, she took a long breath, closing her eyes to gain clarity and courage.

When she opened them, she was already moving.

CHAPTER 89

The Coptic Museum, Cairo

Bursting out from behind the map case, standing full height with the flare gun drawn at chest level before her, Emily powered through the archway and into the gathered fray of Arthur Bell's assembly. Michael sprang out behind her, taking a position at her side.

'Put down the codex!' Emily commanded, her voice authoritative and retaining more control and determination than she'd thought it might. 'I promise you, I won't hesitate to fire.'

The shock on the men's faces was palpable, even in the darkness. Bell swung round from his position near the end of the table, his eyes squinting to catch their identities.

'You!' He spat out the words, genuinely stunned. The grenade he had lobbed into the cave outside Nag Hammadi had delivered its charge. He had watched as the stone crumbled and the sole exit was thoroughly blocked. Their death had been a certainty.

'How the hell . . .'

Emily managed a spiteful look through the adrenaline. She

clenched her fingers around the small flare pistol. Even in the tension of the moment, there was a satisfaction that came with seeing him confronted by his failure to kill them.

Bell's reaction was an indecipherable growl. Emily and Michael pushed forward into the room. She kept the flare gun drawn, its form adequately mistakable for a revolver in the darkness of the museum. Occasionally sweeping it over the whole assembly of Bell's men, it was on the man himself that she compressed her attention, together with her rage.

'Have you no sense of responsibility, of right or wrong?' she asked, glaring at him. 'History means nothing to you. *Life* means nothing to you!'

'They mean everything to us,' Bell answered, defiant. 'They're why we're here.'

'You're here with blood on your hands, that's all I know for certain.'

Bell looked into her eyes, his expression unreadable but hard. 'You're upset about your cousin. His death was an unfortunate accident.'

'An accident!'

'That's right. He came at my men. They had no choice.'

Emily worked hard to fight the urge to clamp down on the trigger and fire a searing flare into the face of the man as he spoke. She felt Michael lay a reassuring hand on her back. 'Breathe,' he whispered softly from the corner of his mouth. She obeyed, reclaiming focus.

'You can justify murder however you want,' she finally said. 'You'll pay for it eventually.'

Emily moved a few steps closer, now facing Arthur Bell

from across the end of the table where the translator had been at work before their arrival. Gazing down at the open codex and the keystone, she steadied her breath.

'You know nothing of what we're doing,' Bell persisted.

But as the keystone glistened in a fluttering glance of torch-light, the way forward became clear.

She looked up again to the man's cruel face, her gun arm steady. 'What I know is this.' Her voice was now calm and controlled. 'You're willing to stop at nothing – including murder – to get what you want.' Bell opened his mouth, but Emily cut him off with a wave of the pistol. She reached down, her hand passing over the open codex and clasping around the ancient keystone. She knew that what she had to do was abhorrent, but she also knew it was the less offensive of two evils. The only real option.

'This stone,' she said, looking up and into Bell's eyes, 'was the cause of my cousin's death. That blood is on your hands. And in tribute to him, I intend to make sure your hands never touch it again.'

Before Bell could register her meaning, Emily thrust her arm downwards with all the force she could muster and slammed the keystone onto the metal ribbing at the corner of the display table.

'No!' Bell shouted, his face panicked, but it was too late. As the ceramic substance of the man-made stone met metal, the keystone shattered. A cloud of powder shot through Emily's fingers as the old stone disintegrated, and before Bell's exclamation had fully left his mouth, a hundred shards of shattered clay clattered to the floor.

'*Bitch!*' he screamed. 'What have you done?' The redness of his face was visible in the cold darkness, his fury frantic. '*What have you done?*'

Emily took a breath to answer, but seized when she felt Michael's body slam into her shoulder from behind, then fall to the floor at her side. She looked down at his fallen form, momentarily confused; but before she could turn to see what had caused his fall, a blow struck her head from behind. The dark room suddenly sparkled with a fiery white light as her vision blurred. She felt her clutch on the flare pistol release, vaguely heard it clatter to the floor, felt her knees buckle and her own body start to fall.

As her blurring vision saw the strangely beautiful pattern of the parquet floor come closer to her face, Emily heard only the echoes of Arthur Bell's pained cries.

'*What have you done?*'

Then there was the thud, the floor, the pain, the blackness. And at last, nothing.

CHAPTER 90

Downtown Chicago

The sun was just starting to crest the skyline, bringing brightness to the concrete and glass cityscape of central Chicago, as the group of four closed in on their target. The Tribune Tower was situated towards the front of tomorrow's parade route, which made its position ideal. The greatest crowds always gathered along the front of the route.

The service entrance on North Saint Clair was to be their entry point. A series of text messages with the brother working with the night janitorial crew confirmed that the internal arrangements were ready.

Maintaining as casual an air as they could manage, Ammon and his team approached the doorway, the two Arab men keeping a steady lookout for any local law enforcement or prying eyes that might upset their entry. As expected, the metal door pulled open without resistance. Precisely ten minutes after Ammon sent an SMS confirming their entry, the janitor would ensure it was locked again.

In a smooth and seamless motion the team was inside the tower.

The door closed and the SMS sent, Ammon extracted a hand-drawn map from his pocket. The floor plan of the ground level had been drawn by the janitor, red pen highlighting the corridors in which he had disabled the security cameras.

'So long as you keep to this route from the door to the storage room, you'll remain off footage,' he had confirmed to Ammon and his team the day before. 'Just don't wander off this path. The cameras everywhere else are live and they're scrutinized meticulously. You get caught on one, security's gonna be sweeping the whole building before breakfast.'

Ammon rotated the paper in his hand, then glanced down the corridor to gain his bearings. A second later he gave the go signal and they began to move.

The device remained packed on his back.

Ten metres down the corridor he motioned the group to the left and their course was efficiently altered down a connecting hallway. When it terminated a lengthy distance later, they followed the map to the right, and then another left. Though they encountered no one, they kept their weapons at the ready, and each turn was made with military precision.

At length they arrived at their ultimate destination: a door marked 'SC-118', or Storage Closet 118. The name was a misnomer. Positioned next to a cafe opening onto the always busy sidewalks of North Michigan Avenue, the room they had targeted was normally a retail space, only recently converted into a makeshift storage area while the building's managers awaited a new lessee ready to pay the high premiums for street-front real estate at the foot of the Magnificent Mile. Not only was it on the ground level, facing the street, but its front-facing wall was cosmetic in nature, constructed of glass that had been painted over to black out the space prior to renting.

Ground level, facing the parade, with glass walls. For their purposes, ideal.

The door here, too, was unlocked and only seconds after they reached it, Ammon and his team were inside.

'Take up protective positions,' Priscilla commanded, nodding in the direction of her two male counterparts. She set down her pack and began unloading the heavy armament they had brought with them: a number of small handguns complemented by four fully automatic Heckler and Koch MP5s.

While the others worked, Ammon moved to the painted-over glass wall nearest the street. Pulling up a storage crate to serve as a platform, he gently, carefully, removed the burden from his back. Slowly exposed from its pack, freed layer by layer of the protective wrapping that had assured its safe transportation, the device had an awesome majesty about its form. Its two central explosive chambers were surrounded by a fine wire mesh that held in place a collection of old shrapnel – scraps of metal that looked so unassuming, so innocuous, in their eclectic assortment. But with a shock wave behind them, each scrap would become a deadly missile, every shard terrifying in its destructive power.

Entering a carefully memorized sequence of digits into the

keypad, Ammon confirmed the command codes twice. At the final key press, the countdown timer began.

Tomorrow morning, July 4th, 10 a.m. All that was left now was to wait.

CHAPTER 91

The Executive Mansion – Springfield, Illinois

Governor Wilson picked up his office phone and dialled a number across an encrypted line. He hoped this would be the last call he would have to make before the event in the morning. There had been too much communication. Encrypted or not, every contact represented a potential exposure.

The line connected, and his contact in the FBI Chicago Division answered. In the background, a bustle of activity could be heard.

'Yes?'

The Governor spoke without identifying himself. 'Tell me the situation's been dealt with.'

The FBI operative answered in shielded words. 'It's done. I eliminated the prying eyes last night. That line of investigation is over.'

Wilson sighed, relieved. 'I'm glad to hear that.'

'It was messy, and an investigation will follow. But it will come too late. Well after the fact.'

'Can I assume, then, that our arrangements are all still in place?'

The FBI operative, who had been a Knower for years, confirmed the plans in professional tones. 'Our squads are about to make the discovery that will lead them directly to the device. The terrorist intentions of the Church of Truth in Liberation are about to be thwarted. Before the day is out, security will be restored.'

Governor Wilson listened with admiration. The Brotherhood's contact in the FBI had sacrificed a great deal in order to see their purposes through. Internal scrutiny within the Bureau was second to none, which meant the contact had been forced to abandon much of the Brotherhood's life and activities in order to remain undetected and rise to a suitable position within its ranks. No attendance at ceremonies, no participation in gatherings. Only a private visitation from the Great Leader twice a year, covertly and distant from the city, had provided spiritual solace during the long undercover placement.

Wilson stood in awe of that devotion. He'd had to practise similar abstention to provide for his own position, and he felt a bond with the FBI mole.

He was satisfied. 'Thank you for your work. Just don't lose sight of the remaining objectives. Defer attention, and when the moment comes, prevent any interruptions.'

There was a slight pause, then the Brotherhood's FBI operative answered in clipped words. 'I know my role. Now, I've got to go. A/V's just sent out notice of a discovery in their footage. It's all about to go down.'

CHAPTER 92

The Coptic Museum, Cairo

'*Get her a sheet of paper and a pen. Make sure the ropes are tight . . . Don't bother with the fragments . . . The photo on the phone is too small to work with, we need to use her . . . Be prepared to do what's necessary . . .*'

Emily's consciousness came back to her slowly, the voices of the men in the room swirling through her head before vision returned to her eyes. The sounds were first of commotion, of activity; but as she began to move, to sit upright in her chair, they began to soften and go expectantly quiet.

Her chair. Emily realized she was sitting, leaning slightly forward at a strange, uncomfortable angle. She tried to straighten herself, but found she could not move. Her arms, bent at the elbows at rigid right angles, were stuck fast beside her. Her legs would not respond.

'Please, don't bother.' The voice was Bell's. Emily blinked her eyes several times, but the figure before her remained a blur.

'You'll find yourself quite securely tied down,' the blur continued, his voice strangely calm. 'We can't have any more of your . . . antics.' Emily pulled at her arms, at last feeling the rope restraints binding her wrists and elbows to the wooden arms of the chair. Her legs were bound twice, at the ankles and just below the knees.

'Where's . . . Michael?' Her words came out slowly, slurred. The blow that had felled her had been fierce.

'Your husband's not far away.' With a hand suddenly on each side of her head, Bell turned her gaze to a position across the table. There she saw Michael, similarly bound; but he was also bloody, his face swollen and contorted.

Emily's rage quickly overcame her pain, drawing fuller alertness back to her senses.

'What the hell have you done to him?'

'Only what has been required.' Bell answered calmly, stepping away from Emily's side. She kept her glance on Michael's face. Through his wounds, she could see his expression was one of concern – not for himself, but for her.

Bell reemerged in Emily's line of sight, placing a blank sheet of paper on the table, and next to it the codex containing the *Gospel of Truth*.

'What I had suspected when I saw the way you remembered the map with such precision, when I saw the way you scanned every detail of your surroundings in the cave, your husband has – somewhat reluctantly – confirmed.' Bell stood over the materials he had set before her, staring down. 'You have a good memory. A nearly perfect memory, if truth be told.'

Emily did not respond. She simply kept her gaze on Michael.

His eyes were discoloured by blood and sweat. What had they done to wrest that small detail from him?

'Obviously, your memory is good enough to remember something as complex as the surface of the keystone,' Bell continued. 'It brought you here, in full knowledge of our actions. Actions you've cut short.'

Suddenly, he took a step forward and extracted a knife from the small of his back. *Chris's knife*, Emily noted. The knife Michael had taken from the car.

She tensed as the blade was pointed at her and Bell took another step closer. Everything she knew about the man suddenly flashed through her mind. *He's ruthless. He shot Chris. He tried to kill us. He killed Andrew.* In a single moment she realized that Arthur Bell would kill her here, without losing any sleep over the act. The blade of the knife he was aiming at her body could be the last thing she ever felt.

Strangely, the thought reinforced her composure. She could not control the other man. She could only accept what came, and act – if and when she was able.

The knife was thrust forward suddenly, strongly, but it did not pierce her skin. With surprising skill, Bell lanced it through both of the ropes binding her right arm.

'You have destroyed my keystone,' he said, keeping the knife held at the ready, 'but fortunately, you're in a position to help us undo what you've done.' He slowed his next words to emphasize the threat they were meant to convey. 'I expect you to help us.' Glaring into her eyes, Bell stood himself upright. He patted down his jacket, returning his voice to a calmer tone.

366

'I am, however, not expecting you to be willing to do so. You are confused, still bitter about your relative. You are . . . unmotivated. That, however, is something we can change.'

He gave a nod to one of the larger men in the group, and the man swept to Michael's side and stood at the ready.

Bell turned his gaze slowly back to Emily's face. There was no need to make the threat. The situation spoke for itself. Action and response were obvious.

She hesitated, trying to register her options, but Bell's impatience flared. With a nod of his head, the Italian brother recognized his signal and pulled a hammer out of a small tool kit at the base of Michael's chair. Even from her vantage point, Emily could see the gleam in the man's eye – a gleam that came from one source. *Pleasure*. She suddenly realized that whatever was coming next was something he cherished, and the realization filled her with a new horror.

Allowing the hammer only a moment of steadiness, more to ensure that Emily saw it than to support his aim, the man arced his strong arm and slammed the metal head squarely onto the back of Michael's left hand. The tormented man's scream filled the room.

Bell leaned down and whispered into Emily's ears between Michael's screams, 'I will do what I have to.'

Emily gaped in shock as Michael clambered to regain control, but his attacker had already laid aside his hammer. He reached down to Michael's injured hand with his own. Grabbing two fingers, he slammed them back until they gave under his force, snapping to lie flat against the top of Michael's hand.

The sound of popping joints and splintering bones again gave way to his renewed shrieks of agony.

'Enough!' Emily cried, her face flushed red with a fiery mix of anger and horror. 'Enough!' She raised her freed hand to signal her surrender.

As if anticipating the move, Bell stepped to her side and placed a pen in her outstretched hand. Michael's attacker stood back in the darkness.

'I'm so very glad we could come to an agreement,' Bell said. He pushed her chair closer to the edge of the display case that had become their worktable. The codex and paper were at the ready.

'Now, I would appreciate it if you would please decode the remainder of my list.'

CHAPTER 93

FBI Field Office, Chicago

As Chris held his cell phone to his ear, the frustrated look on his face grew more severe. Over the last fifteen minutes he'd tried Emily's line three times, Michael's five, but each time the result was the same: the lines went straight through to voicemail. He'd left brief messages on both phones already. They were supposed to check in.

'Michael,' he started as soon as the brief message had played through to its tone, 'me again. The moment you get this, call. Haven't heard from you, and we've got a serious problem here.' He swivelled on his foot as he spoke, unsure of just how much to share on a recorded message.

'Arthur Bell is the man behind the threat here in Chicago. I don't know what you've found out about him, or if you're still following him, but be careful. He's at the head of a religious sect, and the fact that he tried to kill us doesn't even begin to compare with what he's planning over here.'

Chris beat his knuckles against the wall. His conversation with Ted Gallows had left him deeply unsettled, as well as certain that Michael and Emily were in pursuit of a man who was far more dangerous than they had anticipated.

He sped up his speech. 'We're doing background on Bell's Church of—'

He was cut off by a long tone.

'Goddamit!' Chris shouted, slamming his thumb down on the end key of his own phone and shoving it into his pocket. Michael should be answering. He and Emily had been out of contact for too long . . .

He took a deep breath, pushing the thought away, and resumed his pacing.

A few steps later Chris reached the final office in the corridor and turned around, prepared to backtrack his pacing. As he turned, his eyes caught the plaque next to the office door beside him, and he brought himself to a halt. The plaque read 'Special Agent Laura Marsh,' and the name forced Chris's thoughts to a very different place.

He'd known he would see her again the moment the call from Chicago had reached him in Egypt, and that knowledge had been one of the few things that made the unexpected journey sound appealing. Dealing with tragedy and emergency was familiar territory. Seeing Laura was a rare consolation.

So many possibilities, unexplored. Things I wish I'd said and done, ages ago. He reached for the doorknob. *But today, no chance to change that.*

Chris took a breath, knocked, and poked his head through the door.

CHAPTER 94

The Coptic Museum, Cairo

Emily worked at her task with diligence. With Bell's readiness to do to Michael whatever he felt was required to motivate her, she had ample incentive to work to her full ability. The fear seemed to heighten the detail of her memory, and she deciphered the hidden contents of the codex at a slow yet steady pace. Without a lexicon, which she'd had at her disposal during their drive, she was unable to translate the Coptic results into English; but a member of Bell's group possessed more than ample translation skills.

Bell had, for a time, paced the room, his forced composure giving way to a mixture of anticipation, anxiety and religious fervour. Yet focus had been reclaimed, and as Emily worked under the supervision of his men, he retreated to a far corner and switched his attention to finalizing the arrangements required once the revelation was complete.

'It's Marcianus. Tell Praxean and Victor to ready the men on the ground in the city,' he spoke into his small satellite phone, commanding one of the brothers who served as a go-between for himself and the regional Leaders at the great assembly in Chicago. 'Cerinthus won't be seen again until the moment of liberation. Praxean will have to take charge of organizing the brethren into the crowds tomorrow, ensuring they're in the right location when the time comes.'

There was a lull as he listened to the voice on the other end of the line. Emily, though hard at work decoding the remaining ingredients, strained to take in his words. *He called himself Marcianus.* All the names sounded ancient, taken straight from the third century.

'The crowd is set to be as large as we expected – perhaps even bigger. We couldn't have asked for more. Let the Liberation Incantation show these people what liberty really means.'

The Liberation Incantation, Emily repeated silently to herself. It was the first time she had heard 'Marcianus' refer to his intention by name.

She tucked her face into the codex, striving to give no sign that she was cognisant of the ongoing conversation.

'Have Praxean inform Victor of the agreed square. The gathering place is essential. I've been assured it's where the procession will be at its most condensed.'

Another pause, and Marcianus gave a satisfied laugh into the phone. 'Whether they will understand it or not is irrelevant. On our way to freedom, we'll make a statement on religion the fallen world won't forget.'

Emily's body tensed as she heard the words, and at the vindictive tone that suddenly filled Marcianus's voice, her grasp slipped. The codex fell to the table, striking it with a thump that echoed through the room.

Marcianus spun his head towards her. As their eyes met, he realized she had been listening in. But he no longer cared. She would not leave this room alive. He would not make the same mistake he'd made in the desert.

Staring directly into her terrified features, Marcianus completed his conversation with the brother in Chicago. 'We depart this material cage, and leave the world only the echoes of its corruption. What's the death of a few dozen religious leaders, or a few thousand deluded revellers, if not an ultimate sign of their irrelevance?'

The details of Chris's warnings at the hotel in Asyut came flooding back to Emily's mind. The Chicago parade, a terrorist threat. Suspicion of a bomb or large-scale attack.

'Ready the bomb,' Marcianus said, shaking all pretence of secrecy, 'then phone the pilot here in Cairo and get the jet prepared for our transfer over.'

Marcianus slammed shut his phone and walked straight towards Emily, his gaze unflinching.

'You're mad,' she said, horrified.

'So you've said,' he answered dismissively. He approached her side, looking down at the page. 'And you, my dear, are done.' Snatching up the text, complete with Emily's final decoded word, he handed it to the translator who identified the last ingredient. A moment later it had been added to the third tray.

Turning Emily's chair so that it faced the centre of the table, Marcianus bent down and whispered into her ear. 'Before you die, I want you to see what real devotion can accomplish.' His breath was hot, its moisture clinging to her skin.

He rose and motioned to the chemist.

'Do it, now.'

CHAPTER 95

FBI Field Office, Chicago

Laura rose to greet Chris as he entered her office. She walked around her desk, arms already opening, before she caught herself. She held out her right hand instead, took Chris's and shook it.

Chris shook back, over-emphasizing the professionalism of the gesture. 'Chicago's been good to you. Your own office.' He watched her walk back to her desk, then took a seat in a chair facing her.

'More privacy, more responsibility,' she answered. She'd received her own office only a few months ago.

Chris allowed his eyes to linger a long time on Laura Marsh. The silence would have been awkward if they weren't both locked in it. The undeniable attraction between them during the few months they'd been in the Chicago Field Office together had gone unresolved since his changed posting had cut their relationship short before it could be explored.

'I'm sorry it took so long for me to get here,' he finally said.

'I got the call in a little place called Asyut. It took a few transports to make it from Egypt to O'Hare.'

'I've been anxious to have you here.' Laura recognized the double entendre, and forced herself to sit straighter in her chair. 'We're in need of your skills.'

'They're at your disposal. Gallows briefed me on the way here, and I've caught up on as much intelligence as you've got. Doesn't look good.' He was still feeling the frustration of his exchange with the section head.

'No, it doesn't.'

'Where's your focus in the op?' Chris asked. 'You're obviously not on the field teams out sweeping for security.'

The question brought Laura's concentration back to the uncomfortable work that had preoccupied her all morning. The loss of life in the building, the odd direction of her leads, the uneasy tension in her chest.

'Chris,' she said, leaning forward, 'that you're here from the outside means you're one of the only people I can talk to about the line I've been following.'

'Me? You've got your whole team.'

'I've been working on the case's international dimension,' she skipped over his question, 'and there's a major problem with our intelligence. A problem no one is talking about.'

Suddenly, all the joking and flirtation left Chris's mind, and he felt the skin on his face go taut. His own problem, the source of his frustration with Ted Gallows and the bureaucracy of divisional hierarchy, was to do with the case's international dimension. Arthur Bell. Egypt. Cairo. Could Laura possibly know already?

'I didn't think anyone else knew,' he said.

Laura peered up, surprised. 'Know what?'

Chris fidgeted. 'I was told, firmly, that it wasn't meant to be general knowledge.'

Without knowing how, Laura found herself standing.

'*What* isn't meant to be general knowledge? What are you talking about, Chris?'

He hesitated, but Chris had to share what he knew with someone other than Gallows, and Laura Marsh was an agent he knew he could trust. It was enough for him.

As Laura listened, eyes wide and hardly breathing, Chris recounted his experiences in Egypt with Michael and Emily, his encounter with Arthur Bell, the discovery of the keystone and his friends' current intention to track Bell to Cairo.

Only when Chris had finished the whole of his narrative did Marsh finally open her mouth. 'My God, I knew there was something up abroad, apart from Iraq.'

The pieces of her day were starting to fit together, confirming her instincts and painting a worse picture than before.

She realized she had to tell him about the morning.

'Chris, there's something else I need to fill you in on. Something far closer to home, and something I can only tell you.'

He waited, and Laura Marsh brought him fully into her confidence.

'One of our agents has been murdered. And it was someone in this office, working for me.'

CHAPTER 96

The Coptic Museum, Cairo

It took the chemist only a matter of minutes to complete the third solution with the final ingredient. Powdered Acacia root bark, two tablespoons. A commonplace herb in the fourth century and a supply his men had at the ready. Then the suspension of equal parts water and palm oil was added to bind them together, but to a far smaller ratio than had been required for the solutions that decoded the map. Rather than producing three liquids, the chemist stirred in the suspension to create three thick pastes.

Emily, bound to her chair, watched the process with a horrified yet enrapt fascination.

When the chemist had brought the three pastes to his desired consistency he gave a nod to another of the brethren. The man picked up the Nag Hammadi collection's Codex II, containing the world's sole copy of the *Gospel of Thomas*. Opening it to the first page of the unique tract, he set the volume on the table.

Without spoken command all the brethren huddled

close, their eyes glued to the event about to take place before them.

The chemist took up a small paintbrush with a one-inch wide, flat head and swirled it in the first paste. Lifting the readied brush from the tray to the codex, he lowered it onto the papyrus page and pulled it over the surface in smooth strokes – first one, then another, the rusty-red colour of the suspended powders covering the ancient text with a translucent hue.

'Thirty seconds, counting.' His assistant clicked a stopwatch as the solution was applied. All stared on in silence, gazes transfixed. Even Emily could not bring herself to protest. There was little point, and though their act was a desecration of history, she could not take her eyes off it.

'Mark,' the assistant announced. The chemist took up an L-necked plastic bottle filled with distilled water and rinsed the surface of the page. The paste washed away, revealing the papyrus and its writing without any visible changes.

The second thick paste was applied like the first, the papyrus surface now taking on a dirty-brown colour. The assistant announced a 45-second wait, and once again the room fell into tense silence. The paste was too dark, too thick, to see through it to the page, making the wait all the more expectant.

At last the count mark was announced, and again the chemist began to rinse. Emily's horror grew as the solution dripped away from the page, revealing the surface of the papyrus.

Blank.

The ancient text, the sole copy of one of the earliest fringe interpretations of the Christian message, completely erased.

'Bastards,' Emily said, her voice filled with dread.

Marcianus did not look up, but spoke with notable irritation as his men continued their work. 'Quiet, please, Dr Wess. I don't particularly want to gag you.'

The moment the second solution was off, the third, yellow paste was applied.

'One minute and thirty seconds,' came the count and the start of the timer.

As the time passed, each second seeming to draw out longer than the one before it, Marcianus pushed aside his brethren so that he could stand as close as possible to the codex. His eyes were wide, his brow raised. For those long moments it appeared as though there was nothing in the world apart from the text before him – the words he was about to see.

'Time,' the assistant finally called. The chemist took up his bottle and began to rinse. The solution thinned, formed rivulets on the page and dripped away.

Within a few seconds, the surface was fully exposed.

It was no longer blank.

Emily leaned into her restraints, straining for a closer view. What covered the ancient papyrus was no longer the text of the *Gospel of Thomas*. Nor was it a map, as she and Michael had discovered beneath their French manuscript in London. It was a new text, written in an elegant, bold hand.

Marcianus stared at it in wonder, but it was one of his brethren who announced the sight to the room.

'The Liberation Incantation.'

Marcianus nodded, his eyes never leaving the page. 'At last.'

CHAPTER 97

FBI Field Office, Chicago

'This is an entirely new dimension to our situation,' Chris stated, leaning towards Laura Marsh from the opposite side of her desk. For ten minutes she had spoken without interruption of the details that had consumed her past twenty-four hours, culminating in Agent Scott Lewis's murder.

'It means you have a mole. Someone inside the FBI, working for the Church. Someone with enough influence to derail one of the Bureau's biggest operations.'

'And whoever it is,' Laura added, 'is not above stooping to murder, much less erasing computer records.' She looked into Chris's eyes, her synapses firing through the possibilities. 'Killing Lewis . . . that means it has to be someone who knew I'd taken him on board to help me.'

'Who'd you tell?'

'I only filed the tasking up the chain of command. There was no need to inform anyone else.'

'Which limits the pool of potential leaks to senior staff in the Field Office.' There was a note of dread to Chris's voice.

The more senior the leak, the more problematic the situation became.

'That's just it,' Laura said, 'the list of names above the heads of squads is pretty small. There are the sectional heads, Mayfair, Gallows and Smith, and then only Deputy Director Dawson herself.' She hesitated. 'I had conversations with all of them.'

'It's a pretty small shortlist. Out of the four, who do you make as the most likely traitor?'

'I'd narrow it down to the three section heads.'

'Not Dawson?'

Laura shook her head pensively. 'I think we can rule out the Deputy Director. She's been a respected force in the Bureau for years. She's measured, rational, always looking out for her teams. I don't see her as a mole and a traitor.'

'Traitors are rarely the people you suspect,' Chris countered, 'and almost always turn out to be people you thought could never fit the mould.'

Laura clenched her fists, forcing herself to contemplate the possibility of the Deputy Director's involvement.

'Dawson has access to everyone. She certainly has the power and clout that would be required.'

'And pretty free authority over an operation of this sort,' Chris added.

'But she's used that reign to run it aggressively. Dawson's been unstinting in countering this attack and gathering every available ounce of intel on the group involved.' Marsh's hesitancy resurfaced. 'I really don't think it can be her. Dawson is one of the good guys.'

'Okay, for the moment let's keep the Deputy Director from the top of the list. That means we're down to three.'

'Mayfair, Gallows and Smith. They've all been pushing me fairly hard to prioritize street-level work over the secondary intelligence trail.'

So, Chris noted, *there's more than one person trying to keep alternative routes of enquiry from gaining ground.*

'Any suspicious behaviour?'

'Hell, Chris, my mind what it's been these past few hours, I've started to see everyone's behaviour as suspicious.' She threw up her hands in frustration. 'The short answer is, they're all tight-lipped and closed-mouthed. Of the three, I only know Ted Gallows reasonably well, and he's too much of a diligent tight-ass to pull off a national betrayal.'

Chris gave pause. 'I don't know, Laura. It was Gallows who muzzled me on Bell. And he'd have known you tasked Agent Lewis to advance your research.'

There was only a slight hesitation to Laura's response. 'I told him I planned to bring Lewis on board,' she confirmed, 'but the others would have found out quickly enough. And Brian Smith was the most aggressive of the group when it came to trying to get me off the European dimension and onto street sweeps and preventative measures. He was not exactly subtle in reminding me where my priorities should lie.'

'He was pushing you?'

'Pretty firmly.' She pondered, then spoke with more certainty. 'If I had to take a guess, my suspicion would rest with Smith.'

Chris sat back in his chair. 'It's a start, but we're going to need something more concrete. And until we've got it, let's not rule anyone out. Keep everyone in the pool till we're dead sure we know who's been derailing the Bureau's work.'

CHAPTER 98

The Coptic Museum, Cairo

'O world, behold! I will reveal to you my mysteries! For you
are my fellow brethren, and now you shall know the All.
We are knowledge, we are ignorance;
We are shame and boldness.
We are shameless, we are ashamed;
We are strength and we are fear –
We are war and peace: give heed!
We are the disgraced: we are the Great Ones!'

Marcianus could not help but let his lips give voice to the
ancient text as it became visible, page by page, under the
gentle and talented hands of his chemist. As each page was
revealed, he passed it to the translator, who transformed the
Coptic phrases into English as fast as his skills would allow.
Words that had been hidden for centuries, the better part of
two millennia, artfully concealed just out of view on pages
that had become among the most famous in the scholarly

world – they were suddenly given shape, their utterance at last a possibility.

His tongue naturally followed as his eyes flowed over the phrases, the revelations, of his most desired incantation.

'Ignorance has brought about terror and fear,
And fear became a dense fog that none was able to see.
Because of this, error became strong;
Yet truth shall burst forth a great, new Light,
And as fog fills the sky, so our fire will burn the air
And lungs, the eyes and heart –
Each breath a death and gateway to life.'

Still bound to her chair, Emily watched Marcianus exult in his find. Her reaction was a mixture of conflicting emotions, hard to define. There was horror at the very sight of this man who had been responsible for murder, pursuit, fear, death. There was angst each time the chemist, who appeared less and less concerned with the fragility of the ancient pages of the codex, tore them out of the antique leather binding after each folio had been submitted to the chemical treatments. But then, there was wonder at the fact of so ancient a mystery, exposed; awe at the reality that new words did come, a new piece of history unfolding before her eyes.

The translator lifted another page from his tablet, handing it to the Great Leader: the latest folio, transcribed and translated. Marcianus received it like an eager child.

So will Truth be known!
If one has knowledge, he gains what is his due and draws it
*   to himself;*
But he who is ignorant is deficient, and woe to that great
*   deficiency —*
For he lacks that which will make him perfect.
Our Light shall burn as fire and be carried upon the
*   breath!*
Each inhalation the gasp of liberating separation.

In the dim lamplight of the group's torches, together with the soft back-lighting of the display cases, Emily could not be certain, but she thought she caught a sheen of moisture in Marcianus's eyes as he read. His wonder was almost limitless, his joy seemingly unrestrained.

CHAPTER 99

FBI Field Office, Chicago

The primary A/V suite of the Chicago Division had quickly become the central hub of the office's activity. CCTV footage had been constantly under review on all the main buildings along the Magnificent Mile, with a bank of nine agents constantly poring over the more than 1,000 combined hours of camera footage flowing in every thirty minutes, covering almost every external facade of the city's commercial hub. Everything from shoppers to suppliers, to merchants and mere passers-by, all caught on digital tape every time they passed near a door, presentation window, ATM or access route. It was a monumental undertaking, but there was no substitute for dedicated manpower.

It had paid off.

Fifteen minutes ago, Deputy Director Dawson had been called into the suite with news that a pertinent discovery had been made. She had phoned Special Agent Gallows on the way, along with his fellow section heads, Mayfair and Smith.

News of the monumental discovery spread through the

building like wildfire. Five minutes after Dawson's leadership team had entered the room and verified its importance, an announcement of the new video lead was passed to Laura Marsh in her office, together with a summons. Within seconds she was on her feet and on her way to join her colleagues, Chris Taylor in tow.

As they entered A/V, the tension in the room was palpable. Laura pushed her way towards the front of the assembled group. She nodded when her eyes met the Deputy Director's. Then they met Gallows's and Mayfair's. When they met Smith's, her stomach tightened. Chris was close behind her, and she could sense a similar reaction. Their three principal suspects were all in the room together.

Ted Gallows turned to Marsh and Taylor, along with the small huddle of other agents who had entered the room. When he spoke, his tone was grave. 'CCTV surveillance has spotted a short clip that has a direct bearing on our present operation.' He motioned towards the men at the bank of monitors. 'Roll the footage again.'

They watched as the gravelly footage frozen on the screens looped back and began to play. Though their motion was made choppy by the low frame-count, a group of four individuals were nonetheless clearly visible, making their way towards a service entrance on what Marsh recognized as the side-structures attached to the famous, neo-Gothically inspired Tribune Tower.

'Stop it there,' Mayfair ordered.

'At 5.37 this morning, these four individuals entered the

door you see here. Though it appears to have been unlocked, their behaviour is indicative of an illicit entrance.'

'Three are men, and one is a woman.' The voice belonged to Brian Smith. 'We don't have IDs on any of them yet, but two facts can be determined from the footage itself.' He pointed closely to the monitor. 'Those two men are clearly Arab, and that –' he pointed towards a bulging backpack worn by the third, non-Arab male '– is a pack that could easily be the right size for an improvised explosive.'

Gallows turned and looked pointedly at Chris. 'We've found our threat, and our attackers. Special Agent Taylor's suspicion of a portable IED has proven correct.' He glanced back over the whole room. 'Needless to say, this image fits our intelligence profile exactly: Americans working together with Middle Eastern counterparts, a bomb, and a location on the parade route.'

Angela Dawson once again took on the commanding air of the woman at the helm of a powerful force. 'We're moving out. Get to your teams.' She nodded curtly at the group, and marched out of the room. In an instant every agent on the floor was in motion.

'Both of you get hooked up with the ground teams,' Gallows muttered to Chris and Marsh as he passed them by. 'SWAT will take the action, but we'll need all the expertise on the ground we can get.'

CHAPTER 100

Chicago

Walter Cerinthus pressed the phone to his ear, waiting for a new line to connect. His heart raced, his anticipation heightened to an almost painful degree.

'Yes?'

'Ammon, it is Cerinthus.' His voice rushed with enthusiasm. 'You're in place?'

'The device is in situ, and we've taken up positions around it, as arranged.'

'It's armed?'

'That's an affirmative. The timer is set for the morning. We'll stay with it till the end.' From their makeshift bunker in the street-side room of the tower, Ammon cast a respectful glance over the woman and two Arab brethren who stood fast with him.

'Your reward will be great,' Cerinthus affirmed. 'Stand fast, and find your peace.'

CHAPTER 101

The Coptic Museum, Cairo

During the whole process of decoding the ingredients for the solutions, attention had fallen away from Michael. He had been brutalized by Marcianus's men prior to Emily's regaining consciousness, and on her waking, his torment had been increased. But then, once she had begun to comply, he had been left alone, ignored and abandoned to suffer in ignominy. It was Emily's skills, not his, that they required. Michael was a broken man – crushed, defeated, used for a necessary purpose and no longer of significance.

It was a blind assumption that Michael realized was his only advantage.

Rather than protest, he employed the darkness and the distracted interest of Marcianus and his men to conceal the movements of his remaining good hand. The up side to the severity of his earlier beating had been that his attackers had not bound him as securely as his wife: his legs, thoroughly pummelled, had not been tied down, and his arms were fastened to the chair only at the wrists. The presumption that

391

he was too wounded to escape would have likely been correct, had they not threatened his wife before his very eyes.

Quietly, patiently, he writhed his uninjured hand back and forth in its rope restraint. With each motion, the knot gave slightly – only a fraction of a millimetre, but persistence was something Michael was ready to offer. The long work of decoding, Marcianus's phone calls and the teams' preparations, these took time. Throughout, with gentle, consistent regularity, Michael loosened his bond.

At last he pulled his hand free and began using it to loosen the bond over his left wrist. Fierce darts of pain shot through his torso with every tug and pull, his fractured bones scissoring through flesh and nerves as he worked, but his determination did not wane.

By the time Marcianus used his phone the second time and made contact with his chief partner in Chicago, Michael was free. And one thing was clear: the man had to be stopped.

Waiting for Marcianus's gaze to be lowered, consumed in terminating his call and returning the phone to his pocket, Michael found his moment. The chemist was absorbed in applying his potions to a new page, his partners huddled around him, their gaze singularly on the task to hand. The translator's head was down, his mind concentrated on his charge. There would not be a better opportunity.

Mustering every ounce of his strength, Michael stood up from the chair and thrust himself forward in a single motion. His sole aim was the waistline of the translator, where a small pistol was held in an unclasped holster. Slamming his body into the other man's to stop his fall, knocking the wind out of him in the process, Michael played the element of surprise and grabbed the gun with his good hand. It took him less than a second to locate the chemist, halfway down the table, and fire two rounds, one into each of his legs. Extending the arc of his arm, he swung the gun towards Marcianus.

'Don't move!' he commanded, his breath rough, the pain from his injured arm shooting throughout his body, his battered legs throbbing beneath him. He nodded towards the chemist, now buckled on the floor. 'Hitting his legs wasn't an accident. Next time, I aim higher.'

It hadn't been an accident, but it had been damned lucky. He hated guns, but it didn't mean he couldn't use one.

Marcianus gaped at the sudden intrusion. All around him, his men froze.

'You,' Michael ordered, waving the gun at another of the men, 'release my wife.' There was a brief hesitation, but the man capitulated. Emily glanced up to Michael, relief and gratitude in her eyes. His own were bloodshot and swollen, but satisfied. 'Take his gun,' he ordered when she was finally free. Emily complied, and an instant later she and Michael both held the team at gunpoint. He tried to reach his free arm up to touch her, to give her face a consoling touch; but the pain of the wounds was too great. She reached out to him instead.

It was then that Michael heard the bustle in the darkness to his left. Spinning towards the sound, Michael caught sight only of Marcianus's back as the group's leader moved away into the shadows. The sounds of crumpling paper highlighted the possession he grabbed as he fled: the translation of the Liberation Incantation that his men had produced, together with the torn-out pages of the codex that had revealed it.

'Stop!' Michael shouted, aiming his gun. He had never killed another man, but he found himself acting without hesitation. Bell had proven what he was capable of, and what he was planning to do. Michael squeezed the trigger tightly, firing two shots into the darkness. The suppressor softened the noise, but the bursts of light from the muzzle lit up the dark room like a strobe light.

Neither shot found its mark. Marcianus disappeared from sight.

'Go after him!' Emily cried. 'He's taken the codex!'

Michael limped to follow Marcianus, fighting against the pain, but as he reached the door into the main corridor two facts simultaneously flashed into his mind: he had not seen which way the man had run after leaving the room, which meant he would be following blind in the darkness; and no matter how adept she might be with a firearm, eight-to-one against were not odds he was willing to risk leaving Emily alone with. Marcianus's team were likely as desperate as he was, and there were more guns in the room than just the two they had confiscated. He couldn't leave Emily to face the remaining men by herself.

He turned back, returning his gun to a general sweep over Marcianus's team.

'Mikey, what are you doing? You have to stop him!'

He stepped up to Emily's side. 'He's gone, Em.' She stared wildly into his eyes, incredulous. But Michael could only repeat the truth.

'Marcianus is gone.'

CHAPTER 102

The Tribune Tower, Chicago

The footage from the city CCTV cameras demanded an alteration of Chris and Laura's immediate priorities. The revelation that a group of four unknown individuals had entered the Tribune Tower only hours ago, toting what could easily be a bomb, sent the FBI's ground forces into motion.

Two SWAT teams had assembled for the operation, and after a swift transport to the location both were now inside the ground floor. Deputy Director Dawson, who oversaw the operation from a make-shift assembly at the door, continually issued orders through a digital headpiece. The first team was to be the strike force, taking the room and its occupants by whatever means were required. The second, to which Marsh and Chris had attached themselves, would sweep in after the room had been cleared, to assess and disarm any device. Two explosives experts were part of the crew and a supplemental supply team, stationed just outside, had brought materials for every conceivable type of explosive. They would be ready for anything.

Ted Gallows had ensconced himself in the follow-on to the primary SWAT contingent and followed a few steps behind as the highly skilled agents swept through the ground floor, clearing each room as they went. Gallows was convinced that the most likely location for a bomb would be on the ground level, street side, opening onto the Mile where the crowds tomorrow morning would be at their thickest. The sweep had started, accordingly, at the opposite side of the building, gradually moving across the vast space until it reached the corridor that granted access to the street-front shops. The team was now positioned outside the door of the last remaining room: a storage space that their schematic showed was in fact an unleased retail shop.

The security cameras that would normally have given the team a visual on the interior had been disabled.

The chief of the principal SWAT team spoke almost silently into his throat mic, which picked up the vibrations of his vocal cords and translated them into perfectly audible sounds in the ears of the entire crew.

'On my mark we enter. Standard tactical sweep. Configuration of targets unknown. Possible device last seen with the non-Arab male. Eradicate any threat immediately.'

Chris heard the transmission come across their headsets. He had been involved in many tactical operations in his time, but nothing could remove the tension that always swelled just before the go was given and the FBI's SWAT operatives burst into action.

He glanced across the corridor to Marsh, whose features showed the same anticipation. Whatever their suspicions of a global conspiracy might be, it was looking more and more like they would end up being something for the post-op analysis. Due diligence was prevailing. The bomb would be safely disarmed before the parade even began.

CHAPTER 103

The Tribune Tower, Chicago

With a simple motion of his hand, the SWAT team leader gave the go order and the siege on room SC-118 began.

Once a small steel ram had shattered the latching mechanism, the six-man team poured through the door and into the storeroom. The large space was mostly vacant, though piles of boxes littered the floor in various locations, chiefly along the walls.

They had made their approach silently, giving no cause for immediate alarm to the group inside, but the first thing the team leader noticed was that they were already positioned in a kind of formation. In his immediate field of vision were two men, behind boxes on either side of the door. On the far wall stood another man. He could not see the woman.

The group was prepared to be attacked.

At the first sounds of the team's entrance the two Arab men snapped to alertness at their posts, taking up the fully automatic MP5s they had slung at their sides. They appeared more than ready to die fighting for their cause.

The efficiency of the FBI team was, however, too much for even such dedicated opponents. The ammunition from the agents' M4 carbines pierced through the packing boxes as if they weren't there, cutting through the men on either side. Before the initial push through the door had even ended, both Arabs were dead on the floor, pools of reddening blood seeping slowly from their positions behind the crates.

'Clear right!' one team member shouted. Two men side-stepped to the right, clearing the space behind each pile of boxes.

The team leader kept his gun trained on his man at the far side of the room. It was the street side, and next to the man was a crate, atop which sat what was quite clearly a bomb.

'Right side clear!' came a shout.

'Clear left!'

A duo swept left, mirroring their colleagues' work. 'We still haven't found the woman,' the leader shouted, without removing his gun from the third man.

No sooner had the words left his lips than a scream erupted from a corner to his left. Before he saw the woman's hair, he heard her gun fire: the quick, irregularly patterned explosions of a handheld pistol being discharged as fast as fingers would allow. Every agent in the room gave a practised duck and side-step, transforming themselves into moving targets. The team leader dropped to a squat, still unwilling to let the third man out of his sights.

'Man down!' an agent cried.

'She's in the south-west corner!'

The attention of the team converged on the corner and

the tall stack of crates behind which the woman was installed and continuing to shoot.

Through a series of hand gestures, the team leader conveyed his instructions. Two of the team kept concentrated fire on the boxes from the front, sustaining the continual response of the woman. A third man tended to the agent who had taken a bullet at the shoulder, pulling him out of the line of fire. A fourth quietly stepped to the side, working his way out of sight and to the right.

'It's over! Surrender yourself and throw down your weapon!' one of the agents cried out between volleys of fire.

The woman responded only with a feral, guttural scream and the remaining rounds from her clip. As she reached to her side for another, she heard the last sound her ears would ever take in. From the far side of the room, the hidden SWAT agent fired two rounds in quick succession. The first entered her temple, the second her cheek. The woman's death was instantaneous.

'Clear it!' the man shouted. The agents swept forward, moved around the crates and ensured no one else was present. 'Clear!'

With that confirmation, all attention switched to the third and final man, still standing in his original position next to the device. The team leader stood fully upright. The man's forehead was squarely in his sights.

'Step away from the bomb,' he ordered. The man didn't move. 'Do you speak English? Get away from the bomb, or I'll blow your fucking head off.'

'I speak English,' the man answered. 'You've got it wrong. I'm military.'

The team leader gave a momentary start. *Military?*

'I'm a staff sergeant in the Army.' The man kept his eyes drilled on the agent's.

'I don't care,' the team leader answered. Military or not, he had seen this man enter the building with the other three.

'You've got to understand,' the sergeant continued, beginning to take a step forward. 'I'm ju—'

'Not another move!' The guns of the other agents all rose to attention, each trained on the man.

'I need you to understand that this isn't what you think it is,' the soldier said. He continued his forward motion.

It was then that an agent to his right spotted the handle of a handgun, positioned beneath a bag on a crate just two steps away from the man. The object of his movements was suddenly clear.

'Gun!' the agent cried.

The team leader could not see a weapon, but he did not flinch in his trust for his men. What he could not see, his team could. When the cry came, he squeezed his finger over his trigger, and fired two rounds into the soldier's chest.

Staff Sergeant Paul Johnson, known to his brethren as Ammon, hit the ground only three feet away from the device he had transported halfway around the world.

'That's everyone,' the team leader said a moment later, rushing up to confirm that the man was dead. 'All clear. Bring in the second team.'

The second SWAT unit, together with the pair of explosives experts, poured into the room, Chris Taylor and Laura

Marsh following at their heels. Ted Gallows had already entered.

'Get on the bomb,' Gallows ordered, motioning towards the device as the two experts swept up to it. 'Do whatever it takes to make sure it's disarmed.'

CHAPTER 104

The Coptic Museum, Cairo

The police had arrived at the Coptic Museum only twenty-five minutes after Michael had phoned them. His charge had come at the right time: the group had been so focused on their work that what might have been an unstoppable force for a two-man team had been caught off guard. Their arms had not been at the ready, and they'd given up the remainder after the first two were pointed at their heads.

'You say his name is Marcianus? Or was it Bell?' an inspector asked Emily.

'Both. Arthur Bell must be his actual name, but within his group he identifies as Marcianus.'

'It's taken from the second century,' Michael added, standing alongside his wife, his left arm newly supported in a sling that a medical team had provided before the questioning began. 'A variation of a name in use among the early Gnostics. Bell must have taken it on as a mark of association.'

The Egyptian inspector's brow was raised, as it had been for most of the interview. The majority of details Emily and

Michael shared were utterly strange – keystones, encoded texts, invisible ink, secret names, mystical incantations.

The police were at first as suspicious of Emily and Michael as anyone else in the security-compromised museum, particularly once they saw the crude rope restraints applied to the collection of foreigners in the manuscript room. A check of their backgrounds, however, confirmed them both as respected academics with no records of violence, and the sheer amount of physical torture that Michael's body had borne was enough to convince them that he was a victim rather than a perpetrator.

After twenty minutes of questioning, Emily and Michael were dismissed and the officers' attention turned towards the captured men.

'You've got to call Chris,' Emily said, once they had stepped aside of the others. 'Now.'

'He's been trying to get through to me,' Michael answered. 'He's left half a dozen messages, and I've got twice as many missed calls from his number.' He hadn't had a chance to listen to the messages, but thought it best simply to call Chris directly.

Emily grabbed her own phone and looked at its display. 'Mine, too.' Michael was already dialling.

6,100 miles away, Chris opened his phone with relief. 'Mike! Thank God. You're okay?'

'We're fine, Chris,' Michael answered. 'But it's been a bit of an adventure over here.'

'You're not the only ones.'

Michael pressed forward. 'Listen, Chris, we found Arthur

Bell and his men at the Coptic Museum, just as we suspected. They had to force Emily's cooperation, but—'

'Force?' Chris interrupted, worried.

'She's okay. They used her to complete their decoding. Their target was one of the Nag Hammadi Codices, just as we'd suspected, and it revealed more hidden text. This time, what they uncovered was an incantation.' Michael took a deep breath. 'You were right to be suspicious before, Chris. I couldn't tell you precisely what the incantation means, but it's got all the signs of being a kind of death ritual. Bell is most definitely planning an attack. He specifically mentioned a bomb.'

'Mike, calm down,' Chris finally interrupted. Michael was speaking at a racing pace.

'The threat is real, Chris,' he persisted. 'You've got to act.'

'That's what I'm trying to tell you. We already have.'

The comment finally cut through Michael's warning, and he listened as Chris filled him in on the operations of the past hours – the CCTV footage, the raid on the storage room, the discovery and disarming of the bomb.

'Our explosives experts say it was a fairly simple device, though it would have been deadly. An explosive core wrapped in wire mesh that contained nails, metal scraps, screws, bolts. It would have been carnage.'

'Good God.'

'These shrapnel bombs are a favourite of suicide bombers.' He let out a thorough sigh. 'Our intelligence may have been piecemeal, but the pieces fit together perfectly.'

Michael felt a physical rush of relief, visible to Emily as she listened to the words passing between them.

'The FBI want the two of you over here immediately,' Chris continued. 'Now that the threat has been eliminated the priority is on sorting out the conspiracy that created it. One of the agents here, Laura Marsh, and I have a few suspicions; but we want your take on everything that's happened in Egypt and the UK. Can you fly over tonight? On the Bureau's tab.'

'Absolutely, Chris. Of course.' Michael answered without hesitation. Chris relayed information on a workable flight and a few minutes later they had said their farewells.

Michael turned to Emily. 'They want us in Chicago as fast as we can get there.'

'There's no point in our lingering here,' she answered. Her face conveyed her desire to stay involved. She still wanted to get to the man responsible for Andrew's death.

Michael took her hand in his uninjured arm and they surveyed the scene before them a final time. Marcianus's men remained bound, each being interviewed in turn by the local police.

As they made to leave, Michael caught the gaze of one of the bound men. Something about his expression chilled Michael to his core. The man sat bound and tied, his future incarceration ensured and the larger plot of which he was a part soundly foiled, yet his face looked . . . content, stuck in a strange grin.

As they moved away it became an enormous, satisfied smile.

CHAPTER 105

Downtown Chicago

Evening in downtown Chicago was like an electric version of day. Shops radiated glistening lights, street lamps illuminated everything around them and the glass fronts of the buildings reflected the light like mirrors.

The Italian Leader took in the sight with awe. The crowds in the evenings were almost as active as those of the mid-afternoon retail rush, and there was more noise than usual on this night as city officials continued the process of cordoning off North Michigan Avenue for the morning's parade. The buzz was as electric as the glamorous illumination of the Magnificent Mile itself.

As he passed a wandering glance over the sights surrounding him, the Italian Leader's assistant arrived at his side and they walked slowly, aimlessly, along the street.

'I've just had news,' the assistant said, speaking in soft Italian. 'The American FBI has discovered the device. The four guardians have been killed. The bomb is diffused and in their custody.' He allowed a brief pause to punctuate his words. 'The plot has been foiled.'

The crowds around them were thick, people milling between restaurants, theatres, bars. The Leader allowed both the sights and his assistant's revelations to linger in his attention.

'So,' he finally said, 'everything has gone according to plan?'

The other man did not reply, but a slow smile started to curl his lips.

The Leader gave a nod, affirming the hoped-for news. Then without further words the men parted ways, continued at their casual pace, and disappeared into the crowds.

CHAPTER 106

Ancient Egypt, AD 373

Tarasios hovered over Markus's shoulder, watching as he inscribed the final letter on the page. The young man had worked for over two weeks on the project, and at last the encoded document was complete. The leather cover into which it would be bound was already prepared and sat, as if expectantly, on the table's edge.

Markus gazed on as his mentor revelled in the sight.

'The list's three parts are encoded in those words,' he confirmed. 'If someone has the keystone and knows how to use it, they can reveal the instructions. If they do not, they'll only get my slightly revised version of the Gospel.'

Tarasios nodded. 'It's absolutely perfect.'

Finally, Markus's curiosity got the better of him.

'What is it for?' he asked. 'The incantation. Why is it so precious to you?'

'It is precious to us,' Tarasios corrected him, reminding the younger man that he was a welcome recruit to the Brotherhood's ranks, 'because it gives voice to the truth. What has been hidden away are words for another generation. Words that, when spoken,

open the spirit to reality. *The incantation changes the soul. When it is rent from the body, it finds freedom.*'

'But they're just words,' Markus countered.

Tarasios met his gaze with a look as deep, as wild, as any the younger man had ever seen.

'They are words that have power,' he answered. 'Mystical words.'

He leaned close to his disciple's face.

'They are words that can alter the destiny of man.'

Part Four

WEDNESDAY, JULY 4TH

CHAPTER 107

FBI Field Office, Chicago

On a table covered by bank lighting, lay the device. The bomb had been meticulously disassembled by the explosives experts following a relatively simple disarmament. Laura Marsh, together with Special Agent Chris Taylor and a select group of others that included Deputy Director Dawson and the three section heads, Mayfair, Gallows and Smith, were assembled in the early hours to hear the explosives team's report.

'The arming mechanism was surprisingly simple,' one of the explosives technicians announced to the group. Marsh recognized Karl Jasper. He spoke efficiently and dispassionately, like a school teacher describing a textbook lesson.

'We were able to deactivate the device after only a few minutes. There were no internal redundancies. Looks like it was something they thought they could deliver without threat of intervention.'

'They should have thought a little harder,' the Deputy Director announced. A few of her men gave satisfied, proud grunts of assent.

'What's most important,' the technician continued, 'is that the device conforms to our intelligence almost exactly. We've been on the lookout for the handiwork of a cooperative alliance between Americans and a bona fide Middle Eastern terrorist cell. This fits the bill perfectly.'

Jasper leaned over the table, pointing to various components of the disassembled device as he spoke.

'These structural components are common stock in regional IEDs we've seen more times than we can count. The way they've been fashioned together, with a double-cylindrical centre and metal fencing pegs protruding to support the wire mesh – it's an almost point-for-point match to a number of devices we've recovered in Iraq and Afghanistan. Could almost have been manufactured by the same hands.'

'Could it have come from anywhere else?' asked Brian Smith.

'Possibly, but trace analysis definitively places it in the region. We've got dust on various components,' he indicated with a smear of a finger on a metal plate, 'and from that we can get a good chemical match on the soil, which helps narrow down a geography. There are also the metals used, and so forth. But the most glaring evidence is the writing.'

'The writing?' Marsh queried.

'There are assembly notes handwritten on various components,' the technician answered. He took out a pencil and used it to point to three separate places where small scribbles had been written on metal and plastic elements of the device. 'They're all in standard Arabic.'

The gathered team looked at the device closely, processing the technician's data.

'Lines up with the intel on all counts,' Gallows finally offered.

'A threat that had real substance,' added Mayfair.

'But a threat eliminated,' Smith concluded. *End of story*.

Laura and Chris looked uncomfortably over the senior team that surrounded them. The bomb was no longer a threat, but a threat still remained. Someone in this room had still played the part of a mole, betraying the Bureau. Betraying the people.

Someone was still dirty.

CHAPTER 108

In Flight between Cairo and Chicago

'Relax, Mike,' Emily smiled comfortingly. 'Have another drink. They'll keep them coming as long as you ask.'

She and Michael had settled into adjoining seats in EgyptAir 9231's business-class cabin a little over four hours before, and though the flight had been smooth since departure, neither had been able to rest.

Michael took her advice and ordered another double gin and tonic. His bandaged left hand, kept at chest-height through a tightly applied sling, was a constant source of throbbing pain, muted only slightly by a prescription painkiller that he took in half-doses.

'What is it?' Emily finally asked, watching him squirm. 'Don't tell me you've suddenly developed a fear of flying?'

'No,' he answered, giving her a small smile. 'It's not the flight, Em. It's not even this.' He signalled towards his injured hand. 'It's Cairo. I can't clear my conversation with Chris from my mind.'

The raw ending to their encounter at the museum had left

Michael lingering. They had not been able to catch the fleeing Marcianus, they had not been able to reclaim the stolen text. On top of it all, the sudden end to the threat that was announced through Chris's phone call had thrown Michael off guard.

'What's still troubling you?'

'They found the bomb, that's all well and good,' Michael answered. 'But the specifics of Chris's comments to us are troubling.'

Emily brought her left leg underneath her and turned to face Michael more directly.

'What in particular?'

'It's his description of the bomb. You remember the details?'

'Major explosive wrapped in shrapnel. An ugly thing.'

'Ugly, yes. But as awful as it sounds, it doesn't sound . . . right.'

'*Right?*' Emily hesitated. 'What could be more "right" for a terrorist weapon?'

Michael ran his fingers through his hair, trying to bring his thoughts into order. Then, without warning, he jumped to a different topic altogether. 'You heard the incantation with me, right? When we were tied up and Bell started to read aloud?'

'His "Liberation Incantation"? Of course.'

'Do you *remember* it?' Michael asked. Emily merely nodded.

'Then I'm sorry to have to mimic the request of a madman, Em,' Michael said, 'but I need you to take advantage of that memory of yours.' He reached into his carry-on bag and a

417

moment later handed her a paper and pen. 'I need you to write down every word you heard.'

Emily handed Michael back his sheet of paper five minutes later, covered with her recollection of the opening lines of the 'Liberation Incantation' that Bell/Marcianus had read aloud as it was revealed on the pages of the ancient Nag Hammadi codex.

'That's everything I can recall,' she said. 'I think it should be pretty close to the original, assuming that his translator was doing his work accurately.' The event had burned its way into her mind with dramatic clarity.

Michael snatched up the page and began to pore over each line. Emily watched as his eyes grew wider, then narrowed as he read and reread phrase after phrase.

'Come on, Mike, what is it?' she finally asked.

Michael didn't look up as he spoke. 'I'm not sure, but the details Chris relayed to us, and my reading of this text . . . the two just don't feel like they fit together.'

Emily could only continue her expectant look.

'Here it is,' Michael suddenly blurted out. He set the paper on the drinks tray between their seats and pointed towards a section of Emily's handwriting. 'Read that bit aloud for me.'

Emily leaned into the page and did as he instructed.

'Ignorance has brought about terror and fear,
And fear became a dense fog that none was able to see.
Because of this, error became strong.'

She looked up at Michael, her face a question mark. 'I don't understand. The text is mystical in tone, but doesn't have anything to do with a bomb.'

'Just keep reading,' Michael pointed her back to the text.

> 'Yet truth shall burst forth a great, new light,
> And as fog fills the sky, so our fire will burn the air
> And lungs, the eyes and heart –
> Each breath a death and gateway to life.'

'There,' Michael stopped her. 'You see?'

She didn't, and her expression telegraphed that fact with clarity.

'Concentrate on the imagery, Em. The incantation is describing a great, cataclysmic event, just as Bell suggested. The "bursting forth of a great light". That might easily refer to a bomb.'

'Okay,' Emily hesitantly affirmed. 'I can see it. I'm with you so far.'

'But listen to what the text describes the effect of that light to be: "Our fire will burn the air, and lungs, the eyes and heart. Each breath a death and gateway to life." Tell me, Em, do those sound like the effects of exploding shrapnel to you?'

She hesitated. 'No. For that, I would expect images of carnage, of torn flesh, dismemberment.'

'Right, but here we have totally different imagery. The incantation talks about breath, fog and wind. It sounds more like a poison, or a gas.'

Emily looked back down at her transcription of the

Liberation Incantation. The lines that came a little later seemed to confirm Michael's point.

> *'Our light shall burn as fire and be carried upon the breath!*
> *Each inhalation the gasp of liberating separation.'*

'This "Marcianus" and his group are obsessed with bringing to life their interpretation of this ancient mantra,' Michael offered when she was done. 'My guess is that its authors never intended anything like what he's been planning, but this text is his guiding document all the same. If his followers were intending to unleash a device on Chicago that fulfils *this* imagery, how would that have been accomplished with a bomb that functions in an entirely different way?'

Now it was Emily who needed a drink, and she reached over to Michael's tray, grabbed the remainder of his gin and tonic and threw it down the back of her throat.

'And then,' Michael added, his voice taking on a different tone, 'there was the farewell glance I received from one of Bell's men in Cairo. Just as we were exiting the museum.'

'He said something to you?'

'No, there were no words. It was only his expression. I'd had my telephone conversation with Chris close by; he must have overheard it.'

'And?'

'And he looked . . . content.' Michael remembered the man's facial expressions with a crystal perfection worthy of Emily's eidetic memory. 'And then he looked all but happy.'

All at once, the combination of factors came together in

Michael's mind. His skin went clammy, and he gripped the armrest as he turned to Emily.

'Em, I don't think the bomb they discovered in Chicago is the real bomb at all.'

'Chris seemed to believe it was real enough,' she protested weakly.

'No,' Michael answered, 'it can't have been. That bomb would have been hell, but what Bell is really planning, it's . . . it's . . .'

His words faltered. The words on the page started to flash as images in his mind. *Fire that burns the air. Burns the lungs, the heart. Every breath a death. Every inhalation a gasp.*

He reached across the armrest and grasped Emily's hand, squeezing hard, his face pale.

'I know exactly what he's planning to do.'

CHAPTER 109

Central Chicago

By a delicate candlelight, Cerinthus engaged in the final acts of preparation that would lead to his greatest work. There were electrical lights in his basement workroom, but for this he chose the natural, mystical illumination of bare flame. He worked slowly, deliberately, with long breaths attached to the words of the Truth Incantation which he chanted to himself one final time.

'We are come to proclaim what is, and what was, and what will be.'

He took up the vest in agile fingers, inspecting the linked series of vials that were sewn all around the exterior surface of the thin fabric. His eyes knowingly checked each for the tightness of its fastening, ensuring none were loose.

'We are come that man might understand the invisible world beyond that which is seen.'

His body swayed gently as he worked, the combination of sight and words overwhelming his senses.

He gently, carefully, turned the vest inside out. The interior was covered in thin blocks of C4, sewn into the lining. Cerinthus checked the wiring that ran through each block, ensured that the power source was connected and the battery pack fully charged.

> '*He who is ignorant is deficient*
> *And his deficiency is his terrible ruin.*'

He inverted the vest again, returning it to its proper configuration. Then, standing lithely, Cerinthus slid it over his shoulders and onto his torso. He fastened the four buckles he had sewn onto the front. The vest was light. A cord dangled from the right side with a trigger switch at its end.

The twenty-five vials of toxic chemicals would cling close to his chest, hidden from view until that moment when they were unleashed on the masses. The death they would bring would be agonizing, tormenting, except of course to those who were prepared for release from this physical world – prepared by the sacred words that had finally been disclosed and which would be on the lips of the Brotherhood's great assembly. Their end would be peaceful, liberating, free.

The FBI contact had already called with the final check-in. '*The diversion continues,*' the report had come. '*I'll carry on making sure they do not see what's really in front of them. Ensuring you are free to act will be my final offering.*'

Cerinthus's heart was now entirely at peace. He had

witnessed the end of all things. Now he would witness the birth of true life.

> 'For the ignorant world lacks that which would make it
>   perfect –
> But this we shall give.'

In reverent tones, he added his personal modification to the ancient text.

'No, this *I* shall give.'

Cerinthus stood, and walked towards the door.

CHAPTER 110

O'Hare International Airport, Chicago

Cardinal O'Dowd stepped off the jetway into the bustling arrivals terminal of O'Hare. The flight had been short, but he was still grumpy. Chicago was the last place he wanted to be.

'If you're not going to smile, Eminence, at least try not to glare.' His assistant, Mary, carried the small duffel that was more than they would require for the brief visit. The Cardinal carried his own briefcase.

'This is a waste of my time,' he answered back, his face retaining its displeasure. 'You know I hate these things. Politics and Church, they don't mix.'

'Extra crowns in heaven for your long suffering,' Mary answered back sarcastically.

At last the prelate smiled, but the good Catholic humour did little to ease his annoyance. Harmony dinners, fellowship marches, or the Chicago Governor's 'unity procession' – they all amounted to pointless political games. The fact that Governor Wilson was so insistent made the Cardinal dread the political nature of this event all the more. Two calls from a state governor in as many days. Ever since he'd confirmed that he would, in the end, be able to participate in the parade, he'd been given bizarrely attentive treatment. *Most unexpected.*

'There's that scowl again,' Mary snapped, observing his drooping features. 'Do try to be sociable. You're a special guest. Try to look a little less like you'd rather be delivering your own last rites.'

Cardinal O'Dowd merely sighed, then quickened his pace through the terminal. With any luck, he could be out of the city again before suppertime.

CHAPTER 111

FBI Field Office, Chicago

Chris sat awkwardly on the small settee in Laura Marsh's office. Both had taken in the tangible sense of relief that permeated the Chicago office, though tensions still remained understandably high. That tension was nowhere higher than in Marsh's office.

Following the climax of the previous evening's assault and taking of the bomb, Chris's mind had lingered in a sustained way on the arc of details of the operation, from its beginning to its end. An undefined discomfort he had felt since his arrival began to take definable form.

Chris had been in intelligence long enough to be innately suspicious of any scenario that played out too smoothly. His experience of real-world enemies was that they were just as complex, conniving and disorganized as real-world friendlies, and engaging with them was always an act of trial and error, false stops and starts, hard-and-fast fact mixed with guesswork and chance. The experiences of the past thirty-six hours, however, bore very different markings. They had gone

– Chris almost hesitated even to think the word – *smoothly*.

A, B, C, D . . . all in nice order, each detail confirming every other, Chris thought to himself. *It's far too neat and tidy.*

Across the office, seated behind her desk, Laura Marsh's thoughts followed a not dissimilar track. There was still the unanswered question of the second strand of the Church of Truth in Liberation's international activity. The bomb confirmed everything the FBI had discovered about the group's Middle Eastern connections, but they still could not account for its apparently unconnected European activities.

And there's still the matter of Lewis. His death was a constant reminder of the presence of a traitor.

'The mole,' Laura suddenly blurted out. 'We still have to sort out the leak in the Division.' She looked across her desk into Chris's eyes, already alert and nodding his agreement. 'That we found the bomb doesn't rid us of the fact of Agent Lewis's murder. Our list of suspects still hasn't been resolved.'

'Smith was at the top,' Chris answered. 'He was pushing you away from your investigation early on, and his comments at the post-op this morning were insistent. It's like he was trying to hammer home that the whole case has been wrapped up and finished.'

'You think he's capable of murder?'

'You think he isn't?' Chris shot her a probing look. Once treason entered into a game, the stakes quickly went high – and high costs had to be met.

'But why Special Agent Smith, or any of the rest of them

for that matter, would want to cut short Lewis's investigation, I still can't figure that piece out,' Chris confessed. 'The plot by that stage was local. What were they trying to prevent him from finding?'

'Anything beyond the Middle East line was shrugged off. It was push for that, and nothing else.'

Chris reflected a moment, then asked, 'Which, specifically, were the regions being ignored?'

'I have reason to believe we should have been tracing out Italy,' Laura answered immediately, 'where the phone had come from that was used in the local call to confirm the video's release. And Germany, where that phone had been registered. And France, and –' Laura clicked a few keys on her laptop and opened the email she had sent herself the day before, containing the listing of SMS recipients Agent Lewis had tracked to Church members, '– and we have the text-messaging activity of the group's members to numbers in Spain, Greece, even Macedonia. The list is extensive.'

'But it's also incomplete,' Chris replied. Laura lifted a brow.

'What do you mean?'

'You haven't mentioned Egypt.'

Marsh turned back to the computer and scanned over the listing. Egypt was not among the country codes of the numbers Lewis had assembled. 'It's not here.'

'But it *is* a country connected to the Church of Truth in Liberation, through its leader, Arthur Bell. It's where I met the man.' He locked his eyes on Laura's.

'And of the Division's three section heads, there's only one I told about that encounter.'

429

Marsh stared back. She had resisted before, but suddenly Chris's earlier instinct seemed impossible to deny.

Chris sat back in his chair. 'I think we've narrowed our list of potential moles down to one.'

An unexpected knock on Marsh's office door broke the silence that followed Chris's comment. Deputy Director Dawson twisted the knob and entered.

'Special Agents Marsh, Taylor. I need you to—' She cut herself off as she saw the troubled expressions on both their faces. 'What is it?'

Before they could answer their solitude was interrupted yet again, this time by the electronic notes of the *Navy Blue and Gold*. Chris felt the mobile phone in his pocket start to vibrate and slid his hand to extract it.

The ID displayed a cryptic source for the number: 'EGYPTAIR IN FLIGHT.' Chris gave a mild start. Michael was on a flight at this very moment. The call could only be from him. He knew he had to answer and raised an apologetic hand to the Deputy Director, indicating its importance.

Chris held the phone to his ear. 'Buddy,' he said calmly, trying to keep the gravity of his expression off the line. 'How close are you to arrival? We need you and Emily here in the office now.'

'We're on our way,' Michael answered. 'But this couldn't wait. We have a serious problem.'

CHAPTER 112

Central Chicago

Marcianus stood proudly on the wooden platform at the centre of the temple. All around him the brethren from every region of the globe assembled. There were so many expressions, mouths speaking so many languages, so many skin tones and builds. The temple now contained countless heritages and backgrounds, lineages ancient and diverse.

All of them superfluous, the Great Leader mused. *All of them so soon to be transcended. The common spirit will be set free. We will be one.*

Surveying the gathering, he wondered a moment whether they were truly ready. Would they be able to manage the action to come – to embrace the tearing away from the physical that true liberation really required?

As he beheld their expressions, the anticipation in their gestures, Marcianus knew that they would. He watched as they shook out their velvet robes, casting their other baggage into piles spaced throughout the warehouse. Worldly things were no longer required. They had been necessary en route in order to maintain the ruse of ordinary, unpresuming travel; but now that they were here the brethren could cast them aside.

All that the members kept with them was a small rucksack here, a backpack there, an oversized handbag or briefcase, their robes and cinctures folded loosely inside.

And in their hands, the words of freedom. Marcianus's closest aides were distributing photocopies of the Liberation Incantation now, handing a page to every member of the Brotherhood. *We will speak our words together, and enter into eternity.*

He took up the original translation his men had made in Cairo, folded it carefully, and slid it into his breast pocket. He wanted it close to his heart.

Stooping down, he added a loudspeaker to his bag and zipped it closed. Outside, the sun shone brightly.

CHAPTER 113

FBI Field Office, Chicago

'What sort of problem?' Chris raised a hand, alerting Dawson and Marsh to the nature of the call.

'Hold on, Mike, I'm going to switch you to speaker.' He removed the small mobile from his ear, clicked the speaker-phone button and set it on Marsh's desk. 'I'm here with the head of our Field Office, Deputy Director Angela Dawson, and Special Agent Laura Marsh. You can speak openly with both of them.' He turned towards Dawson. 'This is Michael Torrance, a close friend who, along with his wife, tracked Arthur Bell to Cairo yesterday and nearly had the man in custody.'

Dawson's expression shifted instantaneously. She had been informed that Torrance and Wess might have intelligence critical to their post-operational investigation, but this was the first that her teams had told her of any direct encounter with the sect's leader.

'Why didn't I know about this?'

'I'll explain that in a minute,' Chris answered, glancing

towards Laura. 'Right now, Michael's en route to us, calling mid-flight.'

Michael's anxious voice crackled out of the speaker. 'We tracked Bell, whom we now know also goes by Marcianus, to the Coptic Museum in Old Cairo. They've uncovered a new text, a kind of Gnostic chant that Bell called the "Liberation Incantation". Emily and I think his group believes it to have a mystical power over the moment of death, providing a kind of freedom to their souls and releasing them into the spiritual realm.'

'Shit,' Dawson muttered. '"Liberating souls from matter".' She quoted the words that the FBI's anthropological specialist had used to describe Gnostic aims.

'Bell intends to enact this incantation publicly, with a large audience.' The voice coming through the phone was now Emily's. 'His tone when he described his aims, it was . . . vengeful. I think a kind of secondary goal is to show the world just how little physical life really matters. And especially religious life. To this man, religion itself is deluded. His truth is the only reality, everyone else is preaching lies. He seems intent on making a statement with his death – in the moment of his "liberation" to take out as many emblems of religion as he can.'

'If that's his aim,' Marsh interjected, processing the details, 'it fits with his choice of location. There will be thousands at today's parade, including the nation's largest contingent of religious leaders.'

'Bell specifically mentioned disrupting Governor Wilson's "Unity Procession",' Emily added.

Chris leaned towards the speakerphone. 'But he can't do that, not now, Emily. We found the bomb his group had planted for the parade. It's disarmed and disassembled. His run is over.'

On the plane, Michael grabbed the phone back from his wife, the pain from his injuries matched only by his level of urgency. 'That's where the problem lies. Emily and I heard Bell reciting parts of his incantation, and we're convinced they're orientated to something else.'

'Else?' The Deputy Director's face betrayed her concern. 'What else?'

'It speaks of creating a mass of death, but uses the imagery of breath and inhalation. In short, they're images of inhaling some kind of poison.'

From the aircraft, Emily leaned into the phone. 'Our suspicion is that the bomb you found is not their genuine weapon. I'm not sure what its role was in their greater plot, but it may have simply been a distraction.'

Stunned silence was the only response she received. It lingered long, until finally it was broken by Dawson.

'That sounds incredibly unlikely,' the Deputy Director answered, though not without her mind still considering the facts. 'Let's not forget that it was guarded by four of their group, all of whom defended it with their lives. That's a long way to go for a distraction.'

Laura's mind was racing. 'Hold on a second,' she interjected. 'This is where my own investigation has me suspicious about the same things. The data that led us to the Tribune Tower wasn't our only strand of intelligence.'

'But it was accurate,' the Deputy Director countered. 'It led us right to their bomb.'

'*Exactly*. Right to it. As if we were being deliberately . . .' Marsh let her voice trail off. It came back to her with full force. 'That's precisely what Scott Lewis meant.'

'You got a lead from Lewis?' Dawson asked.

'His final note was that the Middle Eastern connections looked like details that "wanted to be found". Like someone was leading us on.'

'Whoever this Lewis is, it sounds like he came to the same conclusion as us,' Michael announced. 'Maybe Bell knew the FBI would be looking into them and needed a way to give you something to follow, to keep you at bay. His group concocts some fabricated Middle Eastern motivated, anti-American attack that they know will draw your attention—'

'While they pursue their real intentions through their own networks in Europe and here in the States.' Marsh finished the thought for him. Finally, all the intelligence was making sense.

'Then they lead you to discover their dupe bomb, causing you to believe the threat is foiled. Meanwhile, they're able to ready themselves for their real attack.'

There was a long, silent pause as the Deputy Director pondered what she'd heard.

'How the hell did we get this far,' she finally asked, her voice tense, 'and not know more about this?'

'But we did,' Marsh answered. 'That's what Special Agent Taylor and I were discussing when you entered the room. The Church of Truth in Liberation has an inside man here at the

FBI. A man who knew about the connection to Cairo, and a man I firmly believe killed Agent Lewis in order to silence his investigation.'

When the name came, it was announced by Marsh and Taylor together. 'Special Agent Ted Gallows.'

CHAPTER 114

FBI Field Office, Chicago

'He's one of our finest section leaders!' Angela Dawson's shock was palpable. 'I've worked with him for years. And you want to mark him a, a *traitor?*'

'We've been considering multiple options,' Chris clarified. 'Anyone higher than Marsh on the food chain. That list has been short, but it's included Ted Gallows, Alan Mayfair, Brian Smith and . . .' He hesitated.

Dawson's glare narrowed. She stared straight into Chris's eyes. 'And me,' she completed the listing for him.

Chris said nothing, only meeting her stare.

'You had to have been looking at me. If you think there was a mole that high on the totem pole, then I would have been a candidate.' Her eyes bore more deeply into Chris's, awaiting confirmation.

'That's right,' he finally affirmed, speaking slightly more softly.

'How do you know I shouldn't still be at the top of your list?'

'Everything points to Gallows,' Chris answered. He listed the details that had convinced both Marsh and himself, the Deputy Director taking them in, almost motionless.

'It's all circumstantial. Merely suspicion,' she finally said.

'There was also the SWAT operation yesterday,' Laura objected. 'Gallows was on the ground with the first team and led them right to the room where the bomb was located. It was as if he knew where he was going. It fits with a plan to lead us astray by guiding us to a dupe device.'

They awaited a reply. Dawson paced the room, scanning the floor blankly as her mind computed the information.

When at last she stopped her pacing and spoke, her tone was determined.

'Charges like this aren't to be built on hearsay, and internal staff investigations are well above either of your pay grades.' She stared into each of their faces, her features an indistinguishable blur of accusatory, angry, and concerned.

A moment later, her expression changed. She had made her decision.

'Dammit, it's enough to call him in for questioning. And if you're right, there's no time for a normal investigation before we do it. We'll bring him in, see what he knows. Immediately.'

'Where is he now?' Laura asked, her relief palpable.

'In the field, leading one of the final routine crowd sweeps before the parade begins. I've assigned all our teams to standard grids along the route.'

'Then we need to get out there as well.' Chris was already moving towards the door.

'I'll relay commands to all the ground teams on the new

threat,' Dawson said, moving towards the phone on Laura's desk. 'Our primary target now is some form of dirty bomb. Focus on the most concentrated areas in the crowd: squares, hubs of onlookers. Wherever a released toxin could affect the largest number.'

'As well as a location with ample public coverage,' Marsh added. 'Emily and Michael said that Bell was insistent on the world seeing him obliterate the bulk of its religious leaders. It suggests they'll try to find a place with ample television crews around.'

'Take the central square,' Dawson noted. 'The two of you focus on Gallows. I'll have the full contingent of ground teams sweep for the device.' She paused, the words escaping her lips sounding surreal. 'If Gallows has been involved all along, he'll be involved at the end.'

'We'll get to him as fast as we can,' Chris answered. He waited for Laura to reach his side and they left her office together.

At the desk, Angela Dawson lifted the phone and ordered the switchboard to connect her to her men on the ground.

CHAPTER 115

Downtown Chicago

The moment they were clear of the airport and nestled into the back of a Chicago yellow cab, Michael and Emily phoned Chris.

'We're in the city,' Michael said as the line connected, his voice brisk. 'Tell us where you want us to go.'

'As far away as possible,' Chris answered. 'Dawson was convinced by your theory and ours. All the FBI teams, together with the local PD, have been instructed to look for a portable dirty bomb or chemical device. As much as we're going to need your help for the debrief, Mike, downtown Chicago is not the place to be right now.'

'Our leaving isn't an option, Chris.' Emily's squeeze on Michael's shoulder communicated her agreement. 'We have too much invested.'

'No way in hell,' Chris's tone was unbending. 'A device like that goes off in a crowd like this . . . no one lives through it. Not with this many, so close together.'

'Chris, we—'

'It's not happening, Mike! You and Emily head for the Bureau office. I'll call you when this is over.'

Before Michael could answer, Chris had cut the line, the conversation finished.

Michael looked over to Emily. 'He's worried about our safety. Doesn't want us anywhere near the action. He wouldn't even tell me where he was going.'

There was a moment of quiet between them. Then, shifting in her seat, Emily turned to face the driver.

'Where is this morning's parade going to draw the biggest crowds?'

The man thought over the question. 'That'd likely be the Watertower Plaza, I'd think. Big space. Always fills right on up.'

Emily turned to Michael, reached out and took his hand, and squeezed.

'Then that's where we need to go,' she said to the driver. 'Get us as close as you can.'

CHAPTER 116

The Magnificent Mile, Chicago

Cerinthus walked through the milling crowds, his steps light, as if he were only half-touching the earth. The masses of people in the pre-revelry atmosphere of the parade's beginnings created an ethereal backdrop. He felt his senses heightened: he noticed the crispness of the morning air, the bright light of the sky, the vivid and shimmering facades of the buildings. For an instant he was back in his tattered youth with all its degradation, its loneliness, its sorrows; then he was redeemed, restored, about to reach into the sacred future.

He continued walking towards the pre-ordained location. As his steps pressed forward, gentle footfall after gentle footfall, he rubbed his hands along the surface of the shirt that lay lightly over the vest hidden beneath. His fingers danced over the future.

At the parade's staging grounds on Lower Michigan Avenue, the Reverend J. Barry Packard scanned over the faces of the assembling religious entourage. The front acts of the parade were already past the starting mark and making their way down the jubilant Magnificent Mile: a fire truck carrying the symbolic opening flag followed by a marching band from East Chicago Central High School.

The Unity Procession would march at the centre of the parade, forming its heart. This was an intentional symbolism: the faiths of the nation united at the heart of the rally for national spirit. Governor Aaron Wilson's staff had thought through every dimension of the spectacle, ensuring that it exceeded the expectations anyone might set for a symbolic religious gathering. This would be one of the greatest showings of religious unity in modern day America, and the world.

Packard was surrounded by his fellow religious leaders. Many of the faces were familiar: there was his rabbi friend, Veniamin. A few bodies over was the elaborately dressed Roman Catholic Cardinal from Washington DC, who looked none too pleased to be there. *Probably views it as a PR obligation*, Packard pondered. *But at least he's shown up. That's all that really matters.*

He wondered how many of the assembled leaders, who amounted to nearly seventy-five men and women, knew what it was they were really here for. Only a few, like he, were secretly a part of the Brotherhood's Elect. The rest were wholly ignorant of the fact that their procession had nothing to do with demonstrating religious unity and everything to do with destroying the pointless myth of worldly belief. That they were actors on set for the final act of the world's ignorant spiritual delusion.

Good riddance to the lot of them.

Packard fiddled with the small bag he carried at his side.

His robe was folded within, his cincture ready to be tied around it.

At last, at the head of the group, a push of black-suited security officers signalled the arrival of the Governor: the man who had organized the entire event. The very man who had sold the nation on the need for a demonstration of religious tolerance in which he himself hadn't the slightest interest.

'Welcome, gentlemen and ladies,' he said, shouting to be heard across the assembly. 'I'm so very glad you could be here. What we do today, the whole world will see.' He gave a beautiful smile to the crowd of religious leaders, who smiled back.

Stepping aside and taking up his place for the start of their march, Governor Wilson straightened his suit and stood tall. The Reverend J. Barry Packard noticed his proud demeanour. He also noticed the duffel bag his aide carried at his side. A bag that looked exactly like Packard's own.

CHAPTER 117

The Magnificent Mile, Chicago

The cab now two blocks behind them, Emily and Michael were at as close to a full run as they could manage in the dense crowd. Michael's injuries continued to restrict his speed and motion, and Emily attempted to keep a step ahead of him, shoving aside the parade-goers so they wouldn't slam into his injured arm. The same crowd tugged at Emily's conscience. There were so many faces, unassuming and unaware. Children clung to their fathers' shoulders; a mother offered a bottle to a baby; a teenage couple stood locked in an almost pornographic embrace, taking the parade as a welcome excuse to get away with publicly displaying their unrestrained affection. Hot dogs were in hand, plastic flags flapping from enthusiastic wrists.

So much happiness. Innocence. None of them aware of the terror that was so close by.

The intersection of East Pearson and North Michigan was a main hub of activity, and there was very little space not filled by the mob. It was only Chris Taylor's peculiarly focused behaviour that enabled them to spot him. He was scanning the crowd, his head moving in long arcs across the whole, vast space, seeking some unknown target. A female counterpart followed suit, only a few paces away.

'Over here,' Emily yelled, tugging at Michael's shoulder, keeping him close. 'That must be Laura Marsh.' The woman beside Chris was obviously fit, and just as obviously anxious. She was pressed almost to Chris's side, the two of them dividing the surveillance of the square.

Emily and Michael dodged through the crowd to make their way towards them.

'The hell are the two of you doing here?' Chris spurted out, clearly stunned to see them. 'I told you to stay away!'

'And I told you we had too much invested in this not to be here.' Michael held Chris's gaze. 'We know it's dangerous.'

It was then that Chris noticed Michael's bandaged arm and scabbed face. The encounter with Bell in Cairo had clearly been more physical than Michael had shared on the phone.

There was no time, or point, in protesting further. They were here. Chris looked to Emily, then back at Michael.

'All our men are on the ground. They're on watch for anything that might be the kind of device the two of you described. But it's one helluva project.'

The magnitude of the sweep was fully apparent from where they stood. There were thousands, even tens of thousands, in the streets. Buildings reached skyward on all sides. The device could be anywhere. Emily's mind reeled.

'Our teams are sweeping as thoroughly as they can,' Laura added, 'but our immediate task is that man. Ted Gallows.' She raised an arm and pointed across the busy street. On the far side, a jacketed Special Agent was surveying the masses, speaking to a partner at his side. His gaze was professional and diligent.

'He's the agent we've determined is the internal link to Bell's group. If anyone knows what's about to go down, it's him. We've been monitoring his gestures, watching for any contacts in the crowd. He's got to know who else in this melee is part of the group.'

Laura was cut off by the sudden arrival of another woman, who stepped through a wall of bodies and joined the huddle.

'Deputy Director,' she acknowledged.

'It's time for your surveillance to stop,' the woman ordered. 'The religious procession is making its way into the plaza. Get Gallows in hand immediately. We can't let him interact with anyone in the procession.'

Chris kept the Deputy Director's gaze. 'We need you with us. Laura and I are his juniors. He'll pull rank to keep us back.'

The woman pondered the comment only a moment. 'Fine. We'll take him together.'

She stepped forward briskly, pushing past a fence barrier and into the street itself, Chris and Marsh immediately following.

Michael tried to push forward and follow, but Emily held him at bay.

'Let them go.' Her expression was forceful. Michael stared back quizzically, but did not interject.

As the FBI team moved off, Chris turned back and tossed him a radio. 'Stay in touch with this. You spot anything suspicious, let us know.' Without another word, Chris, Marsh and Dawson pushed across the street towards Gallows's position.

Michael turned to Emily, his face a puzzle.

'Why wouldn't you let me follow? You think we're going to be any safer here than twenty feet over there?'

'It's not our safety I'm concerned about,' Emily answered, 'it's everyone's.'

CHAPTER 118

The Magnificent Mile, Chicago

Marcianus at last came to the spot where his life would culminate. A concrete plinth along the roadside, towards the centre of the large public square, would allow him enough height to be seen over the sea of bodies.

He sensed the greatness of the moment. For all that the deluded woman in Egypt had taunted him for despising history, he knew that at this very moment history was finding its culmination. The work of ages was about to be fulfilled.

Marcianus deposited his bag at his feet, then reached down and unzipped its top. Subconsciously he passed a hand over his chest, feeling to ensure that the paper containing the Liberation Incantation was still in his pocket. As his hand descended along his side, he felt the knife sheathed at his hip. With the arrangements they had made, the chances of being intercepted were all but non-existent. The kabar, which had belonged to Mustafa Aqmal, was a personal memento. A reminder that costs had been required in Marcianus's sacred work, but that all was now being fulfilled.

Across the plaza, he spotted his close brother: a true Knower who had been with him through the planning of their entire work. He stood watch now, his eyes affixed to the Great Leader, awaiting the signal.

Marcianus took a deep, slow breath, closing his eyes.

When he opened them, he gave a firm nod to the brother, his palm flat on his chest.

The final signal was sent.

Without hesitation the brother turned and passed the signal to another man, stood at a distance across the street. The man in turn passed it to another, and then another, and in a matter of seconds the signal spidered throughout the massive crowd – a chain reaction sweeping across the densely packed grounds.

CHAPTER 119

The Magnificent Mile, Chicago

Emily and Michael were now surrounded by the crowd, and Emily's gaze passed frenetically from one person to the next as she moved, Michael at her side. She paired the task of searching for anything that might amount to the sect's device, with a preoccupation with sorting out how they intended to bring together their incantation and the outrage meant to follow it.

The end result they're seeking may be liberation, her mind raced, *the freeing of spirit from matter. But they still have to recite the incantation first. They can't just blow off their bomb without some sort of recitation.*

Assuming there's only one bomb. Her stomach tightened. If there was more than one . . .

Suddenly, she eyed a man with a strange, misfitting poncho that hung loosely over his frame. Emily's eyes were suspicious: there could easily be a bomb beneath – but in a sudden fit of patriotism the strange man raised both arms high above him in a cheer, revealing nothing but a Chicago Bears jersey underneath.

452

Emily's eyes went back to darting over the crowd.

Bell wants his group's 'departure' to be visible, and wants the crowd to see what's happening – to know what's going on, before he takes them out. That can't happen if they aren't drawn into the action. The incantation can't be a private affair. It won't be the members just reciting it to themselves.

Another suspicious man, this time sat atop a large picnic cooler. *Too large*, came Emily's first reaction. She veered towards the man, but even as she stepped closer he rose, opened the cooler, and extracted a canned drink from a nest of ice and identical cans. Emily steered away, dragging Michael with her. He, too, scanned the crowd diligently.

The recitation needs to become a focal point. They need to draw attention to themselves. Then will come the words, and then, then . . .

She didn't allow her thoughts to continue. If they couldn't stop Bell's Brotherhood before they finished their public recitation of the incantation, what would come next would be suffering and death on a massive scale. In such a densely populated milieu, even a poorly designed chemical weapon would yield thousands of casualties. And somehow, Emily did not believe Bell's group would have gone for a poor design.

It was then that a strange flash of dark colour at the corner of her vision caught Emily's attention. Turning, she watched as a diminutive woman, strangely frozen in her tracks, pulled a long velvet robe from her rucksack and began wrapping it around herself. A white rope dangled from her hand, and once the robe was in place she affixed it as a belt.

Then, just beyond her, a taller man, similarly frozen in his place, removing an identical robe.

Emily's skin started to go cold.

She turned on the balls of her feet. Behind her she could see three more people, all removing identical garments and robing themselves in the midst of the vast crowd. She turned again. Two more, then three. As she spun her vision around the great plaza, velvet robes appeared all around her, nearby as well as deeper into the fray. Tens, then dozens. More than she could count.

My God. She swallowed hard. *It's happening right now.*

CHAPTER 120

The Magnificent Mile, Chicago

Ascending the concrete plinth, Marcianus took up his final position. He stood a good three feet taller than the crowd, his velvet robe wrapped around his body, tightened at his waist with the white cincture.

As he looked down on the masses his heart raced. For the first time in history, they were fully in the public eye. The open space was their new temple.

The Brotherhood, revealed in the light of day at long last.

At the far edge of the plaza, the religious entourage began to appear. The denizens of fallen religion poured into the square, surrounded by their mindless followers. Perfectly timed. Marcianus could clearly see the Governor, and a few steps behind, Reverend Packard. The Brotherhood's two followers within the assembly, who had ensured that it came together. They each had bags in hand, and each were already beginning to dig into them. In a moment, they would be robed with their fellow brethren.

Marcianus picked up the loudspeaker and switched it on.

With a sense of power, he unfolded the white sheet of paper on which the precious words were written. In the crowd, every member of the Brotherhood began to do the same.

The strange actions of so many parade-goers were now attracting the attention of others in the crowd. Dark velvet robes speckled the entire square. Little children who had moments ago been enrapt with floats and dancers, were now pointing questioningly at the people all around them, dressed in strange garments. A marching band that had been perfectly in synch began to falter as first its chief drummer, then student after student in its ranks, fell away from the music, captivated by the bizarre sight. The faces in the crowd were mixed: some were amused, thinking the spectacle was a staged event, an unadvertised addition to the morning's entertainments. Others were starting to look worried, unsure what to make of the peculiar interruption.

But all seemed compelled to watch what was happening. Thousands of eyes scrutinized the strangers, and those eyes followed their gazes to the man atop the concrete block.

Marcianus glanced at his page, then cast it into the breeze. He had read the incantation a hundred times during his flight. Every word was clear in his memory. He needed no text, only to speak.

He raised the loudspeaker to his lips. In booming voice, he spoke the ancient song, joined by countless others.

'O world, behold! I will reveal to you my mysteries! For you are my fellow brethren, and now you shall know the All.

We are knowledge, we are ignorance;
We are shame and boldness.
We are shameless, we are ashamed;
We are strength and we are fear –
We are war and peace: give heed!'

CHAPTER 121

The Magnificent Mile, Chicago

Emily yanked the radio from Michael's pocket, but the unfamiliar device was more complicated than time allowed. She swapped it for her BlackBerry and located Chris's number, clasping the phone to her ear.

'Chris!' Emily rushed her words. 'It's happening right now.'

'Godssakes, I know that, Emily,' Chris answered back. His voice was clipped and anxious. 'We're steps away from taking Gallows.'

'Not your mole, Chris, the attack! Mike and I are in the middle of the plaza. All around us, men and women in the crowd are robing themselves in identical garments. *Ceremonial* garments.' Sect members were now in their attire on all sides. 'They're everywhere, Chris. There's no more time. They're beginning to recite their incantation.'

Across the square, Chris's eyes went wide. He shouted forward to Dawson and Marsh.

'It's starting!' They spun to face him. 'Emily and Michael

458

are in the middle of the square,' Chris continued. 'Bell's group are beginning their mantra.'

Even as he said the words, the group of FBI agents could see individuals in the nearby ranks of the crowd donning velvet robes, as if sparked into action by some unseen command.

They were only feet away from Ted Gallows. At Chris's exclamation, the Special Agent turned, his brow raised in surprise to see them all so close to his location. When he heard Chris's remarks, his eyes scanned over the crowd and he beheld the same sight as the other agents.

Chris pushed towards him. Gallows would have to be taken quickly, and then . . .

Suddenly, his gaze fell on something else.

'Shit, look up!' he shouted, extending an arm and pointing across the crowd – and high above it. The heads of his colleagues, including Gallows himself, swung around to face what he'd spotted.

'There, cresting the top of the Old Water Tower. Right at the peak!' Chris thundered his words. In seconds, they saw what he saw.

A man stood atop the tall tower which rose like a Gothic stone spike in the midst of the parade. Far above the revellers, the man moved slowly and deliberately.

In a smooth motion, he removed the light T-shirt from his chest.

Beneath it was a vest. Even from their distance far below, the FBI agents could see it was covered in vials and explosives.

They had found their dirty bomb.

CHAPTER 122

The Magnificent Mile, Chicago

Ted Gallows immediately switched into command mode. 'Special Agent Marsh, take Special Agent Taylor and head round the back of the Water Tower building. I'll take the main entrance. We have to get to the top of the tower and stop that man.'

'That's not going to happen, Ted,' Chris boomed back. 'Your role in this is over.' Despite the need for action, he knew that if Gallows was allowed to take the lead, as the sect's mole in the FBI, the attempt to stop the bomber would be over before it began.

Gallows's face instantly turned a fiery red. 'What the fuck are you talking about?' He stared into Chris's eyes with barely controlled rage. 'That wasn't a request, and we don't have time to argue. Get your ass moving!'

'We know you've been involved,' Marsh interjected, stepping up to Chris's side. 'We know, Ted. We know you learned about Bell's activities in Egypt from Chris, and kept them hidden from the rest of the Bureau.'

Gallows started, enraged. 'That was a tactical necessity. I thought—'

'And you're the only person I told about Lewis working on intelligence networking for me,' Laura continued, her face red with anger at the betrayal of her peer, her voice was at a full, accusatory yell. 'The man was dead the same day!'

'You think I *killed* one of our agents?' Gallows spat out the words with anger and contempt. 'We don't have time for this! Why on earth would I do such a thing?'

'Because you're an inside operative for Bell's group,' Chris answered. 'God help you. We weren't sure at first, but it's come together now. This group has had a connection inside the FBI all along.'

Gallows almost laughed back, towering over Chris. 'You're damned well right about that!'

Chris and Marsh stared at him, baffled at the admission.

'But it sure as hell isn't me!' Gallows yelled.

'I didn't tell anyone else about Lewis,' Marsh repeated. 'Not a soul. The only one who knew about his work was you. You, Ted!'

'For God's sake, Laura, don't you remember a damned thing about your basic training? We follow a chain of command!'

Marsh's rage was high, but she fumbled at the remark.

'You . . . told someone else?'

'Of course I damned well did!' Gallows bellowed back, exasperated.

'Who?' Chris demanded.

'*Her!*'

CHAPTER 123

The Magnificent Mile, Chicago

At the end of Ted Gallows's outstretched arm a finger pointed past Chris and Laura, directly to Angela Dawson. With one hand the Deputy Director pulled on a long, velvet robe. In the other she held her sidearm, aimed directly at her former agents.

'That's quite enough, Special Agent Gallows,' she shouted, the Beretta unwavering. 'This operation is over.'

'Like fuck it is!' Gallows boomed back. His own firearm was still holstered at his chest, and he knew he would be unable to reach for it without her getting off a clean shot. He could only engage her attention.

'There's a man on the top of that tower with a bomb. A dirty bomb, Angela. Unless we stop him, this crowd is going to be slaughtered.'

Dawson's usual composure was nowhere in evidence, her expression filled with zeal, an impassioned gleam in her eye. It was as if, in donning the sect's ceremonial robes she had donned a completely different personality.

462

'None of you understand what this is about. You're so scared of death. None of you realizes you're already dead. This whole world – dead. Over. All we can do is escape into something better.' She took a step towards Gallows, her eyes wild.

'Christ, you can't be serious,' Ted answered back. He stood with his feet wide, his hands out at his sides, palms open. 'You can't actually believe this, actually be willing to commit to *this*! You're talking about the mass-murder of the citizens you've sworn to protect!'

'You know nothing about commitment. Eight *years*, Ted! Eight years I've worked, and *all* for this! Deprived of fellowship with these people – *my* people – who have shown me love and purpose in a world filled with terror and lies. Eight years I kept that truth hidden inside, a secret, so that finally, finally, I could play a part in something great.'

'You've gone fucking mad!'

The barrel of Dawson's small pistol shook with her nervous excitement, but she maintained its aim at the man who had served her. 'I knew you'd never understand, Ted. That's why I had to lie, to keep you in the dark. Your world is over, but we will be free!'

Gallows stared boldly into her frenzied features. 'That's not going to happen, Deputy Director. I'm not going to allow you to exterminate innocent people.'

Dawson only smiled. 'You don't have a choice.'

The firing finger of her right hand began to pull back on the gun's trigger. The slightest squeeze, and Gallows would no longer present an obstacle to the Brotherhood's aims.

Sensing her split-second of total focus, of that concentrated moment of deliberation in which one human being ponders that ultimate act of ending the life of another, Chris Taylor bolted into action. Shoving Laura Marsh to the side, an act of protection as much as to ensure a clean shot, he ripped his firearm from his hip and fired two shots, directly into Angela Dawson's chest.

Her eyes bulged and she spun towards him, but the blow of the shots had already toppled her balance. Dawson fell backwards to the pavement beneath her, her velvet robe fluttering in motion. She hit the ground, her features still frenzied, a betrayer no more.

CHAPTER 124

The Magnificent Mile, Chicago

Across the plaza, Emily and Michael heard words booming out over the din of the crowd and the increasingly disjointed background music of marching bands and choruses. Bell's recitation was joined by the voices of every robe-laden figure in the massive plaza, reading from their own copies of his text. Soon it was the only thing Emily and Michael, or anyone else, could hear.

Emily turned to locate the source of the amplified chanting, and a few metres away saw Arthur Bell, now the fully ceremonial Marcianus, standing atop a cement pillar, chanting through a megaphone. Without conscious command, Emily's legs sprang into action and an instant later she was at the man's feet, standing aside the concrete plinth.

'You have to stop this!' she cried up to Marcianus. 'You don't have to be the cause of so much death!'

Marcianus ignored her and continued to chant.

'We have come down and reached into chaos;
We have stood with those who were in that place —

465

*We were hidden with them, empowering them, giving them
    shape.'*

Emily realized her pleas were getting her nowhere and glanced
desperately at Michael. His injuries wouldn't allow him to do
what she knew needed to be done. Turning squarely towards
Marcianus, she grabbed at the plinth and started to climb,
scrambling for his position. A thrust of her legs, and she was
almost there.

Spotting the motion below him, Marcianus looked down,
his eyes suddenly filled with anger. Forcing all his physical
strength into his left leg, he slammed his foot into the side of
Emily's head. Her grip immediately gave, her body flying backwards and downwards to the pavement. Michael reached out
to grab her as she fell, but his one good arm only managed to
ease the impact with the ground.

'Nothing can stop us now!' Marcianus roared, holding the
megaphone away from his mouth and glaring down at them.
'It is all accomplished. The words are being spoken in their
glory!' To make his point, Marcianus raised his free hand and
passed it grandiosely over the crowd. Without the Great Leader's lips moving, the words of the Liberation Incantation still
came, rising up from the masses.

*'Now we shall grant glory to those who are ours:
We shall reveal ourselves and so reveal the mysteries,
Becoming before you the Sons of Light!'*

Emily scrambled back to her feet, scanning through the crowd desperately. The sect's members were everywhere. She glanced to the centre of the plaza, where the movement of the parade had come to a halt, and where the gathered religious leaders were assembled in formation. There, in their midst, a minister stood robed: and at their head, the Governor himself, clad in velvet, chanting their common words. *Is there no one who isn't a part of this?!* Emily's mind cried out.

Just as conspicuous was another fact of which she was suddenly aware: with the whole of the FBI's Chicago Division out on the streets for the threat, there was almost no sign of any force presence here. The plaza was filled with parade-goers and Bell's followers, but there was not a visible sign of an FBI presence anywhere.

Gallows, Emily thought accusingly. The man Chris and his partner had identified as an inside agent at the FBI. *He must have had a hand in organizing the search grid, keeping surveillance away from the heart of the action.*

Desperate for a way to intercede, Emily again took up the radio Chris had given Michael. She forced herself to concentrate on the button-laden control panel for the surprisingly complex device, until she finally found a key marked 'Broadcast'. Holding her thumb over it, she shouted into the police band transmitter: 'The ringleader of the sect is on a concrete podium at the centre of the Water Tower Plaza, leading the run-up to their bomb. We need help to stop him. Anyone!'

Marcianus had returned to his recitation through the megaphone, his whole body reflecting his mind's mantra-like concentration on the words he spoke.

'We will separate the visible from the invisible world;
We will show forth the salvation of hidden wisdom.
For we are the first and the last;
We are the honoured and the scorned ones.
We are the whores and the holy ones.'

From his own place in the centre of the street at the front edge of the Unity Procession, Cardinal O'Dowd looked on in horror at the disgusting display taking place all around him. Only a few feet away, Governor Wilson had absurdly clothed himself in a ridiculous velvet garment and was now joining what appeared to be hundreds of others in a ridiculous chant that was taking over not only the square, but seemingly the whole parade. Television cameras there for the procession were having a field day scanning over the uncommonly clad sectarians and piping their drivel across the nation.

The Cardinal had been right to be suspicious of this event. His only problem was that he had not been suspicious enough. He had anticipated that it would be a PR-inspired bit of ceremonial dross. What it had turned into was some kind of spiritualist stunt by a group of fanatics – fanatics who apparently included even the Governor himself. It was a travesty. He had inadvertently become an object of public mockery; he, and all the religious leaders who were part of the now confused assembly.

Cardinal O'Dowd's tone changed, however, when he heard the shouted appeal broadcast over the police radio that clung to the hip of one of the security guards standing near the

Governor. Though the din of the crowd and the low fidelity of the radio made the words difficult to understand, a frantic voice could still be made out, crying for help, crying out that this whole nonsensical incantation was the lead-in to something unimaginable. A bomb, in this midst of the crowd.

The Cardinal knew there was a time for anger, and there was a time for action. He could not let this event become an unhindered rallying cry that led to death and destruction.

Breaking from the group, he turned and ran into the crowd.

Governor Wilson was now fully clad in the Brotherhood's ceremonial best, ready for his liberation. The men and women around him were stunned, utterly confused by his behaviour, but he had known that would be their response. Even his closest aides had known nothing of his real affiliation or his genuine intentions. He had become a masterful keeper of secrets, and a certain delight came in the confusion covering the faces of the unenlightened in the last moments of their sorrowful lives.

But a moment ago the radio had crackled, and the Governor had heard the woman's cry. The Great Leader's position was under attack. She had begged for help. She was trying to stop them.

And then the Cardinal had broken ranks and run.

What good would the Brotherhood's work of infiltrating the FBI and state agencies ultimately be, with their success in ensuring a security-free zone around the plaza at the moment of action, if a renegade cleric managed to help a random woman stop what history proclaimed must not be stopped?

A. M. DEAN

The Governor could not let that happen. He hiked up his velvet robe, shoved through the line of his baffled aides, and followed the Prince of the Church into the centre of the square.

CHAPTER 125

The Magnificent Mile, Chicago

Emily regained her position, but she realized that time was nearly up. She waited until Marcianus was once more entranced in his incantation, his eyes rolling up in his head in something close to ecstasy, and she charged again. Her hand grabbed the upper edge of the plinth and she tried to pull herself atop it before he could react, but the man caught sight of her approach and delivered another vicious blow to her head. His conviction seemed to give him strength, and once again he sent her reeling back into the crowd.

Marcianus's chest filled with a great breath as he turned again to his recitation, and came upon the concluding phrases of the Liberation Incantation, bellowing them out for all to hear.

> 'Ours is the day and this moment our own:
> Behold now what light and force shall split the world –
> Now choose your death, and we, our glory!'

At the very moment the final words left his mouth, a man in crimson-fringed black garments, a large gold cross suspended from his neck, appeared at Emily's side. Cardinal O'Dowd looked up at Marcianus, then passed a determined glance at Emily and Michael.

'You're the ones who called for help?'

'We are. He's the leader of this sect. They have a bomb.' Emily pointed up at Marcianus, her head still spinning and her breath gone. The Great Leader's eyes were closed, his arms raised heavenward in glory.

The Cardinal pulled up the sleeves of his cassock. The arms underneath were covered in short, grey hairs, but they were muscular. He stared up at the man he knew he had to stop, readying himself with a series of deep breaths. His posture was ready to charge.

Before he could lunge, a body burst through the nearby crowd and threw itself at him, toppling the prelate and crashing down on top of him. A heavy velvet robe covered the attacker's frame, concealing his features, but as he rose upon the winded Cardinal his hood fell over his shoulders and the man's familiar visage was laid plain before them. Governor Aaron Wilson was red-faced, frantic, and lacking any of the political restraint that all politicians normally bore. He was a man enraged.

Pulling back his right arm for a blow aimed at the side of the Cardinal's head, the Governor made the mistake of leaving his midsection exposed. Cardinal O'Dowd was no more used to hand-to-hand fighting than the politician, but he knew an opportunity when he saw it. Buckling his knuckles into a fist, he drove his arm into the Governor's stomach. Reeling forward, Wilson's eyes bulged as the air was knocked from his diaphragm, and the Cardinal drew up his right knee into the Governor's groin, simultaneously landing an upward blow to the left side of his head. The combination was enough, and Governor Wilson, his body tensing only a moment, collapsed on top of him.

Cardinal O'Dowd rolled the Governor's body off his and stood upright. The confrontation had taken only a manner of seconds, but more remarkable than the fact of the Governor's behaviour was that the whole brawl had not seemed to distract the man atop the concrete plinth. Marcianus still had his arms raised, his eyes elevated, and his lips continued to recite his chant.

The Cardinal pulled straight his garments, glanced at Emily and Michael, then turned back to Marcianus.

'Let me show you how to negotiate with a heretic.'

Taking his cassock in hand, Cardinal O'Dowd took three large steps back, then charged at the concrete plinth at a full run. Using the rounded rim at its base as a step, he propelled himself upward with all his force and barrelled into Marcianus. Wrapping his encrimsoned arms around the shocked Great Leader, the two men went flying off the mount and crashed onto the pavement below.

Twisting instinctively as he fell, Marcianus misjudged the distance and fell face first, wheezing as the air was knocked out of his lungs. The Cardinal's full weight came down on top of him, and the sound of breaking ribs registered in his ears.

The prelate pulled himself off the other man's body and rolled him over.

Marcianus was stunned. There were not meant to be any interruptions. The incantation was paramount. Arrangements had been made.

He forced his mind to attention. The Cardinal was rounding on him. He was a surprisingly strong man. He would not stop his assault.

Marcianus reached down to his hip. Aqmal's kabar was in its sheath, and he unsnapped the leather restraining strap, wrapping his fist around the grip. Man of the cloth or not, the Cardinal was not going to interrupt his work.

Governor Wilson sputtered as his breath returned, blood filling his mouth from the Cardinal's blows. His vision was blurred, the sky above him swirling. He lay on his back. The cleric had dropped him and moved on.

He forced his mind back to attention and squinted until proper vision returned.

And then he heard the sounds to his left.

He rolled himself onto his side and saw an impossible sight. The Great Leader lay on his back, his face bloodied, the Cardinal rising from the ground near his feet, making ready to attack again.

It was something that simply could not be allowed.

Cardinal O'Dowd forced his knees to straighten and reclaimed a standing position near Marcianus's ankles. The man was still moving. He had to be stopped, completely. Pulling back his fist, he leaned down and pushed all the strength he could muster into a blow aimed at Marcianus's face.

It was then that he saw the flicker of light at the man's side, and the convulsing of muscles at Marcianus's shoulder. The Cardinal's mind processed the information instantly. A knife. The man was fighting back.

At the same instant, a guttural cry tore through the air behind him. Even with the rage it now possessed, O'Dowd recognized the voice. The Governor was back in action, lunging at him from the rear. He was about to be pinned between two men, one of whom was already raising a blade towards his chest.

The Cardinal's instincts took over, and he contorted his body to the right just as he was about to land atop Marcianus. Buckling as he hit the ground, he tucked his knees upwards and rolled.

Governor Wilson saw the cleric's body shift to the side, but it was too late for him to stop his lunge. His body plummeted downward, intractably aimed at that of his Great Leader, whose knife was now pointed directly at his chest.

The Governor fell upon the knife, his eyes as wide as Marcianus's. The blade stood firm as his body hit it, ramming the knife deep into his chest, deflecting off his ribs and coming to rest in the centre of his heart. For an instant, time froze, and neither man moved. Then Wilson coughed, staring into Marcianus's eyes, and a second later his lifeless body went limp.

Emily and Michael raced to the bodies, Michael pinning down Marcianus by the shoulders as Emily rolled the

Governor's dead frame off him. The crowd had parted at the fight and now gathered in a ring, encircling the action. Television cameras appeared as if from nowhere, honing in on the strange activity that had, almost beyond belief, claimed the life of a sitting Governor.

A moment later, ground reinforcements from the police flooded into the circle, responding to the same radio call that had alerted Cardinal O'Dowd. A uniformed officer approached Michael, still pinning down Marcianus, and put a strong hand on his shoulder.

'Sir, we can take him from here.'

His eyes still locked on Marcianus's, Michael gradually released his hold, then stood over the fallen man.

It was then that Marcianus began to laugh. Gently at first, but soon with deeper, fuller conviction. His face shimmered in a great smile.

'You're too late!' he shouted with maniacal joy, blood spattering from his mouth. 'It is already done. And now, the great light comes!'

He lifted his arms skyward, his fingers framing the tower from which deliverance was about to flow.

CHAPTER 126

The Magnificent Mile, Chicago

'Where the hell are all my men?' Ted Gallows swept his gaze anxiously across the plaza. The body of Angela Dawson lay at his feet, unmoving. He'd already cuffed her hands, and in the absence of the proper equipment to do more, had fastened her ankles together with a second set of cuffs. Her flak jacket had stopped Chris's two bullets from piercing her chest, but he'd been at such close range that they'd knocked her to the ground and forced the breath from her lungs. Gallows had dropped a knee onto her midriff and cuffed her immediately.

The brief panic caused by the gunshots had been quelled with the sight of their FBI vests and badges, but the effort that had taken had drawn Gallows's attention to a disturbing fact. The plaza had almost zero FBI presence.

'They're everywhere else,' Marsh answered, 'but not here. We thought you'd manipulated the search grid to keep teams away from the site.'

Gallows's gaze came down on Laura, then moved to Chris. 'You're not the only ones who suspected an inside link,' he shouted. 'I've been operating under the suspicion that someone in the Bureau was part of the Church of Truth in Liberation for the past two days. *That's* why I didn't want you spreading your information on Bell.' Gallows looked directly at Chris. 'I didn't know who could be trusted.'

'Christ, you could have said as much,' Chris shouted back.

'You were only a few minutes on the scene. Forgive me for not rushing to confide my every suspicion in you!'

'Boys,' Marsh interjected, 'the fact remains, we have to get to the top of that tower. That man is still up there. We've got to move, now!'

Gallows gazed upwards, then at the masses surrounding them. 'The two of you start up the tower. I'll get Dawson into the hands of our team, and track down reinforcements for a full assault.'

'It'll be a tight manoeuvre up top,' Chris said, scoping out the scene. 'If the bomber's got anyone with him, it'll be hard for the two of us to keep him at bay.'

'It'll be easier with us behind you.' Michael's voice suddenly broke into the group. He stepped up to Chris and Marsh, Emily beside him. 'We've just left Arthur Bell in the custody of the local PD. A little outside help, but the "Great Leader" is no longer leading.'

'Who the hell are these two?' Gallows motioned to Michael and Emily, his face an anxious blank.

'Friends,' was all Chris answered. 'There's no time for introductions, Ted.' He turned to Michael.

'We've met up with Bell's men before,' Emily shot out. 'We

can follow you up, Chris. Provide a little extra manpower until your reinforcements arrive.'

'They're law enforcement?' Gallows demanded. He glanced back up to the tower. Time was running out.

'No, but they're—'

'Then fuck no. They stay here. The two of you get moving.'

Emily saw his resolve. There was no way this man was letting her or Michael join Chris and Laura on the tower. She understood: no FBI protocol would allow civilians to take part in an active siege.

The agent was right. But she wasn't about to accept it.

Taking a quick step forward, she reached down to Angela Dawson's body. The gun that a few moments ago had been aimed at Chris's head lay on the pavement, a few inches from her hip. In a smooth motion, Emily scooped it up, locked it in her grip, and slid back the action for a quick check. The Glock 22 was loaded and ready.

She looked straight into Ted Gallows's eyes before he could object.

'We have no time, your men need backup, and this isn't the first time I've held a gun. Protest all you want, but I'm going up that tower.'

Their expressions locked, words almost forming on Gallows's lips, but Emily's eyes were on fire. A split second later, she broke the stare and turned towards the water tower, already moving towards their target.

'That makes us four,' Chris announced. 'With four, we can at least contain him.' He took a second, smaller pistol out of his chest holster and passed it to Michael. He knew how his friend loathed guns, but he'd also heard of how Michael had fired on Bell's men in Cairo. It was enough to make him an asset, in the circumstances.

'Just get help up after us quickly,' he said to Gallows. 'And get snipers in position. We either talk him down or take him down, and with that vest already on him, it's going to have to be a clean, fast kill.'

And then he was running, chasing after Emily with Michael and Laura in tow, racing for the tower.

The main entrance at the base of the Old Water Tower building was jimmied open. The man at its top had broken his way in, and though he'd attempted to cover his tracks by closing the door behind him and engaging what little of the locking mechanism he hadn't destroyed, it offered little in the way of resistance. Chris levelled a kick squarely at the latch and the door gave way freely.

Emily and Michael stayed behind Chris and Laura as they raced up the steep, winding staircase towards the tower's summit, moving as quietly as they could. With any luck, the bomber's attention would be on the crowds below, and they could try for the element of surprise.

The tower was magnificent. The eclectic, quasi-Gothic structure began at the ground level as an ornate, castle-like structure of pillars, turrets and arched windows, rising to its triumph in the water tower itself: an octagonal limestone spire reaching 154 feet up into the Chicago skyline, with a spiralling staircase ascending to the summit where a cupola once housed the control room.

Run! Emily's mind raced. *The ascent is taking too much time.* When they'd taken Bell, with the Cardinal's help, the Great Leader had been near the end of the incantation. The followers' chanting would be nearly over. *How long will the man wait to act?*

She pressed forward with all her energy, taking the steps two and three at a time. Chris and Laura led with trained precision.

A minute later, they were faced with a door at the top of the staircase. Beyond it was the surface of the tower, and the bomber.

'You two take up positions behind,' Chris ordered. He and Laura flanked the door. They still did not know if the man outside had reinforcements or arms other than the vest he wore on his chest. But whatever the possibilities, their small group was going to have to confront them directly. There was no time to wait for Gallows to get snipers into play.

Chris drew in a deep, controlled breath. Then, pressing his left hand to the metal bar that ran across the door, his gun drawn in his right, he pushed.

The door opened into the brightness of the morning sun. The roar of the crowd hit their ears suddenly, like a wave of sound.

Before them stood a man, perfectly calm. Around his chest he wore his makeshift weapon, and in his hand he held its trigger.

CHAPTER 127

The Rooftop

'Drop the trigger!' Chris's words to the bomber were forceful, but spoken in even tones without jolting command. The last thing he wanted to do was spook the man – a man whose torso was wrapped in enough toxic chemicals to kill the whole crowd below – into setting off the explosive that would deliver them into the air they breathed.

Chris kept his eyes steady on him. The man was breathing erratically, his eyes like orbs. He looked enraged, entranced. Despite the fact of the weapon he wore and his intention to kill so many, he seemed feeble. Sad. Pitiful.

Behind Chris, crouched on either side, Emily and Michael trained their sidearms on the bomber. Laura side-stepped out onto the platform.

'It's time to put a stop to this,' Chris continued, taking a cautious step forward, his gun still raised and supported now by both his hands. 'It's over.'

The man caught sight of Emily and Michael behind Chris, and tensed. His opponents were not two, they were four. His eyes darted wildly between them, his thumb bobbing over the trigger. He started to sway nervously, his breathing more shallow and rushed.

'Nothing is over!' he cried, the words coming out with a spurt of nervous, defiant laughter. 'Haven't you heard the words? The glorious words?' He signalled towards the air around him. Sounds of the Liberation Incantation continued to waft skyward from the crowd below, the masses having taken up their captured leader's charge. The tones reached up to the decorated spike of the Water Tower's summit in ominous unison. As if spellbound by the rhythmic phrases, the man's eyes fluttered in a trance-like rapture.

Emily's boldness flared. They couldn't allow him to get fully caught up in the chant and its meaning. Frantic, she stepped through the door, walked to the edge of the platform and looked down from the tower's height to the crowd below.

There, towards the centre of the plaza, was an opportunity. *Break the spell*, her mind commanded. *Don't let the trance run its course.*

'Your words have come too late,' she suddenly announced. The man was startled by the woman's voice and his eyes snapped back open.

'Look closely,' Emily continued, 'your leader is taken.' She removed a hand from her gun and pointed downwards, over the edge of the spire. Her other hand kept his head in her sights.

The man hesitated, but followed the line of Emily's gesture. Far below, he saw a circle of bystanders, newly formed at the heart of the plaza. At its epicentre was the Great Leader, shackled in the hands of law enforcement officers and FBI. Beside him, the body of Governor Wilson lay dead on the pavement.

Fallen.

He swallowed hard. 'Marcianus falls,' he whispered to himself, as if narrating a story playing out in front of him. His expression betrayed thoughts that seemed to struggle to accept the next act. Then, he spoke a little more firmly. 'Marcianus falls, but Cerinthus rises.'

When his gaze returned to Emily, it had gained resolve.

'Even this cannot stop us now. The sacred words have been spoken. The incantation is complete. What comes next is release.' He began to raise his right arm, the vest's trigger grasped tightly in hand.

Emily took another step forward, willing the man to meet her gaze. His eyes were so wild now, almost inhuman. But there, just in the instant before he blinked, the confusion of a child caught up in something too vast for him.

'Please, think of what you're doing,' Emily implored. 'You don't need escape. The world may be suffering, but you won't help it like this. It needs repair. Do this and you'll only be adding more despair, more pain.' She waved her gun towards his vest. 'Your life can still amount to so much more than this!'

Emily stopped. She was out of words. The force of human compassion was the only hope against the grip the sect's message had over this man's mind.

There was a long, lingering pause in which Cerinthus seemed to reflect on her words. Time seemed to slow, the roar of the crowd softening into an indeterminate swell of noise. The wind that normally howled over the tower's height seemed to go absent and the world reduced itself to the gravity of this man and his choice.

And in a flickering moment, it came.

Cerinthus slowly closed his eyes, his trigger arm descending lower. His head began to sag forward. He took a deep breath. Then, with a sudden gaze of unworldly intensity, he bored his terrorized eyes directly into Emily's. With bestial force he cried out at the top of his lungs the only word that mattered.

'*LIBERATION!*'

An explosion of sound followed a millisecond later. Emily felt it, rather than heard it; and then the concussion wave slammed into the right side of her face, burning with a fiery heat.

The wave did not, however, come from Cerinthus's vest. Chris sprang forward and fired a single shot squarely into the man's shoulder. The movement brought his gun to within inches of Emily's ear, and with almost instantaneous effect it began to bleed from the unexpected burst of sound and heat.

Cerinthus spun backward, the round shattering his right shoulder and thrusting his body against the low stone ledge. He immediately lost muscle control in the injured arm, the vest's firing trigger falling from his grasp and dangling six inches below it from a single electrical wire.

Refusing to lose his focus, Cerinthus reclaimed his balance and lunged for the controller with his left hand. Another gunshot broke the silence, this time from Laura's weapon. The bullet entered Cerinthus's left arm, high above the elbow. His body pushed back again.

He looked up, his eyes wild, as if all humanity had left him and only a raging beast remained. Knowing he wouldn't be able to reach the trigger without more bullets stopping every attempt, he could think of only one way to proceed. Mustering his strength against the rapidly increasing dizziness of shock, he pushed his weight backwards against the waist-high wall.

'He's going over the side!' Laura cried out from her post. 'For God's sake, don't let him jump! With or without an explosion, if those vials around his chest are crushed, hundreds of people are going to die!'

Cerinthus marshalled all his remaining strength into his legs and thrust his body up and back. He could feel the upper rim of the stone ledge collide with his calves, flipping him backwards and over the edge of the 154-foot precipice. It was not how he had intended the end to come, but the woman was right. Crushing the vials on impact would still have an effect. The brethren were gathered close together, in range of his fall. He could offer them their exit.

Liberation could still be accomplished.

Emily threw her gun aside and leapt forward. As Cerinthus toppled headlong over the wall, she lurched at him, wrapped her arms around his legs and dropped her own out from under her, using every pound of her bodyweight to counter his fall. But his substantial body mass had already gained momentum and she felt her own body being tugged into his descent. Her knees slammed into the ledge, her footing starting to slip.

Chris dived forward. Keeping his pistol clenched in one

hand, he wrapped his muscular arms around Emily's waist from behind, anchoring her in place.

Locked in Chris's grasp, Emily's forward plunge came to a sudden halt.

Cerinthus hung upside-down from the edge of Old Water Tower's spire. The symphony of sound from the crowds far below had converted into terrified screams as the gunshots had pierced the revelry, and as the flurry of activity atop the tower came into public view.

'Don't let him go, Wess,' Laura repeated, holding her voice steady. 'Whatever you do, hold tight!'

Michael rushed to Chris's side and took over the role of anchoring Emily in place. He concentrated as much weight as he could in his right arm, his left shooting fire through his body from the injuries he had sustained the day before – but his will, coupled with a heady dose of adrenaline, steadied him against the pain.

Freed from providing support, Chris moved to the edge of the platform and reached over to Cerinthus's dangling form. Together, he and Emily pulled him upward and towards the ledge.

The man squirmed violently, and Emily quickly realized that if he made his sudden jerks and movements in contact with the stone, the vials could still shatter. They wouldn't be able to risk bringing him over the angular, stone wall.

It's time to end this once and for all, her thoughts suddenly commanded. Ensuring that Chris had him firmly in his grasp, Emily removed her hands from Cerinthus's legs and held them out towards her husband.

'Mike, give me your gun,' she ordered.

'Emily, think before you—'

Before he could complete his sentence, Emily wrested his gun from him. Spinning on her heels, she looked down on the man dangling in Chris's grasp. She would put a stop to this.

She clutched the Glock tightly in her fist. The nylon polymer grip was warm, and as her fingers wrapped around it, every emotion from the past days pulsed through her vision. She saw Andrew's face, she heard his laugh. She heard the cold, disinterested words of his killers. She saw Marcianus's deluded, unyielding features. She felt the pulse of so much life, far below them. But most of all she saw her cousin's eyes, joyful and bright, trimmed in the smile she had seen so often during their childhood summers together. Eyes now closed forever.

The vision took only a fraction of a second. When it was over, Emily raised her gun arm.

'Emily, this isn't the way.' Michael's voice called out, but her hands were already in motion.

Spinning the gun in her palm and grasping it by the barrel, Emily reached down and swung. The grip slammed squarely into Cerinthus's skull. In an instant the man dangled motionless, unconscious.

In that instant, the world paused. The man swayed in Chris's grasp. The breeze started to blow.

It's over. The words resonated in Emily's mind.

Motion returned a moment later. Carefully avoiding any contact between the stone ledge and the vials on his vest,

Emily and Chris pulled the limp Cerinthus fully back onto the tower's landing. Beneath them, the sounds of terror were replaced by cheers, and a moment later by the sirens of police cruisers speeding onto the scene.

Laying his unconscious, limp body gently on the stonework balcony, Emily gazed down on his fallen form. Here, the man behind the worst that Bell's plot was to have offered – the evil fruit to be gained from Andrew's murder – was finally stopped. Emily's heart pulsed with more than merely the adrenaline of the act.

She stared at the vest that Cerinthus had fastened around him. The man who had thought he would stage the way to freedom was now shackled in the device that would ensure he remained a captive the rest of his life.

It took less than a minute for the scene in the plaza to change dramatically. Hundreds of confused members of the Brotherhood, still sporting their velvet robes, found themselves the object of a very different kind of attention than they had anticipated. Officers swept in, targeting everyone in the ceremonial attire, eager to arrest anyone who had been a part of what amounted to the largest single act of attempted terrorism in the city's history – an act that had claimed the life of the Governor, even as it seemed to involve him. The television cameras and reporters that the brethren had hoped would broadcast their final act abroad, sharing with the masses their message of condemnation to the fallen world, instead rushed to report on the overthrow of yet another extremist sect, one amidst the hordes of madness that inundated the modern world.

His wrists still shackled behind him, his face still bleeding from the unexpected clerical intervention, Marcianus/Arthur Bell was pushed towards a squad car by the police. Nearby, the cuffed form of FBI Deputy Director Angela Dawson was shoved into the back of a black sedan. Marcianus would be taken in by the authorities, but Dawson had betrayed her own, and her own had no intention of letting the privilege of recompense go to anyone else. The black sedan was moving even before the door was slammed shut behind her.

Marcianus's eyes wouldn't leave the rooftop as the officers pushed him forward. He was trapped in disbelief. It was over. Their cause, their mission. Their hope for good.

Their deliverance.

Cerinthus's fruitless cry of 'Liberation' still echoed in his ears, but the hope of millennia was now lost.

This world, he realized, was one he could not escape.

CHAPTER 128

Ancient Egypt, AD 373

As he placed the keystone into the small jar, Markus cast a final glance over its tooled surface. Tarasios had told him it was in this that their hope for the future resided. They had taken every precaution conceivable to preserve the words of freedom for the future. The key would be hidden, secreted away, the books kept separately, innocent in every outward appearance. They would await the day when their revelation could come.

Markus covered the mouth of the jar with a small bowl, setting it into place with bitumen he had heated over the flame that burned in their courtyard. He pressed firmly, sealing the keystone's protective shell.

Turning, he handed it to Tarasios.

'You have done well, young Marcianus,' the older man said.

Markus inclined his head. He had been initiated the week prior and was still growing used to his new name.

'But now you must go. Go as far as you can. Go north, to the coast, then cross the sea. Find another land – and do not forget our brethren here. We will be overtaken, but you will keep the

Brotherhood alive. You will make certain that the knowledge o
secret is not lost.'

Tarasios pulled the jar close to his chest, and with his other
reached out and gently squeezed Marcianus's shoulder.

'One day, our work here will bear its fruit, my brother. L
the decades and centuries, when the world is ready. Others
come, bearing the names of the brethren before them. Perhap.
will even bear your name, as the years unfold.'

The young man looked up. 'And then?'

'When the time is come, the secret will help them find the w
and they can put them to use. Learn what it means for the so
be free, and to find peace in the midst of the world.'

Marcianus allowed a smile to flush across his features. '"
will find our words, and make them the rallying cry for war.

'I should hope,' Tarasios answered, gently, 'that they woul
them for peace.' His eyes sparkled in the firelight. With pat
care, he raised the young disciple to his feet.

'Now, young brother, it is time for you to go. May your
find liberation.'

He pressed his open palm to Marcianus's chest and both
inclined their heads in a silent bond. Then, without another u
the new recruit turned and walked alone into the darkness.

EPILOGUE

Logan, Ohio – July 12th

The body in the open casket looked calm, even peaceful. There was no sign of the tragedy that had marked the end of his life, and the trauma from his fatal attack had been artfully covered up by the Logan funeral home, located only blocks away from the Wess family house. He lay almost as if he were asleep, as he had been only minutes before the attack had come – before the sounds that had roused him from his rest, propelled him into the role of protector and defender and ultimately taken his all too short life.

Emily stared down at the body of her cousin, unsure what emotions she was supposed to be feeling. It was hard to believe that it was with Andrew that everything had begun – at least, the part she, Michael and Chris had come to play in foiling the Brotherhood's designs. By Arthur Bell's own admission, killing Andrew had been an accident, an unintended response to a situation his men had not foreseen. And yet without it, Emily and Michael might never have learned what was taking place. How many thousands might have died, if they hadn't been drawn into the Brotherhood's saga and helped to put an end to its madness?

Andrew was dead, but many continued to live. The sadness Emily had expected to feel here at his funeral was tempered by that knowledge. He had played a part – unwittingly, perhaps – in stopping a madman. He hadn't hesitated to rise up to defend her. He had always been her protector, and he had protected her at the end. Perhaps he would be happy, knowing that his death had helped defend so many others as well.

Chris Taylor gazed on from a position to the side of Andrew's immediate family, Laura Marsh clinging to his arm, supportively. They had not expected to be invited to the funeral, but Emily and Michael had been insistent. They were part of the story of the end of Andrew's life, and they wanted them close.

As Chris watched Emily gently caress her cousin's cheek a final time, he felt he finally understood Michael's objections to the worldview of those they had pursued during those frantic days. The tenderness of her touch was a material thing, yet even in the presence of death – perhaps especially in its presence – it was something strangely beautiful. It was far more a mystery than the escapist incantations any Gnostic cult could devise.

Michael stepped forward to Emily's side and wrapped his arms around her shoulders.

'You've done well by him, Em. Andrew would be proud of you.'

Emily gave a gentle smile. 'I know.'

A lingering gaze and a final prayer offered, husband and wife turned and walked through the funeral home's aisle of chairs, out of its double doors, and into the waiting world beyond.

AUTHOR'S NOTE

Like *The Lost Library*, this book takes genuine historical events and discoveries as the bedrock on which its story is constructed. The history of ancient Gnosticism, together with the remarkable trove of documents found at Nag Hammadi, are subjects of mystery, ambiguity and intrigue among both scholars and the general public, and provide more than ample territory for the kinds of speculations that fuel *The Keystone*.

Gnosticism

Chris Taylor's intellectual struggle during the flight to Cairo gives some sense of the complexities involved in studying the mélange of traditions summed up as 'Gnosticism'. Though a conference was held in Messina as far back as 1966 in order to settle on a common definition of the term, historians and academics today still debate nearly every aspect of what Gnosticism really was or is.

The basic contours of ancient Gnosticism, according to most interpreters, are a radical dualism that claimed the spiritual realm was holy and the physical realm evil, partnered with a belief that specific mystical, often secret knowledge (*gnosis*) would allow a soul to be liberated from its 'material captivity'. While extremely diverse in terms of particular teachings and doctrines, Gnostic groups regularly embraced esoteric, mystical and secretive traditions that served to foster the 'secret knowledge' that might liberate the soul from its suffering – releasing the soul into the realm of spiritual freedom. They were deeply text-driven, producing many writings of their own as well as Gnostic versions of existing texts (such as the writings of Plato, or Old Testament and early Christian documents).

The Christian Church reacted strongly against Gnosticism in the second to sixth centuries, for reasons that include those summarized by Emily and Michael in the course of *The Keystone*. While there is a resurgence of interest in Gnosticism today (particularly since the discovery in 1945 of the Nag Hammadi Codices), and while certain scholars seek to deconstruct Christian history in order to yield greater importance to early Gnostic groups, the response of Christianity to Gnostic concepts and ideas remains today essentially unchanged from the response given by the Church in the early centuries, which identified it as a movement that runs counter to the fundamental teachings on a creator-God. The essential incompatibility of Gnosticism with Christianity does not, however, stop people from continually trying to merge them, and, rather as Emily and Michael discuss, Gnostic thought has been hugely influential on many strands of New Age spirituality in the twentieth and twenty-first centuries.

496

The great Lisbon earthquake of 1755

The 'Great Earthquake' referred to by Mario Terageste as a reason for the mood shift in eighteenth-century Italy was a historical event that rocked Portugal at 9.30 a.m. on November 1st 1755. Though measurement instruments did not exist at the time, scholars today estimate that the earthquake was 9.0 or even 9.5 on the Richter scale, with an epicentre some 200 kilometres off the Portuguese coast and a shaking duration of nearly ten full minutes. Cathedrals and churches in Lisbon, which were packed for All Saints Day mass, were levelled, as was most of the city, and tens of thousands died both in the quake itself and the fire that swept through the city afterwards. A tsunami generated by the quake battered the coast with three distinct waves, killing countless more who had fled for safety to ships and barges on the coast and rivers.

The tsunami affected Britain, France and Belgium and reached as far as Antigua and Barbados, where sea levels were said to have risen by over a metre. It is estimated that the shock waves from the earthquake were felt over an area of some 1.3 million square miles, reaching inland to Spain, France, Germany and Italy, and even as far abroad as Sweden. In northern Africa, Algiers was obliterated, Tangiers hobbled and some 10,000 died in Morocco. In Italy, as reported by Mario, the great volcano called Vesuvius ceased erupting when the earthquake hit.

Natural disasters of this sort were often taken as signs of divine displeasure in the middle ages, and given that this particular catastrophe took place on the morning of All Saints Day, at precisely the time the faithful were gathered into the churches, all the more so.

The Nag Hammadi Codices

The thirteen codices found near Nag Hammadi in 1945 (actually twelve codices, plus remainders of a thirteenth) contain some of the only first-hand Gnostic writings from antiquity. There is heated scholarly debate over just what the collection represents (is it the library of a Gnostic sect? of a Christian monastic community with Gnostic leanings? of a private adherent?), but there is little question that it is one of our earliest – and certainly our most substantial – collections of texts considered important in a Gnostic milieu.

The history of the Nag Hammadi Codices, provided to Chris by Emily and Michael, is an accurate portrayal of the actual discovery of this remarkable collection. The strange history of its discovery, together with the long feuds over ownership and scholarly rights that kept its contents mostly inaccessible to the wider world for decades, is one of those rare areas where truth presents just as compelling (and bizarre) a story as fiction. The entire collection is now available in an affordable English translation for any who wish to read it (published by James M. Robinson as *The Nag Hammadi Library*); though, regrettably, Emily and the Brotherhood's easy access to online scanned versions of the original is at this stage only the figment of a hopeful literary imagination.

Highlights of the Nag Hammadi collection are on display, as the book suggests, in Room 10 of the Coptic Museum in Cairo. They remain among the most important documentary possessions of Egypt's Supreme Council of Antiquities, and an incomparable resource for the study of the complex early centuries of the Christian era.

The 'incantations' in The Keystone

The three incantations employed by the Brotherhood in *The Keystone* are drawn from authentic Gnostic documents from the first centuries of the Christian era – principally from the Nag Hammadi collection itself – interjected to a limited degree with phrases of my own invention that unite them fully into the action of the novel.

The 'Initiation Incantation' (chanted by the Córdoba brethren in chapter 3) is drawn from the Nag Hammadi tract known as *The Dialogue of the Saviour* (found in Codex III), with slight modifications.

The 'Truth Incantation' (chanted in the Chicago temple in chapter 39, and again by Cerinthus during his final preparations in chapter 109) is drawn from two Nag Hammadi sources: the first stanza from the *Apocryphon of John* (Codex II), the second and third from the *Gospel of Truth* (Codex I, with a second copy in Codex XII) – the same text which figures heavily in the plot of the novel. In each case I have slightly altered the wording for dramatic effect.

Finally, the 'Liberation Incantation' itself is a mélange of refrains from throughout the Nag Hammadi Codices: namely, from the tracts known as *Thunder: Perfect Mind* (Codex VI), the *Gospel of Truth* (Codices I, XII) and the *Trimorphic Protennoia* (Codex XIII). Only a few lines of this incantation are literary constructions composed for *The Keystone*; the remainder are all authentic Gnostic refrains.

ACKNOWLEDGEMENTS

Throughout the writing and production of *The Keystone*, I have been fortunate enough to have the support, expertise and enthusiasm of many of the same people who were essential to the success of *The Lost Library*. My thanks once again to E.F. for his early readings and comments, which are always of tremendous help. My principal editor is also my superb agent, Thomas Stofer, whose precise eye and creative mind strengthened this book immensely. Later in the process, two enthusiastic and critically conscious readers helped make this book far better than it would otherwise have been: Kate Atherton, one of the few people I know who actually reads more books than I do, ensured that I never got lazy with the parts of this book that really mattered; and Miles Orchard, whose eye for detail and creative suggestions were so strong that they forced us both to learn how to make a Skype call in order to discuss them more easily, was especially influential in spotting creative possibilities with the story that I might not have found without him. All of these readers have my profound thanks and respect; and, of course, any deficiencies that remain in the book are entirely my own doing.

My thanks are also due to Dr Malcom Choat and Dr Victor Ghica of Macquarie University, Sydney, for their assistance with the Coptic transliteration employed here.

I'm fortunate to be able to play in the vast publishing garden of Pan Macmillan, which is tended by wonderful people who produce beautiful books. My gratitude especially to Wayne Brookes, Director of Publishing, who puts an extraordinary amount of energy into these books; and to my principal editor at Pan, Louise Buckley, whose notes always come in multiple colours and make for the best-possible versions of whatever she touches.

My agent, Thomas, is supported by Luigi Bonomi and all the experts at LBA. These are the finest agents around, responsible for taking the words I manage to write and transforming them into books that have sold in over sixteen countries and made their way onto lists all over the globe.